OUTSTANDING PRAISE FOR RIDLEY PEARSON

HIDDEN CHARGES:

"Epic in scope . . . Strongly c

"A fine thriller."

"Engrossing . . . A page-turner

PROBABLE CAUSE:

"Pearson writes in the smooth style of Lawrence Sanders, Robert Ludlum and other very successful storytellers."

—*Los Angeles Times Book Review*

"Fascinating . . . Breathless." —*Chicago Tribune*

"Ridley Pearson is a natural storyteller who keeps the thread going—twisting the details . . . Dancing the forensic shuffle without missing a step."

—*Richmond Times-Dispatch*

UNDERCURRENTS:

"Pearson writes with a knowing eye and he builds suspense with a masterful touch." —T. Jefferson Parker

"A real winner. A taut, clever plot. Ridley Pearson can write!"

—Tony Hillerman

"Intense . . . in the line of Wambaugh and Caunitz."

—*South Bend Tribune*

What a strange place to die.

He could picture the thousands of people in the new pavilion tomorrow. What a sight. He sat in the tunnel, legs crossed, and continued twisting wires together. In all he had laid nearly a mile of wire. He had already set his timer for tomorrow at four o'clock. Now, even if they caught him, his plan would be carried through. The timer would detonate the main charges, and the pavilion would fall like a house of cards.

He pitied the poor bastards inside the pavilion if they didn't pay the money. It didn't matter to him anymore. He would give them a chance. If they chose to ignore him, like the judge had ignored him, then that was fine. As far as he was concerned, he had a score to settle: his father's life for two hundred grand.

They deserved to die. . . .

HIDDEN CHARGES

(previously published under the title *The Seizing of Yankee Green Mall*)

RIDLEY PEARSON

ST. MARTIN'S PAPERBACKS

Hidden Charges was previously published under the title *The Seizing of Yankee Green Mall*.

HIDDEN CHARGES

Copyright © 1987 by Ridley Pearson.

ISBN: 0-312-92959-5

Printed in the United States of America

St. Martin's Press hardcover edition published 1987
Worldwide Library edition/July 1988
St. Martin's Paperbacks edition/May 1993

10 9 8 7 6 5 4 3 2 1

Dedicated to the hardworking women of the Community Library, Ketchum, Idaho: Librarians Dottie Thomas, Ollie Cossman and Ellie Lister, and the Board of Directors. Many thanks for the endless hours of research devoted to this project.

1

THE CONSTRUCTION CREWS began work at seven-thirty, an hour before the doors to the other pavilions opened, two hours before the stores opened. This was possible in part because not a single worker on the project was union. The union had been broken in the early days of the new pavilion's construction, following a walkout protesting fifty-hour work weeks with no overtime pay.

Jim McClatchy climbed the stepladder. One of the ceiling fixtures was not working; he'd been told to fix it. The row of lockers to his left provided temporary storage for the workers. This small concrete room would be a utility area once the construction boys had left, and if everything went according to schedule, that meant Saturday—the day of the new wing's grand opening.

Having already thrown the circuit breaker in the panel room, McClatchy moved an acoustic ceiling tile out of the way and aimed his flashlight at the overhead J-box. *There* was one good reason the fixture didn't work: It wasn't hooked up.

McClatchy went about his work with annoyance written on his thirty-five-year-old face. It was not the first foul-up he'd seen on this job. The trouble with hiring nonunion labor was that you often got nonunion quality. He knocked the punch hole out of the junction box and attached a piece of flex with a locknut, running the fixture's two wires to the box. Three half-inch conduit pipes entered the J-box, each with one black and one white wire pulled through. The light fixtures were connected in series.

The presence of an extra set of wires made him realize that something else, somewhere else, wasn't working either.

Making a mental note to check the plans later, McClatchy cleaned the ends of all the wires, twisted the blacks together and then the whites, and covered them with wire nuts. He worked the stubborn wires inside the J-box, finally capping it with a blank plate.

He replaced the acoustic tile and descended the stepladder.

Down the hall he entered the panel room and threw the appropriate breaker. All in a day's work. McClatchy's wife was studying in Hartford for her teaching certificate. As a result, he saw her only on weekends. For the past few months, life without her had become a little too routine, too boring. That woman meant more to him than anyone would ever know.

He ambled back down the long, drab utility hallway and checked his watch. He'd been on the job a total of one hour and ten minutes and was already bored.

He pushed open the door and casually threw the light switch, his eyes on the overhead fixture he had just connected.

A tongue of orange flame uncurled toward him, pinning him helplessly against the doorjamb. The intense pressure of the explosion whipped the steel-edged door on its hinges, cleaving his head open, killing him instantly.

Amid a swirling cloud of charcoal smoke, debris from the lockers settled onto the floor like feathers from a pillow fight. The fire alarm cried out, strangely mechanical and inhuman.

Jim McClatchy's wedding ring rolled twenty feet down the long hallway before tilting to one side and falling over. The ring danced on the smooth concrete surface, a tiny bell chiming, and finally came to a stop only inches from a small drain.

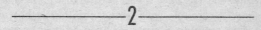

2

As THE RUMBLE of the explosion rolled through the building, the short stocky man looked up from his work. He eased his finger off the trigger of the star-bit drill and listened to the eerie pulse of the fire alarm, its sound dulled by his earplugs and the wall of

ACKNOWLEDGMENTS

The author wishes to thank: Joe Wohandler, Jackie Green, Hollis Turner, Laura Dodge, Mab Gray, Helen Bennett, Stan Silverman, Jerry Danzig, James Daverman, John and Jaimie Borton, and Randi Myrmo for their help and inspiration.

Technical information on explosives supplied in part by Special Agent John C. Killorin, Chief Public Affairs Branch, Bureau of Alcohol, Tobacco and Firearms, Washington, D.C.

Special thanks to Howard Moster, Director of Security of the West Edmonton Mall, and Deane Eldredge, Director of Public Relations. And to the other malls used for research: The Beverly, Los Angeles, CA; Northgate Mall, Seattle, WA; Clackamas Town Center, Portland, OR; Northbrook Court, Northbrook, IL. To each of these malls, Yankee Green owes a debt of thanks.

To Franklin Heller, whose idea this was, Brian DeFiore, who patiently edited the story, and Colleen Daly, my wife and best friend—there would be no novel without you.

Architectural drawings created by Jonathan H. Marvel and drawn by Craig Keller.

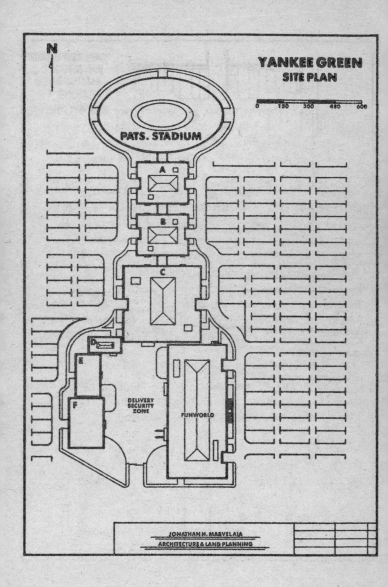

N

YANKEE GREEN
SITE PLAN

0   150   300   450   600

PATS. STADIUM

A

B

C

D

E

F

DELIVERY
SECURITY
ZONE

FUNWORLD

JONATHAN H. MARVELAIA
ARCHITECTURE & LAND PLANNING

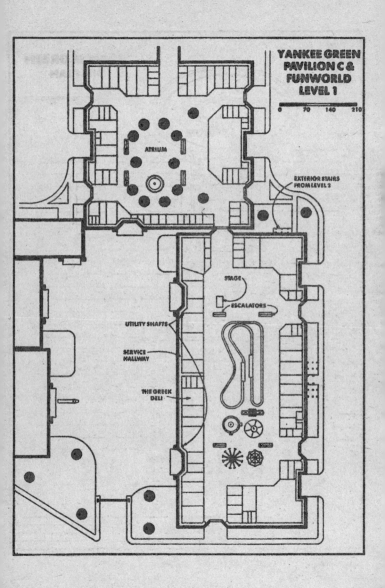

YANKEE GREEN
PAVILION C &
FUNWORLD
LEVEL 1

0   70   140   210

ATRIUM

EXTERIOR STAIRS
FROM LEVEL 2

STAGE

ESCALATORS

UTILITY SHAFTS

SERVICE
HALLWAY

THE GREEK
DELI

Tuesday
August 18

cement between this area and the utility room. The explosion had happened nearby. He spent a moment debating what to do. How could he stop now? He made a hasty decision and leaned his weight against the butt of the heavy drill, simultaneously pulling the trigger. The drill screamed into action, its special bit chewing through the hardened cement.

The man wore unusually thick eyeglasses which distorted his eyes and the sides of his face, giving his head an ungainly figure-eight shape. Thin gold-colored wire rims hooked around his oaf-ish ears, holding the heavy glass onto his face. He had a narrow chin with a day's stubble on it. An oddly shaped scar, barely visible, ran from the edge of his left eye into the coarse brown curly hair at his temple. Still drilling, he crooked his neck to mop his brow on his shoulder, the sweat staining his faded cotton shirt like the stroke of a careless paintbrush.

He heard the bit strike the electrical conduit that ran up the center of this column. He withdrew the bit and, with the aid of a small penlight, peered inside the long cylindrical tube he had drilled. It took two more gentle efforts with the drill to shred the conduit without damaging the wires held within.

This was the third of three such drill holes in this column, each uniformly distanced from the other, like spokes of a wheel. Using a special hook he had fashioned from a garden tool, he had snaked his No. 12 THHN wire from the conduit into the first hole he had drilled. Two spliced wires made connections to the other drilled holes possible. He placed the dynamite inside the drilled tubes, connecting the wires from the blasting caps to the No. 12 THHN with wire nuts. When each of the three sticks was in place, he opened his small Tupperware container filled with wet cement and plugged the drilled holes. In a few short hours the cement seal would cure. By the next day at the same time, after a little work with sandpaper, it would be damn near impossible to spot the plugs.

He had the disconcerting habit of breathing from an open mouth, brought on by two deviated septums, the result of the same accident that had scarred his face. He snorted as he hurried to collect his tools and organize himself.

The fire alarm continued to cry on the other side of the wall. This area was a dead space in the architecture accessed from a crawl space below the utility room. All the pavilions were riddled with such crawl spaces, known to the maintenance crew as utility tunnels and shafts.

The man with the thick glasses slipped through the open space, over a low cement wall and found himself crouching in a dim utility tunnel. Bare bulbs hung at intervals of twenty feet, as far as the eye could see. He pulled his tools over the wall, and then moved slowly in the same low crouch, avoiding banging his head on the overhead pipes. The slightest bump to his head caused him excruciating pain because most of the top of his head was platinum. He'd sometimes laugh to himself about how rich he'd be if he could only melt his own head down.

He didn't much care for darkness. It brought upon him a sensation of choking. Drowning. He was never without his penlight.

He was quite accustomed to traveling around these tunnels. This column was the sixth. Five to go. Four wall charges after that and she was all set. Ready to go. He would have the columns finished by later this afternoon.

What really worried him now was that explosion. He knew without investigating what had happened; if there was one thing this man knew it was the sound of an explosion. He convinced himself it was no big deal. He couldn't let himself worry about it; he couldn't stop now. One charge by itself would do little structural damage. It was the combination that would have the desired effect.

Any explosion would certainly bring the cops, however—and Toby Jacobs; he worried about the Director of Security, a man he had never met and hoped never to meet. Jacobs seemed to have the ability to be in several places at once. It was unnerving.

It wouldn't be long now, he reminded himself. It was almost time.

He reached a door, turned the knob, and pushed it open, quickly shoving his tools into the drab hallway.

He would avoid the site of the explosion at all costs. But he had to appear curious. He left his tools and hurried over to a group of painters. Painters always struck him as a bit short on brains—too long in the fumes.

"What the hell's going on?" he asked as the alarm stopped.

The thinnest of the three replied, "Explosion in the locker room. Maybe gas or something."

"Terrorists," said the one with the potbelly, looking frightened.

The man with the glasses shook his head in disgust. "Terrorists? Here?" He turned and hurried back to his tools, appearing appropriately anxious.

There was much work to do.

TOBY JACOBS PAUSED on Level 3, Pavilion C, Administration Concourse South, overlooking the Atrium, where a group of nearly forty senior citizens walked briskly in unison, headed toward Pavilion B. Ten of them wore the color-coordinated T-shirts of their walking club, the Greyhounds.

It was something of a sociological phenomenon, this walking craze. Seven months earlier, in this hour before the shops opened, the concourses would have been nearly empty. Recently however the "pre-open" hour had swelled in attendance to several hundred. Nearly all were over sixty; all walked energetically for forty minutes to an hour, taking advantage of the empty, environment-controlled space.

Waves of blue hair moved below him. Rotund individuals, alongside bodies deserving the Greyhound logo, pushed themselves to an enviable pace, driving their hearts and lungs.

These elderly walkers gave him a daily sense of purpose: it was like having several hundred grandparents to look after. He had never met his own grandparents, though he'd heard plenty of stories. He appreciated the bright eyes, the pumping arms, the hungry slap of rubber on the polished stone floors. The bluehairs were a wonderful addition to the mall.

He reached up to massage the base of his neck. He yawned. He'd been up half the night working on the spars and rigging to the *Angel*, a ship-in-a-bottle project that had consumed his evenings for the past several weeks. He longed for two weeks on the Cape, with the lazy slap of surf and a cooler at his side. No

chance of that. No time for it. There never seemed to be time for
it.

He studied the Atrium's central chandelier, twenty feet across
at its widest spot, boasting some two thousand individual pieces
of cut glass. It hung above the computer-controlled fountain that
displayed fifty-five separate streams of water in varying heights
and combinations, creating a reported 440,000 possible different
patterns—a promotional claim Jacobs found difficult to believe.
Placed around the fountain were six maturing elms and ten
whitebark birch. Below, and in the shade of these trees, several
dozen varieties of annuals encircled a small rose garden and were
flanked on four sides by hanging baskets of flowering begonias.
The combined colors and smells were intoxicating. All of Yankee
Green was intoxicating.

Suddenly, the building rocked beneath his feet.

He reached for the small radio handset he kept clipped to the
inside of his suit coat. Its two-foot coiled cord ran to the light-
weight walkie-talkie hooked to his belt. From the walkie-talkie
another tiny wire led up between his jacket and shirt and out
between the collars, attached to a clear plastic invisible earpiece.
All his guards carried similar equipment.

"Dicky, what was that?" Jacobs spoke in a pleasant tenor. A
tall lean man, he wore a light suit. A brimmed hat, like something worn by Elliot Ness, sat cocked at a gentle angle over
bushy black brows. The hat provided two functions: it gave him
the appearance of a visitor to the shopping center, a customer
perhaps, and at the same time made him immediately identifi-
able to his security staff—easily spotted in a crowd, even at a
good distance.

He looked up through the immense overhead skylight and
spotted yet another set of steel-wool clouds billowing down from
Boston, toward Providence, trapping the city of Hillsdale and the
Yankee Green beneath an August umbrella of heat and humidity.

Still looking up, he noticed the small antenna protruding from
the wall. Because of interference caused by the tremendous
amount of steel in the huge complex, Security's radio signals
were bounced to these nearby relay stations. From the relay stations the signals were transmitted by coaxial cable to the roof and
then radioed across the street to another set of relays, which

deflected them back across the street to the far end of the mall, where again they ran via coaxial cable to the Security Dispatch Control Center—all this accomplished in less than a thousandth of a second.

Considering where Jacobs stood, there was a certain irony in the complexity of this technological feat: the Dispatch Control Center was just across the way, on the other side of Pavilion C's third level.

Installation of the sophisticated radio relay system had been one of his first recommendations. The old system, riddled with dead spots, had been too inefficient and prone to failure. The new system had cost over twenty thousand dollars. One of the early joys of his job had been spending someone else's money.

He pushed up the sleeves on his poplin suit and tugged at the cuffs of his shirt. He jerked his tie. It felt like someone had tied him up. The jacket was often kept hooked over the back of the chair in the office marked DIRECTOR OF SECURITY AND SAFETY, but not during summer, when air conditioning kept the Green's seven pavilions as cool as meat lockers. Out of habit, he dragged his shoes across the backs of his pants leg. His efforts failed to restore the shoes' original luster.

In the instant of time it took to release the call button, he studied the lush, attractive setting below. The Green's architects had specifically designed the complex to direct customers' attention to the inside, to move the foot traffic deeper and deeper into the heart of the multi-pavilioned maze, and to mesmerize shoppers with exotic sensory experiences, diverting them from the problems of everyday life. It was, in essence, a giant trap: inviting, alluring, seductive. For patrons, an hour passed in a matter of minutes, an entire day in what seemed more like an hour. For employees, this same distractive atmosphere, this purposely controlled confusion, the perpetual temptation for the mind to wander, proved to be a miserable environment to work in.

At 3.5 million square feet, Yankee Green was the second largest enclosed shopping complex in the United States, the third largest indoor amusement park in the world, In New England it was already the stuff of legends.

The voice of the dispatcher, Dicky Brock, came through his

earpiece. "Fire alarms are activated in the new wing. It felt like an explosion."

"Agreed. Get DeAngelo on the horn and find out what's up. I'm headed over there. Keep me informed." Jacobs was moving toward the escalators as he spoke. This central pavilion, Pavilion C, was immediately adjacent to the newest wing.

At the bottom of the escalator, Jacobs turned right. As he dodged his way through a cluster of Greyhounds, several of the seniors said good morning to him. He waved, his concentration on his earpiece.

A huge banner, blocking the eight doors to the new wing, read: GRAND OPENING—FUNWORLD—AUGUST 23RD. PUBLIC INVITED. Below in slightly smaller letters it continued, DON'T MISS YANKEE GREEN'S FIRST LOTTERY DRAWING—$200,000 C*A*S*H—2 P.M. Jacobs ducked around the banner and pushed through one of the fireproof glass doors. When locked magnetically, these doors could sustain an impact of 6,000 pounds of force—another of his security modifications. All doors were now equipped with similar mag locks, under the control of Dispatch's central computer.

The angry pulsing of the fire alarm drove him on.

The final details of the pavilion's construction were being attended to. On Saturday, ribbon-cutting ceremonies would open this latest amusement wing to an expected crowd of five thousand. The Giant's Tail, the world's largest indoor roller coaster, loomed before him. A twelve-foot-diameter solar-powered clock dominated the far wall, a black rack of photovoltaic cells to its left, fed by sunlight through the pavilion's glass canopy.

Today, FunWorld's concourses were nearly empty as a few dozen workers scurried about, dressing up the storefronts, working on electrical fixtures, planting foliage, and installing awnings. Several retailers were busy inside the stores as well, though clearly in the way of the workers.

Jacobs broke into a run.

The monotone beeping in his ear caught his attention. Its pitch clashed with that of the alarm, causing an ugly dissonance.

"The fire is down in Utility Room Five on Sub-level Two," Brock informed him. Jacobs opened the door to the emergency stairway and leaped two steps at a time. The alarm stopped.

He turned left, the bitter smell of fire enveloping him and raising the hairs on the nape of his neck. His heart banged in his chest. He threaded his way through onlookers, sensing the death before he saw it. A chilling silence hung over the normally bois-terous construction workers. He stopped, panting, facing a bloodstained T-shirt that covered McClatchy's crushed head and chest. Inside Room 5, the blackened, smoking remains of what had been a locker room. Several workers finished emptying fire extinguishers on the debris.

"What the hell happened here?" Jacobs inquired of the bare-chested worker to his right.

"Who knows? Whatever it was, it blew McClatchy here to high heaven. I covered what remains of his head with my shirt. His brains is all over the place. Never seen nothing like it."

"Touch anything?"

"No. The boys have been real careful."

"Seen DeAngelo?"

"I hear he's on his way down."

"Okay. Why don't you stick around. See if you can't get somebody to break up the show. We don't need a lot of specta-tors. And why don't we hold any discussion of this down to a minimum until we know exactly what happened."

Jacobs stared at the charred contents of the room as the worker hollered to the men to get back to work and keep their mouths shut until they knew what they were talking about. The hallway emptied quickly.

Jacobs called Dispatch on his radio. "You better notify down-town. This is one for their people."

"What happened down there?" Dicky Brock's voice was anx-ious.

"Explosion of some sort. We lost a man." Toby walked down the drab hall, stooping to stab the errant wedding ring with a pen. He held the ring at arm's length, a glint of fluorescent light sparkling off the edge. "You better notify homicide."

4

HANK STEVENS HAD a delivery to make at the mall. Because of an unexpected, ferocious summer rainstorm in the Atlantic, off the Jersey coast, the driver of the heavily laden Peterbilt had had too little sleep. At five this morning—six hours late—he had made his first deliveries in New Haven. At seven, he had dropped sixteen cases of cod on the outskirts of Providence.

He had yet to eat breakfast and his stomach continually reminded him of that fact, pained by too many coffees and a sticky Milky Way chocolate bar. He kept his hands from shaking by gripping the wheel tightly. He wanted some sleep and a square meal, knowing full well that he still had dozens of deliveries to make in the Boston area, as far north as Marblehead, before this long day would be over. All because of a goddamned New Bedford fishermen's strike.

He steered the rig left at the light and followed a long line of cars into a four-lane access road. He'd heard about this mall, seen pictures of it on the tube, but he'd never been here before.

At its north end was the covered sports stadium. The Boston Patriots had moved here from Foxboro last season, in a deal worked out by the Sullivan brothers. But the stadium was just the beginning. Stevens could see another four structures—damn near as large as the stadium—each connected to the next, all with glass canopies bubbled out of their centers. It looked like a NASA drawing of a space colony.

Thousands of cars were parked in the carefully labeled parking lots. An open vehicle, constructed to look like a San Francisco cable car, turned in front of his rig, ferrying customers from the outlying parking lots to the mall. A sign on its side read: TO PAVILION C. It was packed with women and kids. Stevens couldn't help but notice the number in back. She was built like a centerfold, her thin T-shirt sawed off above the navel. A bright red impression of a kiss hung between her breasts. He couldn't take his eyes off them. Jesus.

She ran some deep red lipstick around her open mouth

and checked herself out in a tiny mirror she fished from her purse.

He followed the trolley. His first delivery listed on the manifest was for a restaurant, the Fish House, in Pavilion C. He figured the trolley would lead him there.

He wanted to reach out and touch her. Firm little buttons, hardened from rubbing against the soft fabric.

Suddenly, without signaling, the trolley made a sharp right into the semi-darkness of the pavilion's underground parking facility. Stevens didn't react quickly enough. The cab's front rubber caught the curb. He jerked the wheel sharply to the left in order to avoid construction scaffolding, but, before his right foot reached the brake pedal, the front of the Peterbilt struck the vertical steel posts that supported the underside of a large cement stairway. The posts fell away like matchsticks. As the front bumper slammed into the concrete stairway, he heard the refrigeration unit connect with the overhead landing.

A large chunk of cement was crushed to dust by the rig's bumper. More cement, from overhead, spilled down the windshield and onto the shiny hood.

It was over in a matter of seconds.

---------- 5 ----------

MARTY AND JESSICA RAPPAPORT started out from their condominium on the north side of the city of Hillsdale. They were late. Marty drove the yellow midsize Cadillac that he had bought equipped with electric everything. Jessi had blue-white hair held in a pink scarf. Her fingers wormed inside a tissue as she checked her seat belt for the third time.

"I get the message, honey," Marty drawled. "There's no need to tug on it every time you think I'm driving too fast. You can just tell me." Marty had grown up in a Jewish neighborhood on Manhattan's West Side, though he spoke without a New York accent. Many of the local residents of Pawtucket, outside of Providence, had a stronger "New York" accent than New Yorkers.

"Okay, I'll tell you," she quipped. "You're driving too fast."
He slowed down.

Even so, she tugged at her seat belt. As a young girl of seventeen, madly in love with the stout and handsome Martin Rappaport, she had ignored her mother's warnings that marrying a Jewish man would make for a difficult life. Difficult in some ways, perhaps. But she had no regrets. Martin Rappaport was about as special as they come. Odd in his own way. Rebellious, even in his late sixties. But there was no other Marty.

Marty eased back on the pedal without argument. Jessi had wanted to sell the Caddy, but he wouldn't ride the city bus no matter what. Going to the shopping center was about all they used the car for anymore, what with everything the mall offered, but she could not persuade Marty Rappaport to ride the bus. He thought that riding the bus was for the really old, and the really poor, and he didn't think of himself as either of those.

"You're never going to be elected president of the Greyhounds if we're always late," she reminded. "We should get an earlier start."

"If I could control the timing of my bowel movement, I would, sweetheart. What am I supposed to do?"

"Less coffee, I think."

She'd been envious of his ability to still drink coffee ever since the doctor had ordered her off it. It was a sensitive subject, one Marty chose to avoid. "Look at that lamppost there. That thing's going to fall over one of these days and kill somebody."

"Everything is unsafe to you. Ever since that trip to Mexico you think you're the expert on everything. Why you had to go to Mexico I'll never know."

"Because our government asked me, that's why."

"They asked you because one of your brothers arranged it."

"Ahh . . ."

"Stay in your lane."

"The lanes are too narrow. They should have made them wider and painted them better."

"There you go again."

"That's not complaining."

She reached out and touched his arm. "Sorry, honey. I just don't like being late."

"I know. I understand."

He reached over. They held hands. Marty smiled and sighed. "Love you, sweet thing."

"Love you, too."

Jessi looked at him. His face was age-stained, his lips a pale white. Since the firm had requested his retirement ten months ago, her Martin had not slept well, did not eat well, and had signs of prostate trouble. His problem was that he couldn't face retirement; he couldn't face the long, empty days and he hadn't found much to replace them with.

In the last few months he had somehow convinced himself that to remain active was to find fault in anything and everything ever built, that remaining active kept one young. She knew only too well that nothing would ever change him. Thank the Lord. She loved him just the way he was—irreverent, strong, loud. Even abrasive. Martin Rappaport knew what was what, and he wasn't afraid to say so.

She had grown comfortable living with him, like learning to sleep with the sound of loud traffic outside your window.

He had always been like this: wound up tight, fully coiled, filled with a straining nervous energy that attempted to escape through a tapping foot, a scratching hand, or running-on of the mouth. His mouth had gotten him in trouble too many times to count. Early on she had tried to point this out to him, but what was the point of trying to change another person? He was an alarmist, plain and simple, and the older he grew the worse he got, now complaining about anything that caught his eye, as if by identifying any fault at all it reinforced his own existence.

There was more than a bit of jealousy in Martin. The youngest of three sons, his oldest brother had inherited the family business, a tray manufacturing company established in the Bronx at the turn of the century. The middle brother, Abraham, became an influential Washington attorney, after handling the family company's expansion. Too young for the big war, Martin had enlisted in the Army and become part of the Army Corps of Engineers just before the Korean conflict. From then on his life had been numbers and drafting, stress ratios and slide rules.

Jessi had met him at a USO dance in Wells, Nevada, four days before he had shipped out: a strong, handsome man who drank well and knew all the best jokes. For three days they had enjoyed a passionate romance that culminated with champagne in bed and the loss of her maidenhood. Off he had gone to war. Three months later she had miscarried, and complications left her unable to bear children.

Martin joined an engineering firm in Dover, Massachusetts. His promotions went slowly (they both agreed this was due to his heritage), to unimportant positions in unimportant divisions. In all, he had spent the last thirty-four years in six firms. He remained envious of his older brother's control of the family company and the large growth the business experienced under his direction. Martin received a small check from his father's trust each month; his brothers elected to reinvest their cash into company shares. Martin had missed much of his brothers' financial success due to his own failure to reinvest.

Now it was the two of them and the Greyhounds. Nearly every day was spent at Yankee Green.

"This is the short cut I was telling you about." He swung left and down a residential road, the houses identical boxes with identical roofs. "You don't get caught up in all the arriving traffic. So much more traffic these days."

She looked over and studied his hawk-nosed profile.

He angled his way through a grid of back streets, finally pulling to a stop sign. Ahead of them was the south side of the sprawling mall.

Ever since Jessi's triple bypass they had used the Green for morning walks. Doctor's orders. Stay out of the heat. Stay out of the cold. The Green's controlled air system was the perfect answer.

So it was that each and every morning at this hour Jessica and Martin Rappaport entered through the doors of Yankee Green, running shoes bound tightly to their feet, shoulders square, a youthful lilt to their stride, heads held high. Marty wore his usual white ever-press shirt, Jessica her pink scarf and khaki walking outfit: an anonymous elderly couple in a sea of stiff-legged septuagenarians.

"Look at that, Jessi!" he exclaimed, pointing to the truck wedged beneath the stairway.

"First we walk, dear. First we walk." She knew he'd be over there within the hour.

———————— 6 ————————

DETECTIVE DOUG SHLEIT stood behind a pair of dirty glasses that dominated his hard face. He was as tall as Jacobs, and his broad shoulders had the same look of being carved from oak. His fore-head reminded Jacobs of a sheer granite cliff rising to a short-cut field of corn-stubble auburn hair. His voice had the sound of a two-packs-a-day smoker and came through lips that barely moved, like those of a character in a low-budget Saturday morning cartoon. He had all the animation of a chiseled stone statue. He walked as if nursing a bad case of hemorrhoids. His suit was wrinkled, the jacket missing a button. He had the deliberately unkempt appearance of a longtime bachelor.

"Jesus," he said, standing at the door to the utility room, Jacobs to his right, "even blew a chunk out of the wall." McClatchy's body had been taken away only moments earlier. Other than the coroner, Shleit had been the only one to lift the T-shirt and look at the man's crushed head.

"No threatening calls, nothing like that?" Shleit asked.

"Not that I'm aware of."

Shleit turned to one of his men. "Can we go in there?"

The man nodded. "Long as you don't disturb nothing, Lieutenant."

"Right," he replied, stepping into the room. "Wanna look at this?" he asked Jacobs, who followed him inside.

The room smelled strangely bitter, confirming that the explosion had been the result of a bomb, not gas. A tremendous hole in the middle of the lockers showed the concrete of the wall. "Any way to tell whose locker was in the middle?"

"Already checked. It was DeAngelo's. He's the general contractor's supervisor."

"Runs the show?"

"Essentially. The contractor spends most of his time split between four or five jobs. DeAngelo keeps this one running."

"I think I'd like to speak with him."

"One thing doesn't track."

"What's that?"

"If someone was after DeAngelo they'd blow the trailer outside. He practically lives in that trailer."

"But his locker   in the middle?" Shleit asked, stepping forward. "No question that bomb was in the middle locker, is there?"

"Looks that way to me."

"Harvey!" the detective shouted into the hallway. "How much explosive we talking about?"

"To do that kind of damage to the wall, I'd say four ounces of plastique or two to three sticks of dynamite. Know more soon. Could have been worse."

"So maybe it was just a warning," said Shleit, fishing for a comment from Jacobs, who had knelt to examine a piece of stretched, scorched metal from the lockers.

"Could be."

"Any guesses who would want to scare the shit out of this DeAngelo?"

"I've been thinking about that—not necessarily DeAngelo, but who might want to do this."

"And?"

"Unfortunately, it's a rather long list."

The two men looked at each other. There was a heavy silence in the room. The hallway had emptied of all but a few police who stood around talking. "I'm listening."

"You'll want to check DeAngelo as well."

"Don't tell me my job, Jacobs. Tell me your long list."

The lack of light in the room and the blackness from the explosion gave Toby the feeling of standing in a cave. "How about in my office?"

"How about in DeAngelo's trailer?"

On the way to the trailer, which was kept on the south side of the new pavilion, Toby received word of the truck accident. He told Brock to inform Traffic Control to reroute cars entering at entrance six.

"What's up?" Shleit asked, waddling along uncomfortably.

"Tractor trailer jumped the curb and struck one of our new stairways."

"Not your day."

"Not that unusual. We get our share of work out here."

"How long you been here?"

"I came on a little over five years ago. Been Director for a little over two."

"You like it?"

"Has its ups and downs. I came out of repo. It's better than repo."

"Anything's better than repo," Shleit said, smiling as he opened the door to the white trailer.

Jacobs smiled back.

DeAngelo was on the telephone, pushed into a corner behind a small desk littered with paper. He had a hook nose and half-filled inkwells beneath his eyes. He held the phone pinched against his stubby chin and waved the men inside, pointing to two chairs that were covered with construction plans.

Shleit moved the plans carelessly to the floor. Jacobs rolled up the set on his chair and placed them on the desk.

DeAngelo ended his conversation, hung up the phone, and greeted Shleit after Jacobs introduced the detective. "Making arrangements for McClatchy's insurance. Goddamned companies love to cover you until they gotta pay up."

"Was he with a sub?" asked Shleit.

"Right. Most of the job's subbed out."

"You had the center locker down there?"

"Right."

"We think it was a bomb. We think it was in your locker."

"What's that mean?"

"You tell me."

Jacobs looked at Shleit curiously. Shleit flashed him a quick glance to silence him.

"Are you saying that someone was trying to kill me?"

"Would someone want to?"

"Jacobs could answer that as good as I could. This place seems to be everybody's favorite target."

"Meaning?"

The big Italian shrugged his shoulders. "You know the situation out here. We busted the unions about four weeks into this project. We pissed a lot of people off. Some of our crew comes from as far away as Fall River. The local boys don't like that too much."

Shleit took out a pad and scribbled down a note. "Anyone in particular?"

"I'm not going to go naming names, if that's what you mean. I might have a couple of guesses, but that's all it would be."

"So who are they?"

"Like I said, the unions."

"That's a little vague." Shleit glanced to Jacobs for support but got none.

"That's all I've got for now." DeAngelo looked over at Jacobs. "You could fill in the rest better than I could."

"So, let's have it," Shleit said.

"Downtown has had us marked since the first pavilion went up. I assume you've read about our battles," Jacobs told him.

"Downtown? You think the downtown merchants would do something like this? I have a hard time believing that."

"They're desperate. It's worse each month on them. We've had threats in the past."

"When I asked you earlier, you answered no to that question."

"Not for some time. No threats for quite some time. Not since they voted Peterson out of the Chamber. But before that, it got pretty nasty."

"Then there's the downtown politicians," added DeAngelo. "Everyone who's anyone knows that the mall is supporting Campagnola's bid for mayor."

"I don't buy that," said Shleit.

"Just thinking out loud," admitted DeAngelo.

"You don't seem very worried by any of this," the detective commented.

"If someone wanted to kill me they'd blow this trailer up. A warning maybe. My guess is the union. You dig hard enough and you'll find your man."

"You're pretty sure of yourself."

"This is a hundred-and-fifty-million-dollar job, detective. The way things have been going in Hillsdale, the unions needed this job."

"Why'd you break 'em?"

"They didn't like the deal."

"Which was?"

"We work six days here, a fifty-hour work week. We only pay overtime after fifty hours."

"I can see how the unions wouldn't like that."

"We had a schedule to keep. We knew what the job would take. They voted a strike. It wasn't our choice. We filled the jobs with scabs. Couple of weeks later we had most of the workers back—they couldn't stay out forever—but without the approval of the union. We made a few guys sore."

"So I would imagine."

"It got nasty for a while, but Christ, that was well over a year ago."

"So it could be organized or it could be some pissed-off worker who lost his job. It could be the Chamber of Commerce," he said, glaring at Jacobs, "or downtown politicians"—offering the same look to DeAngelo. "Anyone else you want to throw into this pot?"

"It has to be someone who knows explosives," suggested Jacobs.

"I've considered that," said Shleit.

DeAngelo's brown eyes narrowed above the dark sacks of sagging skin. "Didn't do any blasting on this job. Too much risk to the other pavilions. A little hammer work is all. Not much of that." He tilted his heavy head and, after a moment of consideration, told Shleit, "You want a name? Bob Russo. Russo was head of the union when we busted it. I've heard rumors for years that he's connected to the Providence families. You might want to talk to him. But it doesn't make much sense, does it? Why would a guy like Russo wait until the job is nearly over to start the threats? It's too late. There's nothing to gain here now."

"Revenge is powerful motivation, Mr. DeAngelo. People do things for the damnedest reasons. Six months ago we had a fifteen-year-old kid shoot his mother for not letting him go to the movies."

"Christ."

Jacobs said, "Russo's well connected."

"That's supposed to be news to me? So am I," reminded Shleit. "You fellas think of anyone else, I'd appreciate hearing about it. This is a big town, gentlemen. If we're going to stop it, we have to stop it at the source. One other thing to think about, Mr. DeAngelo. They've killed a man now. Probably didn't mean to, but they have. That means there's less to lose. And that means they can take more chances." He shifted in his chair. Even sitting down, Shleit looked uncomfortable.

7

THE SMALL MAN'S GRAY EYES tracked the sweep hand on his wrist-watch. He held the watch close to his face despite the thick glasses. At exactly the seven-second mark he threw the elevator's bright red EMERGENCY switch, stopping the descending car with a *thunk* between floors.

From his toolbox he removed a headlamp and a piece of nylon fishing line with a rubber band tied to it. He strapped the head-lamp around his wide, pale forehead and placed its battery pack in the pocket of his faded blue jeans. The elastic band of the headlamp covered his scar.

Too small in stature to reach the elevator's low ceiling, the man pushed it open with a long screwdriver and, after pushing it to one side, used the same homemade tool he had used for snaking wire to hook the foot ladder that was stored on the roof of the elevator car. With the ladder dangling from the ceiling, he wrapped the rubber band around the EMERGENCY switch and tied the fishing line to his belt loop. He pushed the toolbox through first. Then the heavy drill. Finally, he ascended the ladder one last time and pulled himself through the hatch and up onto the roof of the car.

Elevators raced past on either side of him, dangerously close. The elevator shaft was extremely dark, lit only by the narrow beam of his headlamp and the bright blue flashes of sparking electricity high overhead.

He had timed the stop perfectly: the utility tunnel was directly behind him—a deep, dark, four-by-four-foot hole entangled with pipes and lit periodically by bare bulbs. He drew the ladder up and returned it to the roof. Quickly he set the tools in the tunnel behind him. He replaced the ceiling panel, leaving a tiny unnoticeable gap for the rubber band to pull through. He moved into the humming utility tunnel, water pipes and aluminum air ducting overhead. Phone lines, gas pipes, electrical conduits.

He checked the glowing hands of his watch. The drill had slowed him down. One minute, five seconds. He gave the fishing line a good strong tug. As the line tightened, the EMERGENCY switch inside the elevator flipped up, engaging the car's electric motor once again. The car fell away.

The rubber band pulled off the red switch and slipped through the small gap he had left between the escape panel and the ceiling. He took a moment to remove his thick glasses and clean the sweat from the thick lenses, then hooked the wire-frame stems carefully behind his oddly shaped ears. He gazed down into the deep shaft. The elevator hummed away from him, its heavy steel cable glinting in the low light of his headlamp.

Squatting in the tunnel, the man coiled up the fishing line, lifted the drill and toolbox, and hobbled, hunched over, down the congested tunnel.

Fifty feet inside this second-story utility tunnel he paused and tried to tune his ears to any nonmechanical noise. Since the accident, the hearing in his right ear had actually improved. He supposed it had something to do with his going deaf in his left. The doctor had told him that the body has ways of adjusting.

He had grown accustomed to the sound of the tunnels the way a motorist grows accustomed to the sounds of an engine. He heard nothing unusual today, except the faint resonance of banging on a pipe, so faint it had to be at least one level down.

He reached up and dislodged a cinder block and set it in the narrow tunnel. Two more came out as well. As he peered over the lip of the hole in the wall, his headlamp filled the oddly shaped dead space, packed with materials and tools of all kinds, many stolen on site. The space was about the size of a large car trunk. There was a stack of boxes of No. 12 wire, over a thousand feet in all. A pile of scraps lay scattered in the corner. He placed the drill in with his stash, shoving it as far back as he could.

A box of No. 12 barely fit through the hole left by the cinder blocks. He struggled with it to get it through. He replaced the blocks and brushed away the cement dust. He pushed the box of wire along in front of himself and carried the toolbox awkwardly.

Ten minutes later he was at the farthest end of this tunnel. A conduit outlet from one of the nine weight-bearing columns was located here. He began fishing the wire down the conduit immediately, roughly measuring the length he fed out. At fifty feet he stopped, cut the wire with room to spare, and bent it around a pipe to hold it in place. The remaining fifty feet belonged in column number seven.

He continued to re-create the plan in his head. He checked his watch again—a runner monitoring his lap time. Everything was on a certain predetermined schedule. Each aspect of the complex plan had been budgeted a specific amount of time—it allowed him to know exactly how much time he had to make up or how much time he had gained.

Today he had time to make up. He was twenty minutes behind schedule.

8

JACOBS OFFERED SHLEIT his office, so the detective could have a telephone with some privacy. He then checked on a reported purse-snatching at the north end of Pavilion B, but by the time he got there his guards had found the purse which had merely been left behind in a department store dressing room. He decided to check on the damaged staircase located at the northeast wall of the new Fun World pavilion.

Problems requiring his attention seemed to come in six-packs. One of the predictable things about his job was its unpredictability. It never failed that when something went wrong, more problems were soon to follow. First the explosion, then the truck accident. What next?

The idea of walking from the north end of Pavilion B, clear to the south end of Pavilion C, didn't appeal to him at all. His feet hurt and, even at a fast pace, it would take him at least ten minutes—ten minutes he didn't have. He decided to ride a parking trolley instead.

The sign read: WARNING—EMERGENCY EXIT ONLY—ALARM WILL SOUND. He unclipped his plastic ID card from his coat pocket and inserted it into a slot alongside the door. Its magnetic strip alerted the Chubb computer in Dispatch to disable the door's alarm mechanism.

As Director of Security, his card allowed him access to any area in the shopping center at all hours—including all the stores and restaurants. Other cards, whether maintenance, janitorial, security personnel, or retailers, only allowed their holders specific passage to particular areas at certain times, all preprogrammed into the Chubb.

As the reinforced door to the emergency fire stairs hissed and clicked shut behind him, he headed for the basement level where he could catch a ride on a departing shuttle trolley. He bounded down the well-lit stairway effortlessly, hand sliding along the cool steel banister. Next month he would turn thirty-three. He felt about ten pounds overweight. He stood five feet eleven inches, though with his hat, lean look, and rigid posture he appeared taller. He was clean shaven. He had brown-black hair, cut somewhat short, and inquisitive chocolate eyes.

He pushed through the bottom door and out into the underground parking facility, which was filling quickly with cars (the sub-level garages were always full by ten fifteen, leaving parking available only in the outside lots). Thirty yards away, by a cluster of elevators, six trolleys awaited departing passengers. As on any day at this hour, not many people were leaving. Instead, a group of about twenty, just delivered by one of the trolleys, waited for an elevator.

He rode a trolley toward the east lots. As the minibus rounded the corner, Jacobs spotted the demolished stairway. One of his older guards, Phil Robinson, a potbellied man with slumped shoulders and basset-hound eyes, was speaking with a much younger man who had to be the driver. Jacobs was relieved to see the driver had not been injured—not only for the driver's sake, but because of the Green's insurance situation. Liability insurance had tripled in the last two years. The board claimed that if it got much worse the Green would be forced to close. Forever.

Two lawsuits, already in the courts, which had arisen from accidents on one of the rides, threatened the Green with losses of over three million dollars. The cases were due to be wrapped up by mid-September.

Jacobs tugged on an oily plastic cord, sounding an electronic chime, and disembarked, nodding to one of his women guards who was rerouting traffic. The Peterbilt appeared stuck beneath the cement stairway.

He was glad to see his men and women already on the job. It proved the value of Dispatch. Security, at first merely a cosmetic department aimed at dispelling fears of patrons and local politicians, had evolved into a small police force as the Green had expanded. Now, more than two hundred thousand people passed through its doors each week. The parking facilities held more than ten thousand automobiles. What had started out as a few uniformed guards was now a force of nearly eighty.

"What have you got?" Jacobs asked Robinson.

Robinson introduced the truck driver as Hank Stevens. Jacobs shook the man's hand.

"I don't believe this," said the frustrated Stevens.

"All the workers accounted for?" Jacobs asked, pointing to the overhead scaffoldings.

Robinson nodded. "Everyone's fine. No one was anywhere near at the time."

Stevens reviewed the accident for Jacobs, animated and obviously deeply concerned over where the blame would fall.

The Green's electric powered first-aid cart arrived. Jacobs sent it back and then used his walkie-talkie to tell Brock to call off the city fire crew and ambulance. He was too late. Fire truck, ambulance, and a police car arrived only minutes later, sirens blaring.

Two uniformed police along with the head of the fire crew inspected the perimeter of the pile of concrete and twisted reinforcing rod. The policeman put up red Day-Glo tape as a temporary barricade. Bold black letters repeated POLICE LINE——ACTIVE INVESTIGATION——DO NOT CROSS.

Jacobs tugged at his tie. Low gray clouds swirled overhead. The air smelled of cement dust and impending rain.

The fire truck left a few minutes later, as did the ambulance. The two city cops who remained behind loitered by their car, both smoking cigarettes, glancing in Jacobs's direction from time to time.

Jacobs stepped to one side and spoke into the walkie-talkie. He then addressed the driver. "I'm told we can't move your rig until the accident has been inspected by our insurance companies. One covers the mall; several others cover the construction."

The driver scratched his head. "And how long will that take?"

Jacobs shrugged. "An hour, maybe two or three."

"I got perishables in there. Fresh frozen fish straight off the Jersey coast." He pointed. "That beam there smashed my freezer. Lost my freon. Another couple hours, my ice melts, my fish rot, and I got big problems."

"One other thing," Jacobs added. "We have to ask you to run downtown for a tox scan."

"A what?"

"Tox scan: alcohol, drugs, that sort of thing."

"You son of a bitch," the driver snapped. He leaped at Jacobs, swinging. Jacobs dodged the blow by leaning back, caught the man's arm and swung it up behind his back, pressing the man's wrist toward his shoulder blade. Stevens' face contorted. "Okay, okay!" he pleaded. Jacobs eased off and released him. Stevens spun around and tagged him hard on the chin. "Asshole," he yelled.

Jacobs dropped to the sidewalk intentionally, though it looked like a fall. His hat fell off, revealing a thinning patch of hair on the crown of his head. He swung his leg back and connected behind Stevens' knees, knocking the man down. Again he jerked the man's arm up high behind his back. "Stupid thing to do." He forced the man's wrist even higher.

"Don't bust it," Stevens begged.

The two cops tossed their cigarettes, jumped off the hood of their cruiser, and hurried over.

Jacobs said, "You better pull yourself together. These cops look like they're itching to thud someone over the head. Summer heat does that to people."

Stevens saw them coming. "Hey, I'm sorry 'bout the pop. Tired, is all. Come on . . . come on."

Jacobs released him, ready this time.

Stevens threw up his hands. "No problem, guys." The cops collared him.

"Our insurance people require a complete tox scan," Jacobs explained. "Would you please escort Mr. Stevens over to County?"

"You pressing charges on the assault?" the younger one asked.

Stevens turned his head to try and see Jacobs, who hesitated before saying, "No."

The three went along peacefully, Stevens hollering over his shoulder at the last minute, "Tell your boys my freezer is busted. I gotta move that rig or they'll be hearing from *my people's* insurance company."

Jacobs nodded. Robinson checked to make sure no diesel was leaking. When he finished his inspection he said, "Some water's leaking from the trailer, but that's all. Nothing flammable."

Jacobs nodded and said, "Do me a favor and go see how much freezer space the Safeway has available. Ask Popolov to check the various food concessions as well. Also find out how much ice we can dig up on short notice. I doubt these insurance companies are going to be here real soon. If it drags on too long, then maybe at least we can save the perishables."

A crowd began to develop around the accident. With its rides and side shows, the Green aimed to entertain patrons; the collapsed stairway proved to be yet another attraction. Jacobs walked over to two of his traffic guards and asked them to set up some barricades to reinforce the Day-Glo tape. He didn't want any souvenir-taking before the insurance adjusters arrived.

9

THE TWO TEENS began to laugh as they passed the pickles. Both had Afro combs sticking out of the back pockets of their jeans.

"Good morning, Mr. Oreo," one of them said, addressing Verne Greene, who was looking for sliced dills with no garlic. Greene stood as tall as these boys though he was two years younger. They teased him because he worked hard at school, because his mother cleaned the white people's homes, and because his stepbrother had just become an attorney. "Don't call me a lawyer," his brother had said. "I'm an attorney."

Greene wouldn't be baited; he said nothing as they passed. *Sticks and stones*, he thought to himself. He thumbed through the barrel-shaped glass jars, reading labels carefully.

What he really wanted was to pop one of those guys right in the chin.

The fight broke out as he was thinking about it.

THEIR DIVERSION WORKED like a charm. As the two boys began to fight, the butchers rushed to break it up. The other boys stepped up to the long expanse of meat coolers, leaned forward, and started slipping steaks inside their shirts.

Carmichael, a plainclothes security guard who was pretending to shop the dairy cases, responded to the fight immediately; he depressed the walkie-talkie call button three times, signalling Dispatch that he had trouble.

One of the shoplifters, a tough black kid named Frankie, managed to fit two New York Strips up his shirtfront. He turned around and shoved a lamb chop up his back, tucking in his shirt quickly. The fight was over.

Heading down the long aisle toward the checkout lines, Frankie looked for something cheap to buy. Buying something created less suspicion.

The steaks felt nice and cold against his skin. He decided to buy some A-1 sauce and a bag of frozen French fries.

10

LAURA HAFF'S HUSBAND, Tim, had been sixty-five feet above the Hailey tract about to resplice a 180,000-volt power line when the gust of wind hit.

High-voltage tower workers wear a special grounding suit for such work that actually clips into the power line, allowing the huge amount of electricity to pass "through" them, dispelling any chance that contact with the line will electrocute them. Tim Haff had been just about to clip in when the gust hit. Equipment at a nearby weather station measured the same freak gust—a wind sheer—at seventy miles an hour. As the wind hit him, Tim accidentally clipped onto the tower, not the power line. His neck hit the 180,000 volts first.

Laura had been told he had died of a heart attack from contact with the line, but it had been a closed casket, so she had assumed the worst: her husband had fried to a crisp at sixty-five feet, held aloft by a wire mesh suit designed to protect him. He wasn't the first. "Part of the job is the risk," he had told her. Tim Haff had been a risk taker, a brave man with a zest for life few others had.

And Tim was gone.

He had died one year, two months, and one week ago. Laura didn't need a calendar to know that.

Her two daughters had been too young to fully understand. Laura had simply told them that daddy had gone away and wasn't coming back. Some day soon she would have to explain. Shelly would turn five next month. Someone was bound to tell her first if Laura didn't get around to it; but Laura had spent the last year and two months trying to rebuild, not dwell on Tim's death. "Done and gone," is what he would have said about his own condition. Done and gone and buried.

She reached down sadly and picked up the package of bacon. Tim had liked bacon with his eggs.

Last September Laura had been rehired, after a six-year absence, as a third-grade teacher in East Hillsdale Elementary School. The life insurance had been paid out just after Thanksgiving. She had put nearly all of it into several certificates of deposit. The interest on the CDs had allowed her to place Keze, age three, and Shelly into a morning summer camp where they could learn arts and crafts, swim, and play with friends. In truth, the camp was not solely for the benefit of the girls. Laura had had a rough year. She needed some time alone in quiet. Time to get the house together. Time to have coffee with her friends and talk. Time to shop.

The Safeway at Yankee Green was the single largest food market in the Northeast. Thousands of penny-conscious housewives like Laura made a special twenty-minute drive once a week from either Boston or Providence just to shop the market. The savings would pay for the gas and then some, or so read the full-page daily display ads in both cities' newspapers. Nearly everyone in the greater Hillsdale area shopped the market.

Pavilion A contained over twenty amusement rides for the kids' enjoyment. While Mom shopped, the kids played. Each pavilion had its own day-care center—the Green employees called them Puppy Patrols—staffed by scores of trained and certified teenage girls, each of whom took charge of no more than two children at a time. Although the service was only provided full-time in the summer months (afternoons during the school calendar), an independent survey conducted by a marketing firm out of Boston had shown the day-care concept had resulted in a fifteen percent increase in mall attendance and a twenty-five percent jump in retail sales.

Today was Laura's second trip to Yankee Green. It was nice to shop without having to keep track of the girls. She felt a little pang of guilt as she dropped the package of bacon into her cart. Was it fair of her to put the kids in camp? She wasn't sure they liked it. She had difficulty admitting that it might be more for herself than for the girls.

Bent over, she looked at the reflection of her face in the mirror that doubled the impact of the meat in the long line of open refrigerator space. Twenty-seven years old going on thirty-five, she thought. More lines this year than before, lines that wouldn't be there if Tim were still alive. Pale skin. Need more tennis, or maybe a bikini and some pool time. Dream on. Barely time to shop. No way for pool time. Soft green eyes. Lifeless. Hair still holding a two-month-old perm. Everyone always complimented her on her hair. She hated it. Decent cheekbones, thin little neck. Boobs sucked dry by two children. They looked better when she was pregnant. Tim had joked about how she should stay pregnant all the time. Jokes. Tim. Time. Too pale. Lifeless.

The fight broke out to her right. Two black kids were really going at it. She took three brisk steps toward the commotion and stopped herself. Tim had always encouraged her to participate. "Don't watch life go by, Laura. Get in there and do something." But he had also warned her against her habit of biting off more than she could chew. Could she stop the fight? Or would she just find herself in the middle? Despite her small size, Laura Haff had

unseen strength. She'd grown up with two older brothers, and
she was tough. One year, two months, and eight days ago she
would have charged right in there and taken her chances. But
what if this time her efforts failed and one of the boys shoved her
or even hit her? What about the girls? She stepped back to her
cart, hands clenched at her sides.

When Frankie and friends approached the meat counter and
began stuffing their shirts with meat, she couldn't believe her
eyes. Good God, there were at least ten of them. She realized the
two closest to her were meant to screen the others from view,
and the fighting was no doubt an attempt to distract management.

She looked around, her earlier reservations about becoming
involved suddenly vanished. Through a small window in a
swinging door she could see an aproned man signing for a delivery. She pushed through the doors and grabbed the man by the
arm. His apron was sky blue and dirty. His bald head was sweating. His name tag listed him as produce manager. Good enough
for Laura Haff. She pulled on his elbow, her teacher instincts
emerging. "Come with me."

The man had no choice. Laura dragged him through the
swinging doors. "Lady," he finally objected.

"You won't believe this," she announced.

"Lady! I've got a delivery."

"This is more important." She steered him up an aisle. The
shoplifters had dispersed from the meat counter. Frankie was
searching for the A-1 sauce. She led the produce man up to this
boy. "Young man," she said, catching up to the young hoodlum.

Frankie didn't look over.

Laura Haff reached out and yanked his shirttail out of his
jeans. The packaged meat fell onto the floor. "See?" she asked.

"Hold it," the aproned man demanded as Frankie took off at
a fast run down the aisle.

The boy stuck out a long arm and raked a ten-foot run of
bottles from the shelf. He grabbed a cart from a shopper and
launched it down the aisle at the approaching man, who fell
down and shouted again for the boy to stop.

"Thief!" Laura Haff yelled at the top of her lungs, leaping over the downed manager and jigging her way through the fallen bottles in hot pursuit. "Stop him!"

As she rounded the corner at the end of the aisle she ran smack into a security uniform.

─────────── 11 ───────────

CARMICHAEL'S INITIAL ALERT triggered a chain reaction by Dicky Brock in Dispatch that included notifying Toby Jacobs of the trouble. A three-pulse warning meant there was an engagement under way. At the very least, a "three-click" meant a fight; at worst, an armed robbery or a hostage situation.

Jacobs left the scene of the truck accident immediately, choosing to jog outside along the sidewalk rather than inside, where he strictly enforced a no-running law.

It took him several minutes to run the east perimeter of Pavilion C, and another few to go the length of Pavilion B. Over time, the facility seemed smaller and smaller, a deception brought on by familiarity. But at moments like this, the Plaza seemed gigantic.

"You're about to run into Captain Blow Dry," Brock said into Toby's earpiece as the Director of Security yanked open a door to Pavilion A. Brock had been monitoring his boss's run via the Dispatch monitors responsible for parking lot surveillance. His warning came perfectly timed.

Peter Knorpp, the mall's general manager, wore a tailored suit that fit snug against his lean body. A thick gold-plated bracelet sparkled on his thin wrist, sliding under his tailored cuff. Knorpp's blond hair held its shape perfectly, no doubt thanks to a hairspray or mousse. The California native's teeth reminded Jacobs of a toothpaste ad; his artificially low voice, of a B actor long since forgotten. "What's this about a bomb?"

"Later, Peter," Jacobs said, pushing through the swelling crowds. "Not the best place to talk about it."

Knorpp caught up to Jacobs and grabbed him by the arm. "If this Safeway thing is those damn niggers again, some heads are going to fly, and the first'll be yours. I warned you about them."

Jacobs glared at the mall manager and shook his grip free. "One of these days that mouth of yours is going to get you into trouble you can't get out of," he warned sternly. "Why don't you go upstairs, Peter, and let me handle this?"

"Not a chance. I've seen the way you 'handle' these situations. You can't play buddies with them forever, you know."

The automatic door whooshed open. Groceries lay strewn everywhere. Several security guards had bloodied faces, as did many of the youths they had collared.

A few of the kids shouted at Jacobs. "Mr. Jacobs, they got the wrong guys." "Mr. Jacobs, we didn't mean nothing. Just having a little fun."

"I'm innocent," Verne Greene yelled over the objections of the others. "I had nothing to do with this."

"Friends of yours?" Knorpp asked sarcastically.

Carmichael approached Jacobs and Knorpp, reaching for his handkerchief to dab away some blood from his lips. "It came apart on us, Toby. We were ready and waiting, but the produce manager spotted one of them and started a chase. All hell broke loose."

"That much is obvious," interjected Knorpp.

"Why don't you handle Atkinson?" Jacobs suggested strongly, gesturing to the frantic manager of the supermarket. "I've got this."

Knorpp swelled out his chest, ready with a comment, but trudged away instead.

Carmichael described for Jacobs the series of events. The chase had led to food coming off the shelves. A collision and a fight broke out. In all they were holding seven of maybe ten or twelve kids. Only one had actually been seen with meat hidden on his person.

Jacobs caught up to Knorpp and Chuck Atkinson, the bald, aging store manager. "We don't have enough to hold them on," Jacobs began.

"Enough to hold them on? Are you out of your mind?" Atkinson pointed. "Look at this place. Look at the inventory I've lost. I'll be closed the rest of the day. Maybe longer. Nothing to hold them on?" He turned to Knorpp. "I've been over this with you a dozen times. These hoods are nothing but trouble. They hassle every damn retailer in the mall. You know it. I know it. Christ, something has got to be done! This is ridiculous." He took a deep breath and announced, "I demand something be done!"

Knorpp looked at Jacobs. His black leather loafers reflected the overhead lights like two oddly shaped mirrors. "Call downtown. Arrest them," Knorpp demanded of his head of security.

"It's about time." Atkinson ran a hand across his head, a response from when he had once had hair.

Jacobs pulled Knorpp aside and whispered harshly, "Do *what?*" He threw his jaw forward in disbelief. "One kid was caught with a steak. One out of seven. What are you going to do about that?"

"Arrest them," Knorpp hissed.

"We can throw them out, Peter. We can put them on our shit list and keep them out. This mall is everything to those kids. Don't you think that keeping them away is punishment enough? Why bring in the cops? Why give 'em a police record? We have bigger worries today, Peter. Think it over. Who needs the added hassle?"

"Your Big Brother approach hasn't worked, Jacobs. Face it. You keep trying to make peace with these kids. But they're troublemakers, plain and simple. They'll always be troublemakers."

"They're bored unemployed youths, most from broken families. I agree they've worn out their welcome, but we're not helping anyone by giving them criminal records."

"I want them arrested. Every last one of them."

Jacobs glared as Knorpp went over to console Atkinson. His attention fell on Verne Greene, who declared his innocence again. He moved over to the group of youths and addressed the leader, a tall black kid with a short Afro. "Who's he, Earl?"

"How should I know? He's a *sophomore,*" Earl said, to the amusement of the others. "Sophomores don't mean shit."

"I'm innocent. I had nothing to do with this," Greene declared.

"Is he with you?" Jacobs asked.

"Him? Hell, no. You think we'd hang around with a sophomore?"

"Pretty big for a sophomore," Toby said suspiciously, eyeing Greene.

"Cut him some slack, Mr. Jacobs. He didn't do nothing. Honest."

"I swear," Greene said hopefully.

"Okay," Toby nodded. He cocked his head. "You can go. But you stay away from the mall for a week. You got that? I see you in here, you won't get a second chance."

"No sweat, mister. Who'd want to be in this place anyway? Good riddance." Greene stepped out of the group.

Jacobs paid him no mind. He said with anguish, "Why'd you do this to me, Earl? I thought you and I understood each other. You screwed up. Now I have to bring you all downtown."

"The cops?" The leader was clearly horrified.

"Orders from management."

"Mr. Slick over there?"

"He runs the show, Earl."

"Hey!" Knorpp shouted, seeing Greene at the door. "Stop him." A guard stopped Greene. Knorpp hurried over to Jacobs. "Just where the hell is *he* going?"

"He wasn't a part of this," Jacobs said.

"Says who?"

"He wasn't a part of it, Peter."

"Arrest him. The cops can decide who was and who wasn't a part of this," Knorpp instructed loudly. "Take them all out of here. We're pressing charges. Him too."

"Peter—"

"I'm overruling you on this one, Jacobs. You're too soft on these kids. They all go downtown. It can be straightened out down there."

"You'll be sorry about that, Slick," Earl said.

Knorpp bristled. Jacobs pushed Knorpp away from the bunch and whispered angrily, "You're arresting that kid because he's black, Peter. Think about it. How stupid is that? He had nothing to do with this. He's not a part of their group."

Knorpp pushed past his Director of Security. "I want these kids out of here now!" he shouted.

12

THE WHITEWASHED GREEK DELI occupied a retail space on the east concourse of Level 1, Pavilion A. Mediterranean-blue letters spelled out the name in oversized pseudo-Greek typeface. Like most of the retail stores in the Green, there were no doors across the front of the deli. At closing, the shop owners rolled metal lattice cages down electronically and locked them shut. For the Greek Deli the open look worked especially well.

Mhykloteus "Mykos" Popolov, the proprietor, short and round with a dark weathered face, wore a white apron at all times, his stumpy legs protruding from beneath it to reveal wide sandaled feet and his trademark white socks. His teeth twisted inside thick red lips. He had hairy ears, bushy eyebrows, and tufts of white hair escaping from the T-shirt he wore beneath the apron. His shoulders were strong and broad. His right arm stopped just above the elbow, the amputation a constant reminder of his service in Italy's underground resistance during the Second World War.

Rarely a day passed that Mykos did not recall that nightmarish experience. Even now, with the radio droning in the background, his attention was split between the guest on the talk show and his memories. Nineteen hundred and forty-three. The German patrol closed the gap quickly, the sharp barks of their dogs piercing the silence of dawn. Then the rumble of a train nearby. Popolov pushed through the woods and came face to face with a slowly moving freight train that seemed endless. He could sense the patrol was gaining on him despite the overpowering noise of the train. He had nowhere to go. No way to escape. He debated diving under the train as he ran along the clearing that edged the tracks. Then a gunshot from behind. He studied the gaps between the wheels and established a rhythmic count. Another gunshot. He distinctly remembered crossing himself as he stooped and dove under the clacking steel wheels. He landed face up, the underside of the train rushing only inches above him. The wheels roaring in his ears. Screaming in his ears. He counted and rolled out the other side, his right arm trailing behind him. . . .

He wiped at a stain on his apron. Looking up he spotted a girl of seven or eight standing with her mother at the counter. He smiled and the child giggled, burying her face in her mother's skirt.

When the store was empty, he turned to his plump Italian wife. His voice resonated like an opera singer's, carrying rhythms even when speaking. "Have you been listening to this, Mother?"

Popolov's wife—"Mother," he called her—was as round and short as he. "Mother," to Mykos Popolov, meant Gaea—the supreme Greek goddess who bestows all good things to all people. Unlike the old man's white hair and brown eyes, Gaea had graying black hair and sharp blue contented eyes. She wore flowered print dresses, usually containing a shade of red, and shiny black shoes. Her legs were mapped by varicose veins so she had taken to wearing flesh-colored tights. She shuffled stiff-legged when she moved about, pushing her feet noisily across the floor. She shook her wide round head. "I can't listen to him." She continued wiping down the wooden tables that occupied the front quarter of the large delicatessen mini-market.

"I understand," he said compassionately. Popolov positioned himself by the clock radio, listening intently. A young thickly accented male voice spoke stridently.

"Who wants junkies and pimps in their back yards? Answer me that. These half-breeds aren't worthy of dog pounds. They think they can run fear into our lives and drive us into hiding with their violence and filth. They're nothing but street scum—sewage—meat scraps that should be flushed down the toilets and out of our lives. Why should we put up with needle freaks who corrupt our children just to maintain their own habits? Dog hair like that should be shaved and burned, if you ask me. I don't see that there's any choice, is there? Are we all a bunch of you-know-whats content to roll over in the face of a few greaseballs who think they can ruin the beauty of American life? Is that what we've come to?"

The talk show host's voice cut in. "But isn't a citizen's protection group simply a euphemism for a vigilante group, Mr.

Civichek? We have the Guardian Angels. Some would say they cause enough problems already. Why do we need the Flock?"

"Excuse me, one minute," said the same Bronx-accented voice, "but the Guardian Angels have my respect until the day I die. You're committing a sin by putting them down. These are people, just like the Flock, who volunteer their time to walk our streets, ride our subways, and patrol our schoolyards."

"Then what's so special about the Flock?"

"Listen here, the Angels can't be everywhere, can they? They do their best to take care of the larger cities in this country. The Flock is for places like Hillsdale, Springfield, Providence, Portland, and the dozen other smaller cities we're already located in. Our bylaws aren't so different than the Angels'. We have dress codes. We ask our people to look nice. Many of our people are specially trained in CPR. Not even the Guardian Angels can claim that. We aren't afraid of being tough—maybe a little tougher than the Angels, because sometimes you have to crack one of these goofballs over the head—and we aren't afraid of the lawsuits. I've been to court many times over the last three years, and I'm here talking to you, aren't I? I'll let you be the judge of how the courts decided. You don't see me in jail, do you? The goofballs, the greaseballs, the meat scraps are the ones still in jail. They can try and slow us down with lawsuits, but the Flock will never crawl; we just run slower, that's all."

"You say we don't see you in jail, but in fact you were once in jail for grand theft, were you not? Didn't they call you the Elevator? Weren't you a so-called second-story man?"

"Sticks and stones, Mr. Commons. You dredge up my past and try to spread it around over your airwaves like so much crud. Yes, yes, yes. You think I'm going to sit here and deny it? Sure, I went the way of the environment I was raised in. I don't deny anything. But where am I now? I recognized the very ingredients that led me down the wrong path, and I'm back to put an end to those influences that corrupt and degrade the minds of our youths. The Flock travels under the eyes of the Good Lord, not the Devil, Mr. Commons. Your listeners can certainly recognize the difference."

Mrs. Popolov had stopped sponging the tables. Now she

looked up at her husband, who was bent over the radio. "You see, Mykos, he *is* a criminal."

"I read in today's paper that he was arrested once. Can you imagine? A criminal! And now look. He claims he wants to clean up the streets, get the junkies out of the alleys, and give the kids a chance. Who can trust him? Answer me that."

On the radio Civichek said, "The Flock is what America is all about."

"Mother of God," Mrs. Popolov gasped, making the sign of the cross, "he frightens me."

Popolov switched off the radio. "If I had any guts, Mother, I'd chase him out of town. No good can come of this."

The thought of her husband's bravery renewed her concern over the letter. For weeks she had been awaiting the letter. Where could it be? Certainly the Italian government would award him the Medal of Honor for his work in the underground. How could they not? And for him it would mean so much—a simple acknowledgement of a country's appreciation. He never spoke of it, but for years he had been waiting for that medal.

Chuck Atkinson, the bald manager of the Safeway, stood in the doorway. "Peter has ordered them arrested!" he said gleefully. "My store is ruined, but we're finally making some progress."

"The children?" Mrs. Popolov asked.

"The *gangs*, yes," acknowledged Atkinson. "I thought the president of the Retailers' Association should know."

"That's great news. Come in, Chuck. Have some coffee."

Mrs. Popolov glared at her husband. Their opinions differed sharply on finding a solution to the gangs of kids who roamed the mall and often scared away potential business. She was of the same opinion as Toby Jacobs, who advocated hiring the youths instead of trying to force them out.

Her husband, the go-between representing the retailers to management, had taken a firm stance against the gangs, though mostly, she knew, because he felt the democratic obligation of representing the wishes of his constituency. Deep down inside Mykos was rooting for the kids, though he never showed it.

"I can't stay." Atkinson explained the fight and the trashing of his store. "It will take us all day, maybe longer, before I can reopen. I don't need to tell you what that means. The store is a mess."

"I'll help you clean up."

"Nonsense."

"It's the least I can do. Mother, you watch the store." She nodded. It did not surprise her that her husband would offer his services—insist on helping a neighbor—as he just had. Helping others was at the very core of his personality. It was what he lived for. It was what had attracted her to him thirty-seven years ago, on a stormy night in the middle of an air raid. Mykos Popolov thrived on helping other people.

"You're kind to offer. . . ." Atkinson hesitated, not knowing what a one-armed man could do.

"Of course I will help. You will see. We will have you back in business in less than an hour." On his way out the door, Mykos turned and said, "Mother, call Bill Dramboski and see if he can't send some of his Puppy Patrol over to help us out. It's almost noon. Most of the mothers pick their children up around now. The young ladies are probably standing around with nothing to do. Tell him we'll have them back in no time. Tell him it's a favor." Popolov slapped his meaty left hand around the shoulders of Chuck Atkinson. "We'll have you back in business before you know it." His big voice was fading into the roar of the rushing crowds, but his wife heard him say, "Have you heard anything about a young man named Les Civichek? He's a dangerous man. He plans on speaking in the mall tomorrow. I don't think that's such a good idea. . . ."

13

"I'M AWFULLY BUSY, so let's get right down to it."

Marvin Haverill looked British. He sat at the head of the conference table, his gray pencil-thin mustache and black eyebrows giving him a distinguished look consistent with his Ivy League background. He wore a blue silk handkerchief in his coat pocket, matching tie, gold collar pin. His hair receded from a widow's peak above a broad forehead with tire-track creases across it. His large ears wiggled as he spoke, an annoying and distracting occurrence that somehow contributed to his intimidating presence. He had the voice of a man who shouted too much.

The conference room's indirect cove lighting and hardwood appointments reflected Haverill's professional attitude. There was no artwork on the walls to distract the participants. Each place at the table held an inverted water glass, a microphone on a flexible arm, and a small felt-padded paperweight embossed with the Yankee Green logo. The African-hardwood conference table was surrounded by ten chairs, though only three were occupied. Knorpp and Jacobs flanked Haverill.

"What about this explosion?" the big man asked of Jacobs.

"The police are conducting their own investigation, headed by a Lieutenant Shleit. He seems competent enough, but if you agree, sir, I'd like to conduct my own investigation as well."

"I'm listening."

"I'd like to turn over a good deal of the everyday management to Brock, freeing me to poke around some."

"The explosion is going to hurt our grand opening," added Knorpp. "No question about that. I'd say we should step up our advertising in these last few days to try and overcome the negative publicity."

"Should we even open?" Haverill asked. He paused. "Toby?"

"At this point there's no indication the two are connected. No one has claimed responsibility for the bomb, probably because of the death."

"We certainly can't stop the opening *now,*" interjected an irate Knorpp.

"We most certainly *can,* if we have to," corrected Haverill.

"We'd lose what, a hundred thousand dollars in advertising and promotion fees? How can we justify that?"

"A man was *killed,* Peter." He turned to Jacobs. "I think you have a good idea. The sooner we know what's going on, the sooner we can make a rational decision on the opening."

"But this could be exactly what the bomber wants!" objected Knorpp. "He could be trying to close us down."

"Who else would do something like this?" Haverill asked Jacobs.

"Shleit and I discussed the unions with DeAngelo. Shleit thinks this is a little too obvious for Russo. He thinks Russo would try something a little more underhanded, something more subtle."

"After my dealings with the man, I'd have to say I agree. I don't put revenge past a man like Russo, but nothing so blatant. He strikes me as a constrictor, not a venomous snake. He's the kind to squeeze you to death. Who else?"

"I mentioned downtown to him."

"I hardly think that likely," commented Haverill. "They dislike us, yes. But bombing us? I don't think so."

"I wouldn't be so sure," said a disagreeable Knorpp. "They're getting desperate. Their second quarter sales were off another eighteen percent. That's twelve straight quarters of losses. They can't sustain that. Nothing would help them more than to have people afraid to shop the Green."

"I just can't believe they'd resort to this kind of thing."

"They're desperate. Desperate people are unpredictable."

"Toby, what do you think?"

Jacobs felt uncomfortable constantly contradicting Knorpp, a position he often found himself in. "Peter's right about the downtown merchants being desperate. And desperate people are unpredictable. But that particular group of men just doesn't strike me as the criminal kind. I could be wrong. A few of them might have hired a professional to try and discredit us, but if I had to make a guess, I'd say this isn't their work."

"I agree." Haverill scratched a note to himself and asked, "What about people with past grudges? There's certainly a long list there."

"That's part of the reason I'd like a chance to investigate. The police won't cover the long shots."

"I'll expect daily reports."

Jacobs nodded.

"But we continue as if we're opening on Saturday, don't we?" Knorpp wondered.

"I think we should. Yes." Haverill looked inquisitively at Jacobs.

"I agree."

"And what about security arrangements for the lottery money?" Knorpp asked.

"It's worked out as we discussed. It's the state's responsibility. It's their lottery after all, not ours. They've hired an independent security firm to handle the movement of the cash. It'll be placed in the display on Saturday around noon and guarded heavily. I have a meeting late Friday with the company handling the job, and I don't foresee any problems. I'm still uncomfortable with that much cash on hand—it's simply too tempting a target—but I've said that before, haven't I?"

"There was little we could do," Haverill said with the uncommon sound of apology in his voice. "The cash makes it such a good media event. After all the tax concessions city hall's given us, we couldn't very well turn them down."

Jacobs grunted. He didn't like the situation, but there was nothing to be done about it.

"It's terrific PR," interjected Knorpp, who had supported the idea all along. "Who the hell's ever seen two hundred thousand dollars in cash? It's gonna bring us a lot of business."

"Anything else?" asked an impatient Haverill, stealing a look at his wristwatch. Knorpp checked his Rolex.

"There's the truck accident outside the new wing," Jacobs reminded. "If we could lean on those insurance inspectors it would help out the situation. We have nine tons of fish about to go bad. If we don't move that truck before tomorrow—"

"What about off-loading the fish?" interrupted Haverill.

"My people contacted the parent company. They're reluctant to try and move the fish. They'd rather move the trailer."

"Christ, it'll smell up the place something awful," Knorpp pointed out. "That's all we need."

"If they take much longer, the insurance companies are going to get themselves in an interesting situation," said Jacobs. "By dragging their feet they're going to get us sued, which, I assume is what they're trying to prevent by making the inspection."

"Good point. I'll run that by Phil Huff and see if we can't light a fire under them. . . . Speaking of lighting a fire under someone. Where exactly do we stand on our anchor space, Peter? Any progress there?"

"Is that all for me, sir?" Jacobs asked. The new wing's biggest anchor, Northern Lights, a regional department store, had gone bankrupt without warning two weeks earlier. The result was an empty space the size of Fort Knox in the new wing. Empty space was a mall's biggest curse. For two weeks Knorpp and Haverill had been struggling to fill the spot. Rumors were rampant that they would give the space away if the right tenant came along. Knowing Haverill, Jacobs thought that was stretching it a bit. Haverill didn't give anything away.

Haverill nodded.

Jacobs stood to leave. Knorpp had the weasel face of a man about to announce failure, and Jacobs had no desire to stick around.

14

IN TOTAL DARKNESS he began to feel queasy. He switched on the headlamp, despite the noise in the distance. He felt as if he were underwater, swimming at night toward the target, still several hundred yards ahead of him.

A simple training routine was all it was. SCUBA his way across the bay, plant the charges on the hull of the old freighter being used as a dummy, and swim back to a checkpoint. It had later been explained to him as an "operational miscommunication." The Navy's airmen were on a training mission too, that night. And their mission was to bomb the same deserted freighter that had been towed out for target practice.

Instinctively he touched his head where there should have been skull. All he remembered was the darkness of the water and the blinding flash. From that day on, total darkness made him queasy.

He threaded the No. 12 wire into the wide conduit that ran the length of the narrow utility tunnel. These two wires would serve as his master trunk line for the detonators. His work on the last column had gone quickly, the cement softer than he had encountered previously. He had picked up a half hour.

He was anxious to see the damage caused by the accidental explosion. It had a specific purpose, and a quick look would tell

him if he had calculated its effects correctly. But the look would
have to wait. That area would be far too hot for the next few
days.

His efforts consumed his every moment. For the past eight
weeks he had worked furiously to accomplish all that had to be
done. As usual, he had been sleeping very little. Now, with just
days to go, each minute seemed more exciting than the last.
Timing was everything. His moment was at hand.

At first, entering the construction site had made him nervous.
Then, after just a few visits, he realized there were too many
subcontractors' crews working intensely to finish up the project
for anyone to notice him. Hundreds of workers were scattered
around the three-hundred-thousand-square-foot pavilion, from
construction supervisors to installers and testers of the numerous
rides that would comprise FunWorld. He blended right in. He
wore blue jeans, a T-shirt advertising Mepps fishing lures, and a
tool belt. He looked no different from any of the others.

Once he overcame his initial fears, movement through the
facility had become easy. He had stolen three different sets of
plans and, over several weeks, all the materials he would need. All
but the explosive gelatin, which he made in a homemade lab in
his apartment, a copy of *The Anarchist Cookbook* at his side.

He had a job to do, and he intended to do it correctly.

He had just finished snaking the No. 12 when he heard the
sound of a voice not far behind him. The utility tunnels inter-
sected throughout the complex, not only with other utility tunnels but with vertical utility shafts as well, the basement-to-
rooftop chimneys that carried the same piping and conduits. He
had to be careful. As the project neared completion, more and
more legitimate electricians and inspectors would be traveling
these tight passages. Where construction workers would not realize he was not a hired electrician, other electricians most likely
would. He had to avoid them at all costs.

With no way to tell who might be approaching, the man set
off quickly down the tunnel. With practice he had become quite
agile at moving through the tunnels, which to the laymen
seemed almost impassable. He reached an intersection and
turned left—north—now facing the older Pavilion C. These two
pavilions were separated by a twelve-foot gap between their out-

side walls, except for the walkway on Level 1 and Spanner's Drugs on Level 2. Their utility tunnels were not connected, as some other utility tunnels in the complex were.

Reaching a vertical utility shaft a moment later, he hurried down the ladder grips mounted in the cement, the moist smell of clay filtering through his battered nose. He paused and listened. He was all alone. He had ditched whoever had been behind him.

At Sub-level 1 he joined up with another tunnel and headed toward his stash. It was nearly midday. Nearly time to go to work on another column. For the past several days there had been some jackhammer work going on outside just after lunch. The noise made the perfect cover for his star-bit drill.

He pulled down the cinder blocks carefully and aimed his headlamp into his makeshift storage area. He grabbed the drill and his longest extension cord. He had to discard the small amount of cement from the Tupperware and mix himself a fresh batch, using water from a plastic jug hidden there. After five minutes and a quick polish of the thick lenses, he was on his way again, the extension cord across his chest like a bandolier.

15

LAURA HAFF FOUND a place to sit down. The fight in the grocery store had rattled her. She checked her shopping list. Tim had taught her to write notes, and a good thing, too, now that she was single. So much to do just to stay on top of things.

She checked her list:

Take girls to camp
Food—milk, cereal, margarine, veggies, noodles, Kool-
       Aid, orange juice, tuna, popcorn, hot dogs,
       hamburger (1#), hamburger helper
Drugstore—aspirin, Keze's med., Tampax, dental floss
Sandals?

The nice thing about Yankee Green—even if it was too big, as everyone claimed—was that absolutely *anything* could be found within its walls. *One-stop shopping,* she thought, reminded of the many ads for the mall she saw every week: billboards, radio, television, newspapers.

She had shopped closer to home until last week, when she had read about the frozen food and vegetable prices at Safeway. That was all it had taken. She changed her allegiance in one week from small store to mega-mall.

On her one previous visit she had had no time to explore the enormous six-pavilion complex. Today, the kids would not be ready until noon and it was just after ten, so why not?

The sound of the towering fountain relaxed her. It had taken her a full ten minutes to walk from the Safeway in Pavilion A to the Atrium in Pavilion C. She had passed replicas of New York streets, a life-sized model of the space shuttle, a few hundred stores, and few dozen restaurants. Like a movie scene of Paris, hundreds of shoppers sat around white patio tables, reading, eating, drinking, and chatting. The sound of the voices seemed to be absorbed by the relentless fountain.

Laura had nearly passed this area by because as she arrived a large crowd had been watching a pair of costumed jugglers. She was not in the mood for crowds; she was feeling lonely, and crowds only made her feel more alone. When Laura felt as she did now, she longed for some quiet, reflective solitude to let her mind wander and grab what it would. The background hum of the fountain was perfect for that.

But her mind focused on her children. Keze would need a doctor in a day or two if her cough didn't improve. Laura wouldn't let her swim until it did. The thought of a doctor made her think of money, which in turn reminded her of the large insurance settlement and what to do with it. Her father had suggested she invest it in mutual funds. Her brother, a broker, trusted the stock market and advised avoiding aerospace and buying blue chips: "Good steady growth potential and strong dividends," he had told her.

Tim had liked certificates of deposit. That's where her money was now, growing at a modest rate. The account had earned nearly thirteen thousand dollars in interest. How strange, she thought, that with Tim gone the family now had more money than when he had been working. Her teaching salary, combined with the interest on the CDs, brought in over thirty thousand a year. They had a new car, a new VCR, and morning camp for the girls. All she needed now was Tim back.

She worried for the girls. They would have to be told the truth. Shelly had come through it well so far, though Laura thought that perhaps she knew. Keze still occasionally asked where Daddy was.

Laura glanced up at the changing patterns of the fountain. Beautiful. It seemed never to repeat itself. She wondered if she should repeat herself. Should she go on a "manhunt" as her friend Georgine constantly suggested? All the arguments were there, most importantly that the girls could use a man around the house. At their age, the loss of their real father had not yet had too much impact on them. In a few more years, acceptance of a new man around the house would be difficult for them.

It had been over a year. For the first six months there had been no urges whatsoever. Lately, however. . . . Her physical desires were returning, no matter how hard she tried to keep them at bay. Her denials were finally being denied by nature. It hit her in waves, a week or two apart. Flashes of desire. Glimpses of guilt.

In her heart she believed that no one could ever replace Tim. So what was the use? Georgine kept telling her that replacing Tim was not the idea; starting over was the idea. But starting over would require a change of heart.

She looked up to the second level, well aware of the shoe store and the fact that Sam Shole worked there. Her palms began to sweat. Georgine had found out about Sam Shole and suggested to Laura that she simply walk into the store and buy a pair of sandals. "Check it out," she had said. "What can it hurt? You're old friends who haven't seen each other in years. What's wrong with that? You can't shelter yourself forever." Easy enough for Georgine to say.

"May I get you something?"

The sound of the waiter's voice startled her. He wore a white coat with epaulets and a black bow tie. He looked silly. "The Garden Restaurant," he explained, waving an arm dramatically. "We cater these tables. Would you like to see a menu?" He held it out for her.

"No, thank you."

He nodded and walked on. He was young, perhaps twenty-two, broad-shouldered and handsome, yet he did nothing for her. She decided to move on. What good was sitting around here? She had errands to run.

To Laura, a relative newcomer to the Green, it seemed as though every living person in the state of Massachusetts was shopping here. What astounded her was that the crowds were made up almost entirely of women like herself. Many dragged children along by one hand, a shopping bag in the other, a purse slung over a shoulder. And they all seemed to know where they were going. Could it be that she was the only woman new to this place?

She located a large INFORMATION placard, which was bolted into the cement against the far wall. The color-coded map displayed a blue curved arrow marked YOU ARE HERE. It showed her which concourse of which pavilion she was on and listed, by number codes, all the retail stores in the entire complex.

Spanner's Drugs was located on Level 2, East Concourse, the south end of Pavilion C. She tried to ignore the fact that it was only a few doors down from the shoe store where Sam Shole worked. She took her bearings and looked around the large structure. It had begun to rain, she deduced from the tangle of water streams that were being shed from a vented glass canopy high overhead.

She wondered if someday people would live in cities like this, never seeing the out-of-doors, protected from a polluted environment, supplied with all the necessities and luxuries of life. She then recalled having read about penthouse apartments at the Green. It had already begun. Little numbers at first. But how long until this was the norm and a house on 6th Street the exception?

She rode a glass-sided escalator up to Level 2, where a decent-sized crowd had gathered to watch a performance by two white-faced mimes. There was entertainment everywhere, she realized. Yankee Green truly was an amusement mall; it wasn't just part of the advertising hype to lure people here. First the jugglers, now this. She glanced back at a large clock, the word TIMEX printed in boldface. She hadn't seen a clock that size since Grand Central

Station. An hour had passed since the grocery store. Incredible, she thought.

After Spanner's Drugs, she glanced again at her list. The bourbon and rum were for Georgine, who was throwing a party this weekend and knew the booze here was less expensive. Everything was less expensive here. Laura rarely drank alcohol, and then only a glass of wine. The liquor store was near the car. She made a mental note to pick up the booze later.

Sandals? she read off her list. Shoe store, she thought. Why was she doing this?

Georgine had convinced her that new clothes helped one to change attitude, start fresh. Georgine was big on starting fresh. Recently she had begun to tease Laura. "Sure haven't seen that blouse before. . . . Get that skirt when we were in high school? Nice shoes, Laura. Those are from the Stone Age, aren't they?" So Laura had been coaxed into shopping for a nice pair of white sandals to wear to Georgine's party this weekend, *if* she got up the courage to go to it. She had a sneaking suspicion that George —as she called her—was more interested in matchmaking. First she had heard an awful lot about Tony somebody-or-other who worked with George's second husband. Laura disliked the name Tony; she didn't even want to meet the man. Then George had mentioned Sam Shole.

Sam. . . .

What could it hurt to look at a few pairs of sandals?

Laura edged closer to the store and scanned the dozens of shoes displayed, noticing a pair of white sandals she liked. He probably wasn't even working today. Why worry about it? The sandals were on sale. She shrugged and headed for the open entrance. On sale. Why not?

There he was.

She stopped cold. He stood by an inside display, speaking to a salesman who wore a bright red name tag. The sight of Sam triggered a flood of memories. He hardly looked any different— the same Sam she had been madly in love with at the grand old age of seventeen. The same Sam with whom she had skinny-dipped out at the Corwin farm. Sam the basketball player. Sam the school vice-president. Sam, her last real heartthrob before Tim.

She stepped back, away from the entrance, and moved to the side. She couldn't go inside. She just couldn't do it. She put her hand to her chest. Her heart was running out of control. *Slow down, lady.* She moved back against the railing and turned around, looking down at the Atrium with its trees and fountain, its mirrors and lights and miles of brass railings. The table she had been sitting at was now occupied by two women and three children. The same waiter was asking them the same question. She turned, took one step toward the shoe store, stopped, stepped back, and leaned against the railing again.

Rain drummed against the overhead glass. She suddenly felt warm. She fanned herself, thinking, *It's just a pair of sandals.* From here she couldn't see inside the open store. She felt foolish. What could be wrong about buying a pair of sandals? What's the big deal? He probably wouldn't notice her anyway, and if he did, he'd never recognize her. She was a mature woman now— women change in ways that men don't. Men are easy to recognize ten years later. Not so with women. Anyway, that had been years ago. It wasn't as if they had feelings for each other now.

Then why was her heart still racing?

She spotted a sign indicating a public rest room a few doors down. She found her way down a short hallway, entered the cavernous lavatory, and headed straight for the mirror. She chastised herself for being so vain. She applied a fresh coat of nearly invisible lipstick. She brushed her hair. She tucked in her blouse and smoothed out the wrinkles. Ridiculous. She smiled and checked the spaces between her teeth. She wanted to pry herself away from the mirror, but brushed her hair once more before she did.

"Got a date, hunh?" asked a woman to her right, also preening herself in the mirror. This woman wore bright red lipstick, no bra, and a shirt with a huge kiss on the front.

Laura shrugged, uncomfortable with the woman's looks.

"Me too," said the woman. "Sort of," she added with a shrug and a forced smile.

He won't even notice, Laura thought.

"You look great, hon." The overbuilt woman slipped the lipstick into her purse and walked out of the rest room with full control over her lower half. Laura wondered how you could walk like that without dislocating your hips.

She straightened her skirt. Her hands were clammy.

A minute later she hesitated by the open doorway to the shoe store and then edged her way inside, quickly turning to face one of the displays.

"Laura!" he called out from clear across the room. She wanted to run. Oh, God! She felt her face warm.

She pretended to be searching for his name. She blurted out, "Sam . . . Sam Shole. Good grief!" He had already crossed the room to her. His strong, confident hands took her gently by the shoulders. He was quite tall, and nearly as fit as he had been ten years ago. Even more handsome. He bent down and kissed her cheek.

She felt lightheaded.

His expression changed to sympathy. He said softly, "I read about Tim. I'm so sorry." He lit up. "But I'm certainly not sorry to see you. Let me look." He stepped back, and his piercing blue eyes ran from ankle to earlobe. She thought her neck might set fire to her collar.

"You're lovely," he said sincerely.

"And you're the same old charmer you always were." She stepped aside to allow a patron to leave.

"How are you doing?"

"Okay, I guess." She shook her head and looked him in the eye. "It comes and goes." She had always been able to talk to Sam about anything. It felt good to slip right back into it. "Listen to me. It's like we've been friends for the past ten years. A lot has changed."

"A lot hasn't."

They stared at each other, eyes searching.

"How about you?" she asked, her heart drumming.

"Partner in Fleet Street Shoes. Really hit the big time."

"Still putting yourself down, I see."

"It's all right."

"It looks terrific. It's gigantic."

"Twelve hundred square feet." He paused. "Pun intended," he added.

She forced a giggle. "Still making terrible jokes."

"Yeah." He grinned. "Same old Sam."

She couldn't believe that two grown, mature people were staring at each other in a shoe store. She had two children, for heaven's sake; why did she feel so damn vulnerable and young? "Sandals," she finally said, breaking his stare. "I'm after a pair of those white sandals."

"Right." He took her gently by the elbow. "Have a seat. What size?"

"Five and half, six," she said, sitting down and adjusting her skirt.

"White? You're sure? Red's more your color; red or a bright blue. White's too . . . too simple for you."

"White, I'm afraid." She blushed. "Yes. I need them to go with yellow slacks."

"White it is. Don't move a muscle. I'll be back in a flash."

She caught her breath, noticed herself in a mirror that faced her, and adjusted a sprig of hair. Better now.

He came out of the back with three boxes stacked in his arms. His size made the boxes look small. He set down the boxes and pulled up a stool to face her. "Okay," Sam Shole said. He reached down and touched the back of her ankle to lift her foot.

Laura experienced what felt like a bolt of warm fluid rush up the back of her calf to the inside of her knee, up her thigh, through her crotch, and into the hollow of her stomach, where it floundered and cooled. Instead of tensing, she felt her whole body relax. He had already pulled off her shoe and set it on the floor. He fiddled with a box, removed a left sandal, and took her foot softly into his hand again.

The same thing happened all over again. She recalled how tender he had been with her, on that night at the Corwin farm, ten years before when they had been nervous teens in the first throes of petting. Perhaps that night was why she had sought him out. Was she after affection, or was she just testing the waters?

"The only way you get into this business is by having a foot fetish." He forced a smile.

She wanted to say something, but couldn't.

He attempted an accent. "I've seen a lot of feet—miles of feet, as we say in the business—and yours are the nicest."

"I bet you say that to all the girls."

"Only past high school sweethearts whom I've never forgotten." He looked up quickly and then back down to the foot he held. "Stocking running time." He tugged on the toe of her stocking and ran his finger between her big toe and the next toe over to make room for the stem on the sandal.

She jerked slightly as his finger touched her there.

"Ticklish," he said.

"Yes," she lied.

"Here we go," he said, slipping the sandal over her foot and running the strap behind her ankle and then across her arch. He fastened the small buckle and sat up on his stool.

Laura noticed the salesman to her left, who seemed perplexed The salesman took her glance as a cue. He approached and said, "Excuse me, Mr. Shole, the strap's twisted," and dropped to one knee to fix it.

"I'll get it," said Shole. He grinned at Laura and shrugged "I'm new at this. Only been in the business seven years." He smiled shyly. "To be honest, I'm out of my league. That's why the funny looks from Henry. This is his turf."

"Why the special treatment?" She felt stronger.

"Take a guess." He paused fixing the strap. "You're a special woman." He set her foot down. "How's it feel?"

Laura nearly said, "Wonderful." But that would hardly describe the sandal. "New," she said. And even that held a special meaning to her.

"The other?"

"Why not?"

He moved his stool a matter of inches and repeated the procedure. His touch felt equally stimulating. When the second sandal was on, Shole said, "Got the strap right that time."

"You always were a fast learner."

"So were you," he said, his reference having nothing to do with academics.

She felt herself blush. She was beside herself. "Perfect fit," she mumbled, wondering if she meant the sandals. "Exactly what I'm looking for." She suddenly felt like buying another pair. Anything to keep her here. "Well, I guess that's that," she said, leaning forward to unbuckle the sandals. "They're perfect." He leaned forward simultaneously, and their faces were close.

"Allow me," he said. She acquiesced.

He removed both sandals and slipped her back into her shoes. She was thinking of Cinderella.

"We carry . . . these, too," he said. "Which isn't to say you need a new pair—"

"They're a disaster. I know."

"It's the businessman in me. Always looking for a sale."

She couldn't believe she said, "If I buy them now, I don't have another excuse to come see you."

Without so much as a pause he followed with, "Sure you do. How about lunch tomorrow?"

She stuttered. "Sh-sh-sure."

"Twelve o'clock sharp. We'll meet by the fountain downstairs. Sound all right?"

"I don't know. . . ."

"No fair reconsidering. We're all set."

"Sounds great."

"Good."

She paid at the counter. She started to pay by credit card, but then decided on using a check. Her checks had her phone number on them. And her address. She wondered if he had noticed her changed decision.

"Twelve noon. See ya," he said.

As she was halfway out the store, he caught up to her. "Don't forget these." He handed her the box containing her new white sandals. "I still think you're a red or a blue."

"Maybe tomorrow." She shrugged. She could still feel a tingle between her toes.

THE LITTLE MAN REACHED the far end of the utility tunnel and paused to listen for any movement below. Hearing none, he switched off his headlamp and peered out of the tunnel's exit and down into the cement room below, a room filled with the dark shadows of racks of telephone switchers, snaking cables carefully laid out and color-coded.

Seeing no one, he switched the headlamp back on and descended the series of hand grips. The room, a cement vault, echoed his movements. Pavilion C had been built several years before, so much of the telephone equipment was of the older variety, despite the bank of new switchers that had obviously been installed recently, as additional phones had been added.

He checked the schematics he carried in his toolbox and moved over to the third rack of switchers, each rack housing dozens of pairs that provided phone service to the hundreds of stores and offices. He propped open the hinged, gray metal cover to the electromechanical switching matrix. His headlamp lit the maze of relays inside. He checked his schematics, removed the telephone handset from his pack, and hot-wired the appropriate relay, one of the five active relays that led to the Security Dispatch Control Room high overhead.

He had personally requested the two lines from the phone company himself, claiming to be a new businessman at the mall, giving mall addresses of two empty spaces in C. Everything was all set.

He dialed the first number from his hot-wired phone and watched for the tiny electromechanical switch to connect. It was three relays away. The sound of a ringing line filled his receiver.

He smiled. He dialed the second number and the next relay connected. Again he heard the line ringing in the handset. Again he smiled. It was all so simple, he thought: a dialed number, the tiny pulse of electricity, a switch thrown, an explosion.

Simple.

Climbing back up to the utility tunnel with the toolbox in hand was awkward. He moved a few yards down the tunnel and set the box down. Contorting his body, he slipped around the overhead pipes here. Carefully he moved back toward the room he had just left, but this time he entered the false space between the hung acoustical paneling and the true cement ceiling above. He had to lie prone and crawl carefully, using the pipes for support. One slip and a foot would go through the paneling. At the far end of this dead space he reached three small cassette recorders. All three were the same model, voice-activated recorders made by Sony. Tiny wires ran from boxes that looked like transistor radios to the cassette recorders. A single extension cord, spliced into a power line overhead, furnished the electricity.

The man removed the three cassettes and replaced them with blank tapes, depressing the RECORD buttons on all three. Now, when someone spoke, the hubs would turn, the tape would roll and all would be captured on tape.

He pocketed the recorded tapes. Later tonight, as he worked in his apartment, he would listen to what was being said in the overhead offices. Intelligence, he knew, was ninety percent of the game.

17

TOBY'S FEET ACHED—they always began to ache around midday. His job required constant movement throughout the complex. He was still upset about the trouble at the Safeway and Knorpp's orders to arrest the kids. It was true that the kids had provoked their share of trouble at Yankee Green lately. But the kids also had their ears to the ground. On several key occasions they had supplied him with inside information that allowed him to prevent gang brawls on the premises. Now he had paid them back by having them arrested.

The threat of violent crime was a constant worry at the Green. Nationally, shopping centers were epidemic with juvenile violence and crime. Babies were stolen from their mothers, purses were snatched, elderly people mugged. The challenge to keep these three and a half million square feet free of violent crime never ceased. It was what made the well-paid job interesting.

Jacobs had been extremely lucky thus far, and he knew it. The Green had had just one attempted child abduction (foiled by an alert guard at an exit) and one armed bank robbery. No rapes. No assaults. But the odds were against the Green. Statistics implied that it was long overdue for a wave of serious crime. It was what kept Jacobs working late, working Saturdays, worrying.

He looked outside through the drizzle, where a pair of uncomfortable city cops stood guard over nine tons of thawing fish. He had no idea why the cops had been posted there, but trying to figure out the local police was an exercise in futility. Sight of the truck reminded him to ask Knorpp to nudge the insurance companies. It had been several hours, and still no one from either company had showed.

He pushed through the door and out into the drizzle, driven by curiosity. He walked over and introduced himself to the cops. A minute later he opened the back door of the large trailer. The smell of fish overpowered him.

As a child, he had often gone out with his father and uncle on their trawler. By day's end the two men would be drinking beer and singing songs in Portuguese, the tangy smell of fish and salt water permeating the air. The smell of this truck took him back. He could see the bow of the ship splitting the swells of the sea, could hear the slippery sound of the dead fish shifting in the open hold, the occasional final slap of a tail fin as a defeated cod surrendered. He could smell the beer on his father's breath and recall almost word for word the dirty stories of whores the two men would tell each other, thinking young Tobias did not understand. The stench in the trailer reminded him of how long ago it had been.

The trailer was dark. Frozen fillets sat on milky ice. They wouldn't last long; in the absence of refrigeration, the August temperature was making quick work of the ice. Jacobs wondered about the liability, knowing that of all the problems the Green's management faced, insurance was at the top of the list. A trailer this loaded with fish didn't come cheap.

A strike by fishermen in his home town of New Bedford had left New England without fish for twenty-two days. Restaurants from Stamford, Connecticut, to Bangor, Maine, were having to truck their seafood in from New Jersey and points south. He wondered how the strike was affecting his father and uncle.

He jumped down from the trailer and called Dispatch on his walkie-talkie. "Dicky, this is Jacobs. Check with Administration. Have someone over there call a company called Interstate Transport," he said, reading from the door of the cab, "and find out who is responsible for the fish in this trailer. Most of it's still frozen, but it's going to go fast. Find out if it's our responsibility or the shipping company's. What's the estimated value of contents? Can the company send another refrigerated truck and off-load the fish? Something has to be done immediately. Okay?"

"Got it," said the confident voice of Dicky Brock.

The bell of one of the trolleys sounded as it passed. A motorcycle roared down the street in the distance. The drizzle continued.

Jacobs noticed an old man beneath the stairway. He laughed privately to think that the only job the two cops had was to keep the curious away from the accident, and here was someone poking around. Jacobs walked over and interrupted him.

Marty Rappaport's aging face spun around, his dull-green eyes penetrating. "Hello there, son."

"Are you with the police?"

"Me? Hell, no."

"Insurance?"

Rappaport shook his head. "Nope."

"Just exactly who are you?"

"Marty Rappaport. How 'bout yourself?"

"Toby Jacobs, Yankee Green Security. I'm afraid this is a closed area."

"Take a look at this." Rappaport held a chunk of the broken concrete in his hand.

"It's a closed area, sir. I'm afraid you'll have to leave."

"I'm doing harm, I suppose? And here I am trying to help. Look here." Rappaport pointed to the large chunk of cement that had broken away from the underside of the stairway in the collision. "That's a hell of a lot of damage, even for a rig this size."

"That's why it's a closed area."

"You're missing my point. A truck this size shouldn't have caused this kind of damage. At least I don't think it should have. I won't be absolutely certain until I've pushed a few numbers around."

The man looked vaguely familiar. Perhaps one of the early morning walkers. Jacobs heard the banging. He turned around to see a blue-haired woman pounding on the safety glass of the doorway to Pavilion C. Rappaport obviously saw her too, because he was off toward her in a hurry, a dog with his tail between his legs. Jacobs smiled.

"Excuse me?" said a high, smoky voice from behind.

Slowly he turned his head around.

———————— 18 ————————

SUSAN ANNE LYME wore a peach windbreaker and peach sweatpants. The pale blue leotard stretched tightly around her torso was damp with a large orb of perspiration between her modest breasts, a telltale sign of the level of activity she had been engaged in for the past hour. Her hair was pulled back and held off her face by an Adidas sweatband. The exercise had pinked her cheeks and whitened her eyes, giving her a wholesome, vital look. Toby was a sucker for wholesome, vital women. She was remarkably put together, the exercise obviously paying off. Her face was lovely, but not classically beautiful. Pink lips, white teeth, and dimples.

The raindrops drummed loudly as she managed to pop open an umbrella. She stepped boldly forward, reaching to hold the umbrella over the two of them. She was considerably shorter than he was.

Well aware of the large overhang only a few yards away, he made no mention of it. Standing out here was more fun.

"Toby Jacobs?" Her tiny hand released the hooked handle of the umbrella as she switched hands. They shook. "My name's Susan Lyme. Pardon the appearance." She glanced down at herself and seemed suddenly embarrassed. She fumbled with the zipper of her windbreaker, which was partially zipped up but now jammed as she yanked at it one-handed. Jacobs reached down, took the zipper in his fingers, and ran it up the length of her jacket. He stopped and looked into her eyes. Both stood silently under the umbrella. "Thanks," she finally managed to say softly.

"My pleasure."

"I was in class. Aerobics class. Someone said something about a bomb going off in your new wing."

"You're a reporter."

"How'd you know that?"

"Writer's bump," he said touching the middle finger of her left hand. "A southpaw reporter at that."

"And you must be Sherlock Holmes." She hesitated and altered her tone of voice to imply he might already know the rest of this. "Free-lance, these days. Used to work for the *Times*." Noting his inquisitive look she offered, "It's a long story."

"Unfortunately, it's a busy day, Miss Lyme. It *is* Miss, I hope?"

She chewed on her tongue. He couldn't tell if it was a nervous habit or an attempt to suppress a smile. She nodded. "The bombing?"

"Too soon, Miss Lyme."

"It's Susan, Mr. Jacobs."

"It's Toby, Miss Lyme."

"It's Susan, Toby."

"Too soon, Susan. 'The dust has barely settled,' I guess you reporters might say."

"Actually, we *good* reporters try to avoid clichés," she said more distantly.

Oh, no, Toby thought. *She's feminine and she's tough.* He felt a sudden urge to run, like a married man who can sense an affair long before it begins.

She had the tiny nose of a mouse and the large gray eyes of a wildcat. He could see the strength of her personality in the hard line of her jaw, and the tender girl in the faint freckles that bunched on top of her high cheekbones.

He said, "You'll want our public information office."

She continued undaunted. "No, it's you I want," she said deadpan. "You're head of security, aren't you?"

"*Director* of Security," he corrected. "Our public information office is in Pavilion C, on the third floor."

"Can't you tell me anything?"

"I just did."

"No need to be a prick, Mr. Jacobs." Rain continued to drum on the umbrella.

After a long pause, he apologized. "No, I don't suppose there is. I've been trained to distrust the press," he said by way of explanation.

"And I've been trained to distrust cops."

"I'm not a cop."

"I'm not *the press*. I'm free-lance, remember?"

"The *Times*."

"I *used* to work for the *Times*."

"Right." He smiled. "Got it."

"You *don't* trust me, do you?"

"No."

"Well. Then it looks as though we have something to work on, doesn't it?"

"I suppose so. It really is a bad day."

She had long legs and a high waist.

He added, "A detective by the name of Shleit is in charge of the investigation. You might try him."

"Shleit?"

He spelled it for her. "No one knows anything at the moment. Their lab people have been going over the room all day."

"A man was killed—"

"Yes, a worker. An electrician."

"Did you know him?"

"No. Detective Shleit may be able to tell you more. Otherwise, I'd try our public information office later in the day." He had read once that people made their final judgment of other people within the first five seconds of their initial meeting. He had never really believed this until now.

"Please? Five minutes. I'll even buy you a cup of coffee as a bribe."

"I can't accept bribes." He wanted to accept.

"Please." She grinned. "I won't take much of your time. Promise."

"Maybe later." He wanted her to take much of his time. Feminine but strong. Like a lioness.

"Dinner? Good!" she said not waiting for his answer. "Dinner it is."

The penetrating look in his eyes caused her to take a step back, and in doing so, the runoff from the umbrella poured over his head and down his neck. He jumped back and took advantage of the sudden opportunity. "Nice meeting you." He ran toward the door and hurried inside, glancing one last time over his shoulder. She looked somehow vulnerable, standing in the rain.

He thought he saw her lips mouthing the words "Damn you." Susan Lyme was clearly used to getting her way.

—————19—————

THE HOUSE WAS PERCHED high atop a hill, overlooking downtown Hillsdale. The lawn smelled of being recently mowed. The gardens surrounding the one-story sprawling home were perfectly manicured, though many of the flowers seemed to be struggling. Detective Doug Shleit announced himself at the gate to the estate and was immediately allowed inside.

He drove the unremarkable sedan around the loop in the driveway and parked in the shade of a towering elm. At the front door, he was greeted by a uniformed maid and a moment later was ushered to the pool, where Robert Russo's trim abdomen collected the sun's rays. The cement was still drying from the showers that had passed over less than an hour before. The pool was large, its water still.

"Nice view," said Shleit, looking past the rock gardens that clung to the hill.

"Goddamned pollution is killing some of the hybrids. Not a thing a guy can do about it."

"You heard about our little problem out at the mall today?"

"Word travels fast in a small town."

"Hillsdale's not so small anymore."

"Why don't you have a seat, Lieutenant." The host sat up, pulling the back of the chaise lounge to accommodate him. He was a middle-aged man still trying for twenty-two. He made Shleit uncomfortable. "You look like a man too long on his feet." He added, "Iced tea?"

"Thanks."

Russo signaled with two fingers for a maid.

"Nice place. Never been up here."

"It doesn't matter what you make, does it, Lieutenant? It matters how you invest it."

"I wouldn't know. Never get ahead enough to invest."

"The tragedy of public service."

"You're a powerful man, Mr. Russo."

"Retired. You overestimate my situation."

"The bombing killed a worker. We've got a murder on our hands."

"So I heard."

"Of all the men in this town who might want to see Yankee Green in trouble, your name seems to head quite a few lists. It did, after all, cause your early retirement."

Russo's face tightened. "An oversimplification of the situation at the time, Lieutenant."

"At the time you said, and I quote, 'Some heads will roll.' Now we have an explosive device placed inside the locker of the construction supervisor, one of the key men who broke the strength of your union."

"If I'd wanted DeAngelo, I'd have placed razor blades up the cunt of that whore he sees. You know me better than that."

"I hardly know you at all."

"My reputation, then."

"Yes. I'm not accusing you—"

"That's not what your tone of voice says. You sound pretty sure of yourself."

The drinks arrived. They came complete with frosted glasses, a slice of lemon, and a sprig of fresh mint. Shleit chugged the first half of his and placed the glass on the damp cement. He pushed the hat back on his head. "You tell me. Who would want to do a thing like this? And remember, it's not your everyday Joe who has access to explosives."

"So that's it. You think because I once ran the construction union that I might be able to snap my fingers and have someone dump some powder in someone's locker. Come off it, Lieutenant. You're not thinking clearly. Do I look like Marlon Brando? I have some money; I have some friends, it's true, but my finger-snapping days are over. So maybe you people busted me once for having a couple of people persuaded to change their minds. A killer I am not."

"Those people ended up in the hospital. One of them nearly died."

"It's over and done with. It's behind us. This is today. I didn't blow any locker, Lieutenant." He sobered. "If I wanted Yankee Green, I wouldn't go tossing bombs in the windows. If you're familiar with my reputation, as you claim you are, then you know that much is true. I learned a long time ago that violence has its limitations. Even fear has its limitations. But pressure? Pressure just keeps building and building. I'm a man who's come to love the complex nature of applied pressure. For instance, if you want to call on me again, you can contact my attorney. I, meanwhile, will have a short talk with Tommy Dunn and find out why one of his detectives is invading my privacy without the common courtesy of a phone call. I could have been banging some bitch out here. As I understand it, you and your captain have problems to begin with. You may be on your way out, from what I hear. Just too damn independent, isn't that it?"

Shleit rose from the chair.

"You haven't finished your iced tea. Stay. Please, be my guest."

"If you're involved with this, Russo, in any way, we'll put you behind bars for it."

"Now my guest threatens me. And so dramatic. Perhaps you had better leave."

Shleit turned and headed for the side gate, rather than walk back through the house. He picked a wilting flower and studied it closely. He said convincingly, "It's not pollution. It's slugs. You must know all about slugs with the company you keep. Try garlic and chalk around the base of the plants. The slugs don't like the smell of garlic. You know something, Russo? Neither do I."

"Much too dramatic, Lieutenant," Russo said as Shleit disappeared around the corner. He spit a lemon seed back into his glass and grimaced.

JULIA HAVERILL HAD the long, slender figure of a fashion model, an innocent face, and the provocative eyes of an all-knowing woman. Her walk exuded the warm ripeness of her sexual awakening, enthusiasm and excitement evident in her alluring smile. At seventeen, she looked twenty-one or -two, her womanly qualities fully developed, the baby fat that often plagues teenagers long since gone, driven away by a frenetic metabolism and constant swimming, which had once been her passion but which had recently taken second place to a decidedly more indoor activity.

Many of her outward charms had been learned from her cosmopolitan mother, absent from her everyday life for the last three years but the person, nonetheless, who had indirectly taught her how to dress like a woman, how to charm, how to flirt. The older boys had been after Julia Haverill for years; but she had not been interested in older *boys*. She had saved herself for a *man*—someone who recognized her as more than a charm on a bracelet or a night at the movies—she had saved herself for a lover. This, too, she had learned from her mother.

She wore a khaki skirt, blue and white wide-striped blouse, and pale sandals. Her hips pumped gently side to side, bouncing the large purse that hung from her shoulder. She avoided clusters of patrons, commanding an envelope of space around herself, assuming royal stature as she strode proudly along. Her sandy-brown hair, perfectly cut and curled under, swung across her shoulders as she moved. Rarely did a male eye miss her entrance to a room—certainly never her entrance poolside, where she wore a skin-tight Lycra suit cut high on the buttock, low in front, and even lower in the back. Like her mother, Julia believed in showing what you had while you still had it; like her mother she knew that youthful beauty, especially for women, passed much too quickly. Other women in the Green, bland and dreary by comparison, watched with envy as she drew the attention, misjudging her age by several years. She often walked with her hands in her pockets, as she did this noon, to hide her short stubby fingers and the nails she often chewed ragged. But few paid attention to her hands. Most were attracted by her more obvious attributes.

Marv Haverill had taken custody of her after he won the divorce case by default. Despite the sordid nature of events surrounding the divorce proceedings, and despite her vulnerable adolescence at the time of her mother's abrupt departure, she gave the impression that she had not suffered badly. She had half expected the divorce. She had always loved her mother's keen sense of independence and had actually been consulted before the night her mother failed to show up from "shopping." Perhaps it was this being privy to her mother's secret that had stemmed the grief she might have otherwise felt. Perhaps it was the camaraderie of being included in the decision. Perhaps it was the crying and hugging, the tenderness, and the simple explanation, "In a few weeks, dear, when you go away to college, you'll be free of him too, except summers. When you turn eighteen you can join me if you like—there's nothing he can do about it except threaten to cut off your funds, and you know I can take up any slack there—and we'll start all over, together." She knew that such an improbable rendezvous would never take place, never work out, but accepted this truth maturely and with little regret. Her mother had never fully grown up, spoiled by a family with too much money and too many choices. A corporate wife, Kate Haverill was not. She had taken on the role like a poor understudy. The simple truth of the matter was that Julia loved her father, despite his fourteen-hour workdays six days a week, despite his trite patting of her head and fatherly warnings about drugs and sex.

He was old-fashioned. Julia knew all about drugs and sex. She had an appetite for both.

Her father had suggested Julia take a summer job, on this, her last summer before college, but Julia had convinced him—an art she had mastered—that just for this reason it was a summer to swim, play tennis, catch up on reading, and reestablish friendships. Marv Haverill had gone along with her, showing none of the argumentative skills he was famous for in business. Patting her head.

Her real motivation had been her lover.

She took what looked like a credit card from her purse and inserted it into the slot in the polished brass molding of one of the bank of private elevators. A light flashed and the elevator doors opened for her. She stepped inside and pushed P, for Penthouse.

The ride was short, the elevator quiet.

When the elevator stopped she blew into her palms, stepped into the hallway, and looked both ways. She loved the thrill of it as much as anything. The thrill of adventure was, to her, as stimulating as a line of coke, and that was something special.

The hallway was empty. Her father's office was just around the corner, something that added to the thrill and enhanced her excitement. She felt herself grow moist just thinking about the upcoming encounter. She moved briskly two doors down and used a key he had given her to open the door of the penthouse suite. This was one of two models still for sale.

The air conditioner kept the room cooler than the hallways. Her lover had explained that one of the problems inherent in the use of concrete in the construction of the Green was that the summer sun warmed the walls beyond the ability of air conditioning to cool the rooms. The air conditioners had plenty of power for this purpose, but no way to cool one side of the building more than the other. The problem only affected the upper floor. The result was that in the mornings all the suites to the west seemed overcooled, those facing east, a few degrees warmer.

Standing before the bathroom mirror, Julia Haverill removed her jacket dramatically, impressing herself, her eyes traveling down her body slowly. She then unbuttoned her blouse's two topmost buttons and pulled the shirt open to reveal her firm youthful cleavage. She ruffled her hair slightly, and ran her hands down along her sides to her waist as if tightening her skin. She unhooked and partially unzipped the waistband to her skirt, ready to slip easily out of it. As she stood in the mirror picturing herself naked and him behind her, grasping her gently as he rocked his loins against the back of her thighs, she located the vial in her purse and spooned a small amount of coke up toward her nose and sucked it up. She pinched her nostrils together and returned the vial to her purse. Just right.

She visualized the entire seduction, step by step, as she had read in a book written by Dr. Seymour Klaus. She tried to feel his warmth as he pressed against her, hands searching her, ticklish breath on her neck. She bent slightly, imagining the intercourse, her small stubby hands gripping the edge of the countertop, her eyes focused on the mirror.

They would not use the bed today; she would not have him sit in a chair while she lowered herself onto him; they would not make love in the elevator. Today it would be here, standing in front of the mirror, from behind.

She heard the key rattle in the door. She lightly stroked her breasts in tiny, neat circles, hardening her nipples. She felt wildly in love. He was so handsome, so mature. So knowledgeable. Recently she had even fantasized about running away with him. For him she would excite her breasts as he liked, she would wiggle and squirm as he liked, she would coo and grit her teeth, inevitably out of control by the end. He had taught her much, including how to recognize her own point of no return, where his determined efforts took her beyond any ability to rationalize, to a point where her mind swam in a warm, heart-beating frenzy, and where he dictated her final movement. A point beyond which he controlled her. She loved him.

Peter Knorpp stopped mid-stride as he caught sight of her out of the corner of his eye.

"Darling," she said. She lowered her eyelids over her bloodshot eyes, doing her best to appear as sexy as possible.

He stepped closer and pulled her zipper down the last inch. Her chest heaved in long, heavy, dramatic breaths. The khaki skirt fell to her ankles. She wore a lace garter belt, matching bikini, and dark silk hose. He dropped to one knee and pulled down her panties. As he kissed her chestnut hair, he groaned.

He fumbled with his belt and pulled his pants off.

"I've missed you," she said, watching them both in the mirror.

HER CLOTHES LAY SCATTERED across the countertop, his clothes dumped in a pile on the tile floor. Her upper chest was stained a fleshy pink, her breathing just now returning to normal. "Did you like it?" she asked.

"It was good," he said. "You?"

"Couldn't you tell? I loved it!"

"You do trust me?"

"I do. I do. Always. Always, my love."

His look was vague.

"Does it remind you of anything?" She paused, waiting for a reaction. "Our first time?"

"Of course."

"You took me into your office. I thought you were going to tell Daddy about me smoking that joint. I was really freaked out. You put your hands on me. God, it was a maximum high." She turned and looked at him. "We made love standing up. Don't you remember? We faced each other, like this."

He turned her body toward him, took her hand, and gently pressed it against him. She kissed down his chest, and then even lower, and aroused him.

"You've never told anyone about that, I hope?"

She hummed against him and then giggled. "You practically raped me," she said.

He gripped her arm strongly, hurting her. "You haven't told anyone, have you, Julia."

"Hey, no," she said, puzzled, pulling her arm free.

He pulled her to her feet and they joined; she reached around his strong shoulders and laced her fingers together and then wrapped her legs around him so he supported her entirely. He held her tiny buttocks in his strong hands and moved her gently against him.

Her eyes blinked shut. He studied her face as he thrust deep within her. "You feel good," he said softly. "Does this feel good?" he asked, lifting her higher.

"Oh, yes. Umm. Right there. Yes. Right there, my love." She pulled him tighter and kissed him. She looked up into his eyes. He was smiling.

21

"Mr. HAVERILL, I'm Roy Walker," said the young black man, jumping up from his seat. He wore a coat and tie and wire-rimmed glasses.

"I told him an appointment was impossible today, sir," Haverill's secretary apologized.

"I'm sorry. I'm terribly busy. Perhaps next week." Haverill forced a smile, stuck out his hand, and when Walker didn't offer his own he pushed past.

"I thought you might prefer to settle out of court."

The comment stopped Haverill. "I beg your pardon?" he said, turning to face the handsome young man.

"I'm an attorney, Mr. Haverill, I represent Vernon Greene."

Haverill's face was blank. "I don't know any Vernon Greene. Perhaps you want our legal department. Madge can arrange an appointment, I'm sure."

"As I said, if I have to go through your legal department, then we will handle this formally."

"Madge, call Carl up here, would you? Come in, Mr. Walker."

The two men entered the spacious office. Haverill pointed for Walker to take a seat, which the young man did. Only a few minutes later Haverill's private elevator opened and Carl Brick stepped into the office. Introductions were made, and Brick, a redhead who had once played football, took a chair alongside Walker's.

Haverill said, "Mr. Walker represents a Vernon Greene, is that right?" Walker nodded. "And the case involves?"

"False arrest, assault, and harassment of a minority."

"When did this alleged incident occur, Mr. Walker?" asked Brick.

"This morning."

Haverill and Brick looked at each other.

"Your security people arrested seven members of a teenage

gang that had allegedly been shoplifting in the Safeway. I'm not here to dispute those arrests, gentlemen. However, my client, despite repeated objections and attempts to clarify the situation, was arrested right along with the others. The reason for his arrest is obvious. My client is black, gentlemen. He is not a member of that gang. He was not shoplifting. He was manhandled by your security people, and charges were pressed against him."

Brick sighed. Haverill knew Brick well enough to know it meant they had trouble. "And what damages are you seeking, Mr. Walker?"

"I assume Yankee Green doesn't need negative racial publicity. You have had a campaign on for years trying to lure minorities into this mall. The reason I am here—the reason I came to Mr. Haverill instead of moving through normal channels—is because I have an unusual request."

"I'm listening," said Haverill.

"I have a rock-solid case, Mr. Haverill. It just so happens that the young man your people arrested is an honor student, had forty dollars cash in his pocket, and a shopping list half completed when your people forcefully grouped him with the others. They picked the wrong kid."

"What is it you want, Mr. Walker?" Haverill looked at his watch impatiently.

"When this mall was built, this land was condemned. Over one thousand people were moved off this site by city hall, with a promise they would be relocated. That never happened. What I want from you, Mr. Haverill, is an effort to obtain the housing that was promised those people."

"I'm not a miracle worker, Mr. Walker. As you'll recall, the city government made that proposal in good faith. It was only the passing of the one percent initiative that removed any funds available for a project of that size."

"This mall, your company, single-handedly put three people in office two years ago. You are not without influence downtown. Have you been on the other side of Washington Street lately, Mr. Haverill? Have you seen where those people are living? I grew up on the other side of Washington Street. I know first hand what it's like. Conditions have worsened. What you have is an explosive situation. The people want action. I'll phone you tomorrow, Mr. Haverill. I just thought you should know where I stand." He stood. "Mr. Brick," he said, nodding before letting himself out.

Haverill huffed from behind his expansive desk. The well-appointed office, four stories up, had a good view of downtown Hillsdale in the distance. "Well?"

"I'd say we have ourselves a young crusader. He's seen too many clips of Jesse Jackson."

"Has he got anything?"

"I'll have to look into it, Marv. On the surface, I'm afraid he does. The false arrest and assault wouldn't hurt us too much. It's that harassment-of-a-minority charge that could do us the most damage. It's a new law. Untested. It would bring one hell of a lot of publicity, and our Mr. Walker knows it. If he's right, we'd lose the case. The last thing we need is to appear racist."

"Damn bad timing, too."

"One other thing to consider."

"What's that?"

"Did you notice his phrasing at the end? He said, 'explosive situation.'" Brick paused for effect. "Maybe this false arrest has nothing to do with anything. Maybe Mr. Walker wanted to deliver a message to us."

"This morning's explosion?"

"It was a peculiar choice of words, was it not?"

"He was threatening us? No, I don't believe that."

"There have been several attempts to stage protests about the housing situation. We both know that. The police wouldn't grant them the proper permits. Maybe they've taken a more direct approach. Bombs have a way of waking people up."

"You think we should have Mr. Walker checked out?" He waited for a response. Brick's silence was enough for him. "Okay, I'll ask Toby to look into it. Why don't you have a talk with the police, see what's going on. Did we screw something up?"

Brick knew by the tone of voice that the meeting was over. He closed the folder carefully and neatened the stack with a final tap on Haverill's desk. He stood to leave.

"One other thing, Carl."

"Yes?"

"Let's keep a lid on this."

"Understood."

22

THE GREEK DELI was mobbed.

Jacobs waved to Susan as she entered. Dispatch had told him that she had been asking around for him. She sat down across from him. "You've changed clothes," he noted.

"I went home."

"Where's home?"

"Brookline."

"Hmmmm."

She raised her eyebrows. "My parents' home actually. My mother's sick. I'm taking care of the place."

"I'm sorry—about your mother, I mean."

"Life has a way of running out on people at the strangest times. It's actually been good for me, on one level. I've learned a lot. It helped me to reestablish my priorities."

"Which are?"

"My career used to come first. Now it's health and happiness. At least that's what I'm shooting for."

Her words stabbed too close to home. "A noble effort."

"Listen to us."

"It's okay, we're allowed to talk about things other than the weather and politics."

"Like the bombing?"

Toby smiled. "You're sharp. I'll give you that."

"And persistent," she added. "I did track you down here."

"An investigative reporter?"

"You got it."

"The worst kind." He smiled. "You're the ones who are always finding skeletons in the closet."

"Haven't found any skeletons yet. I do criminal reporting. Dig up background information, that sort of thing. Research, mostly. I find out about bombings in malls and who might have wanted to blow them up."

"And?"

"Later. I don't give things away for free."

"Pity," he said, signaling Mrs. Popolov. Susan, shocked by the implication of his comment, cocked her head and gave him an inquisitive look. He leaned forward on the table. "How about for the fun of it?"

She blushed and quickly looked at Mrs. Popolov herself. "Service isn't exactly lickety-split, is it?"

"I recommend the pouch sandwiches with feta. Whatever you order, order feta with it. And Greek beer. The beer here is fantastic. I drink it with a slice of lemon. Have you ever had beer and lemon?"

She shook her head.

"Feel like trying it?"

"Why not?" she asked.

When the beers arrived, Jacobs poured them and crimped lemons into the foam. Susan tasted hers and smacked her lips in approval. "Takes the edge off the hops."

"Exactly."

"I understand Bob Russo is one of your suspects."

Toby glanced over his glass. "Where'd you get that?"

"I've done a number of pieces for the *Globe* and for the *Herald.* You make friends fast in this business."

"And enemies."

"Those too."

"Russo's not a suspect. His name came up in an informal discussion, that's all."

"Everyone knows he hates the Green. And Carmine De-Angelo. I'm surprised Carmine DeAngelo hasn't had some sort of 'accident.' It was his locker, wasn't it?"

"Was it?" he answered, cautiously.

"That's what I hear."

"You're scaring me. Maybe I should suspect you. You seem to know an awful lot."

"Maybe you should."

"Did you plant that bomb?"

"Not that one, no." She held a straight face for a few seconds and then broke into a wide grin. "I have trouble lighting the fireplace, to tell you the truth."

"I've always liked the truth," he fired back.

The sandwiches arrived. She dumped hers out on the plate and set the pouch aside. "I'm watching my waistline," she said.

"Me too," he said, raising his brow comically. "It's a great waistline."

"Since you won't talk to me about the explosion, how about that truck accident?"

"It's under investigation."

Mrs. Popolov stopped by to make sure everything was all right. Her facial expression revealed her adoration of Toby. The café was full, and she and Mykos were scurrying about.

When she left, Toby said to Susan, "No one was hurt."

"Had the driver been drinking?"

"No. He says the steering malfunctioned. We'll see."

"You don't believe him?"

"My guess is that he'd been up all night. That's how he looked."

"Fell asleep at the wheel?"

"Can't quote me. Just a guess."

"No quotes. This is an informal interview."

"When do we get formal?"

She glanced at him cautiously and didn't attempt an answer. She spun the beer bottle and tried to read the label. "So tell me why they're bothering with a new wing. This place is obviously big enough as it is."

He noticed her reading the label. "Did you know the various restaurants in this place serve beer from something like twenty different countries?"

"I'd like to say that surprises me. It doesn't. You didn't answer my question."

"I thought this was informal."

"It is."

"Yankee Green is no different from any other business. It has to keep growing. West Edmonton set the example. It's grown to five-point-two million square feet, four hundred and forty thousand people a week."

"But this place is gigantic. Who cares?"

He shrugged. "We're in the entertainment business. We've gone beyond a shopping center. We're a phenomenon. We have to maintain that status."

"Biggest is not necessarily best."

"We have to attract people here, in order to stay in business. The bigger you are, the more different you are, the more press. The more press, the more tourists. The West Edmonton Mall, for instance, has become a huge tourist attraction."

"So has this place. From what I hear it's basically saved downtown Hillsdale."

"I wish someone would tell that to the downtown merchants."

"You say that West Edmonton is bigger than this?"

"You wouldn't believe it."

"You've been?"

"Yes. I came to the Green first as a security consultant. Later on, when we were establishing our dispatch booth, we wanted to cover every base we could. I went up to Edmonton to have a look at their system."

"Dispatch booth? That sounds interesting."

"I'd just as soon we skip that for now."

"You're not on the record."

"Just the same. There are some things you want the public to know about. Others are better kept secret." He thought about his own past, about his father and uncle. How long would he keep that buried?

"You don't trust me?"

"You seem very nice. You'll have to forgive me. Part of my training involves dealing with the press—or, more specifically, not dealing with the press."

"But this is off the record."

"Just the same."

She speared a piece of feta and chewed it, washing it down with beer. "This is good."

"Tell me about yourself."

"You first."

"You mean how'd a nice guy like me get in a crazy place like this?"

She laughed a musical laugh, like a singer practicing scales. "That'll do."

"Graduated from SMU—"

"Which one?"

"Massachusetts. I worked as a repo man during my college years."

"Stealing cars, that sort of thing?"

"You make it sound criminal. I was hired to steal cars back from those people who weren't paying for them. It put me through college."

"Dangerous work."

"It had its ups and downs."

"Such as?"

"It's boring. Nothing newsworthy about repo."

"I know. But I'm interested nonetheless." She looked at him strangely. She stabbed another piece of cheese blindly.

He said, "When I got out of college I continued the repo work."

"Go on."

"A job opened up here. It paid better. Better hours, less risk. They had a pretty high turnover rate of guards and a lot of shoplifting. I told the then Director of Security that the system was at fault. Out of date. I bet him I could break into this place without anyone the wiser. I'd had a lot of practice in repo. High Star had just bought us out, and the mall was growing in leaps and bounds."

"And?"

"I broke in and called my boss. He refused to believe I'd done it so I called the CEO, a man named Haverill, from inside his own office. I read him a few confidential memos."

"That was nervy."

He shrugged. "To my surprise, he promoted me to security consultant, doubled my pay, and gave me a sizable budget to get this place in order. A year later he offered me Director of Security and I accepted. That was three years ago."

"I'm impressed."

"Don't be. I'm still just a rent-a-cop." He added, "And you? What about you?"

"Not tonight. I'm not in a 'me' mood tonight."

"I can respect that. Your mother?"

She nodded. "My father, too. He's taking it badly. It's not easy."

"I don't imagine."

He watched her sip another tiny amount. "So what was in the truck?" she asked.

"Nine tons of fresh-frozen fish. But our insurance people won't let us move the truck. The shipper is sending another refrigerator truck up tomorrow. When it has off-loaded its cargo, it will take on the fish and quickly distribute what remains."

"What *remains?* Just what does that mean?"

"It's hot out there. The freezer refrigerator was broken in the accident. The fish will go bad, if it hasn't already."

"Can't you do something?"

"I did. I called the truck company and gave them the options."

"But it's food. How can they let ten tons of food go to waste?"

"Nine tons."

"That's criminal."

"I offered to ice the fish. I gave them an estimate of what it would cost. They said the insurance would cover the loss but not costs of attempted recovery. I did what I could."

"If you had done what you could, Mr. Jacobs, that fish would be packed in ice."

"Toby, remember? Do I sense a crusader?"

Mykos Popolov delivered the bill.

"You're damn right," Susan said. "I refuse to see good food go to waste. What can we do?"

"We?" He stared. "My day's over."

"Was over." She took the bill from the tabletop.

"Was?"

"I'm buying dinner. You're going to help me contact the trucking company."

"Me?"

"And I'm going to tell whoever is in charge that if they don't try to save that fish the *Globe* will run a front-page story that mentions the name of their company a dozen times and tells our audience—and quite possibly the wire services—how their company sat back and watched nine tons of perfectly good food go to waste. Tell me that won't make good copy."

"Listen. I admire your . . . determination on this. Really. You're right, all the way. But the chances of budging these people is extremely faint. I wouldn't get my hopes—"

"You, Mr. Jacobs, are underestimating the power of the press. Never underestimate the power of the press."

"Or a woman."

"Or a woman," she agreed. "Well, are you going to help me?"

"I wasn't aware that I had a choice."

"Are you talking about that truck?" Popolov's cherubic Greek face hovered over the two of them, his wild eyebrows arched in curiosity, his bad arm tucked out of view.

Jacobs introduced Popolov to Susan Lyme, and the man took her hand in his left and kissed her knuckles. "Such a pretty girl," he said in his thick accent. "The reason I ask is that Brock called earlier today, wondering if I had enough refrigerator space to handle the fish. I told him I did not." His apron, covered with colorful smudges and streaks, bulged at his middle. "But as you know, Toby, many of us will be permitted to finish stocking our new space in FunWorld beginning tomorrow. It slipped my mind earlier, when Robinson asked, but just now"—he winked at Susan—"I overheard Miss Lyme and it occurs to me that my new walk-in is cold. We turned it on yesterday. It is empty and available, if you promise to me that by Friday it will be empty again."

"That's terrific!" She looked over at Jacobs.

He nodded, feeling his evening lost to the strong will of Susan Lyme. "We'll see what the company says. Thanks, Mykos."

"You bet. Now, I wonder if I could bend your ear for a moment back in the office."

"Sure. I'll be right with you."

The old Greek nodded. "Nice to meet you," he said to Susan and then shuffled away.

"What a sweet old guy."

"Mykos will do anything for anyone. You've never met a more giving, hard-working man in your life. For two years he's been president of the Green Retailers' Association. Any complaints to management come through him. He fought for the Italian resistance in the Second World War. He's one of a kind."

"Did he lose his arm in the war?"

"Dove under a train and rolled out the other side to escape the Germans. His arm didn't make it."

"And that's his wife?"

"Yes. He calls her Mother. That woman is one sharp cookie. Now," he said, deftly snatching the bill from her hand, "I'm going to put a couple of coffees on here and speak with Mykos. You haven't tasted coffee until you've tried this stuff. Be right back."

"That was underhanded. What's the matter? Can't you handle a woman paying for dinner?"

"No, I can't."

Her eyes followed him as he walked to the counter, pulled out his wallet, and ordered coffee from the plump Mrs. Popolov. After a minute, he and his hat disappeared into the back.

THE ROOM, a cluttered combination of pantry and office, barely held the two of them. "We are good friends, you and I," said the aging Greek.

"Yes."

"I am concerned . . . no, I am worried about something, and I want to know how you stand on it."

"Go ahead."

"It's this Civichek. The Flock. I hear him on the radio this morning. I spent the best years of my life fighting Hitler's army. This man Civichek is no different. He is clever, and he is dangerous."

"But how—"

"The reason I talk to you is because he mentioned the Green in his talk this morning. He is going to come out here to talk to the people. I ask you as a friend, as a man, not to allow him to come to this complex."

"I understand. I feel for what you're saying. But I can't stop a person from walking the mall. You know that, Mykos."

"He is evil."

"If he draws a crowd, if he passes out literature, that's another story. No petitioning permits have been filed for, or we would have heard about it. But you know the new law: If they file for the right to distribute political information, any group has the right to do so here."

"As long as it's approved by downtown."

"True."

"Yankee Green has friends downtown. My God, Haverill and his people got some of those councilmen elected. He must have influence. Deny this Civichek the permits. He's trouble for all of us. Today he seems insignificant. Tomorrow we'll be wondering how he rose to power. I've seen it before."

"I'll do what I can. Great dinner, Mykos. Good night."

"Thank you. . . . Oh—one other thing."

Jacobs paused at the door.

"That woman, Susan Lyme, is very pretty. Be nice to her. She likes you. I can see it in her eyes."

"We just met," he said.

"It happens to the best of us." Mykos Popolov smiled broadly, revealing his imperfect teeth.

23

DURING DINNERTIME at the Green, the concourses were nearly empty.

Across from Haverill sat Forest Long, a limited partner in Haverill's High Redevelopment Partners, and the managing trustee of the long-established New England Real Estate Investors, a real estate investment trust, which had loaned Haverill over $93 million and was also a joint venture partner in Yankee Green.

Haverill laid down his fork and sipped from the crystal water glass, holding it by its stem. Ice tinkled against the sides.

His daughter Julia had just excused herself from the table, and Marv noticed again how much she resembled Kate. He thought of the past. He did mind. They had been a family then. They had known joy, and even innocence. He knew little of that anymore. Work filled the void. Work took over. Even now at a gourmet dinner, work was the main course. Haverill lived for his work. With Kate gone off, what else was there?

Julia would give them five to ten minutes to discuss their business matters. She would then reappear and wait on the edges for a signal from Marv to return to the table. Business as usual.

Long sobered and lowered his voice. "Now what about this anchor? Can you get The Hauve?"

"Peter's been working on it. I'd say we're fifty-fifty."

"Brad James pulls me aside after a meeting the other day and tells me he heard you had inquired about Alex Macdonald's position on the Treemont building. Any truth to that?"

Haverill stabbed a sliced carrot. "All we did was to look into whether or not Alex had the capital to finish his buying spree." He could sense Long's disapproval. "Listen, Forest, you know me well enough to know I would not break the law—"

"Just stretch it," Long interjected.

"If Alex is low on funds then we have other options, do we not? You can hardly fault me for trying to see all sides of a situation."

"You're one of Hillsdale's good old boys, Marv. You point to a spot on the rug, someone cleans it up. You ask around in a certain tone if Alex Macdonald can get his hands on a loan, and some people will make damn sure he can't." He looked across at his friend. "You follow me?"

"We need an anchor, Forest, immediately. Northern Lights screwed us. The media people will jump all over that empty space in the new pavilion. You know it as well as I. We've done everything but beg Mann to sign up with us. He knows our position. Christ, everybody knows about Northern Lights thanks to the *Journal.* Mann's going to try and talk us down to next to nothing, which is where we were three weeks ago. I'm simply trying to enhance our position. Nothing illegal. I just want to see all the cards before I go making any bets."

"I know you're in a rough position."

"Rough? I'm up the proverbial creek. If I get The Hauve and word gets out that I've given the space away, like what happened when we opened the sports pavilion, then I've got the Green Retailers' Association screaming at me to play fair. They'll all demand a reduction. They see the pattern developing. You know how it works. We practically give space away to our anchors and take a small percentage of net. At the same time, we sign the smaller shops to a stiff lease and take a good percentage of net. They're organized now that they have this association. They'll scream bloody hell if we end up rolling over for The Hauve."

"You're saying it's a no-win situation."

"I'm saying it's damn tricky. If I have to involve Alex Macdonald, I will." Haverill looked intensely into the man's eyes.

"Oh, Christ."

"It's all aboveboard, my friend. If negotiations stall with Mann and The Hauve, which they already seem to have done, then hopefully I'm in a position to buy the building out from under them and send them packing."

"You can't evict them."

"Everything but."

Long sighed, bringing the napkin to his lips. "I think I've heard enough."

"Fred Pinkham once told me that the bigger stick you swing, the less times you actually have to hit something with it. We're just making sure we have a big enough stick." Haverill shrugged indifferently. "You wouldn't like retail, Forest. We need some stability. We need some stability soon. I'm protecting your interest as well as my own. Macdonald may come to you for the capital he lacks to finish off his plan. I just wanted you to be aware of our position. No reason to bite the hand that feeds you."

"Who knows about this?"

"People look at Yankee Green, they see a success—as well they should. Growing pains is all it is. We'll adjust. This new wing is just the ticket. It'll pull us out of this slump."

"I mean about your intentions to buy the Treemont building. Who knows?"

Haverill winced. "Nothing to worry about." He sipped some water and spotted her. He scratched his ear and Julia moved toward the table. Long and Haverill stood as a waiter seated her. "What do you think, sweetheart? Are you ready for the grand opening?"

She touched Forest Long's hand gently. "Isn't it exciting?"

"Charm him to death, won't you, sweetheart? I've just spotted someone I've got to speak with. Won't be a minute. Excuse me, please." He wanted to give Long a chance to think things over. He pushed his chair back with some difficulty and stood quickly. "Be right back," he said.

Julia turned to Long and said, "Now tell me all the juicy gossip of the inner circles of Boston's big money world." She pressed toward Long and laid her hand gently on the back of his wrist.

For the moment, Forest Long was breathless.

24

AT ONE O'CLOCK in the morning, four security men, Susan, and Jacobs were still loading crates of fish onto the electric golf cart that served as an ambulance.

"Only a couple of trips left," said Susan enthusiastically. "How's the refrigerator space holding up?"

"We went right to the ceiling," said the driver of the golf cart. "I think we'll fit it all in, if we're lucky."

Jacobs was already sore. He bent over and jerked another heavy crate up to a position where he could carry it. At the far end of the trailer he handed the crate to his guard, who handed it to Susan, who loaded it onto the cart. Jacobs took a long pause to admire her. She had the strength of a man and the self-discipline of a writer. She had not lost a bit of energy over the last three hours. She seemed to love to give orders, and people seemed to like taking them from her. It was her energy that made her so lively, and her quickness to joke that made the situation so bearable. What really surprised him at first was her willingness to tell lewd jokes. He supposed that after several years of pressrooms crowded with men, one grew accustomed to lewd jokes.

It was one of the things he liked about her: She was feminine and masculine at the same time. This morning her curves had been mixed with a big orb of sweat at the breasts. *Men sweat, women perspire.* Baloney. She had been sweating. She was strong —able to handle the heavy boxes—and yet delicate. When

Mykos had kissed her hand she had seemed positively regal. Radiant.

He tried to stop thinking about her, but seeing her silhouette in the light thrown from the side of the pavilion didn't help any. She worked with a permanent smile, eyes darting, ready with a joke if the troops appeared to be sagging.

"Last crate," Jacobs said, handing it out to her, a penetrating look in his eyes as he found hers. They both held the crate for a moment, and then he let go.

His father had once told him that you could only judge a man's character once you had worked with him. "Many men drink well together," he had said. "Few men work well together. You will learn more about a man in ten minutes of working with him than in a week of drinking beer." *Women too,* Jacobs was thinking.

"Done," Susan declared triumphantly, clapping her hands.

Only just beginning, he felt like saying.

Wednesday
August 19

--------- 1 ---------

IN THE HARD, early morning August sunlight, Marty Rappaport, bent at the waist and chewing on the butt of an unlit cigar, pulled a short piece of reinforcing bar from the chunk of broken concrete dislodged by the tractor trailer in the previous day's accident. Behind him, an angry Carmine DeAngelo approached fast. Rappaport tugged hard, and as the bar came loose, he went over backwards. His fresh white shirt was smeared with two long streaks of dirt.

"Who the hell are you, and what the hell are you doing here?" The inkwells beneath DeAngelo's eyes gave him the mean look of a boxer.

"I wanted to check out the rebar before I went jumping to any conclusions," Rappaport explained.

"Unless you got more reason than that, you'll have to go. This area is still off limits. Insurance is supposed to take a look at it later on. Can't touch a thing until they do." DeAngelo bit down squarely on his own cigar, which, unlike Rappaport, he held clear back in his molars.

"You're the super on this job, aren't you?"

"That's right. Carmine DeAngelo."

"Marty Rappaport." As the two shook hands Rappaport pulled himself to his feet. "I pushed some numbers around on this last night. I wanted a firsthand look at the rebar before I went shooting my mouth off. When you get to my age and start shooting your mouth off, people think you're nothing but bad gas. How old are you, Mr. DeAngelo?"

"Fifty-two."

"Well, you'll know soon enough."

"What kind of numbers?"

"Oh, just numbers," Marty said cautiously. "Can I ask who oversaw this project from the mall's end?"

"General manager. Guy by the name of Peter Knorpp. He didn't do squat on this job, though. You gotta gripe, you better settle with me."

"Who's in charge of mall safety?"

"Jacobs, Director of Security, as far as I know. What's this all about?"

"Met him yesterday. Can I ask you one other thing?"

"What's to stop you?"

"Who'd you use for your concrete sub?"

"Had two on this job. That's when all our union problems began. With the first, I mean. We used DeGrassi's outfit, Joey DeGrassi out of Dedham, for the first few pours, but his crews wouldn't work the schedule we had mapped out. Not without a lot of overtime pay. DeGrassi claimed the overtime pay hadn't been figured into the bid, which was a pile of crap, mind you, because we had the dates all spelled out real clear. At any rate, it kicked off our battle with Russo and the unions. Russo organized a picket line on the job and we hired scabs."

"I remember reading about it. It got kind of nasty, didn't it?"

"Always gets nasty with the union boys."

"You said two."

"Danny Romanello, from Milford, finished up the job."

"Who poured the stairway?"

"That would've been Romanello. What's this all about anyway?"

"I'm just a curious old fart, that's all."

The two studied each other. "What'd you say your name was?"

"Call me Marty."

"It's a closed area, Marty."

"Yeah, yeah. Okay. I'm going."

As they ducked under the police tape, DeAngelo said, "If you got something to say about the construction, I'm the one to hear it."

"Nice meeting you, Mr. DeAngelo," Rappaport said casually, raising his hand over his shoulder and heading toward Pavilion C.

"How can I help you, Mr. Rappaport?" Jacobs sat behind a modest desk, the comfortable office's large windows looking west toward Connecticut. Two padded chairs faced the desk, each angled slightly. Jacob's hat lay on the typewriter behind him.

"Nice office."

"They treat us well here."

"I can see that. Nice carpet. I've got a brother-in-law in the carpet business. He's got a good friend in the furniture business if you ever decide to do away with that rack of file cabinets and put in a sofa or a convertible. Jessi and I—that's my wife—put one in our den, convertible, I mean. Just the thing for guests with kids. That extra space really pays off."

"I'll remember that."

"You mind if I shut the door?" Rappaport stood up and closed the office door.

Jacobs chewed away a grin. With the unlit cigar the little man reminded him of DeAngelo, but the bowlegged shuffle was all Rappaport's. When Rappaport had returned to his seat, Jacobs looked the man in the eye and said, "Now, how can I help you?"

"Mr. Jacobs, I've spent my life in engineering. Been around the construction business all my life. I study the way things are built, out of habit. I picture how they'd look on the plans, that sorta thing." He lowered his voice. "When I saw that accident out by your new wing yesterday, something didn't sit right. I couldn't place it at first. You know how that goes, especially at my age." Rappaport had a curious grin, both childish and wise. "Then I recalled a similar accident I'd seen on my Army base, God only knows how many years ago." The same grin. "Couple of good old boys tied one on and ran a semi-truck smack into the armory. Busted the hell out of the truck. Barely scratched the armory. Armory was made of cement, just like your stairway. I got to thinking about the huge chunk of concrete that broke off. There was a good deal of crumbling as well—"

"Are you talking about our stairwell now?"

"That's right. So I snuck a look at the manifest and got the overall tonnage of the loaded vehicle. I plugged some numbers into the equation accounting for the stress tolerance of the cement in your stairway. I did it twice, once for a twenty-seven day-old pour, in case that stairway was added as an afterthought, and once for a ninety-day-old pour—"

"Stairway was poured right along with everything else, as far as I know."

"Yeah, I figured that, by the look of it. I was just down there a few minutes ago. It looks to me like they planned on precast for most of the walls and filled in by pouring some of the support structure and your staircases."

"You're out of my league. Carmine DeAngelo would know more about that."

"I couldn't talk to DeAngelo about this. Wasn't even sure if I should talk to you. But he tells me a man named Knorpp over-saw the construction, and that, I figure, leaves you in the clear."

"I'm afraid I don't follow you, Mr. Rappaport."

That same grin. "Son, if the concrete was up to strength, that truck would have had to be going seventy-eight point five miles an hour to do the damage it did." He let the comment sit there. "Checked my figures five times. Got the same thing each time."

"What are you saying?"

"As far as I can tell, someone started your pours with an inferior cement. Part, maybe all, of your new wing is below code."

Jacobs ran his hand through his hair and looked at the man's face. "That's impossible."

"Happens all the time. More often than you might think."

"Below code?"

"When a job is poured, the concrete sub pours a number of cylinders at the same time. A testing lab breaks those cylinders at certain time intervals to check the stress tolerance of the pour. The lab can tell how well the cement is curing according to how much pressure is required to crush each cylinder.

"There are a few ways a guy can get around the testing labora-tory: One, the sub pours his cylinders from different cement and submits those cylinders to be tested. When they're checked, everything comes out fine. Two, the sub simply substitutes cylinders from a different job for the ones he claims are off of this job. Lab checks them out: no problems. Three, the sub has someone in the lab on his payroll. All three get the job done. All roads lead to Rome." That same smile.

"Is there any possibility of a mistake?"

"I wouldn't take my word for it, if that's what you mean."

"What *would* you do?"

"If I were you, I'd lift two samples from that accident and very quietly submit them to two different testing laboratories, maybe one in Connecticut. Someplace away from here. I wouldn't tell them where they came from—which is to say, if they ask, I'd lie. Many of the labs, at one time or another, have been accused or convicted of this same offense. They tend to protect each other. What you do is tell them it's from a precast bridge on a piece of property you're thinking of buying. I checked the books, and the stress tolerance required for a one-lane preformed bridge is just about identical to that of a commercial property the size of your new wing. Quite frankly, your cement should be as strong as anything that's poured these days. Using prestressed forms for your walls puts all the weight-bearing on your pours. As I understand it, there's eight major weight-bearing columns in your new wing. DeAngelo tells me that everything from your subfloor up was poured by the same sub. That includes the stairway that fell apart. If any of your support columns were poured outta the same crap that stairway was, you got problems. Capital P."

"You talked to DeAngelo about this?"

"No. I brought it to you first. No telling who's involved."

"I appreciate your concern. What I'd like you to do is put all your numbers into a letter, including an explanation of your concerns. Make a copy of the letter and leave it someplace safe. I'd like a copy as well. Include mention of this meeting, so we're both covered there."

"You look a little white, Mr. Jacobs."

"Toby," he corrected. "I don't doubt it. That new wing cost a hundred and eighty million dollars. What you're saying could have far-reaching effects."

"Indeed it could."

"I'd like you to get those samples for me, if you don't mind. I don't know what to look for, and it might tip somebody off if I suddenly take an interest in the construction. You, on the other hand, would just look like a souvenir taker."

"I understand completely." Rappaport was doing a fair job at concealing his enthusiasm.

"This is further complicated by the fact that we broke the unions on this job."

"Yes, I've read about it. And DeAngelo filled me in earlier."

"We'll run those tests, and we'll see what we see."

"I know what we'll see," said Rappaport. "The question now is who is involved."

2

DOUGLAS SHLEIT HAD BEEN a lieutenant on the Hillsdale force for the last twelve years. In that time he had personally handled only four homicides: a suicide, a drowning, a hit-and-run, and a firearms case involving an irate wife and a drunken, abusive husband. If it hadn't been August he wouldn't have been assigned the McClatchy case. The more qualified lieutenant for the job was in Akron, Ohio, visiting a sister, so Shleit had it. His real love was the baritone saxophone. He spent his evenings alone, playing along with Count Basie records and drinking beer. From the very beginning he had been a renegade cop. His file listed three fistfights, all the result of a touchy temper.

Word had trickled down that his days on the Hillsdale force were numbered. The fact that people like Bob Russo had heard the same rumor gave it more credence. He had a real problem taking orders, though the jobs he ended up with got done and got done well. They called him independent, but he didn't feel independent; he felt chained to a bureaucracy that needed three forms filled out to wipe its ass. The joke went: How many Hillsdale cops does it take to change a light bulb? Four. Three to fill out forms and one to steal the bulb. Corruption was rampant on the force, nearly as bad as in the rest of Hillsdale's city government. Shleit felt a certain pride at never having taken a dime in graft, though he knew in part this was responsible for his impending "transfer." The Hillsdale force consisted of several cliques. When you didn't play by the existing rules—regardless of their ethics—you were a threat. Recently Shleit had been hit on by several of the captains and had avoided getting mixed up in sticky situations. Now they had collectively decided it was time for him to leave. So he would leave.

Despite the fact it went against everything he stood for, he found himself half hoping that Russo would try to stick some money in his pocket to keep the McClatchy case quiet. It would be perfect timing now. Ten or twenty grand in cash and then a "transfer" a few months down the road. He pushed the thought from his mind as he pushed the door to Jimmy Jackson's book-store open.

As president of the Hillsdale Chamber of Commerce, Jackson knew what the merchants of the town were thinking. Like the upper staff of the police department, the more powerful businessmen in town had their own clique. They played poker together every other Thursday, entertained one another, and, in a few cases, slept with each other's wives. It was part of the small-town flavor that left a bitter taste in Shleit's mouth.

Jackson wore his blond hair a little too long, had a mustache and blue-green eyes that bored into Shleit as the detective entered the store. Like a political figurehead, Jackson stood on the outside of the truly powerful clique, destined never to be a part of it. He was, instead, the man who chaired the meetings, the man quoted in the press. Divorced and a permanent bachelor, Jackson's only known vice was a regular rum-and-tonic lunch and a platinum blonde named Angie who owned and managed the Ten Pin Bowling Alley and Lounge.

"Morning, Lieutenant."

"Jimmy. How's the trade?"

"Slow."

Those in the know knew that Jackson sold triple X-rated novellas from behind the counter. He was protected from arrest by a monthly donation to the captain of the vice squad. "What's the latest smut title?"

"Me? I don't sell smut." After a pause Jackson picked out a book from beneath the register and placed it out for Shleit to thumb through. *Moby Dick* appeared to be about a sea captain.

The badly lit photos that riddled the poorly typeset prose showed grotesquely close-up shots of overused, oversized anatomical parts.

"The captain, no doubt, has a tattoo of a whale on his crank," said Shleit.

Jackson snatched the book back. "You've read it. No fair," he jibed sarcastically. "What can I do for the law today?"

"Hear about the explosion?"

"Talk of the town."

"Know anything about it?"

"Lieutenant, that's hardly appropriate."

"Downtown's been looking for a way to put the Green back a step."

"I can't deny that. But murder?"

"Maybe murder wasn't part of the plan. Just an unlucky complication."

"You're reaching, Lieutenant. You've seen downtown's ad campaign. That's our attack on the mall."

"I'm asking you, Jimmy, because you know what's happening. You know who's been hurt the most by the mall. If I had the time, we could dance around all day. It's obvious you've got the free time. I don't."

"Hurt badly? Christ, Doug, there's not a downtown merchant who's not been hurt badly. You know that. Sales are off. Way off. And there's no sign of recovery. We're getting more organized but it's too late. There's talk, as I'm sure you've heard, of closing off car traffic to a few central streets and making a kind of mall out of a few key downtown blocks. Fine and dandy. Great idea. Only three or four years late, that's all. I don't know if it's possible to bring back downtown. I think Haverill's prediction may be the most accurate. Downtown will develop into an office center, with retail activity out at the mall. Alex Macdonald has the jump on that end of things. Now Haverill's thinking about adding an office center next, because we took so long to provide downtown space. Come to think of it, you may be right—there's plenty of us who would like to see the mall suffer a little, maybe even go under."

"No one's dumb enough to try it themselves. They'd hire it done."

"Right as rain. A couple of phone calls to Providence, and you could set it up in a matter of hours."

"Who would want it, Jimmy?"

"Christ, Doug, you've been here—what, twelve years or more? You walk the fringe. You're sort of famous for that, but you know what's what. You could name 'em as easily as I could."

"Could I?"

"Couldn't you? Sure you could." Jackson flipped over the classical tape that finished and pushed PLAY. Wynton Marsalis flurried his trumpet from behind the nonfiction. "Say, how's the bari coming?"

"Probably about as well as your trumpet."

"That bad?"

"Afraid so."

"We oughta jam sometime. Dennis could play drums, and Cindy plays a pretty good right hand on the ivories."

"We'd need a bass."

"Call around, see what you can turn up."

"For the jam, or for your investigation?"

"Both."

"How about Russo?"

"What makes you say that?"

"Everybody knows Russo would like to nuke that mall. And who has better connections to Providence than a guy who headed the construction unions in five major cities? Russo's got to be connected to the family."

"Never been any proof he is."

"Never any that's been made public, that is. There's a difference, isn't there, Doug?"

"Sticking a bomb in a locker is no way to solve downtown's problems."

"Hey, I agree. That is, unless it worked. . . . Just kidding," Jackson added quickly. "Okay, I'll put out a few feelers. But I'm warning you, I'm going to come up with more candidates than you want to handle, and they're going to be people who are untouchable."

"They need to meet two qualifications. One, they need the motive. Two, they need a connection to someone who could arrange it for them. And I haven't ruled out a group effort.

There are two or three partnerships I can conjure up that might try a stunt like this."

"Doug, I don't know your business. I don't pretend to. But I'd be real careful if I were you. Whoever did this has killed a man, intentional or not. If you get too close, what's to stop them from killing another?"

"The thought's occurred to me, Jimmy. Don't forget to call that bass player. Tell him I've got the charts and all the beer he can drink."

"Where you been, Doug? These kids don't drink beer. They smoke grass and do lines."

"Just call him."

JACOBS LOCATED Vince Wright at the far end of the new pavilion. He was installing one of the large information maps. Wright reminded Toby of a professional baseball player: long, lean, tan, and agile. He was younger than Jacobs, not yet thirty, but already had a wife and two children. Talking to people like Wright made Jacobs realize that a part of his life was quickly passing him by. It seemed lately that each and every day he found himself wondering if his kind of dedication to a job made any sense. Life had more to offer.

"Got a minute, Vince?"

"Sure. Give me a few seconds."

A few minutes later Wright joined Jacobs in front of the doorway of the empty anchor space, a vacant area that occupied several thousand square feet in the southeast corner of the FunWorld pavilion.

"What's up?" Wright had the looks of a Marlboro man and the deep resonant voice of a disk jockey.

"I don't know many of the crew as well as I know you."

"Scratch one up in favor of weekend volleyball. The way our team is playing, that may be the only good thing about it."

"I had a few things to ask."

"About the explosion?"

Jacobs nodded. "Indirectly."

"There's a rumor going around that Jim set the bomb off."

"Meaning?"

"You'll have to talk to the electrical contractor, but what I heard is that someone checked out the circuit breaker in the panel room and it was switched on. It would only be switched on if Jim had finished his work. Not only that but the light switch inside the door to the utility room had been flipped up. I saw that with my own two eyes. So anyway, somebody was speculating that Jim had finished up and then returned to test out his work, and that when he threw the light switch he blew himself away."

"He *was* just inside the door at the time of the explosion."

"It's got the crew a little edgy."

"I'll check into it. What I wanted to ask . . ."

". . . is who would do something like this."

"Right."

"Mind if we sit down?" Wright pointed to a cement bench beneath the nearest escalator. When the two men sat down, they were conveniently hidden from sight from the central area of the amusement pavilion. Jacobs wondered if Wright had deliberately hidden this impromptu meeting. His curiosity was answered when Wright suddenly began speaking in a softer voice. "There's a lot of workers on a lot of different crews. I don't know how much I can help."

"Would you rather do this another time? Maybe someplace else?"

Wright looked around nervously. "No, this is all right. The thing is," he said, even more quietly, "some of us figure that Russo's boys planted some union workers from other towns amongst us. Kind of like spies, you know, so Russo could know what was going on here."

"You believe that?"

"When you're nonunion, like I am, you get so you can spot a union worker. It's an attitude thing mostly. They wait to be told what to do. Hurry up and wait. You know the symptoms. Well, there are half a dozen guys that fit that here. Can't be sure if they're recent defectors or bad actors. Whenever a union is broken, like this one was on this job, you get some guys who have to turn in their cards and accept the nonunion work. That may be all we have here, but I'd just as soon play it cool."

"Russo's retired. Why would they be Russo's boys?"

"Russo's not retired. Not in the true sense of the word. What happened, as I hear it, is that some kind of internal shit prompted him to pull the plug and hang out on the outskirts. He still pulls the strings. He will for years to come, regardless of who is in the top job. This whole thing is mob controlled, T.J., as I'm sure you know, and no one is going to take away Russo's power without killing him."

"So you're saying the bomb could have been planted by one of these 'spies?' "

"Why not? We were damn near right on schedule, delayed about a month and a half, I think, wasn't it? A job this size, full union would have run at least six months over, probably more like a year. That does two things. First, it makes the union outfits look bad. They'd have more at stake here than a guy like Russo. Second, by being on schedule, workers work less. Bottom line is this business is work. Projects that go out on time mean fewer paychecks."

"You're not narrowing my field much."

"On this job? Jeez, it could have been about anyone. If you knew what kind of explosive was used, and how much, it would tell you something—"

"You think like a cop."

"I spent a couple of years running a bedrock drill for a blasting company that worked the interstate circuit."

"You?"

"Yeah. I learned a lot from those powder hounds. First of all, you have to be a little nuts to do that for a living. That's a requirement. I don't care how safe you tell me that work is, people get burned, lose a hand, go deaf, all the time. Bad business. Not for me. Saw a guy get his hand blown off by a blasting cap. I quit the next day. But my point is that not just anyone could have set it up. Sure, about anyone could have planted it in DeAngelo's locker, and there are plenty who might have wanted to, but rigging the actual bomb is another thing entirely. It takes special gear and special knowledge."

"Why the comment about DeAngelo?"

"You kidding? The guy is a workhorse. A slave driver. Not only does he work us too many hours a week—something no one is happy with—but he works us hard. Did you know he just took away our afternoon coffee break? That's something the union would never have allowed. Nothing we can really do about it. Now he has us on ten-hour days with no overtime. There're some pissed-off people around here."

"How pissed off?"

"Not pissed off enough to blow the guy away, if that's what you mean. At least I don't think so. You never know. People get pissed off about the strangest things. Hey, listen, don't look so bummed out. You'll catch the guy."

"I have about three hundred suspects, it sounds like to me. Four or five motives. I'll look into this angle of yours that McClatchy detonated it with the light switch. That would certainly make a difference."

"The thing that gets me is, what sense would it make to wire a goddamned bomb in DeAngelo's locker so it went off when the light switch was thrown? What's the point of that?"

"DeAngelo use his locker much?"

"Hell, no. Hardly ever. The deal is, DeAngelo had a locker down there, sure. But he practically lives in that trailer out there. He keeps all his shit out there. Only reason he kept a locker down there was to try to seem like one of the guys."

"Thanks, Vince."

"That all?"

Jacobs slapped him on the back. "You've been a big help."

WRIGHT'S LAST WORDS were spinning in Jacobs's mind as he sought out the electrical contractor. If DeAngelo rarely used his locker, then it would have made an ideal place to hide a bomb. It could have been in there for a week or two beforehand. The bomber could have placed it well before in order to hide his own involvement. Or it could have been meant for DeAngelo. There was no ruling out any possibility at this point. What Jacobs needed now was more data to help narrow the field. He made a mental note to check with Shleit about any lab results, and the thought of labs reminded him of his earlier conversation with

Rappaport and the possibility of bad cement. He'd made an appointment to speak with Haverill about it before lunch.

After a brief conversation with the electrical contractor, a man too busy to even stop to talk, Jacobs confirmed the rumor Vince Wright had heard. It appeared that McClatchy had finished his work and was testing the lights when the detonation occurred. So was it coincidence, or had the light switch somehow triggered the explosion?

Jacobs didn't accept coincidence as an explanation for anything. He was of the school that everything happens for a reason, acknowledging that occasionally chance was the only obvious reason. Very occasionally.

But it left him with only more questions. If the light switch had triggered the explosion, then McClatchy's task of rewiring a ceiling panel may have had something to do with it. How did that fit in? Jacobs scratched his head and plunked himself down into the chair behind his desk. He picked up the Boston phone book. It was heavy and bulky.

The white pages listed only one doctor's residence under the name of Lyme in Brookline.

AT A FEW MINUTES past eleven on that Wednesday, the man with the thick glasses found himself once again above the suspended ceiling of the telephone utility room in Sub-level 2 of Pavilion C. He exchanged cassette tapes in the three voice-activated, auto-reverse machines that monitored conversations in the offices several floors up. Pocketing the tapes, he moved cautiously back toward the tunnel from which he had entered the dead space above the Armstrong paneling.

These taped conversations had already proved invaluable to him. Knowing what your opponent was thinking was important. He knew, for instance, that the Director of Safety and Security spent the late mornings catching up on paperwork and dictating memos. This made the late morning ideal for work in the sublevels of Pavilion C, because it indicated that at this hour the

Security force was effectively on break. The Director of Safety and Security involved himself in every aspect of the mall's security operations. He was the man to worry about.

The bomber was anxious to hear the new tapes. Yesterday's unexpected explosion threatened the entire operation, though there was no stopping now. He was committed to seeing this through.

A game of cat and mouse seemed inevitable. They would do everything in their power to discover the person responsible for the explosion. He would do everything in his power to mislead them. With only a few days to go, he couldn't be stopped.

Reaching an intersection with a utility shaft, he climbed the metal handholds one flight up to Sub-level 1 and entered an east-running tunnel. At the far end of this tunnel, nearly a hundred yards long, the small space enlarged, allowing him to stand. Each network of utility tunnels in each pavilion had these entrances, though without a card key they were useless to the bomber except as exits. He straightened his work clothes, checked to make sure the cassette tapes were tucked away, and then, with gloved hands, twisted the doorknob, bumping the door open a crack with his foot. The sub-level utility areas rarely saw any action, except an occasional maintenance man who had a job to do. But the bomber took no chances. He peered out the crack in the door, his distorted eye peering into the underground parking area. He glanced at the surveillance camera track overhead. When it faced away from him, he confidently pushed open the door and stepped out, turning his back quickly toward the location of the camera.

The parking facility was completely full, as were all other underground lots. By noon the only available parking was outside, in the heat and sun. Although occasional shoppers entered these underground facilities in search of their cars, the occasional shopper didn't bother this man. To them he was simply a worker doing his job. One of the things that made his job so easy was the size of the mall and the volume of foot traffic. One man, in this continually changing sea of people, would hardly be noticed, especially with hundreds of construction workers on the job.

Still, it made no sense to take unnecessary risks. Only the careless were caught.

JACOBS COULD SMELL the fresh latex paint. He liked the smell. Shleit's precinct had been transferred to a new space in what had formerly been a one-story post office. In the process of conversion, the building had been stripped of any character. Human skin glowed green under the harsh fluorescent light.

The desk sergeant spoke into the phone and then said in a raspy voice, "You can go in now. Third office on the right, just past the water fountain."

Jacobs waited for the buzzer. He pushed open the glass door. The springs were tight because the door was new. He passed a number of uncluttered desks. Plenty of August vacations.

Bolted to the wall behind Shleit's desk was a sign that read: THANK YOU FOR NOT SMOKING—H.P.D. Shleit had a menthol going. Its pale blue smoke spiraled toward the ceiling.

"Got held up," Jacobs apologized, taking a seat.

"I would have come out there, but I'm expecting a couple of important calls and our call-forwarding is screwed up. New offices."

"So I see."

"I feel like I'm in a hospital. Hate the place."

"The old post office, isn't it?" Jacobs didn't feel comfortable socializing with Shleit.

"Why didn't they keep it looking old? I coulda lived with that." The detective took an enthusiastic drag on the cigarette, which he then placed in an ashtray crowded with butts. On the side it read THE SOFT TOUCH LOUNGE.

Jacobs eyed the rising smoke as it was broken by Shleit's words.

"Reason I called is we've got some lab reports on your explosion. Two, possibly three sticks of dynamite were used. We pulled some ash out of that rubble that could have been wrapping. Fluoroscope revealed four numbers on one of the pieces. Could be part of a date-shift code stamped on the dynamite for identification purposes."

"I'm familiar with date-shift codes. Have they checked the numbers yet?"

"Stolen property. We've got a pretty good idea of when and where. ATF investigated it. File's on its way down from Boston."

"How long ago?"

"It's under investigation. Some things I can tell you. Some things I can't. You understand."

"No, not really."

"That's how it is. Thought you might be interested." He sucked on the cigarette and exhaled toward the overhead light, then snuffed out the butt. The ashtray started smoking. Shleit ignored it.

It smelled awful. "I spoke to one of the construction workers. A guy I know pretty well," Jacobs said.

"And?"

"He said DeAngelo works them hard. Too hard. He said any number of people would have reason to rattle DeAngelo's cage. But not kill the man."

"Never know."

"He also said there's a rumor going around that McClatchy finished up the electrical work and detonated the bomb by mistake. Any truth to that?"

"I'll check it out," said Shleit.

"Other than that, I've got zero."

"Give our lab people time. Impossible not to leave something behind in this day and age. What the human eye can't see, fluoroscopes and spectroscopes can. We'll get him."

"What are the chances the bomber will try again?"

"We don't have enough yet. No profile whatsoever. Impossible to say."

"He could strike again at any time."

"That's right."

"He could do a lot of damage, hurt a lot of people."

"Right again. Logan airport is going to loan us a couple of bomb-sniffing dogs, though it'll probably take a day or so to happen. I think we'll both rest easier once the dogs have been through. If I didn't know Marv Haverill's reputation, I'd suggest to him that he close down shop for a couple of days. But that's not his style, is it?"

Jacobs avoided an answer. "You'll keep me posted?"

"We better talk tomorrow."

"Give me a call."

Shleit nodded.

Jacobs rose from his chair. He asked, "Why didn't you just tell me this over the phone?"

Shleit slipped into a hard-boiled detective pose. It didn't quite work. "I wanted to see how willing you were to cooperate. A lot of people on vacation around here. I'm short-handed. Wanted to see if you and I can work together."

"And?"

"You came down, we did quick business, you're leaving. Suits me fine. How 'bout you?"

"Same."

"We'll talk tomorrow." Shleit's voice was sharp.

"Right."

Shleit struck his disposable lighter and lit up another menthol. He stabbed the bottom of the lighter into the smoking ashtray, fighting tiny orange embers.

Jacobs looked around again on his way out. White walls. White ceiling. Not a single splash of color. No plants. Definitely lacking in character.

LAURA HAFF STOOD partially clothed staring into her closet, trying to convince herself she was only doing this because she and Sam were old friends. She knew it wasn't true. When was the last time she had changed her clothes three times? No doubt for some dinner party in town with Tim—another lifetime ago.

She was a new person now, a woman filled with sometimes agonizing responsibilities and often drained of energy. But today her energy level was high. Excitement pulsed through her veins, with a kind of intoxicating selfishness. This lunch was strictly for her own pleasure. How long had it been since she could say that?

She pulled a cherry polyester skirt and a pink blouse off their hangers and laid them out together on the unmade double bed.

When was the last time she had not made her bed? Suddenly confused, she slumped down on the edge of the mattress and put her head in her hands. What was the point of getting excited? Who wanted a widow with two kids?

Then she recalled the local gossip her friend Georgine had passed along last night. Sam had been married too. His wife had left him, though no one was too clear on that point. It had something to do with his sister. "I told you he was available. I knew he'd fall all over you again," she had said. "You've got to take some chances, kid. My God, I remember when you two . . ."

Laura remembered too. So long ago it seemed, but actually only ten years—not that long. She glanced at the empty ruffled sheets.

The refrigerator groaned in the kitchen. Some blue jays on the feeder fought over the seed, only to be chased away by a predatory squirrel who had the same breakfast in mind. Laura had tried about everything to keep the damn squirrels off the feeder. It was the kind of thing Tim had been so good at.

She decided on the pink blouse, white slacks, and her new white sandals. Fully dressed, she looked at herself again in the full-length mirror. She tried on a smile and then pinched her cheeks to bring some color to them. She'd seen a sign at the Green advertising a tanning booth. It might help. Be happy, she told herself. No one likes a sourpuss. Be happy, bright, and intelligent.

Sure, and while you're at it, sexy and charming too. Who's kidding whom?

And with that, she forced herself out the door.

SHE FOUND A PARKING SPACE well away from the complex and rode a trolley to one of the underground lots where elevators carried hordes of housewives and children up and into the heart of the complex. Where did they all come from? Boston and Providence, Hillsdale, Worcester. The suburbs. Yankee Green had become the shopping focal point of this whole area of the Northeast. Five years ago, at the completion of the first pavilion, it hadn't been this way. Malls had had the reputation of being tacky. But the

Green had challenged the image. Now it was an inescapable fact: The Green was charmed.

Their small talk lasted about two minutes; they verbally prodded one another, testing for soft spots or imposed walls. Then Sam said, "You're curious about my divorce, aren't you?"

"A little." She felt herself blush. "Not that I've any right."

"Of course you do. I know your past. It seems only fair that you should know mine." He paused. "Do you remember my sister, Judy?"

"No, I'm sorry."

"Well, anyway, Judy had a stroke about three . . . no, four years ago."

"Oh, no!"

"She was twenty-one and fooling around with pills." He shook his head and swallowed hard. "It crippled her right side and impaired her speech. At that point Tan and I had been married about a year. Maybe a year and a half. I didn't know what to do. My sister and I lost our parents when I turned eighteen."

"I remember."

"There never was a lot of money. I faced putting Judy in the only home I could afford, which wasn't much. It was the pits, to be honest. I just couldn't see her in one of those places. So we took her in."

"Of course."

"She wasn't that bad, really. She had her right side. She could feed herself, dress herself, that kind of thing. She couldn't get around very well. I usually carried her up and down stairs, though sometimes she could manage with a crutch. I obviously paid too much attention to her and not enough to Tan. That's easy to see in hindsight. Tan got jealous. Then she got angry. We started arguing about it, which made me mad because Tan knew Judy could hear our arguments. It got progressively worse." He looked at her with his warm blue eyes. "She left me. Bam. Just like that. No note. No nothing. Filed through a lawyer for divorce. Thank God there were no children." He grimaced. "Sorry about that. That was rather indelicate."

Laura waved her hand lightly and whispered, "So how's Judy now? Can I meet her?"

"Let's talk about that some other time. It really is *great* to see you. The last thing I want to do is scare you away with a lot of morbid talk that won't do either of us a bit of good."

"I think it does help, at least it's helping me," she said, taking over. "Tim and I had everything we had dreamed of. Two kids we couldn't get enough of. A nest egg for travel that Tim planned on using for a down payment on a motor home. Good friends. It was never perfect, mind you. We had little spats. But never anything that mattered—just enough to bring us back to earth. Then a gust of wind changed everything." She hesitated. " 'Gone with the wind,' as a friend of mine joked a few months later."

"That's pretty tasteless."

"She's a good friend. She meant well. Besides, she was right. She didn't just mean Tim. She meant more like one minute everything was fine and the next it had all blown away. It's true. We take so much of life for granted. If there's one thing this experience has taught me, it's to live life to its fullest each day, which is funny, because I don't do that. Between the kids and my work, and the house—"

"It's good you can smile about it."

"I'm done crying. Thank God. For a while there it seemed I might never be done crying."

He reached across the table and took her hand. She accepted it somewhat reluctantly and forced a smile. To her relief the arrival of the salads interrupted them. A few minutes later he asked, "Can you handle some honest talk?"

"I'd like to think I can."

"I spent most of last evening on the phone trying to find out everything I could about you."

"You did?"

He nodded. "I wanted to size up my competition."

"And what'd you find out?" she asked with a smile. "As if I don't know."

"That a couple of guys hound you all the time for dates and that you never accept."

"Not true."

"Bill Prescott and John Floode, to name two."

"They were being polite. You know how it is: Everyone gives

you a couple of months, and then they start feeling sorry for you
and trying to fix you up." She remembered her promise to attend
Georgine's party this weekend.

"That's not how I heard it was."

"It's sweet of you to say so."

"So why am I so lucky?"

She caught his eye. "Just because. That's all."

"Well, that explains it." They both grinned.

Laura searched her mind for something to say but all she
could see was Tim's face in the photo, smiling out at her.

Tim's face. Always smiling.

PETER KNORPP PULLED on the edge of the hinged frame of an oil
painting that hung on his office wall. The painting was a copy of
a Renoir nude. Once moved, it did not reveal a hidden wall safe
but a full-length mirror. Knorpp admired his dark, even tan, the
result of the two-thousand-dollar tanning machine at his apartment; he examined the perfect shape of his blow-dried hair; he
smiled his practiced smile, making certain no foreign matter had
stuck in his teeth. He wanted to impress Chester Mann. He
remembered Haverill's words when he had first been hired. "Peter, if there's one thing you're good at, it's salesmanship. What
I'm looking for is someone who can represent Yankee Green's
best interests and come off looking like he's trying to give the
place away. If you can do that, you've got yourself a job."

Knorpp's theory of sales was to avoid details and concentrate
on impression. Impression was everything. Image. If you could
sell the image you could lease space. Occasionally Haverill had to
step in and close the sale, handle the details, because when you
got down to the fine print of the Green's percentage lease agree-
ments, the deals weren't all that great. The hidden charges
tended to nullify the attractive financial incentives that appeared
to make the complex special. That didn't matter to Knorpp.
Image was everything.

Knorpp took image to the extreme. He owned an extravagant

apartment, wore the finest clothes. Six thousand dollars and a remarkable orthodontist had bought him a Robert Redford smile.

His secretary buzzed him. Knorpp closed the mirror against the wall, walked over to his desk, and said into the speakerphone, "Send him in, please."

Chester Mann, the forty-seven-year-old owner and manager of The Hauve department store, wore a conservative suit and wing tips. He had a broom-handle spine and flat hands with long piano-player fingers that wrapped around and squeezed the blood out of Knorpp's lifeless grip. This was their seventh meeting.

"Nice to get that rain out of the way," Mann began, typically safe.

"Certainly was."

"I do a little sailing on the weekends. How about yourself?"

"Me? No. I'm a racket man, actually."

"Oh," Mann said, uninterested.

Knorpp checked his watch, wondering what was keeping Haverill.

"Golf's my other interest."

"I've never played much golf."

"Marv knows the game. Damn good player, too, from what I hear."

Haverill entered the office as if on cue. His large size, his bellowing voice, his pacing all contributed to the desired effect: intimidation.

Mann and Haverill greeted each other cordially, although an underlying tension was impossible to miss.

Turning to Knorpp, Haverill gestured. "Peter, why don't you sit here."

Knorpp had been just about to lower himself into the chair behind his desk, but he nodded and walked across the room, brushing imaginary lint off his jacket.

He had studied Haverill over the last few years. Here was a man who could win at anything, from college football games to speculative real estate. Haverill had the Midas touch: he had profited from nearly every business venture he had ever entered into. He had the kind of power and finesse Knorpp envied.

Haverill's greatest asset was that he was a people person. He knew how to charm, to entertain, to negotiate. He cultivated friendships easily, giving him an apparently unshakable self-confidence.

"Let's get down to brass tacks," Haverill began in a strong, clear tone. "You know, Chester, better promotion is one of the many benefits of leasing here at the Green. Our retailers have the added advantage that any promotional efforts generated for the complex as a whole reflect directly on their individual foot-traffic figures. You could look on it as free advertising. Of course, our advertising is strong as well." Knorpp learned a new trick: Haverill was purposely mixing two separate concepts together—promotion and advertising—no doubt hoping to confuse the two in Mann's mind. "What are our figures on that, Peter?"

"We direct-mail approximately one hundred thousand flyers each month."

Mann whistled at the figure, as if he had not heard it before.

"We advertise in twenty-seven national magazines, six regional newspapers, including the *Globe* and the *Journal*—"

"I've seen the ads."

"—and radio stations from Philadelphia up to Portland and as far west as Buffalo. This month marks our third month in television ads. But ads aren't our only television exposure. *Entertainment Tonight*'s going to do a short spot on us because a Hollywood outfit is bidding to shoot a film here in off-hours next month. The *ET* segment has a potential viewing audience of twenty-five million, nationally."

Mann straightened his tie. "I must admit, that is more than the Hillsdale Chamber of Commerce does." He had a wry smile and, Knorpp thought, a distinguished, educated look. Though he claimed otherwise, Knorpp's education had stopped with graduation from Menlo Park Junior College.

"It's one of those unseen items that makes space here a valuable asset to any retailer," Haverill added, "especially one as popular as The Hauve."

"Perhaps I can save us both time by telling you that I took your latest offer to the board and they turned it down," Mann said. "It's just too expensive, Marv. Your square-foot price is good, but the space is larger than we need, which means more money on a per-month basis. We would have to fill that extra space with product, and the added inventory would reduce our cash flow significantly."

"Chester, we're prepared to offer you something we have never offered another retailer: six months worth of *free* full-page advertisements in our flyers. We direct-mail flyers twice monthly to all our Hillsdale credit card customers, as well as to anyone who has used a national credit card here in the last thirty days. It's quite a number of people."

"How can you mail to national cardholders?"

His distraction had worked. The last thing Haverill wanted was Mann thinking about lease costs. "Peter?"

"The Green's retailers require 'for security reasons,'" he said, indicating the quotes with a coy smile, "that all credit cards users include their home addresses on the receipt. At the close of each transaction, clerks check these addresses against the database in the mainframe. If it's a repeat customer—and fifty-seven percent of our customers are—then nothing need be done. If it's a first-time user, the address is added to the database. The advertising flyers, unlike our promotional flyers, are sent out to this list, which we call our Retail Intensive List."

It took Mann a moment to digest the concept. "Sounds like a lot of added work for the retailer, to me."

Haverill spoke up. "Not as bad as you might think, besides which, it has had a phenomenal success rate at flushing out bad cardholders. When the clerk takes that receipt and begins punching in the address—well, you'd be surprised at how many times we've caught counterfeits, stolens, and altereds. Cross-checking that address scares the hell out of 'em."

"Gentlemen, the advertising benefits sound wonderful. But the fact is, The Hauve could be lost in a place this size. My question is this: Can Yankee Green—even with all the entertainment attractions designed to lure people here—support the Hillsdale Hauve franchise? We have two other franchises in malls, and in all honesty they aren't doing so well."

Knorpp decided to try and steer Mann toward numbers. The Green looked good in numbers. "But your biggest fear would be gross and net, would it not?"

"Certainly. And foot traffic. We keep careful track of foot

traffic. The number of people entering our store each day is as important to us as the number of people who actually purchase goods. One supplies the other. Our fear, quite truthfully, is that with so much else to do and see at the Green, we won't get the repeat foot traffic and attention we need to sustain growth."

"I think there's some confusion on that point," said Knorpp. Haverill sat patiently, observing the situation like a moderator at a debate. "Actually the rides, attractions, and variety of retail facilities *support* each other. The average time spent at the Green —the *average* mind you—is three hours. More does not mean less for anyone here, I assure you. If it did, the place would have folded long ago. On the contrary, the entire concept of Yankee Green, and shopping centers in general, is to hold foot traffic longer, giving each retail facility more exposure."

He shifted in his chair uneasily.

"We started out as a single pavilion, don't forget. When High Star Redevelopment Partners took over, under Marv's direction, some big changes took place. First, he recognized the need for expansion. At the same time, he saw the need to create something that would help dovetail the expenditure of free time, the customers' desires to be entertained, and retail shopping. The perfect example of this dovetailing is our stadium. Remember, only Pavilion A existed when High Star took over, and it was eventually completely remodeled, the point being that the Green is conceptually *designed* to hold the customers and keep them spending. You won't find that at other shopping centers, and certainly not downtown in a city.

"Take our Saturdays during football season. The men come to the stadium to see the Patriots play. But, unlike when the Pats were in Foxboro, now the women come along too. For three hours, while their husbands are screaming for first downs, an average of twenty-two thousand former football widows wander our concourses and shop our stores. Twenty-two *thousand*. During the play-offs that average soared to *thirty-nine* thousand! Saturday business, always our best day, is up a staggering two hundred and fifteen percent during stadium use. The stadium can be converted for tennis in the summer, and High Star is negotiating for a major NBA franchise."

"The Celtics?" Mann wondered aloud.

Silence. Mann looked to Haverill, who said, "The point being that downtown Boston, just like downtown anywhere, is becoming an *office* center. Retailers are moving out to the suburbs, closer to their clientele. I'm sure that isn't news to you, Chester."

"Of course not. Why do you think we're considering the Green at all?" Mann was obviously under a great deal of stress. "We've seen your figures. But will your foot traffic translate to foot traffic at The Hauve? I realize that at the moment downtown Hillsdale is suffering. Our sales are off, as you are well aware; however, we're still well above the norm. One reason we're able to hold our share is lack of competition. You already have your share of department stores, gentlemen. The Hauve would hardly be alone here."

"What I was going to say a few minutes earlier," said Haverill, "and I wouldn't want it to go beyond this room, is that we're willing to reduce our base lease square-footage costs by twenty percent for your first year in order to give you a chance to see how the Green's customers respond to The Hauve."

"Well, well," Martin said with more than a little interest in his voice. "Twenty percent from what Peter and I discussed?"

"For the first year," Haverill repeated.

"That's an attractive offer."

"We think so," added Knorpp. "You're going to love the Green, Mr. Mann. There's never been anything like it. We're still expanding. What other location can guarantee you—*guarantee you*—two hundred thirty-three thousand in foot traffic per *week*? Answer me that."

Mann took on a serious expression. "As you are well aware, one of our biggest concerns is the image here. I don't mean to be condescending, but you generate a kind of carnival air that grates on upper-middle-class values. Many of our customers are upper middle class. I think it's a legitimate complaint."

"Overexaggerated."

"I wonder. This mall has changed the face of this area forever. The words Yankee Green mean only one thing anymore: the largest mall in the United States. We just spoke about the publicity. Your people have done an admirable job. A super job. But look at what you've done to downtown Hillsdale. Now, granted, it was never a Park Avenue or Cambridge, but it serviced a huge rural market. I don't have to tell you that. I'm sure your people did ample studies before choosing this site. Obviously, the greater Hillsdale area supported the kind of demographics your people deemed necessary to support a retail complex of this scope and size. But as I said, we know for a fact that a large portion of Hillsdale's upper middle class would not go within five miles of the Hillsdale Mall. That's a problem for us. Those are our people."

Knorpp studied Haverill. What was the big man thinking? He seemed lost in thought.

Haverill suddenly countered. "Well, space in the new pavilion is going quickly. Since you and Peter last talked, we have had a query from another large retailer. They too would like that anchor space. Between you and me, I don't like their store and I don't like their management. Another Northern Lights I don't need. I would like to gather some additional information for your consideration. Perhaps you and I could have lunch together tomorrow."

"I'm sure we can arrange something."

Both men rose simultaneously. Knorpp was a beat behind.

"And I'd love to get out on the links with you one of these days. Did you know that one thing planned for Phase Four is an exact replica of St. Andrews? We borrowed the idea from the West Edmonton Mall. An eighteen-hole mini-golf course complete with sand and water hazards."

Mann smiled genuinely. "My word. Will there be a Phase Four? There's a rumor all over town that if there is a Phase Four it will be an office center. Any truth to that?"

Haverill shrugged. "I never pay much attention to rumors, myself."

Very seriously, Mann said, "It would cripple downtown. I suppose you're well aware of that."

Haverill bristled. "I warned downtown what direction they should take. In five years they've accomplished nothing. Nothing. Hillsdale is in a ripe location for divisions of national companies. Somebody's going to do something about it sooner or later. If everybody wasn't so busy taking money out of each other's pockets, they might get something done. Sorry," he offered, lowering his voice. "As you can tell, I'm a bit frustrated with the political structure of Hillsdale. We provide several thousand jobs, hundreds of *years* of construction man-hours, we do over half a billion gross a year, and all we get is bad-mouthed cracks behind our backs. Yankee Green's been the best thing that ever happened to this town. One of these days the people of Hillsdale are going to wake up to that fact. In this country, you either get on the leading edge or you fall quickly behind. There's no in-between. I hope you'll think seriously about joining up with us, Chester. I think we'd be good for each other."

Mann said cautiously, "You've done one hell of a job here, Marv. No one can argue that. My office'll be in touch."

Haverill and Knorpp shook hands with Mann and saw him to the door. "Timing is critical for us, Chester," Haverill reminded him. "This is a sweet deal for The Hauve. By Monday, it won't be as sweet."

Mann nodded and bit his lip, annoyed by the pressure. "I'll see what I can do. Can't make any promises."

When he was out of earshot Haverill said to Knorpp, "Bastard. He's trying to string us along. Contact Alex Macdonald. Tell him I want to speak with him." He paused and looked out into the office space, where five women and two men were busy at computer terminals. "It's time to turn up the heat," he muttered.

8

LES CIVICHEK'S STRONG, confident voice boomed into the quickly developing crowd. "Each and every day we are all victims of violent crime. Oh, we may not feel the actual blows on our bodies, we may not feel the blades open our skin, we may not feel the bullets pierce our skulls, but they penetrate even so.

"The scum and filth that walk our streets do so by our own consent. Whose cities are these, anyway? They are yours and mine. Well, aren't they? Or do those dirt balls own our cities— the same dirt balls we spent forty thousand dollars a year, per man, just to lock up? Do *they* own our cities, or do *we?* What do we want? Is this life of ten locks on the front door and screaming sirens under the hood what we want? Is this what we've come all this way for?"

Civichek hid the pleasure he felt from seeing the crowd collect so quickly. Five minutes ago, no one. Now, a hundred and fifty and growing. The people nodded where they were supposed to nod and shook their heads where they were supposed to shake their heads. It was at spontaneous times like this that Les Civichek knew he had what it takes. People wanted to hear what he had to say—and he said it better than most. They didn't care that he wore a blue jean jacket, a T-shirt, and blue jeans. They didn't care that his hair was slicked back or that he wore the cross of Jesus Christ around his neck. They saw the symbol of the Flock, a green neckerchief, hanging loosely at his neck. They saw the intent in his eyes. They heard the conviction in his voice. And they felt his charisma.

He had it.

"We are sick and tired of the crime and filth that stalk our streets. We are sick and tired of the liberal lawyers and their concern for these barbarians who rape our daughters and feed chemicals to our teenagers. Who cares what happens to this filth? Should they be locked up in government-sanctioned clubs, complete with TV, steak dinners, and volleyball? Is this what our tax dollars are for? Not mine, people. Not mine."

Now the crowd applauded him. It surged closer and people in back strained to hear him more clearly. He was not using a bullhorn or an amplifying system; those, he knew, would defeat his purpose. His image was that of a man from the streets who has had enough. This alone would be responsible for his success. He turned slightly to give the newscam a better angle. His people had notified three of the local stations. Only one had showed up so far. Some print media people had just arrived. A photographer was changing flashguns over by the entrance to the McDonald's.

"What do I do? Who am I? I can see questions on your faces. I can see doubt." He ran his hand over the crowd like a preacher addressing a congregation. And he laughed, to show his own humility. Many in the crowd laughed nervously.

"You're sexy as hell!" one housewife yelled out. And the crowd roared as he looked himself over.

"Not me, lady," he yelled back. "I'm Les Civichek. And I'll

tell you who I am, because you're gonna hear anyway. I'm part of a group called the Flock"—he tried to avoid using the word "leader" in public—"and we think that law enforcement needs a little assistance in making our streets safe." Applause again, right on cue. Brilliant light from the TV crew flooded him, and everyone suddenly paid more attention because television was here. "I'm no saint. I'm the first to admit that. I've seen our prison system from the inside out. I paid for my mistakes. And I'll tell you something. The people inside the criminal institutions in this country would scare the bejesus out of you! They did me. I realized these people *want* to hurt us. They *want* to steal from us. They *want* to rape our girls and addict our boys. I don't mind telling you, that scares the hell out of me. I don't mind telling you, we ain't gonna catch them by driving around our cities in brightly painted cars with bubble gum machines on the roof. We ain't gonna catch them by talking at lunches to the Rotary Club, like half our police chiefs do. We ain't gonna catch them by cutting budgets. Hell, no. The only way we're gonna catch them is to get out in the streets with them, catch them in the act, and throw their ugly you-know-whats *behind bars!*"

The crowd exploded into a roar. Civichek grinned and turned again for the cameras.

"Now some of you may be thinking about the Guardian Angels and wondering, Why do we need the Flock when we've already got the Guardian Angels? Well, let me ask you this: Do you see the Angels around here? Seen any Angels in Hillsdale, in Springfield, in Newton, in Providence? No way. You only see Angels in New York, Chicago, Los Angeles, big cities like that. Why? Mr. Sliwa will have to answer that for you. I can only guess." He paused for effect and repeated, "Safety in the streets. That's what the Flock is going to bring to Hillsdale, just the way we have to twelve other medium-sized cities and suburbs around New England.

"Is crime limited to New York, Chicago, and LA? No way! So it's time we get organized and get the slime out of the streets and put them behind bars and keep them there.

"This ain't no small task, folks. Hey, if you don't want to work for the better welfare of your children, walk away. Go ahead"—he pointed—"pick up your cute little shopping bags and go buy more knickknacks for Grandma. . . . No one leaving? That's good. Because if we don't organize, if we don't get the slime off the streets, if we don't put them behind bars and keep them there, then what the hell is going to be left for our kids?" He raised his voice. "Think about that. What is going to be left for our kids?"

Jacobs pushed his way through the crowd and found himself face-to-face with five green-neckerchiefed young men who had formed a body wall around the display case Civichek was using for a podium. They wore T-shirts spelling out *The Flock* in bold green letters. They looked ghetto-tough, like most other members of the Flock. "Move aside, please," Jacobs requested.

The boys didn't move.

"Read right here," Jacobs said, pointing to his identification tag. "Director of Security and Safety. That's me." One of the tougher-looking boys nudged him. Jacobs moved to within an inch of this boy's face and said. "Back off!" The boy seemed frozen.

"He'll only be a few more minutes," said a young man to Jacob's left.

"Sorry," said Jacobs. "His time is up." He pushed the tough boy aside without resistance and shouted up to Civichek, "You've got to come down from there. Now."

Civichek stopped in mid-sentence.

Jacobs added, "You a lawbreaker or law abider?"

"Ahhh. . . . Ladies and gentlemen, there's a man down here who looks like Indiana Jones in a three-piece suit saying something about obeying the law. He tells me I have to stop."

"No . . . !" complained the crowd in unison.

"Do you want me to stop?"

"No . . . !"

"Well, I don't want to stop! We haven't even started, have we?"

Applause.

Jacobs hollered up, "It's your choice how you come down from there, Civichek. You drag this out, you'll face criminal charges."

Civichek glared and for a brief moment looked as if he might lose control. He clearly loved being in the limelight. "I'm told I'll face criminal charges," Civichek informed the growing crowd. "Hey, do I looked scared? I've faced criminal charges before, and I'll face them again. Truth is, some people don't like the Flock. They don't like the Guardian Angels either. Know why? Because they're scared of us."

Jacobs, realizing he was fighting a losing battle, stepped back and called Brock in Dispatch on his walkie-talkie. He made sure that when the demonstration broke up, anyone wearing a green neckerchief would be detained. He requested ten guards to help him.

Civichek concluded, "So it looks as though my time is up. You'll be seeing and hearing a lot more from the Flock as this week goes on. We're in Hillsdale to gain your support. We need recruits and we need money. Don't think for a minute that we don't appreciate hard-earned money. You fine people go home and think about what you've heard here today. We can't do anything without the support of the people. We all want safer streets and a cleaner life. God bless you all."

As he climbed down, the large crowd broke into a spontaneous rhythmic applause that lasted nearly a minute. His people helped him off the display case, carried him on their shoulders for a few feet, and then set him down. The crowd was still applauding enthusiastically.

Jacobs stepped up to Civichek and shouted above the roar, "You and I are going to talk." He punctuated it with a loud and crisp "Now!"

"YOU'RE TREADING on thin ice." Jacobs sat in the chair behind his modest desk, Civichek facing him.

"You rent-a-cops are just like the city boys. You've never liked us, never will. What'sa matter? Afraid your union dues are going to go up?"

"We both have jobs, you and I. Part of my job is to keep soapboxers out. You have to apply for a permit to petition here. Speaking publicly is forbidden for obvious reasons. If you want to speak to the people without going through the proper channels, use the park downtown. This is a shopping complex built with private money. We have rules against public gatherings, demonstrations, and loitering. Yankee Green is not a political arena. It's a *safe* place for people to shop. People's safety, if I heard you right, is what you're concerned with. That's fine. Check our record. The Green is safer, per square foot, per acre, than your own living room. And that's true whether you live in Orlando, Florida, or Bangor, Maine.

"A crowd, like that one you just had, invites trouble. Too many people, too crowded together. A little confusion, and you have a whole lot of trouble. You want to preach, Civichek, that's your business. You want to preach here, then that's my business."

Mykos Popolov burst into the room without knocking. The plump Greek waved his half-arm in the air frantically and said, "Arrest him. Arrest the bastard. You hear that? He's just another Hitler, that's all he is."

Civichek appeared stunned.

"Mykos Popolov, meet Les Civichek. Mr. Popolov has been following your campaign closely, Mr. Civichek."

Popolov blurted out loudly, "I heard you on the radio. I heard you just now. We don't want you here. Arrest him," he said, addressing Jacobs.

"A warning will have to do, Mykos. A man like Civichek can turn an arrest into another chance to soapbox. Isn't that right?"

Civichek raised his eyebrows.

"Mr. Popolov is president of the Retailers' Association. Any permits that are applied for need his signature to be valid. That should give you an indication of your chances here at the Green."

Civichek rose to leave. "Private or not, the streets of a shopping mall are considered public property."

"Not in this state."

"Not yet. But read the newspapers, Mr. Jacobs. This same thing happened in Maine just last month. And guess who was involved? The only way to effect legislation is to bring people's awareness level up, to show them areas that need change. It took Maine all of two weeks to change their law. How long do you think it will take Massachusetts? Shopping malls *are* public places, like it or not. It's only a matter of time, Mr. Jacobs. Only a matter of time."

"Sell it somewhere else."

Civichek paused by Popolov and stared the man in the eyes. "I hate Hitler as much as you do, old man. My grandparents died in a camp. The name Civichek's not exactly from the Scottish Highlands, you know." He passed by and walked through the door.

"I'll see he gets out," Popolov said to Jacobs without waiting for a comment.

Jacobs looked at the clock on his desk, willing the hands to move faster.

"You rang?" said the smoky voice of Susan Lyme from the doorway.

"Hello there," he said, heart pounding.

"Hello."

"Please come in. I was hoping you might help me out."

"I'm all ears."

Hardly, he thought, standing to seat her as she fought back a smile.

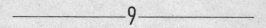

9

"You look dazed," she told him as she sat facing his chair.

He returned to his chair. She seemed far away over there. "I feel dazed. I was wondering why some days seem to go so slowly, others so fast."

"You phoned the house," she said, feeling responsible for his fatigue and trying to change the subject. It had been her idea to do something about the fish, a project that went past midnight.

"Sorry about that."

"That's why there's a phone."

"I wanted to make a proposition."

"So you just said."

"You're a free-lance investigative reporter."

"Free-lance at the moment."

"At the moment, yes. I want to hire you." He thought back to working with her the night before. It had already brought them closer. His father had been right, you did learn more about people by working with them. It bothered him that his father had been right—for years he'd been creating images of the man as always in the wrong. He wondered if this job offer was rationally based or driven by hormones and curiosity.

She twisted a lock of sandy hair around her finger and stared at him, somewhat perplexed. "I'm not sure I understand."

"I need some research done. It has to be done well, preferably by someone familiar with investigative work. You qualify."

"You called me to offer me a job?"

"You sound offended."

"No, I—"

The look on her face told him she had expected something else. They both began talking at once, he apologizing, she defending her surprise.

Then they laughed. "You first," he said.

"No, you."

"I can pay you fifteen dollars an hour and expenses."

"You can pay me twenty-five an hour."

"Twenty."

"Twenty includes drive time, phone time, and an hour for lunch."

"I pay you to eat lunch?"

"I'll be away from home. Lunch will cost me money. You pay me for lunch."

"Lunch comes out of expenses. Work time is work time. Lunch time is on you."

"Agreed."

"Agreed?"

"Shake?" She leaned forward and reached her hand across the desk. Her eyes were oval and large, alluring.

They shook hands. "You're an unusual woman."

"That sounds like a come-on. Is this business or pleasure?"

"Can't it be both?"

"No, it can't. I draw a sharp line on that point."

"That's not what I meant."

"Good. Let's keep it at business. When we're all done, you owe me a dinner." She sat back. "Am I to assume this has something to do with the bombing?"

"You are."

"And just what is it I'm supposed to do?"

"Help me find out who planted the bomb and why."

"I thought you might say something like that. You make it sound so simple. What about the police?"

"They're working on it too."

"We'll come back to that. What about the story?"

"The story?"

"If we solve it, I want the exclusive on the story. I want that up front. If the cops solve it, I need your word that you'll do everything you can to give me the story before the others. Since my mother's illness, I've been off the wires for some time. This is just the kind of thing I need for a comeback. Twelve-fifty an hour pays the bills. The wire services buy me back a career. How 'bout it?"

"I like the way you deal."

"You didn't answer the question. If I'm going to be part of this, I want that exclusive."

"I don't know how these things work. What's to stop someone else from running the story?"

"You are. You clam up until my story's out. Deal?"

"A slight loss of memory?"

"Something like that."

"I think I can handle that."

"Good. You just hired yourself a research assistant. Now, before we get into it, what happened to our fish? I called the trucking company this morning and told them I was with the *Globe*. I waved a front page in their face. They promised to pick up the fish and to contact your office about reimbursing you for the manpower your people contributed last night. Any results?"

"You have power, lady. The fish is on its way to wherever. The trucking company is paying all my help at overtime wages. Nice going."

"The paper has the power, not me. If I'd been honest and told them I work free-lance, they wouldn't have given me the time of day. Very few people like the truth printed on page one. It has much more power than television. Sure, television has a more immediate effect, a sensory overload, if you will. But what's in print stays in print. It's filed away on microfilm, there forever for everyone to see. It lasts. What's on television is there one minute, then it's gone and Road Runner is charging across the screen.

The news becomes entertainment, the entertainment becomes news, its power diminished. That's why I like the printed word."

He grinned, nodded his agreement, and stood. "Can I get you some coffee?"

"Black with one sugar, please."

"No cream?"

"I've hired Leonard Nimoy. He and I are 'in search of' my girlish figure."

"Oh, it's there all right. You just hide it under those baggy clothes."

"Baggy? This is what they call fashion."

"You don't strike me as the type to follow the herd. Why have a nice-looking body like yours if no one ever sees it?"

"How would you know what my body looks like, and just what exactly do I strike you as, Mr. Opinionated?"

"I saw you in a leotard yesterday, remember? You can call off Mr. Spock. You looked great. I was envious, actually." He patted his stomach. "I've picked up some here I could do without."

She blushed. "As long as we're getting picky about fashion, I might point out that this is the first time I've seen you without that silly hat on your head. The thinning hair on top is barely noticeable. You don't have to hide it."

"I'm not hiding it. The hat serves a purpose. It makes me look more like a visitor. I blend in better. At the same time it's easier for my people to spot me in a crowd. Can you say the same thing about wearing clothes that two of you could fit in?"

"Enough. How about that coffee?"

He grinned and left the room.

She looked down at her clothes and tugged at the extra fabric.

When he returned he said, "I hired you for research, but it goes beyond that. I need an observer as well. If you talk to people, I need to know more than what they tell you. If you find something in your research, I need you to read between the lines. What I'm interested in is what the people don't tell you, what the articles don't tell you."

"What are you talking about?"

"Take you, for example. I know that you've already been downtown today. I know that you either woke up in a hurry or you're having an affair with someone. You have an orange cat, so you're an animal lover, but I would guess you don't own a single fur, and wouldn't keep one if it was given to you."

Her face blanched. "You're having me followed?" she gasped.

He laughed. "No, I'm not having you followed. Just a little deductive reasoning, that's all."

"I think you'd better explain."

"Between last night and today, you've had your hair trimmed. The two best salons are downtown—don't tell our manager I said that—so I assume you've already been downtown today."

"Right you are. I see. And the affair? You're way off base there."

"I said that 'either you woke up in a hurry or were having an affair.'" He lowered his eyes to her chest. "You missed a button there on your blouse, like you were in too big a hurry getting dressed."

She looked down, cross-eyed, and noticed he was right. She corrected the problem as he continued. "Orange cat hair on your shoulder—that one was easy; and you're not wearing a single piece of leather, a fact I noticed last night as well. Not even leather shoes. No leather: the telltale sign of a person opposed to the killing of animals. Either that or allergies. Thus you probably don't own any furs."

"I'm impressed."

"It goes with the turf. I need you to see what isn't mentioned —think of what no one has thought of. Notice what isn't mentioned as much as what is."

"That much I'm familiar with."

"In our line of work—yours and mine—you need to notice everything, no? Take Civichek, for example. You passed him on the way in."

"I heard the tail end of his speech downstairs. I know something about him, incidentally, if that will help any. And just for the record, I don't like him either. I interrupted, go ahead."

"He wears what might be called street clothes. But the blue jean jacket was new—and from L. L. Bean. I know because I have one just like it. That makes me think he was in Freeport, Maine, recently. He moves around too much to have ordered it through the catalog. So what will I do? I will call the Freeport police and see what, if any, trouble they had while Civichek was up there. That lets me second-guess him here."

"He *was* in Maine recently. Nice going, Sherlock. Is there anything you miss?"

"Good company," he said soberly. "But I found some last night. And now again this morning." He stared into her right eye and held her there.

"In my business we call those clichés." She couldn't take her eyes off his. "Business, remember?"

"Tell me about Civichek."

"He's an ex-con, a second-story man. I read an interview in *The New Paper*. He was trying to romanticize his escapades, telling the audience how dangerous it was to climb straight up the face of a building. He even claimed responsibility for the investment company robbery they put him away for. He climbed seventeen stories without a rope, broke in through a window, and cracked a safe. A real jack-of-all-trades. He comes from a family of them. His father and brother are serving time in Arizona and California, I think it was. The man gives me the creeps. He uses his willingness to admit past wrongs to sucker people in. 'Nothing like a reformed criminal to know how to stop other criminals.'—that's his angle. He sells it well. There's something dishonest going on beneath the surface. He's a complex man trying to simplify an issue. That's the most dangerous kind. The press seems to love him—they shouldn't sucker so easily. Hopefully, one of these days he'll trip on his own laces. If he doesn't he'll build a power base, and Lord only knows where that'll lead."

"He'll be back. I could see it in his eyes. He wants the trouble. Put him on your list, but not at the top."

She looked at him curiously. "You don't think he has anything to do with the bombing, do you?"

"I'm not a big believer in coincidence. A bomb goes off yesterday. Civichek shows up today claiming to be able to make the Green safer. It's a little too convenient."

She borrowed a pen and some scratch paper. "You said 're-search.' "

He explained. "I need a list of any and all reported thefts of explosives in the rough radius of Providence, New Haven, Hartford, Springfield, Boston. Chronological order, if possible. Go back as far as you have to. I need details, so remember, read between the lines. I need that right away."

"Can't the police help you there?"

"They're in the habit of deciding who sees what when. I need it sooner than later. Is it a problem?"

She shrugged. "Straight library stuff. It shouldn't take long at all."

"Good. I also want to know whatever you can find out about Bob Russo—"

"Robert Russo? *The* Russo?"

"I don't need the front-page material. I know most of that. I need to know what his financial interests are, who he's seen with, that kind of thing. Maybe you could arrange an interview with him. He likes pretty women. Shleit was going to talk to him, but that won't do much good. You'd have a better shot at him than I would. I have a few key words I can give you that I think may get a rise out of him. Like we were saying a minute ago, that's the kind of thing I'm looking for, an unusual reaction, an unexpected response."

"Anything else?" she asked eagerly.

"Any*one* else," he corrected. "I'm not sure what or whom I'm looking for. Your investigative skills will help there. I can come up with some payroll lists of workers who've been on this job. I need to know who, if any, were or still are connected with the union."

"Sounds like you're putting a lot of emphasis on Russo and the union."

"It's the one thing that jumps out at me. DeAngelo broke the union in order to build the new pavilion. Hillsdale's local is suspected of having ties to organized crime, and those in organized crime are famous for paying you back if you mess with them. Russo was the regional boss of the union at the time. He tops my list."

"What about the people who were victims of the mall's expansion? As I recall, some two hundred factory jobs were lost in this area of Hillsdale, and wasn't it two *thousand* people displaced from their apartments, mostly minorities?"

"If you can think of a way to approach those kinds of numbers, I'm with you. There is a lawyer I want you to check out. He busted into Haverill's office yesterday and evidently made some strange remarks. His name—" Jacobs flipped through a pile of loose papers and came up with one—"is Roy Walker. He's about twenty-eight or thirty. The local bar association might have something on him."

"Got it."

"I'll look into downtown merchants."

"That's a possibility?"

"They'd have the most to gain from problems out here. And I'm going to try and follow up on past employees. Someone might be holding a grudge."

"This is a lot of work."

"Yes, it is. And to make matters worse, we need to figure this out by Saturday. Call it intuition, whatever. I have a feeling that bomb was somehow connected to the grand opening of FunWorld."

"Will you go ahead with the opening?"

"It depends on the events of the next few days. The ultimate decision will be Haverill's. He's a reasonable man. By the same token, to call off the opening now would hurt us badly, as you and I just discussed. It would also cost us somewhere around a hundred thousand dollars to reschedule."

"Good God."

"And there are some intangibles. The governors of all three states—Rhode Island, Massachusetts, and Connecticut—are planning to attend. To cancel now would hurt our public relations badly. Incidentally, none of what we've discussed is for print. Not yet. The last thing I need is for the papers to get hold of the fact that the governors are going to be here, so keep that in confidence, okay?"

"Agreed."

"It's bad enough that Knorpp has pushed publicity on this lottery drawing. I don't know who came up with the idea of two hundred thousand dollars *cash*, but it isn't making my job any easier. We have to coordinate security with an outside firm and the police. It's a real headache."

"You know, when you walk around this mall, you don't think of any of this. You don't think about security, or garbage, or cleaning, or servicing. When you get right down to it, this place is a small city, all contained in six or seven gigantic buildings—"

"Eight, including the stadium."

"One thing I should tell you," she said cautiously. "I made a few calls this morning. After meeting you yesterday, it occurred to me that security at a mall might make interesting reading. I put out feelers at the *Globe,* the *Times,* and the *Wall Street Journal.* I think the *Journal*'s the best shot. They run these kinds of pieces from time to time. I'm going to follow up this afternoon. If I get a nibble, would you grant me an interview? Explain how security works here? I realize you probably don't have the time—"

"That's my only consideration—"

"But maybe we could get together some evening or something."

"I do rounds twice a day. Takes about ninety minutes. You could join me on one of my rounds and we could review any progress you've made on your research, and I could explain the security. It would be easier on rounds anyway, because you'd be able to see what I'm talking about."

"That sounds perfect. I should know by this afternoon if anyone's interested in the story."

"I do rounds at eight in the morning and five in the afternoon. Either of those would work fine."

"Perfect," she said.

That was exactly what he was thinking.

―――――――― 10 ――――――――

HE HAD BEEN a frogman in the Navy until the accident. Being in Yankee Green's utility tunnels reminded him of the claustrophobia he used to feel under the water in a wet suit. As a Navy SEAL he had become an explosives expert—a skill that now, finally, was paying off.

He debated sending notes. He had it all planned out what to say. There was a quotation from the Bible that would work perfectly. The Battle of Jericho seemed perfectly symbolic with the walls crumbling down and the army invading and killing every last man, woman, and child. Thousands dead.

Just like Yankee Green.

He left the wires only inches apart, having run several coils to reach this location. Behind him, far away, the elevators that serviced the west side of Pavilion C continued like yo-yos, up and down, up and down. On Saturday he would have to make some final adjustments, but these would only require a few minutes. Then he would be ready.

He was about to become a very rich man.

He still got lost occasionally inside the utility tunnels and shafts. They all looked incredibly similar. When he became disoriented he used the small compass he carried in his pocket, though this was often thrown off by the abundance of steel in the shafts.

It took him twenty minutes to reach the utility tunnel that ran behind the walls of Security's Dispatch Room. Like the cassette machines he used to record conversations in the bugged administration offices, he had rigged a similar listening device here. When he reached the pile of electronic gear, he stopped to clean his glasses on his shirttail. His glasses fogged up when he overexerted himself.

He had discovered the device in the NanoByte section of *Byte* magazine. The article referred to yet another article in a West German magazine that explained how, for eighteen dollars, a person could modify any television set to eavesdrop on any computer that used a cathode ray tube, a picture tube—which meant just about every computer made. The only ones that didn't use CRTs were the lap portables, and the Chubb computer inside Security Dispatch Room was no lap portable.

He had studied the Chubb and knew it well: knew its control codes, how it accessed its memory, how it wrote to disk, how its real-time controller worked. And now, thanks to the computer eavesdropping device he had discovered in *Byte*, he knew the Security director's master password. Each night, while listening to the cassette tapes, he watched the videotapes that had recorded the day's activities on the Chubb computer. Two weeks ago he had gleaned the master password. He now had total access to the brain of Yankee Green's security system. As an added precaution, he continued to run his video machine, taping the activities on the Chubb in case the password was changed or something showed up that might require his attention. He didn't sleep well anyway, and watching the videotapes had become an enjoyable ritual for him.

The modified television set was such a simple device. Each computer emits its own radiation, a low-level radio wave that can be received by the modified television set just like a standard set receives a network signal. All you needed was the right tuner. The eighteen bucks went to purchasing some electronic diodes and transistors which, once installed, changed the frequencies the television's tuner received.

Getting the gear into the Green had required several trips, but one month ago he had finally tried it out inside this utility tunnel and it had worked like a charm. It was just as if he were reading the Chubb's screen. His final stroke of genius was to connect a video cassette recorder to the television set so he didn't have to baby-sit his gadget. He put a fresh videotape in the machine every day, went home, and watched the tape all night. He knew all the commands necessary to perform his job. Everything in order.

He continued to run his eavesdropping equipment and VCR each day, gleaning sensitive security activity information. Two days ago he had gotten a juicy tidbit: maintenance had requested special security clearance to clean the utility hallways in the new pavilion after hours. Without that warning he might have been caught. As it was, he had changed his schedule.

The man smiled in the darkness, his thick glasses glowing from the light of his headlamp. He switched tapes, pushed PLAY and RECORD simultaneously, and the video machine whirred into action.

On the other side of the wall, Dicky Brock punched in a computer command code. The video machine recorded it all.

11

TENTH STREET LOOKED like the back lot of a Hollywood studio in default, blank gray facades of partially empty buildings rising from an oil-stained pockmarked road. Several parking meters had been stolen, leaving behind purposeless steel pipes rooted in cracked concrete.

Marty Rappaport had completed his morning walk at the mall with Jessi and had dropped her back at home. Ever since her coronary he watched over her like a mother hen. Marty had trouble expressing his emotions. He had not vowed his love to his wife in years—not in a way that counted. And if the truth be known, he would be lost without her. She meant the world to him. Life would not be worth living if she passed on.

Standing there on Tenth Street he daydreamed back to a time years before when they had first met. The passion, the romance, the fire flooded into him, and he wrestled with tears. Oh, God, it was hard to imagine what it would be like with her gone. And she had come so close to leaving just a short while ago. Despite his harsh attitude toward Yankee Green, deep down he was thankful there was a place for her to take her miles, for the doctor had made it quite clear that without exercise his Jessi would not last another year, and without the mall she would have been confined to a treadmill in the bedroom, a shut-in, kept from the outside world by the heat and humidity of the summer and the chill of winter.

Seeing this street in disrepair, he realized that five years earlier it would have taken him ten minutes to find a parking space. An American flag snapped overhead in the light wind. The harsh summer weather gagged him. He spat onto the sidewalk.

Wednesday morning and nothing doing downtown. He couldn't believe it. Now he understood why the merchants were moaning about the Green. Many of the same people who now shopped the Green had once shopped the streets of this town. Many of the stores here now sat empty. The blank, pitiful street held nothing but heat waves and bits of trash. The clock over the bank read 9:20, which was wrong; it was 10:47 according to Marty's digital watch. Why spend money fixing a clock when there's no one to read it?

He pushed open the large, heavy door to Wingate Engineering, announced himself, and took a seat in the tiny reception area where an air conditioner's clattering fan roared through what had to be its last days. The ashtray to his right was pitted with cigarette scars. He leafed through a *Time* magazine he had already read, studying photographs he had already seen.

Ten minutes later a portly woman called his name out as if he were one of many waiting for service. He wrote her a check and received a signed sheet of paper, which he reviewed carefully.

He had left the piece of cement off ten minutes before closing the day before. Now, reading the lab's report, he sighed heavily and thanked the woman, whose glued-on fingernails clicked against the typewriter keys noisily.

Across town, on Williamson, he waited again, this time in slightly better furnishings but under the ruckus of another noisy air conditioner.

They kept him waiting a full thirty minutes. Finally he was admitted to the manager's office, a tastelessly decorated fifteen-foot-square room cluttered with paper, its wall crowded with certificates.

Larry Glascock's triple chin reminded Rappaport of a cow's swollen udder. The loose skin of his neck, raw from a battle with a dull razor, hung over his unbuttoned collar. His checked jacket hung in the corner. Big orbs of sweat stained his thin white shirt, despite the air conditioning. "What can I do for you?" He sounded like a candidate for an iron lung.

Rappaport introduced himself. "Your company is listed down at the building inspector's as being the one that did the testing on the concrete for the new wing of the mall."

"What's it to ya?" wheezed Glascock.

"It's fraud, as far as I can tell."

Glascock's eyes were red. "Come again?"

"A truck smashed into a stairway out at the mall yesterday. Tore a good-sized chunk of concrete loose. I pushed some figures around on it, and they didn't add up. The truck did too much damage. I took a sample of the busted concrete and ran it by a competing lab. Got the test results a few minutes ago. There's no way that concrete should have been certified. I just came by to put you on notice."

"I see." Glascock worked hard to inhale. A faint smile parted his lips. He had a bright pink tongue and gray teeth. "So what can I do for you, friend?"

"The pour obviously never fully cured."

"Is that so?"

"That's my guess. I'd say the C-Three-A has been affected by salts, and the result is a weak compound. It's a blatant light pour. A first-semester graduate student could have seen that. Someone in your lab falsified a report."

"I'd be careful about making accusations, Mr. Rappaport. I appreciate your concern, but this lab tests every sample we receive very carefully, as I'm sure you can well imagine. Remember sir, that just because you have discovered an *alleged* problem spot, there are any number of possible explanations. We only test the cylinders we are supplied. Right? There's certainly no reason to infer that the entire structure is at fault.

"I read in this morning's paper that the truck knocked out a supporting post, maybe damaged a second, and we both know those posts are critical to mass support and load—"

"Still—" Rappaport interrupted.

"Still, nothing. Those supports *are* critical. The load of that stairway could have stress-fractured the sample you had tested. It may not be as cut and dried as you think. My point is, Mr. . . . Rappaport"—he groped for the name—"that it was a big job out there—*is* a big job. We don't want to jump to any conclusions before running additional core sample tests."

"Will you call for such tests?"

"Now that you've alerted me to a problem, of course. I assure you I'll contact the sub and we'll get to it soon."

"Because I'd like to know. I'd like to have a look at those tests. As far as I'm concerned, Mr. Glascock, some pretty conclusive tests need to be run here." He looked at the fat man. "Doesn't it bother you in the least that that building might be structurally unsafe?"

"Now wait just one damn minute. Of course it bothers me that your test doesn't jibe with ours. But let's not jump to any conclusions. Why don't you check back with me in a few days. I appreciate your concern. Not many private citizens would take the time to get involved, much less do something about it. I'll have one of my men take a few samples."

Glascock's breathing was loud and irregular. It sounded like a cat scratching glass.

"My secretary will show you out." Glascock pushed a button on his telephone console, and a moment later the door opened.

Rappaport left the office in an angry mood. He didn't like grotesquely fat people. He didn't like hollow promises. And as he stepped into a tired old elevator that reeked of disinfectant, he decided he didn't trust Mr. Glascock an inch.

12

MARY-JO OPENED his office door without knocking. "Hello?"

"What's up?" asked Jacobs, looking up.

"I wondered what to do about your request for public access to our emergency phones. What's this all about?"

"We haven't lost even one child in the last five years. We both know that. Lately, however, we've had some frantic mothers making scenes when they lose their kids. That one the other day was screaming that her girl had been kidnapped—"

"I remember."

"If there's one thing that will kill the Green, it's mothers thinking their children risk kidnapping here. And it just isn't true. Our day-care people have a perfect record. And our security is good."

"So this is essentially a budget request? Should I route it to the comptroller?"

"The problem is, when a mother and child get separated, all hell breaks out. Our people usually handle it okay. It's the parents that fall apart. What kills us is that screaming mother running down a concourse half out of her mind—not that I blame her. Our response time is killing us. It takes us five to ten minutes to respond, and I think our average is something like thirty minutes between the time the child is declared missing and is

reunited with the parent. That's too long. Way too long." He
paused. "What I'd like you to do is type up a memo explaining
that if we placed signs above our security phones that read something like SECURITY PHONE——EMERGENCY USE ONLY, something like
that, maybe the parent would get on the line, contact Dispatch,
and we cut our response time down to about ten minutes total.
That'll draw much less attention. The cost is well worth it. Panic
is what kills us here."

"Sounds good to me. What are the channels for that?"

"The usual. If we get accounting to give us a guestimate, I'll
bring it up at our afternoon meeting."

Mary-Jo said, "It's time for a new rotation."

"Oh, Christ. How long since the last?"

"Over thirty days."

"Okay. Can you handle it, or should I?"

"I will."

"God bless you, mouse face."

She blew him a kiss. "How are the feet today?"

"I'm growing old. The feet hurt bad, I sleep about as well as
an inmate on death row, one of my tropical fish is sick, and I
burned a frozen dessert last night at one in the morning because
I forgot to thaw it out. Other than that, things couldn't be
better."

"You need a foot rub, a back rub, and a microwave."

"Are you volunteering?"

"If we'd met a year earlier I would be."

"You're a tease."

"A married tease."

"Run the schedule by me before you copy it."

"Will do." She gave him a patented Mary-Jo smile and returned to her desk.

Most of his security force consisted of previously unemployed
veterans plus retirees or dropouts from the police and private
investigation agencies. Keeping good people was next to impossible. Much of the security work at the Green involved standing
around. Standing around in jewelry stores, department stores,
and parking lots. Standing around at entrances. Standing
around. Only a few of the guards qualified to carry hand guns.

These were the ones who oversaw cash transferrals or highly valuable retail shipments: furs, jewels, and artwork.

It was a low-paying job with little or none of the supposed romance of police work. One of Jacobs's main jobs was to keep his people from becoming so bored they missed the few crimes that took place. It involved rotating them often and constantly playing cheerleader. The former proved to be a scheduling nightmare, the latter a pain in the ass.

He had been sitting in his chair too long. He stood up to stretch, rubbed his buttocks, grabbed his hat, and passed Mary-Jo as he headed through the recently redecorated combined stenography/reception area that overlooked the Atrium. At the brass railing he looked below at the Atrium's water fountain.

Foot traffic reflected the afternoon lull that the Green experienced each day at this hour. Just past two o'clock on weekdays, thirty minutes before the close of public schools, attendance slumped. Mothers returned home or headed to school to pick up their children.

This was the two-hour period Toby most often used to catch up on his backlog of paperwork. He was about to return to his office when he saw the woman out of the corner of his eye—eyes trained to see such things. His father could spot a school of surface feeders a mile in the distance, where to the untrained eye there was no sign of life at all. Toby spotted potential troublemakers.

The woman moved suspiciously fast through the Atrium, wearing a wide-open blouse that revealed an ample amount of exposed bosom, obvious especially from above. She had no idea he was watching her.

In one deft movement, she plowed into her mark and slipped the wallet out of the man's back pocket. She dropped it into her shopping bag and stepped back to apologize. From where Toby stood, the mark seemed awestruck by her cleavage. He was further bemused as the woman bowed to apologize, giving both him and Jacobs a full view of her breasts.

Jacobs reached immediately for his walkie-talkie's handset and depressed the button. "This is Jacobs. Code Red," he said, alerting Brock that this rated as an emergency. "Check the monitors on the Atrium. Locate a Caucasian female, twenty-three, five foot six, blond hair, white blouse opened in front, carrying a Harvey's shopping bag. She just lifted a man's wallet. Find her and stay with her. Also, keep your eye on the bald guy by the west side of the fountain. Get a guard over to him and detain him. Check your tape on the cameras and see if we caught that area of the Atrium in the last five minutes. I'm going after her." He headed for the elevators.

He bounded down the moving steps, doing his best to dodge patrons riding the escalator. A trained pickpocket would leave immediately, hide from view for a matter of seconds while removing any valuables from the take, and then ditch the wallet or purse on the floor of a concourse so that it appeared to have been accidentally lost.

He saw one of his men approaching the pickpocket's mark, so he didn't bother to stop. He walked fast, eyes searching for the woman. Thirty feet up he spotted the man's wallet on the floor. He cursed as he scooped it up, shoving it into his pocket and looking around for her. There was still a chance that she had stolen a credit card so he continued on. He knew that the more professional pickpockets dealt only with cash so that once they had dropped the wallet or purse they were free of any connection to the crime. He punched a button on the hand-held microphone of the walkie-talkie and asked, "Any sign?"

"I saw her briefly, but I lost her. I think she might have taken the stairs down to a sub-level."

"Got it. Get me some help. Keep watching the monitors. Alert the crews on all sub-levels to keep an eye out for her."

The alarm on the fire stairs had been tripped. Nearly out of breath, he slipped his ID card into the slot by the emergency stairs, gained access, and hurried through the door. He heard footsteps below him. He leaped down two steps at a time, reached a landing, and rounded the corner. No one. He continued down as fast as he could safely go on his tired feet, reaching a door to Sub-level 2 that was just closing. He swung open the door and ran into the parking area.

His eyes scanned the sea of parked cars alert for any movement. Nothing.

A trolley passed, blocking his view. He searched the passenger's faces, leaning this way and that to afford himself a view of all the riders. He didn't see her there either.

In his earpiece a tone alerted him and then Brock's voice said, "We have someone who fits the description on camera C-Fourteen. She just headed into the ladies' room. Should I send someone in after her?" All even-number cameras were mounted on the east wall, facing west. It didn't fit.

"Yes."

He sprinted back up the stairs, out of breath by the time he reached the top. He hurried to the door of the women's toilet and waited. One of his female guards reached the scene quickly. Her name was Pollano. Her face was round and girlish, but she wore fake lashes and thick pencil in her brows.

"You have a description?" Jacobs asked.

"Yes, sir." She went inside.

The woman she came out with a minute later wore a white blouse unbuttoned to the third button. That was where the similarity ended. She was not a blonde but a redhead (the cameras were black-and-white), and she couldn't have been over five foot two (some of the cameras were mounted too high, making a person's height difficult to judge). She wasn't carrying a shopping bag (no excuse for that). He explained their situation, apologized, and asked Pollano to arrange for a free booklet of discount savings certificates, which the woman gladly accepted.

"So where'd she go?" he asked no one, picturing the pickpocket already on her way out of the complex. "Where the hell did she go?"

13

"IT'S TIME TO DO something about the pervasive attitude that continues to oppress Hillsdale's minorities and poor."

Roy Walker's voice carried well. The community center, a cinder-block cubicle painted grass green, with overhead fluorescent lights that flickered annoyingly, held fifty chairs, twenty-five of which were filled. The small crowd listened attentively.

Walker continued. "As a community, we were unorganized

when Yankee Green's expansion began to grab up our housing. We were unorganized as our rent climbed so high we had to move our families every six months just to have a roof over our heads. Well, it's time we got organized."

The group nodded and applauded lightly. "So what do we do?" asked a deep-voiced woman from the back.

"We do what we should have done a long time ago. We make ourselves noticed. We grab their attention. We demand change. We adopt a stance of nonviolent protest. It's the one thing we can do that may have some effect. Our choice is to be unorganized and overlooked or organized and listened to."

"Protests need permits, don't they?" asked a middle-aged Italian near the back. "You think they're going to give us a permit to demonstrate at the mall? They ain't. Maybe for downtown, but not the mall."

"If they won't grant us a permit, then we may just have to get ourselves arrested," Walker explained. "Arrests make the news. Arrests demand attention."

"Arrests cost money," someone shouted. The crowd laughed.

"Which only makes our point more strongly. We're poor because *they* want us to be poor. If we do get arrested, we never lift a hand. You all understand that, I'm sure. We keep our heads, and we never lift a hand. If there's any violence to be done, let them be the ones to do it. That only strengthens our position." Walker looked dignified in his coat and tie. "Besides, we may not be breaking any city laws. Remember, the mall has lobbied heavily in the State House that it is private property. City parade permits are required for public areas. On private property such as the mall, civil charges would have to be filed by the owner or owners. That means the High Star Redevelopment Partners would have to file civil charges against us and then call in the police to have us removed. I may be wrong, but I'm willing to bet the Green's management won't take that route, especially only a few days away from a major publicity event, the grand opening of the new wing. If they do press charges, we can use the media to our advantage—make the mall look real bad—and don't think they aren't aware of that. If they leave us be, then we've overcome our first obstacle.

"The point is, and I quote Reverend Abernathy here, 'You

don't have much, if you don't have your self-respect.' We may not win a change of attitude overnight. It's important we all understand that before we start. But damn it, it's time we did *something*. It's time we win back some self-respect. It's time we stop being bullied and stand up for what we believe in. Downtown *owes* us that housing they promised. The Green is directly responsible for taking away our houses in the first place. The Green has the size, the clout, and the economic power to apply pressure on downtown, so we go after them. This afternoon I filed a one-million-dollar lawsuit against Yankee Green. I intend to win that legal battle.

"People, it's time for change in this city, and it isn't going to happen without our efforts. We owe it to our forefathers, we owe it to ourselves, we owe it to our children. As the legendary Dr. Martin Luther King once said, Our time has come! Our time has come!"

The crowd applauded him enthusiastically.

Ben Parkes, an older man Walker remembered from his childhood, leaped to his feet. "Okay, okay," he said. "So we all gotta call as many of our friends as we can. We don't have enough here. Numbers are what counts. Standing next to that big sucker of a mall, twenty-some-odd of us are going to look like nothing. We need two, three times this many."

Walker agreed. "Everyone call all your friends, explain things to them. On Saturday morning we march on the mall as dignified citizens of Hillsdale. This Saturday things start to change in this city."

The crowd buzzed.

Walker said, "Let's hold hands," and stepped to the front row to join in. He began the Lord's Prayer, and the gathering joined in. Walker concluded by adding, "Dear Lord God, help us to find our self-respect as a community. Help us to understand each other's problems more fully and be ready and willing to sacrifice our own selfish interests for the betterment of our fellows. Help us to follow the path of righteousness. And lead us not into the temptation of violence or arrogance, but lead us toward salvation. In your name we ask you. . . . We, your loving children. Amen."

"Amen," chorused the crowd.

14

A HOPEFUL EXPRESSION on her face, Susan caught up to him in Pavilion A as he began his afternoon rounds. They said their hellos and he quickly explained the physical layout of the mall, how the pavilions roughly formed an inverted Y facing north-south, with C in the center; the stadium, then Pavilions A and B at the top; the sports pavilion, convention center, and convention hotel on the southwest branch; the new FunWorld wing on the southeast. She was familiar with the layout but listened with interest anyway. She found his professional side intriguing. He was all business as he inspected exits, waved to his guards, and peered into the fronts of stores. She could feel how well liked he was by everyone.

She finally got up her nerve and said, "So tell me how your security works."

"First you tell me. You've got something or you wouldn't be here."

"Do you have any Gypsy in your blood?"

"I'm loaded with it."

"I thought so." He walked so fast she had trouble keeping up. She said, "I had luck on both fronts. Which do you want first?"

"The explosives."

She withdrew a handwritten list from a file folder she was carrying. Handing it to him, she said, "Chronological," in a teasing tone. "The most recent theft of explosives, reported in the newspapers, was six weeks ago. Some bridge work was being done just north of the city—"

"Boston?"

"Hillsdale. An entire case of dynamite was stolen from a construction shack. FBI turned the case over to the Bureau of Alcohol, Tobacco, and Firearms. I have a copy of the article for you," she said, lifting the folder, "and a copy of the only follow-up article, which says that the investigation stalled out."

"Others?"

"Eighteen months ago in Springfield. A case of hand grenades belonging to the Army Reserves was reported missing. Turned up three days later in inventory. Record-keeping error."

"I'm more interested in dynamite."

"A few others. They're on the list. They go back several years, though, and in all but one case the explosives were recovered."

"Any details on that one?"

"I'll go to the Boston libraries sometime tomorrow morning. They'll have more film of newspapers than I had access to here. I'll have more details then." She tugged on his arm to slow him down and added, "I've pulled whatever names I could find in the articles and I'm looking into them." She dug through the few papers in her folder. "Here's a list of the arrested and the convicted. You'll notice the difference in size. So much for our judicial system."

"This is good stuff. Thanks. Is that it?"

"On the explosives, yes. For now. But I made an inquiry about Russo, as well."

"Busy girl."

"I prefer 'woman' to 'girl.' And I take my work seriously, just for your information."

Jacobs looked down at her with his warm brown eyes and nodded. Message received.

She told him, "I know an aide to the prosecuting attorney who tried to nail Russo a couple of months ago on a kickback scam. I called in a favor. They never did nail Russo, but as it turns out, they found out quite a bit, and my friend was willing to share. He seems to think that the more bad press Russo gets, the more chance a grand jury will eventually get him."

"I doubt it. He's too well connected."

"I agree with you, but I didn't tell my friend that."

Jacobs waved to one of his guards across the concourse and then held the door for Susan as they passed from Pavilion A into Pavilion B. Ahead of them the crystal-laser display flashed through a pattern of colorful light sequences, and beyond that the gigantic replica of the space shuttle loomed. "So?"

"You'll have to walk slower." She reduced her stride and Jacobs slowed to stay with her. "You're wearing me out." She had a tiny waist and matching feet. She wore turquoise slacks and a pleated white shirt with sleeves partly rolled up. She looked fresh and crisp. "Better," she said.

"Russo came up through the ranks. Started out as a construction gopher. Earned an apprenticeship. Joined the union nearly thirty years ago, at eighteen. The Vinetti family got their hooks in him in the late sixties after he had been elected to a minor union post. He's played their game ever since. His finances are handled by an attorney and an accounting firm out of Providence. I wasn't able to get any specifics, though they should be a matter of public record. He likes to toss his money around. Buys stocks on margins, that sort of thing. Takes big risks. Thinks he's a latter-day Hugh Hefner.

"What I did find out, that I think will interest you, is that he doesn't play hardball."

Jacobs stopped and looked at her. The laser display continued behind him. "Just what does that mean?"

"According to my source, he's not a muscle man. Never has been. That doesn't mean the Vinettis haven't done him some favors. Maybe they have. Maybe they haven't. But Russo is known more for leverage. Pressure. My friend guessed that his attitude stems from the way the Vinettis got ahold of him. The Vinettis don't play rough very often either. They like to get you and squeeze you. It makes it hard for prosecutors, because a lot of what both Russo and the Vinettis do is aboveboard. It's the modern-day mob. The old tactics are left for Jack Nicholson movies."

"You're saying he isn't connected to the bombing?" Jacobs said, continuing on.

"I'm saying it's not his style." She took hold of his arm and slowed him down. "You walk too fast."

She had a strong grip. He felt tempted to place his hand on hers. "I have bad feet. The faster I walk, the sooner I get my rounds over with."

"Maybe you have bad feet because you walk too fast."

He slowed. "Anything else?"

"Hey, don't blame me if I find out what you don't want to hear. I'm just reporting to you what I found."

"Sorry. Does it show that badly?"

"Yes, it does. One other juicy tidbit."

"What?"

"Russo seems to be developing his own 'family.' He's related to three of the biggest contractors in the city by marriage. He married into the Ritigliano family." ·

"*The* Ritigliano family?"

"The same."

"How can that be? Why wouldn't we know that?"

"Married her in a very private ceremony in Atlantic City two years ago."

"But he's a womanizer. He's famous for it."

"A marriage of convenience, I'm told. She has places in Fort Myers and Lake Tahoe. She has a few boyfriends of her own and loads of money. She doesn't like the Northeast."

"If you're the daughter of the biggest builder on the East Coast you have more than loads of money. You have dump trucks full."

"It's all one big happy family. Sam Ritigliano had eight—count 'em, eight—daughters. Number two married Stump Vinetti. Number six is married to Russo."

"Now *that's* interesting. Did you get the rest of the family tree?"

"Working on it."

"That it?"

"That's it."

"You did good, friend."

"Not bad for a few phone calls. Now, what about this place? I got the go-ahead for my article. Give me the run-down."

He opened the door to Pavilion C and admired her as she walked through. She had a tiny rear end, flat and firm. "First my philosophy. Basically, there are two ways to handle security: reactive and pro-active.

"Reactive responds to a crime already committed. That is typically the position urban police find themselves in. They react to an alarm of a phone call and they go after the perpetrator.

"Pro-active, on the other hand, attempts to create an atmosphere or environment that discourages the criminal from committing the crime in the first place. We do that here by making Yankee Green so secure, so patrolled, that the criminal will think twice and go elsewhere.

"We go about it in a number of ways.

"First, we maintain a fairly large uniformed staff, and we make our people as visible as possible. They walk the concourses of the various pavilions constantly. Hopefully if you, as a shopper, stand in any one spot in the Green for more than five minutes, a uniformed officer will pass. That makes shoplifters and others think twice.

"Mind you, this is not the inner city. We don't get the kind of violent crime you would in a city. For the most part we have juvenile crimes, disorderlies, a few drunks, a guy peeing in a fountain . . . nothing major. Shoplifting, paperhangers, and the like present our biggest threats—"

"Paperhangers?" she asked, struggling again to keep up. "Too fast," she reminded him. He slowed.

"Counterfeiters, check forgers, credit card counterfeiting . . . that sort of thing."

"How many uniformed officers?"

"I'd rather not give exact numbers, if you don't mind. Specifics only work against us. We have plainclothes guards working as well, male and female. They provide us with our eyes."

"What about all this high-tech security equipment that has flooded the market?"

"Sure. We have a very sophisticated computerized security system we have just recently installed. It's housed in our Dispatch Room in Pavilion C. From Dispatch we can monitor any number of cameras located throughout the various pavilions. We can run videotape on any of these cameras; we can get an instant printout of a face off any screen for immediate circulation. All the latest stuff."

"Printout?"

"A hard copy. We can videotape any camera. From that videotape we can freeze-frame any image of you and print it out. That gives us a hard copy.

"Each day our people, both in Dispatch and on the concourses, keep their eyes open for specific faces. Again, our attitude is pro-active. If we suspect someone, we pass our hard copies to all our people, and if that suspect is seen again, he or she is followed carefully, all of it orchestrated by Dispatch."

"How'd you learn about all this stuff if you used to work repo?"

"One of the jobs I had after my repo work was to inspect and test private security systems to make sure they did what they were supposed to. I did the work for an insurance underwriter. The Green needed a major overhaul. High Star had just bought it and they wanted improvements made immediately. It was fun for me because I got to shop around on someone else's budget and develop the most effective system I could for the money they made available. Then I was able to oversee its installation. I'd never really done anything like that before."

"So you must know it inside and out."

"Sure. I'll give you an example of the sophistication."

"I'd say tracking people with cameras is sophistication enough."

"There's more."

"Naturally."

"When High Star bought Pavilion A, the entire complex still used keys. You can imagine how many different keys they needed: masters, sub-masters, individual. Every time a master or sub-master was lost, they were faced with the expense of replacing a few hundred locks.

"Nowadays, we run on a magnetic identification tag system. Again, this stuff's been around for years, but it's kind of exciting."

"I'm lost."

He sounded like a man accustomed to giving tours, which he was not. "We operate off a Chubb computer system. Instead of keys, we issue these." He unclipped his ID card and handed it to her. The size of a credit card, it showed a picture of Jacobs and carried a magnetic strip on the back. "The nice thing about the card system is that we can program the computer to allow only certain people entrance at certain doors at certain hours. In other words, the 'keys' are very specific and the system is intelligent, so a card works only when and where we want it to.

"We can use the same system to keep track of our patrols at night. Guards punch in at various checkpoints within certain time envelopes. If they fail to punch in, the Chubb alerts the staff in Dispatch that something's wrong. That way, if a theft involves taking out a guard, we're alerted to the fact that the guard is late to check in.

"In other words, it lets us keep track of employees, shop owners, and security personnel. The computer has a record of when I arrived this morning and what, if any, security-restricted areas I've entered. If someone's looking for me, that may help them find me.

"Another advantage over conventional keys is that if a card is lost we simply issue a new card, and we tell the computer that the lost card is no longer valid. Now, if someone comes along and tries to use the old card to gain entrance, not only will the card not open the door, it will alert the Chubb to an unauthorized attempt. Dispatch can send a guard immediately and apprehend whoever tried to use the stolen or lost card."

"That exists right now?"

"The technology has been around for years."

"So to lock up at night, you just push some button on your machine?"

"That's the idea, but not exactly. The Chubb locks up for us. Automatically. Each door at every exit has what's called a mag lock. Many of our inside doors use mag locks as well. A mag lock is a magnetic locking device that works electrically and requires over six thousand pounds of force to be opened. All wires to mag locks are embedded in the cement so that there's no way to cut them. The entire system is what we call closed. Its default command is to lock the doors. Once locked, even in a power failure our doors remain locked from the outside."

"But if you had a fire or something, couldn't that trap people inside?"

"Sharp thinking, lady, but the answer is no. Typically, each eight-door entrance has one door that we call an ALL-HOURS door, meaning its panic bar will allow it to be opened from the inside at all times, regardless of the condition the Chubb has set the doors to. If a fire alarm is tripped, or the power goes out, the default setting for the panic bars—that is, the *inside* default setting—is for the doors to become ALL-HOURS doors. In other words, when the power goes out or our computer crashes, the Green is locked from the outside, but any door can be used as an exit from the inside, thus ensuring safety exits in an emergency."

"I follow."

"Just to further confuse you, if we want we can override an ALL-HOURS door and prevent its panic bar from working. We use that function rarely: only when we want an exit totally closed.

"This is the boring technical stuff, I'm afraid. What it boils down to is that in a mall this size security is critical. The better your gear, the tighter your security. Again, we'd rather prevent crime than react to it."

"And how much crime is there?"

"Figures on the national average are available. All I'll tell you is, we're well below the national average. We haven't had a child abducted, never had a rape or a mugging. That puts us in our own league. Not many shopping centers can make that claim. The largest proportion of nonviolent crimes in the Green are committed by employees of the retailers. There's not a hell of a lot we can do about that. We also have trouble with juveniles, though I've been trying to bridge the gap there by befriending some of our repeat offenders."

He paused to pull on an entrance to a fire stairs. She handed him back his card, which he clipped to his pocket. Finding the door secure, they continued on.

"It's like a combination of Big Brother and Fort Knox," she said.

"Between the six pavilions it's nearly three-point-five million square feet of shopping center. It requires a sophisticated system to keep it all under control."

"I can see how it would. It's either that or a huge security force."

"Exactly. In the long run, the technology proves much more economical." Out of the blue he asked, "Do you think you can get an interview with Russo?"

She must have expected the question. "I already have. Tentative. Tomorrow afternoon if all goes well."

"You work fast."

"You told me we only had until Saturday."

"I'm nervous about the opening, is all. We have an awful lot to juggle. The opening would make a hell of a target."

"Because of the media?"

"A number of reasons. An event like this is prime turf for

soapboxers like Civichek, that sort of thing. His timing here is anything but coincidental. The Green will receive a lot of press in the next few days. Guys like Civichek are well aware of that and plan around it. The downtown merchants don't want us opening Fun World. For all we know they could have some dirty tricks planned to upset the opening."

"I hardly think they'd do something like that."

"In my line of work you consider all the angles, no matter how unlikely. Again, pro-active. Anticipation. When you don't, something ends up happening that you quickly regret overlooking. Off the record, one of the biggest concerns of shopping center security forces is terrorists. There's simply no way to make a mall antiterrorist. And we're an attractive target."

"That's why all the concern over the bombing?"

"One of the reasons, sure. No one claimed responsibility. That's the best news. It makes it seem more like an isolated incident. That's what you and I are trying to find out."

"Back to something you said about Civichek," she said as they rode an escalator in Pavilion C up toward Administration. "Why can't he soapbox here if he wants? Isn't this place considered public?"

"There's no Massachusetts law yet governing the way the inside of the Green is seen by government and law enforcement. About half the states have such laws. The rest don't. In California it's legal to distribute political leaflets and circulate petitions at shopping centers.

"In New York, the state Court of Appeals held that shopping centers are not public places. There, you need written consent from the shopping center's owners to distribute leaflets. A 1980 ruling by the U.S. Supreme Court, which had previously ruled that the Constitution did not protect free expression on private property, leaves it up to the states to decide for themselves. Connecticut, North Carolina, and Michigan have followed New York's lead. Civil libertarians are throwing a fit. Massachusetts hasn't made up its mind. A couple of bills are pending right now. So we're kind of treading water here."

"Which way would you like it to go?"

"Off the record?"

"Sure."

"Private. If we go public we're going to have one hell of a time enforcing any kind of order. You'll see what I mean this Saturday. The cops and an outside security company are handling security for the cash lottery prize. We handle security for the pavilion. If you want to see a real zoo, be here Saturday. All chiefs and no Indians."

"Wouldn't miss it for the world," she said, stopping at the top of the escalators and checking her watch. "Speaking of chiefs, I have a meeting with one of Russo's former accountants up in Braintree in an hour. Thanks for the tour. Got to go."

"Be careful," he yelled, suddenly worried for her.

She waved from the escalator and then, changing her mind, playfully blew him a kiss.

As she turned around, riding the escalator down, he followed her with his eyes until he lost her in a swarming crowd. He felt tempted to run and catch up to her.

-----------------15-----------------

THE MAN INHALED off the cigarette, fiddled with his thick glasses, and went back to work with the scissors. In front of him on the small table lay a stack of newspapers and magazines. He wore disposable plastic surgical gloves.

His apartment was dingy. The oddly shaped carpet remnant in the center of the small room was soiled by spilled soda and fast food, evidence of which was spread around the room in discarded Styrofoam trash. Newspaper clippings mentioning the mall hung thumbtacked on the wall.

He snipped out the last letter he needed and pasted it onto the sheet of paper. He'd been working on the message for an hour. At first he had thought that sending a note might spoil things. He had listened to the tapes and was well aware of the efforts under way to find him. He had all the pieces nearly in place. He saw no way they could stop him. Now it was a matter of adding the element of threat to the game. It was time to start them guessing. There was no contest if both sides didn't have a chance. Each letter he clipped came from a different paper or magazine, each of which had been bought on local newsstands in the last six months.

The note read:

I MUST PLAY FAIR

He took a swig of soda and studied the page again. It would be enough to confuse them. Just enough to tease. He lit up another cigarette, one still burning in the clamshell ashtray, a long gray ash creeping toward the filter like a dormant snake. On the wall he had pinned several maps of the Green, one of which had been drawn commercially for tourists, as well as several sets of blueprints. He had marked eight red Xs, each representing a strategic stress point in the eight supporting columns of the new wing.

He studied the floor plans carefully, though he had committed them, and everything on them, to memory long ago. He cross-checked his list of things yet to be done.

He couldn't afford any errors this late in his plans. He un-pinned the documents, as he had grown accustomed to doing every night at this hour, and placed them in the back of the open frame lying at the far end of the makeshift desk—an old door propped up on milk crates. He sandwiched the plans between the back of the painting and a stout piece of cardboard, twisting the catches in place to hold all the layers firmly together. Then he returned the framed copy of artwork to the wall.

Still wearing his plastic gloves, hands sweating, he folded his letter carefully and slipped it inside a postage-guaranteed return envelope from the Green's promotion department. He crossed out the printed department number and used his left hand to write the appropriate number for Security and Safety. He wanted this delivered to Jacobs. He licked the envelope.

He swept the clutter of magazines and newspapers off the desk into a cardboard box and added scissors and paste. He then tucked the box into his closet.

He sat down on the saggy bed and sighed, polishing his thick glasses carefully with a clean, soft cloth sold specifically for this purpose. With his glasses off he squinted into the dimly lit room. A few more days.

He flicked off the light, set his glasses on a chair by the bed, and lay back, head on a lumpy pillow, staring blindly toward the ceiling.

A few more days and the job would be over; he would be rich beyond his wildest dreams.

Thursday
August 20

1

TOBY DRAGGED HIMSELF to a sitting position on the edge of his bed and rubbed his eyes. He looked down at himself, annoyed by the small roll at his waist which seemed impossible to shed.

The apartment—a large rectangular loft with hardwood floors, an east wall of windows, gray-painted funnel lights suspended from the ceiling—had once been a sweatshop.

He spooned four heaping tablespoons of coffee grounds in a saucepan, covered them with a mugful of water, and turned the heat on high.

He ambled over to the gurgling aquarium and fed his fish. "Morning," he croaked in a groggy voice, brushing his dark hair out of his eyes.

Why would anyone want to kill fish? How could his father spend his life dragging nets in the ocean and killing fish?

He turned the aquarium's light on and checked the thermometer. A salt-water aquarium, he maintained it at 65 to 70 degrees. His Four-eyed Butterfly passed him with the flick of her tail. She had been sick for the last few days but looked better this morning, which meant the sodium carbonate was finally doing the trick.

On his way to the shower he turned the heat on the coffee to low and added a half mug of water.

Morning had its own ritual. Once in the shower, his thoughts strayed to Susan Lyme. He'd been trying not to think about her, which only meant he thought about her all the more. Same as anything else.

He toweled dry and combed his hair over the thin spot. He strained the coffee into the mug and sipped on it as he waited for a piece of pink Portuguese bread to toast. The bread was a hold-over from childhood; its sweet flavor and light texture made it the perfect breakfast snack when toasted and buttered. He scribbled reminders while he ate the toast and coffee.

On his way out the door, he stopped to have a look at the *Angel.* He glanced back and forth between the partially completed ship-in-a-bottle and his fish in the aquarium, thinking, *You can take the boy out of the sea, but not the sea out of the boy.*

Rather than leave, he took the tweezers in hand, strung a piece of black thread through the hole in the balsa-wood spar, ran it through a hole in the mast, and then tied it off.

A step he had attempted many times, unsuccessfully; it had seemed so easy just now. He placed the tweezers down amid the clutter and stared at the *Angel,* wondering why some things seemed so difficult at one time, so easy the next.

He grabbed his hat and headed for the door.

He filled the twenty-minute drive to the mall with local radio news: the dollar was falling in overseas markets; the Red Sox were two games out; soap opera stars and the governors of three states would be at the opening of the new wing at Yankee Green on Saturday . . . !

He yanked the car to the curb and left it running while he ran into Bowman's Pharmacy for a copy of the Hillsdale *Herald.* The article about the mall was page one. The byline read, SPECIAL TO THE HERALD. A free-lancer. Susan! He tugged his tie loose and shoved his hat back on his head. When he pulled out into traffic, he slammed the pedal to the floor.

As he approached the entrance to the underground parking for Pavilion C, Susan appeared out of nowhere. She was the last person he wanted to see. She had promised to keep the news of the governors' participation in the opening ceremony out of the papers. He felt betrayed. It would make his job on Saturday next to impossible. It was impossible enough without *this*—he had $200,000 in cash to worry about, a possible record attendance, and a dozen major celebrities to protect from adoring crowds. If some crackpot came after a governor—

She stepped up next to the Volvo. "Hi there!"

He handed her the morning paper. What was there to say? It had been years since he had opened his heart to a woman, and that time it had ended in betrayal as well. He threw the *Herald* at her feet. "What the hell? I thought we had an agreement." He faced her briefly. "I even thought we *liked* each other." He slammed the gearshift into first, grinding it, and drove away. The sterile blankness of the near-empty underground parking facility seemed terribly symbolic.

Susan Lyme looked down at the waving pages of the morning paper, dumbfounded.

———————— 2 ————————

PETER KNORPP ARRIVED within a few minutes of Jacobs, early for him.

Like electricity, Knorpp sought the path of least resistance. He always had. When Haverill had "discovered" him in Canada several years earlier, Knorpp had said he was in Canada because of a job opportunity. In fact, he had come to Canada a decade before to avoid the Vietnam draft. Soon he had smooth-talked his way into a public relations firm, his immediate superior a foxy redhead with a French-Canadian accent and long luscious legs. She had taken an instant liking to his California good looks. By the time their three-year affair came to an abrupt end (Knorpp had never been loyal to her, despite his pledges)—a result of Haverill's generous offer—she was executive vice-president and Knorpp was manager.

Knorpp lived for status. His desire to impress drove him to overspend his modest salary.

His vanity and insecurity led him to teenage girls. Women of all ages had always been attracted to his beach-boy looks, but the young ones, so innocent, so full of raw, spirited energy, worshiped him. There was nothing as stimulating to him as introducing a budding, high-breasted young woman to the pleasures of sex.

As he headed toward his office, he tried to talk himself out of the affair with Julia Haverill. It had already gone on too long, could only lead to trouble, and Knorpp was anything but a risk taker. Still, he could not give her up just yet. There was more to teach. More to be done. Besides, she spoiled him with flattery. She would outgrow her innocence soon enough. She would become demanding and self-interested, like the others. But it was nothing to worry about. The Green attracted hundreds her age. Like Julia, most were dying to try cocaine, dying to be considered mature women. They molded in his hands like putty. What others wouldn't give them, Peter Knorpp would.

"JACOBS," he called out, stopping the man. He moved closer. "You don't look so good."

"What is it, Peter?"

"I came in early because my office received a message from Lieutenant Shleit that he wanted to see you and me at eight-thirty. My office, okay?"

"I have to do my rounds."

"What's the matter with you?"

"I'll try to make it." Jacobs went into his office and slammed the door.

Knorpp scratched his head, brushed the sleeve of his suit free of a stray bit of lint, and turned, smiling at the secretaries, despite the fact that most were in their mid-twenties.

3

THE MAN with the thick glasses arrived at Pavilion C early that Thursday morning. He headed straight to the east bank of elevators and waited for number three, passing up two other available cars. This caught the attention of Dicky Brock in Dispatch, who, because of the hour, was not distracted by the typical flood of things to do.

Brock used the first few minutes of every day for dry runs, to test the cameras and computer equipment. Trained to spot the unusual, he elected to keep this little man under surveillance while he went through his morning routine. The test procedure required cueing specific cameras to specific monitors. He anticipated the man's moves, switching between cameras to stay with him. At the same time he ran the video recorder through its morning test by freeze-framing a shot of the man's face and printing out a hard copy on the dot-matrix printer. The printer worked fine. It showed a black-and-white shot of a short, muscular man wearing jar-bottom glasses.

He cued up a camera that showed the elevator area on Pavilion C's Level 2, and another that showed a similar view of Level 3. He waited, ready for the man to exit the elevator on one of the levels.

The elevator arrived at Level 2, and a passenger disembarked. Brock could just see the short man's right shoulder inside the car. When the car then headed back *down* Brock became curious. Why would a person wait for a particular elevator car, ride up to Level 2, and then head back down toward Level 1?

With his curiosity heightened, Brock waited once again to pick up a view of the man with the jar-bottom glasses.

When the elevator didn't arrive at any of the three floors, Brock checked the status line on the bottom of each monitor screen to make sure he had not accidentally cued the wrong camera.

The cameras were right. So where was the elevator car? Now Brock became more than curious. Sure, several times a year different elevators broke down and Security and Safety had to rescue the passengers while Maintenance tried to resolve the technical problem. But this was too coincidental.

Brock leaned over and typed a code into the Chubb computer and pushed ENTER. The screen showed a graphic representation of the four elevators on Pavilion C's east side. Three of the four cars were moving. Car number three appeared to be stuck between levels 1 and 2. Brock, who wore a dispatcher's headset, began to call Maintenance when he suddenly noticed an asterisk on the screen below elevator three. The EMERGENCY switch had been thrown.

He put the call through anyway. "Paul, will you check out—"

He interrupted himself. "Never mind. Sorry to bother you." He hung up. Elevator three had begun moving again.

Brock waited, anxiously watching the television monitors, one eye on the Chubb computer.

When the car reached Level 1 and its doors opened, it was immediately flooded by boarding passengers. He had not disembarked!

Brock reviewed the events of the last few minutes. First, this guy waits specially for car number three. He rides it to Level 2 but doesn't disembark. Then he uses the EMERGENCY switch to stop it between floors. And now he doesn't disembark at Level 1.

He kept a careful eye on the monitors and watched as the elevator reached Level 2 and then Level 3. Still no sign of the stocky man.

He scratched his head and cursed. Had he missed him in the crowd? Owing to the steep angle of many of the overhead cameras, short people were often lost in the crowds. He kept his eyes on the top row of eight monitors, where the pictures switched automatically at five-second intervals. The bottom right monitors were used to isolate a shot from a particular camera. He reset the Chubb computer to its main menu and continued his morning tests.

THE MAN with the thick glasses stared down in disbelief at the elevator as it descended into the dark well. In his right hand he held a piece of broken monofilament. He had yanked on the fishing line; the elevator's motor had kicked on as planned, and the car had begun to descend. But then the fishing line had snapped, leaving him holding a six-foot length of what had been twelve feet of line. The rubber band was still attached to the elevator's EMERGENCY switch. Bad news.

The situation called for immediate action.

In a low crouch he hurried through the utility tunnel. He reached an intersection with a vertical utility shaft and hurried down the ladder toward the intersection with Level 1's tunnel. He followed this tunnel to its end, but there were people just below him. Sweating now, he backtracked, passing the intersection with the vertical shaft.

He found an unfamiliar tunnel that led north. It was more

congested than he was accustomed to. He turned here and
headed north, his headlamp lighting the way. . . .

As JACOBS PUSHED the elevator call button, his walkie-talkie
chirped in his earpiece.

"T.J., as long as you're there, do me a favor and wait for car
number three, will ya?" Brock requested.

"What's going on, Dicky? I'm in no mood to screw around."

"Take a look inside three, will ya? Either its EMERGENCY switch
shorted out a few minutes ago, or we got problems."

NUMBER THREE ARRIVED. Jacobs stepped inside, annoyed at Brock.
Checking switches was a job for Maintenance. The door closed
behind him, but the elevator didn't move because no floor number had been pressed. He spotted the thick rubber band wrapped
around the EMERGENCY switch and moved cautiously toward it,
not wanting to disturb anything. He discovered a short length of
fishing line attached to the rubber band.

Jacobs looked up at the overhead escape panel. He pulled a
pen from his pocket and poked the panel. It moved. It should
have been set firmly in place.

He knelt by the EMERGENCY switch and ran the clear monofilament over the barrel of his pen. He stretched it several feet before
the fishing line ran off the pen and floated to the floor of the car.

The car jerked into motion, summoned from another floor.
The loud *clunk* and sudden motion startled him.

Several times a year, Security caught adolescents prowling the
storm sewers that ran beneath the Green. They had nicknamed
these kids tunnel rats. They had never caught anyone *inside* any
of the utility tunnels or shafts. The thought that someone—
maybe even the bomber—might be inside the labyrinth of service conduits presented a serious situation.

"Next car, please," Jacobs told two heavy women as the door
slid open. The women began to protest until one of them noticed his ID badge.

Jacobs blocked the door of the elevator and unclipped the
microphone from the inside of his sports coat. "Dicky, shut
down number three."

The door slid shut and Brock's voice came into his ear. "Three is shut down. What's up?"

"We've got a tunnel rat."

"Inside?"

"That's how it looks. Why'd you suspect something?"

Brock explained his attempt to keep the man on camera. "I thought I had lost him in the crowd."

"I don't think so."

JACOBS RODE the escalator to Pavilion C's Level 3 and crossed to the east side of the concourse, where he headed down a back hallway and knocked on the steel and glass door to Dispatch. He slid his ID card into the slot alongside the door and, when the red light switched to green, admitted himself.

He told Brock about the rubber band and line. Sliding into a chair, he said quickly, "Put a shot of the utility tunnels on the overhead. Tell me again what you saw." He added, "Let's get one of our people in that utility tunnel right away." He picked up the phone. "Phone book?"

Brock pointed it out, and then said, "Phone number of the police is over there on that list."

"How'd you know that?"

Brock shrugged and went back to his monitors.

Jacobs called the police and left an urgent message for Shleit. Less than a minute later, the detective called back. Jacobs explained their situation as well as he could. No crime had been committed, but even so, he requested the elevator car be dusted for prints. He recalled the detective's earlier questioning of how well they would work as a team. Jacobs found himself wondering the same thing, awaiting a reply.

After the heavy silence of serious consideration, Shleit agreed to send the criminal investigation crew. For now, he had decided to play along. He complained about how much paperwork was involved for a crimeless investigation, and Jacobs offered to file a John Doe breaking-and-entering charge. The compromise seemed to please the detective. *All give and take,* Jacobs thought. They set a time for a meeting later that day.

The electronic map mounted to the far wall of Dispatch could be programmed to show any floor plan, of any level, of any pavilion. It lit up, now displaying the network of utility tunnels and shafts in Pavilion C. Jacobs and Brock briefly discussed how best to try and intercept their tunnel rat and then began electronically locking doors and dispatching security guards to various tunnels.

But they were too late. The man with thick glasses had already left the tunnels. He had, in fact, already left the Yankee Green.

―――――――――― 4 ――――――――――

MARTY RAPPAPORT'S CURIOSITY finally got the better of him. Following their morning walk with the Greyhounds, Jessi had wanted a cup of that good Greek de-caf, so he left her to gab with Mrs. Popolov. He, meanwhile, set off toward the new FunWorld pavilion. He had read in a follow-up article in this morning's paper that there had been "significant" damage to the concrete in the explosion.

He had to investigate. It was in his nature.

He had been around enough construction sites to know how to act and dress: khakis and a white shirt, walk with determination, a worried look on your face, head low in concentration. It gave him the appearance of an inspector, and no one bothered inspectors.

He knew from the newspaper article that Utility Room 5 was located on Sub-level 2. He found the room at the far end of a long drab hallway. It was roped off with plastic tape.

He ducked under the police tape and threaded his way through the debris. The damage was severe. A rust-brown bloodstain darkened the floor by the door.

Concrete had been blown everywhere.

5

ALEX MACDONALD had thin blond hair, bright, eager blue eyes, and an engaging smile. Of all the financial movers in Hillsdale, Macdonald was one of the shrewdest as well as one of the youngest. At thirty-nine he had amassed a small fortune, mostly in real estate. He never wore a tie. Today he wore a collared T-shirt advertising a Maui windsurfing shop, white pants, and sandals. He stood a finger over six two and had the long limbs of a track star. He sat in the chair restlessly.

"What's this all about, Marv?"

"You know the real-estate market in Hillsdale better than about anyone, Alex. We've done a few deals together in the past, and we've both made good money on them."

"Can't argue with that."

"I suppose you've heard about our problems with Northern Lights?"

"Bad break, if you ask me. I hear you got a court case worked up. You'll take them to the cleaners, though five'll get you twenty it won't do you any good. They're tits up. We won't be hearing from them again."

"I agree. The situation left us with an empty anchor space in the new pavilion."

"So I hear."

"That's a space I'd like to fill."

"I can understand that."

Haverill stood from behind his oversized desk and began to pace. "The Treemont building has been for sale for some time."

"Ridiculous price, Marv, you know that. They'd have to come down nearly four hundred K before it made any sense. I've bickered with the Treemont boys a half dozen times over that piece. As you know, it would fit nicely into my plans. They know it too and won't budge."

"So you essentially can't move until you get the building." Haverill turned and looked at Macdonald, who was staring out the large picture window.

"I can't start building. That's true. We're going ahead with the plans anyway." Macdonald looked over at Haverill. "Rumor has it that you'll start an office complex next. Is that what this is all about?"

"You know I've supported the concept of a downtown office center for years. No one but you has made any kind of effort to get something going, and you're stalled because of the Treemont."

"Maybe we had better cut through the shit, Marv?"

"Yeah. Maybe so." Haverill hung his head and returned to his seat. It groaned as he plopped himself down. "I thought we might strike a little gentlemen's deal, you and I."

Macdonald smiled confidently. He had a boyish face but a business mind beyond his years. His security and self-worth left him looking more like thirty than forty: a complacent face void of worry lines or any hint of anxiety. He already knew what the offer was. "I buy the Treemont and make it obvious that I intend to demolish the building. The Hauve is sent packing, looking for retail space. You agree to stay out of the office space business for, say, ten years."

"I was thinking more like five."

"I'll need seven years, Marv. Three to get built, another four to get established. If I maneuver my capital correctly, by then I'll have two or three more blocks downtown. What I'll need then is a cooperative P and Z board to approve closing off those streets and allowing me to spruce it up some. Some tall trees and a couple of restaurants with sidewalk patios in the summer.

"You put Carter in on the P and Z. I could use his vote," he continued.

"I could have a talk with him," Haverill said.

"That's all a fellow can ask. What part of the picture am I missing?"

"Why do you say that?"

"Losing a jump on the office development in Hillsdale is hardly worth a single anchor space."

"I agree completely," said Haverill. "Although The Hauve would give us exactly what we're after, exactly when we need it. We can't very well open this Saturday with our largest space empty. We expect national press coverage. They'll tear us to shreds if our major anchor space is empty."

"What's the catch, Marv?"

"I arrange for the four hundred thousand through First City. For that I promise to stay out of competition with you for seven years. The four hundred grand, plus the promise, costs you a fifteen percent partnership. We work the partnership through a corporation in Worcester. My ownership in the company is so buried no one will ever make the connection."

"No offense, but four hundred grand is hardly worth fifteen percent of that deal. After all, Marv, I've got a solid line of credit. I could go the four hundred if I thought the building was worth it."

"That's my point. It is worth it to me. Doesn't cost you a penny more than you're willing to spend. I make up the difference and promise to stay out of your hair. If it goes the other way, Alex, I can make the red tape bad for you. Five years from now, you won't even have a foundation poured."

"Is that a threat? Not exactly a nice way to treat a possible partner."

"Just trying to make myself clear. You've been stalled downtown for over a year. How much you have sitting on the ground losing you money? One point five, one point eight? What's that costing you a month?"

"I'd have to look at the figures. But I know for a fact I couldn't offer you more than ten percent, and that would be stretching it."

"You have two days to close the deal."

"Impossible."

"After that, I lose interest."

Macdonald scratched his head and rose from the padded chair. "Let me see what I can shake. We agree that you'll hold off of any commercial development out here for at least seven years?"

"My word on it." Haverill knew that this, above all, was his bargaining chip. Macdonald couldn't risk taking on Yankee Green. It was what had stalled the project for the last year. What Macdonald didn't know, couldn't know, was that the new wing had run over budget and increased the debt load to nearly unbearable proportions. There was no way the Green could even attempt expansion for at least another decade, and only then if they were extremely lucky and all the pieces fell into place. It was another reason why filling that anchor space was so important.

A number of the mall's five-year leases would expire in a matter of months. Renewal of these leases depended on a strong financial forecast. Without an anchor in the new wing merchants might panic and leave the Green, which in turn could create a glut of empty retail space—space that couldn't be given away.

Haverill and Macdonald shook hands. "I'll see what I can do, Marv." Haverill smiled.

As Macdonald left the office, Haverill shut his eyes and sighed. If anyone in this town could close a real estate deal in two days, it was Alex Macdonald. The man had a Midas touch.

6

MYKOS POPOLOV KNEW that Mother was right: if change was going to come, he would have to set the example. For the last two months the youth groups had disturbed business in every pavilion.

Security was hand-tied because the techniques used by the groups rarely broke any of the rules, they simply intimidated customers, discouraging them from shopping wherever the young people decided to congregate.

Compromise was needed. And compromise was at hand.

As he rubbed down the tables with his one arm, Popolov looked over at his plump wife, who was busy preparing a tray of pastries.

They had met in a small makeshift hospital in a village in northern Italy. He noticed her immediately, a finely postured woman who never stopped working. The church basement was crowded with young, wounded resistance fighters like himself who had been brought to the small village. The people working there were taking as much risk as the people they tended. If the Germans ever discovered them, certainly all inside would be shot without questions or trial.

One day during her rounds, the then firm and lovely nurse

stopped amid the crowded cots and inquired, "How are you feeling today? You look better."

"You work so hard," he had said immediately.

"No, not really."

"Yes. I have watched you. You should rest every now and then."

"I rest."

"Not enough."

"How is the arm?"

"What arm?" he said, making a joke.

"I didn't mean—"

"A joke. A joke is all it was."

She sat on his bed and looked into his eyes. More than a few of the other boys took notice, several rising up on their elbows. She was one of only three younger women acting as nurses; the remainder were older matrons. Several of the young resistance fighters had crushes on her. "All of you, you're so brave," she said.

"I was running from the Nazis when I lost this," he said, lifting the stump. "I wasn't being brave, I was running. If I was truly brave, I would have turned and tried to kill a few before they killed me. That is bravery."

"No, that is stupidity. Too many young men confuse the two."

"Do you believe in God?" he had asked her.

"Yes, of course."

"So many don't anymore, what with all the killing. I'm glad you do."

"Why do you ask me this?"

"Without God I wouldn't be here," he said matter-of-factly. His eyes lost their focus. He had yet to explain this to anyone. "You see, they were right behind me. I could hear them in the woods. In my fear—yes, in my *fear*—I became disoriented and left the path. I had lost my group. At least I thought I had. I came out of the woods, and I was face-to-face with a train. I knew the Brownshirts were right behind me. I stared at the moving train. I knew what had to be done, but I could not find the courage. It was a strange feeling. I had been on many operations, had never faltered for even a second, and suddenly there I was facing that train, knowing I had to cross the tracks. To me it seemed that Death was behind me and Death was in front of me. Yet I was not prepared to die. I was *afraid* to die.

"We Greeks have a saying, do we not? *If you associate with the wise, you become wise yourself.* So I said a prayer, though a short prayer it was," he said, making her chuckle, "and put my life in God's hands. Then I dove beneath that train and rolled out the other side. I am alive because of the hand of God. He gave me a hand . . . so I gave him mine back." Tears filled his eyes.

She bent down and kissed him on the cheek. "God did not *make* you dive under that train," she told him. "Your love of God, your faith in him, *allowed* you to." Then she whispered, *"Amor con amor se paga."* One pays for love with love. She rose and walked away.

Two months later they were married upstairs in that same church, and a year after that, when the war had finally spent its last energies, they boarded a ship for the United States. Her constitution, her devotion to work, never allowed her a moment's rest. On the ship she helped cook and tended to the ill children, attempting to nurse them back to health before their arrival in the United States, where ill health could mean detention or even refusal.

They worked together in a vegetable market in New York City's little Italy for several months, Mykos, despite his handicap, doing the work of two. Even so, Mykos was fired with the words "There's no use for you here," words that would haunt him the rest of his life.

Several years later, Gaea received an invitation from her brother for the Popolovs to join their cousins in Providence. They took the next train. In Providence, where the four of them ran a pizza shop, Mykos's good nature proved an invaluable asset to business. Customers came in as much to talk with Mykos as to eat. While Mykos worked furiously in front of the ovens, talking a blue streak, Gaea served customers and prepared dessert.

Twenty years later, when Gaea's jet black hair began to show gray, her brother sold the restaurant, split the money with his sister, and moved his family to Fort Lauderdale.

Within a few weeks of her brother's departure, both the Popolovs wanting a change of scenery, Gaea boarded Mykos on a train and rode with him to Hillsdale. When a cab delivered them to a concrete cubicle in a sea of asphalt, Gaea pulled Mykos anxiously through the open—as yet to be completed—doorway and pointed amid the scaffolding, whispering, "This, Mykos, is our future."

That had been seven years ago.

THE GREEN'S MAILMAN arrived and Mrs. Popolov stopped her work and hurried over to receive the mail, as was her custom. She leafed through the pile quickly, hoping to see the letter from the Italian consulate. She had phoned for the third time on Monday, and they had assured her that the committee's decisions had been mailed. She had entered her husband's name for consideration of a medal of honor. After all these years he still secretly longed to be recognized for his bravery. For Mykos Popolov, pride was everything.

She found no letter from the consulate in the pile. She leafed through again, and again there was no letter. She took a deep breath and tried to calm herself. Would they dare refuse a man who had given his arm to the cause? Would they not give an old man the recognition he deserved?

EARL COLEMAN ENTERED The Greek Deli with an Afro comb stuck in the back of his hair. His T-shirt had the word RAD in big bold letters stenciled across the front.

"Mr. Paplav?"

Popolov looked up and blinked. "Mr. Coleman?"

The young black handed Popolov a blue card. "You have to sign that and make a call to Security, or they gonna come looking for me."

Popolov took the pass and excused himself to go to the back, where he placed the phone call to Dispatch, assuming responsibility for Coleman. When he returned they took a seat in the far corner. "It's taken care of," he said softly.

"They say me and the boys ain't allowed in here for two more weeks. It's all that manager's fault. If he hadn't had us arrested, none of this would be a problem."

"That's partly what I want to discuss," said Popolov.

"That man is asking for trouble."

"No more trouble, Mr. Coleman. We've had enough trouble. I was hoping you, as a kind of leader of the young people in the Green, and me, as leader of the retailers, could work out a mutually acceptable solution."

"Mr. Jacobs tried that too. We had a good thing going with Mr. Jacobs. He tried to help us out, and then that manager gone and screwed it all up. What you got in mind?"

"I want to offer you a job, Mr. Coleman. I'll pay you minimum wage for the first two weeks. If you show me you can handle the job, I'll give you a raise. If it works out, I can hire a couple of your friends, maybe find some jobs at some of the other stores. It'll be hard work, and I'll expect you to be on time and work a full day. If you can't do the job, or if you give me trouble, then you're on your own again."

"You know about the fines?"

"What fines?"

"The judge say we got to pay back the market for the cost of cleaning up. Each of us owe a hundred and fifty bucks. Is that what this is all about?"

"I don't know anything about that. I'm offering you a job, Mr. Coleman. This is between you and me, no one else. You've got to give me a decision right now, one way or the other."

"What kind of work?"

"It won't be pretty. Stocking shelves, cleaning the floors. I'm an older man. I need someone with a strong back and two arms. There are plenty of people in Hillsdale who need jobs. If you don't want it I can have the position filled with a phone call to the employment service. What's your decision?"

"I don't know, Mr. Paplav. I need the green, but—"

"Yes or no?"

Coleman looked across the table. "Stocking shelves? Mopping floors?"

"To start out with, yes. If you can show me you're good with people, you can move up to waiting tables."

"I keep the tips?"

"You keep the tips." Popolov smiled.

So did Earl Coleman, who nodded and said, "You got a deal."

The two men shook hands.

——————— 7 ———————

"NICE OFFICE," Shleit said, positioning his chair to face Jacobs, who came around from behind his desk and sat in one of the padded chairs.

"Can't complain."

"You saw ours. Maybe I ought to be in mall security."

Jacobs couldn't tell how Shleit intended the remark. The tone of voice seemed sarcastic; Shleit's facial expression seemed sincere. The more Jacobs got to know him, the more the detective seemed a confusing mix of two different people: the hard-ass and the human being.

Jacobs carefully removed the pasted-up note from his desk, cradling it on a piece of typing paper. "I received this in the morning mail. I kept my prints off it, though no telling how many times the outside was handled." Jacobs leaned forward and shoved it across his desk.

Shleit read the note. "Doesn't say much."

"No telling if it's connected to the bombing, but I thought your people should run the usual tests."

"Could be a crackpot. This thing's gotten a lot of press. I'll have it looked at."

"He scratched out the box number and wrote in mine. Those business-reply envelopes are used by our promotion department—"

"So he knows your box number."

"That's what occurred to me."

"And we've got a handwriting sample. I doubt it's the same guy. No motive apparent in the message. Doesn't make any sense. I'll have it looked at, but I have a hunch it's nothing. Got an envelope that'll hold this?"

Jacobs gave him a legal-size envelope, and Shleit placed the note carefully inside. "I talked with the guys who went over your elevator car," he said. "Obviously, there were hundreds of prints. They're concentrating on that rubber band and fishing line, and on the roof of the car. Found some prints up there. We'll need to print your maintenance people to narrow the field. That okay with you?"

"I'll need the approval of the department head. And Haverill. I don't foresee any problems."

"Good."

"Was the dynamite from the case that was stolen six weeks ago?" Jacobs asked, hoping to catch Shleit off-guard.

"You've been doing your homework," the detective replied calmly.

Jacobs shrugged and waited him out.

"Could be. Fact is, we think so. Yes." Shleit said, "Do you mind?" and held up his pack of menthols.

Jacobs shrugged again.

Shleit noticed there were no ashtrays on the desk and returned the cigarette pack to his pocket. "Shitty habit anyway."

"Anything else from the investigation of the explosion?"

"Not yet. Not that I know of." Shleit toyed with something in his coat pocket. Probably a lighter, Jacobs thought. "I suppose there's no harm in telling you that the ATF lifted a partial when that case of dynamite was stolen. File arrived this morning. It's not a good print. They pulled it from the inside of a torn surgical glove they found on the scene. It's why we're taking this elevator car seriously. If we can pull a good set of prints from the top of the car, we might be able to get a match. It's a long shot, agreed, but we don't have much more than long shots at the moment anyway."

"How about past offenders? I have a small list here." Jacobs searched in his inside breast pocket and found Susan's handwritten list. He held it for a second too long. How close he had felt to her yesterday. How far from her today. He passed it to Shleit, who unfolded it.

"I'm impressed," said the detective, scanning the list. "You really *have* done your homework. As I hear things, I'll pass them on to you so you can narrow your list. Best I can do."

"I'd appreciate it."

"It might be best to leave the police work up to us."

"Might be."

"Okay. I hear ya. Just so we understand each other—it's illegal to interfere with an active police investigation."

"Right. No offense, detective, but I'll do whatever I can to speed up the investigation."

"We've never been known for our speed. Rarely, I should say. But we're thorough. Can't fault us there."

"Just so we understand each other."

Shleit grinned. "You struck me as a real prick at first, Jacobs. I'm glad I was wrong."

"Likewise." Jacobs smiled for the first time since reading the morning newspaper. He'd been preoccupied with thoughts of her all day long. Anger came and went in him like a low-grade fever.

"The more I look around, the more people I find unhappy with Yankee Green. That doesn't make things any easier."

Jacobs let the comment go. "Stolen explosives, surgical gloves —don't those indicate a professional job?"

"Could be. That's certainly one way we're looking at it." Shleit appeared tired. "Could have been hired out, if that's what you're driving at. I have my doubts. A professional would have used a light acid to burn off the date-shift code. We wouldn't have been able to trace the dynamite this way. It was an oversight typical of an amateur. And this elevator thing—"

"Which may not be connected."

"But it *could* be. And if it is, then all the more proof the man's an amateur. Fishing line and a rubber band? You gotta be kidding!"

"Using the elevators isn't so dumb, actually. There are only a few ways into those utility shafts and tunnels. The doors require a security pass. The service hallways are kept under surveillance by camera. Using the elevator shafts to enter the utility tunnels is something I hadn't thought of. Clever, actually. I doubt if it's the work of kids. To make it work, it would require perfect timing and a hell of a lot of planning. That's not typical of the kind of troublemakers we get around here."

"You searched the tunnels?"

"Yes. Nothing. We're reviewing some videotape now—which reminds me. . . ." Jacobs searched through a pile of paper on his desk. "Where the hell?" He continued to dig.

"My guess is that we've either got someone hired to give your Mr. DeAngelo something to think about, or we've got an amateur with an unclear motive. The bomb in the locker could have been a warning. If it was, only DeAngelo knows what it's about, and he hasn't given us squat. It could also have been a mistake. DeAngelo could have put that bomb in his locker for all we know."

"Here we are," Jacobs said, locating the computer enhancement. "My dispatcher got a pretty good picture of a guy who was in and around that elevator this morning." He handed Shleit the photocopy. "I'd sure as hell like to have a talk with this man."

"Ugly son of a bitch. Can I keep this?"

"Sure. It's a copy."

Shleit pocketed it. "Are your people alerted?"

"He sets foot in here again, and we'll have him. All the pavilions are being watched carefully."

The office door opened. Marty Rappaport shook Mary-Jo off his arm and said, "It has to be now."

Shleit and Jacobs looked up.

"I'm in a meeting," Jacobs said.

"Sorry," said Mary-Jo.

"I've got to see you right now," Rappaport insisted. "It's about the bombing."

"Thanks, Mary-Jo," said Jacobs. "Okay, come in." He introduced Rappaport to Shleit and returned to his desk chair.

"What's this all about?" inquired Shleit.

"I have proof the bomb wasn't in that locker," said a breathless Rappaport.

"What the hell?" wondered Shleit, looking quizzically at Jacobs.

Rappaport placed a piece of blackened metal onto Jacobs's desk. "See for yourself," he said. "That's the locker manufacturer's stamp. Company name and address, patent number."

"So?" said the detective.

"So if the bomb was inside the locker, that piece of metal should have been blown into the wall behind it, right? Only direction it could have gone, not to mention that if the bomb was in the locker it should have disintegrated this piece."

"What are you driving at?" asked Shleit, leaning forward in his chair, worry creasing his forehead.

"I found this piece clear across the room. Only one explanation: the bomb wasn't in the locker. It was *behind* the locker. When it exploded, it carried this piece with it. The damage to the cement backs it up. That bomb wasn't in the locker, it was inside the cement wall behind the locker. And if I had to make a guess, I'd say the electrician set it off."

"You crossed a police barrier," said a red-faced Shleit.

"Your people missed it!" reminded Rappaport.

"Sounds to me like we better have the electricians take a look," said Jacobs. "It might give us something."

"Our people will handle it," Shleit said strongly. "Don't look at me like that, Rappaport. I ought to have you arrested."

———— 8 ————

SHE WAS FURIOUS with Toby. His reaction to the newspaper article was completely unfair. Had it been anyone else, she would have immediately quit the job and forgotten all about the incident. But she couldn't force herself to forget Toby Jacobs.

The message had been left on her parents' answering service. She returned to Braintree for the second time in a little over twelve hours. When she entered the apartment she smelled cigarette smoke.

The man was sitting in a chair, obviously waiting for her. "Sit down."

She took a seat across from him. "Change your mind?"

"I got to thinking about what you were asking. I just wasn't in the mood to talk last night."

"I drove all the way up here last night to interview you, Mr. Proctor, on the basis of our phone conversation. You implied you had information on your former employer that I might be interested in. I was a bit disappointed to find out you didn't have anything."

"I do. I do. Like I said, I got to thinking. Russo used me as a scapegoat. Even the papers said so. When the prosecuting attorney needed a fall guy, Russo picked me."

"We've been over that."

"Yeah, yeah. Be patient." The man wore dark green jeans and

a yellow shirt. He looked like a golfer. The cigarette burned next to him. The apartment was furnished in rented motel furniture. "Like we talked about, Russo's not the type to try anything too violent. Not his style. But he sure as hell wanted the mall in his pocket. I can damn well attest to that. Heard him mention it a hundred times. So I got to thinking about a couple of meetings he had with Romanello, and it started to make sense to me."

"Romanello?"

"He's a cement contractor. Pissed off Russo something fierce because he broke his ties with the union and accepted the Green job when DeAngelo broke the union. Only thing is, one time I kind of stumbled in on one of their meetings, they were all buddylike. Know what I mean? Can't explain it. Day before, Russo had been making like he could kill the guy. And, when I step into the room, suddenly Russo changes moods and Romanello plays right along with it, they act like they're angry, but the thing is, two seconds beforehand they'd been laughing together."

"One of the Ritigliano daughters married a Romanello. That wouldn't be the same Romanello, would it?"

"Danny Romanello, sure it is."

"They're brothers-in-law?"

"Danny married the youngest."

"Explain this meeting again."

"It just got me thinking, you know. Why would they want me to think they hated each other? Didn't make no sense. They threw tantrums and Romanello stormed out cursing at the top of his lungs, but that's not the way it was going down a couple of minutes before. I was standing behind the door the whole time, getting up my nerve to give Russo a piece of my mind. I heard Russo say something like 'Our friend at the mall has everything under control,' stuff like that."

"He said that? Those words?"

"Just like that. You consider this cooperating, right? Jesus, my appeals are running out, Miss Lyme. I talked to my lawyer this morning. He says we need every bit of help we can get. They're gonna put me behind bars with a bunch of queers for something I never did. They set me up. You said you'd talk to your friend in the district attorney's office, right?"

"I'll talk to him, but I can't guarantee it'll do any good."

"Something's strange between Russo and Romanello. I'm telling you, the more I got to thinking about it, the more I realized something strange is going on out there. They've got someone out at the mall on their payroll. Maybe I could find out who."

"I think you're in enough trouble as it is."

"If I found out who it was, would that help?"

"That would help very much, but I don't suggest you go breaking any more laws."

"You leave it up to me, Miss Lyme. I'll get you what you need."

9

"DADDY? Am I bothering you?"

"Of course not, dear, come in. Sit down. Can I get—"

"No." Julia Haverill closed her father's office door loudly and sat down. She dropped her purse onto the carpet. Its contents rattled as it landed.

"I meant to tell you, Jules, how proud I was of you the other night with Forest. You handled yourself very well."

"He's kind of like an uncle or something. I like him a lot." The view from her father's office was spectacular. When her father had been away on a business trip once, she had talked Peter into making love to her in Haverill's big leather chair, the city skyline spread out in the distance. It had been one of those risky encounters she would never forget.

"What is it, dear?"

"Nothing."

"You're staring."

"Sorry." She hesitated before softening her voice and saying, "Daddy, could I have another little piece of next month's allowance?"

"Jules, you've already spent September's allowance, and half of October's. That money was supposed to help you get established at school—"

"Well, maybe I won't go to college."

"Just what exactly does that mean, young lady? Of course you'll go to—"

"Maybe I'll get a job up in Boston, like Ellen. I could stay with her. I could earn money instead of going to stupid college. Who needs it, anyway."

"Sweetheart, we've been over this."

"Lots of people don't go to college."

"A college education is more important now than ever. What with the competitive—"

She interrupted, speaking very fast. "No it's not! That's not true at all. I don't know what I'll do. Maybe I'll visit Mom in France. I have her address. She has plenty of money."

"Jules, don't do this—"

"Maybe I'll go to college over there instead, go somewhere a little farther away from Hartford. Only reason I stay here, Daddy, is 'cause I love you, and I think we make a pretty good team, you and I." She faked a few sniffles and rounded the desk, sitting in his lap and throwing her arms around his neck. He smelled like aftershave. "I love you, Daddy."

"And I love you, pumpkin. You know I do."

"And I don't want to leave you. I didn't mean any of that. It's just that there are some things I want to buy and—"

"Not to worry, love. What's money, anyway?" He wrapped his strong arms around her and squeezed tightly. He couldn't bear the thought of her leaving, even though college was just a few weeks away. "I love you."

She was all he had left in this world.

―――――― 10 ――――――

SUSAN SPOTTED JACOBS on the far side of Pavilion D. He was waiting for an elevator. Nicknamed the "Sports Pavilion," D hosted both an overhead running track and a separate bicycle track. Sports enthusiasts lapped shoppers below, some of whom took pleasure watching others work out. Like all the other pavilions, a glass canopy in D allowed natural light to filter down onto the hundreds of potted plants and trees.

The architects had used D's ground floor creatively. Its center island was filled with two unusual items: a jungle gym, "Kiddieland," that rivaled any ever built; and, adjacent to it, an elaborate English maze, a living hedge ten feet high, that spiraled into a garden café, which was served by a set of dumbwaiters from a special kitchen built on the sub-level below.

Escalators rose steeply between levels. Sunlight bit brightly onto the moving steps. Leaving the maze's hedge to her left, Susan hurried through the crowd, passing many people in shorts and jogging shoes on breaks from workouts at one of the various health spas that occupied D.

"Toby," she called, as he stepped into the moving jaws of the large elevator, with several other people. She could feel him willing the doors to close—to shut her out. But she willed them to stay open. She stopped, huffing, facing him. "We have to talk," she said, to the interest of all the passengers but Jacobs. "Well?"

The doors moved noisily, like two great big steel curtains closing.

At the last possible second Susan thrust her hand into the crack and triggered the doors open again. "Ouch." She rubbed her fingers as she stepped inside and stood next to him. She talked into his ear. He looked at the closed doors, trapped. "You've got this all wrong, you know."

"I trusted you. But, it's your job, I should have known better. You're very good at seeming sincere."

A woman tourist in her mid-fifties standing behind Susan blurted out, "Oh, my," unintentionally, misunderstanding Jacobs completely. Her face flushed crimson, and she tugged on the flowered shirt her husband wore. The man brushed her nagging hand away with the automatic response of a horse's tail swatting flies.

"I'm a reporter, and a damn good one." Susan seemed to be telling the rest in attendance.

The doors opened. Jacobs and two others disembarked. He said, "Maybe you're a damn good reporter, but you sure screwed me," and walked on.

Furious, Susan stepped out of the car, the doors groaning closed behind her. She felt the lump in her throat and tried to swallow it away, but her tears won out, and so her voice cracked as she shouted, "*I* didn't write that article. *I* didn't supply the governors' names. Your own people did, you jerk. You self-appointed jerk." She stabbed the elevator call button viciously.

"What?"

"That's right," she said, head cocked, eyes burning. "Mull that over awhile." The elevator bell sounded. The doors slid open and, without looking, she stepped backward; a man in running shorts, wearing a Sony Walkman in his ears, dodged around her and gave them both an odd look.

Jacobs stepped toward her, but she shoved her hand out like a traffic cop announcing "stop." The doors began to close. She held her hand up, their eyes locked together, hers still glassy with tears, his wide with confusion and anger. As the doors were about to shut, Toby shoved his hand inside the crack, splitting them open again. Still looking at her he said, "Ouch," very deliberately.

"No," she told him sternly, not lowering her hand. The doors closed again, leaving him behind.

A minute later, as she got off the ground floor, she saw him sprinting across the Pavilion D's west concourse toward C.

He had used the stairs.

KNORPP'S OFFICE, like Haverill's, had a spectacular view of downtown, several miles in the distance. Its appointments of fine grained woods and leather matched Knorpp's tailored and groomed appearance. Jacobs burst through the door without knocking and caught the mall's general manager doodling on a notepad. Knorpp sat up quickly as the door brushed the carpet.

Jacobs yelled, "So public relations included the VIP names in the press release. What's that all about?"

Knorpp struggled. "I have a secretary. I don't need the intrus—"

"You violated an agreement we had on the release of those names. Why?"

"We need the publicity."

"We're going to have two hundred thousand dollars in cash here for that lottery drawing. That's plenty of publicity."

Knorpp replied, "It's not the same. We need status."

"You know what you've done by releasing those names?"

"I don't have time right now."

"Guarding the governors in a crowd that size will be next to impossible. But do you care? Hell, no. All you care about is cramming another thousand people into that pavilion."

Knorpp rose slowly from his desk, went to the door and closed it. He spoke softly. "My job is to bring tenants into Yankee Green. The bigger the turnout, and the more publicity, the more people are interested in having a store here. Right now we're at a very critical time. You know that as well as I. I capitalized on a rare publicity opportunity. We hope to have three governors here on Saturday. *None* have committed. Promised, yes. Committed, no. I put a little pressure on them, that's all. If it messes you up. . . . I wish I could say I'm sorry. I'm not."

"Your talents are wasted on this place, you know that? You should be in politics yourself." Jacobs stormed out of the office. Knorpp could justify shooting his own mother. What could be expected from a man born with his hair parted?

Back in his own office Jacobs slumped into his chair, feeling guilty about his assumptions. His feet hurt badly. His shoes looked tired. He rubbed fatigue out of his eyes. Everyone had an excuse for everything.

He had made a complete fool of himself with Susan, the one new and exciting element in his life. He phoned the flower shop in Pavilion A. He told them to write on the card, *Ouch. I'm sorry —Toby. P.S. How about dinner tonight?*

-----------------11-----------------

LAURA SIPPED her iced tea. The cool, sweating glass held an imprint of her delicate hand as she returned it to the table. She touched the thin band of pale skin on her finger, the pronounced lack of tan where her wedding ring had been for the last few years. She felt no guilt at having removed it. It was time to move on with her life.

"If there's one thing you need to know about me, it's that when it comes to women I'm a chicken." He pushed the plate away.

"That's not how I remember you."

"That was a long time ago. A divorce has a way of making you feel . . . inadequate."

"That doesn't suit you, Sam." He had never been one for small talk. She remembered him as being the one with the terse and pithy comments that you went home thinking about. While all the other kids had been worried about pimples and looking cool, Sam had been off thinking heady things. It was a difference in him she appreciated.

She and Tim had had a fine, wonderful life together, in so many ways, but rarely, if ever, did they discuss anything of much substance. With their courting days well behind them and the demands of a growing family, their rare discussions had focused instead on logistics and money matters, improving their sex life, fixing the car.

Yes, Sam was altogether different, and that was just fine with her.

"I'm still searching for who I am. That may sound funny at my age, but it's the truth. If you're looking for a rock to lean on, I may disappoint you."

"I'm not *looking* for anything. I'm eating lunch with an old friend."

"I'm certainly not going to manage a shoe store the rest of my life, I can tell you that." He toyed with his food. He had tight-set dark eyes, a straight bold nose, and the neck of an athlete. "I'm sorry, Laura. I'm rambling."

"Not at all. I was just thinking how I've missed our talks. We've lived in the same area for this long and never socialized. Why? We were all good friends not long ago. What's the matter with us?"

He shrugged. "Longer ago than you might think. Besides, we're not exactly in the same town. You live twenty minutes south, I live ten minutes north. People find their own little circles of friends. Isn't that true? Neighborhoods, other couples with children. . . . We get so we have too much to do all the time. Have you ever noticed that? We're always 'too busy.' " He drew the quotes in the air. "We're so afraid of life slipping by, we cram our schedules up, pack every minute so full that life *does* slip by: the exact opposite of what we intended is what happens.

"How often do we go for walks anymore, I mean just a plain old walk, like we did as kids, with no idea where we were going or how long we'd be gone? Maybe you do, but I sure don't. If I go for a walk, I *plan* it. I get up, check my watch, my mind sorts through a likely route I'll take, I prepare for whatever the weather is, and off I go. You know what I'd like? I think I'd like to live way up in New Hampshire or Vermont. Way the hell up there someplace. I'd like to wake up, read the *New York Times* in the morning with a fresh cup of coffee, and then go for a walk; no place in particular, just out into the woods somewhere, no watch, no schedule, just go for a walk and kind of drink it all in. In the fall maybe I'd stop and try to count the colors. How long would that take? In the winter maybe I'd bundle up and sit real still and wait to see a squirrel going after a stash of nuts buried deep in the snow. Christ, now listen to me, I sound like a Grape-Nuts ad.

"I don't know, Laura. I think it's time for a change. I can feel it coming. The more I think about it—I mean, look at this place, talk about an artificial existence—the more that place up in New Hampshire sounds awfully good to me."

She was holding her breath, staring into his eyes.

His tone of voice softened; suddenly he was a different person. "Did I tell you I didn't sleep last night?"

"Me either," she admitted.

"It's weird to feel this way."

"Yes." She spoke so softly even she could barely hear it.

"We're supposed to be adults."

"I know."

"Are we supposed to feel guilty?"

"No."

"I shouldn't have had a beer with lunch. I ramble when I drink beer," he said.

"Then have another. I love it when you ramble. My life has been a little shy of rambling these days."

"You're very beautiful."

"So are you."

He reached over and touched her cheek with his warm fingers.

She placed her hand on his, closed her eyes, and sighed. "That feels nice. . . ."

"Umm," he said, drawing his hand slowly away. "I want to take you for a drive." He raised his hands. "I promise, nothing like that. Are you game?"

"Nothing like what? I didn't say anything. Let's take a drive."

HE WAS QUIET for the first ten minutes. "Where are we going?" Laura finally asked.

"Just for a drive," he replied, concealing something. His mood, all-consuming to Laura, seemed to flicker like a candle left too close to an open window. It struggled to hold on. She felt him slipping from her.

"Where are you?"

"Not far."

"We're adults, Sam." She reached over and placed her hand on his shoulder. He drew her closer to him by clasping her hand, although the bucket seats prevented them from touching further.

He glanced at her briefly, one eye tracking the road. They were well out of town and had climbed a small hill; he swung the car left at an intersection and continued on until a cemetery appeared on their left. He squeezed her hand, and she saw him swallow; his Adam's apple bobbed on his strong neck. He pulled the car over and shut it off, bringing the songs of birds and the rustle of leaves in the afternoon wind. He said, "You asked to meet her. . . ."

The sight of the graveyard triggered painful emotions for Laura. She could remember the day so clearly. The men from the company. The children, so good, but not fully comprehending the situation. Her parents with their warmth and comforting support. Out in another cemetery, not far away, Tim lay still and cold, dressed in his favorite suit—his only suit—a wilted red rose pinned to his lapel. "I'm sorry," she said, pushing her own memories out and concentrating on Sam. In the past year this was one thing she had learned to do well.

He forced a smile, opened her door for her, and led her past the flags and flowers, the names and dates, toward a plot near the back. As they walked he explained, "This is something I would prefer we keep between us, Laura. I hope you understand. I don't mean to be dramatic or morbid—I suppose I'm being both. Why is it we always end up being what we try not to be?" he asked himself. "It's just that if you're to understand me . . . if you're to know me . . . then you should see the full picture. And—well, this is part of that picture. This is part of me." She squeezed his hand. They stopped in front of a gravestone. Newly seeded grass attempted to cover the dark slice of earth laid before it like a welcoming mat. "I couldn't even tell you about this the other day. I still have trouble with it." He knelt on one knee. "She killed herself. That's not what the doctors said, but that's what happened. After Tan left me, Judy went into a shell. She blamed herself for the separation. That much was obvious. I tried my best to explain that it was just as well that Tan was gone. She wouldn't have it. She stopped eating.

"I didn't notice it at first. I was caught up in the divorce and the store; it was easy for her to fool me. She'd been overly thin since the stroke anyway, so I didn't *see* it. She was dumping her food. I didn't notice. She was starving herself, and I didn't notice." Laura moved over and stood behind him, placing her soft hands on his shoulders. She didn't want him to see her tears. He was obviously fighting to hold on himself, and she knew how important that was to the future. Whatever that might hold in store. "She grew weak and nature intervened," he said. He pointed to the stone. "A little over seven months ago she had the second stroke. Then she went into a coma. After four weeks the doctor left the decision up to me. She was technically brain-dead —I *loathe* that term." He shuddered. Laura felt him sob, and she sobbed along with him. "It took me another week of soul-searching to make the decision. I'd been living with it for a month— the doctor had warned me—but it took a few dozen walks, a talk with my minister. At six-fifteen—sunrise—February twenty-seventh, we stopped all life support, and Judith Mary Shole left this earth for points unknown—" He dropped his head.

She hugged him from behind for a full fifteen minutes, her warmth pressed against his, her tears running into his shirt. He had brought back all her feelings about Tim's death. She relived it from a distance for the first time, seeing it through Sam's eyes as she had just witnessed Sam's tragedy through her own. He stroked the back of her hand where she held him around his chest, thankful that they weren't facing each other, thankful he didn't have to show her his tear-streaked face.

This was closer than he had been to any person in months. This one rather awkward moment drew them together, bonded them to one another, and instilled him with the feeling of true friendship. After a while he said in a clear voice, "The president of the Retailers' Association and his wife came to the funeral. They didn't have to, but that's the kind of people they are. He took me aside after the service and held my hands; he's a small Greek man, he lost an arm in the war, short little guy with white hair and a big gut. His left hand is strong as steel. He held my hands together and put what remains of his right arm around me in a gesture of affection, and he whispered real ragged . . . he said, 'We Greeks have an expression'——he has a saying for everything——'He whom the gods love dies young.' That was all he said. He tapped me on the back with that stump of his and kissed me on the cheek. I'll never forget that as long as I live: 'He whom the gods love dies young.' It's beautiful, really."

"Yes, it is." Laura bent over his shoulder and kissed him on the cheek too. He reached back, touched her cheek, and then turned, kissing her lightly on the lips. "When do you have to be back?" she asked. He shrugged. "I have an idea. I'll drive," she announced enthusiastically. "Come on." She pulled him to his feet and began to run toward the car. "The keys," she demanded, hand outstretched; as he handed them to her she kissed him again. "Get in."

She drove quickly, more quickly than she had driven in ages.

After a few minutes of silence he said, "I think I know where we're going."

"Yes, I suppose you do," she agreed, unable to look at him.

The car hurried down the back roads tunneled beneath branches full with wide maple leaves, past cow fields bittersweet with dung, an old red barn leaning into the wind, a roofless silo alongside. Stone walls blurred on either side of the road, carefully stacked and seemingly endless, bordering field after field. It seemed impossible that so many stones could have come from each field and that people long ago had had the energy and time to use the unwanted stones to wall their property. But on and on they went, as if they had been part of the landscape for a thousand years: dark square walls, low to the ground and snaking along mile after mile.

She pulled the car over at a break in one of the walls. "Quickly," she pleaded, "before I lose my nerve." She flew from the car, through the gap in the wall, Sam close on her heels, down the verdant footpath lined with bramble and wild raspberry. They passed a section that smelled of skunk and Laura let out a shriek of a laugh. "Get away, skunk," she yelled. "Get away!"

The leaves overhead, the saplings; she rounded a bend in the path, still running, still laughing; now Sam was laughing too, as he saw the blue-green water of the pond before them. She unbuttoned her blouse on the run. As it came off, she tossed it into the air; it lifted and flew in a flutter, then floated in loops and tumbles to the moss-covered rocks. She chortled to herself, coming to a stop by the pond's edge, shedding her clothes furiously, unabashed at his expression as he struggled to keep up with her, giggling nervously, childishly, and saying wide-eyed, chest heaving from the run, "Remember? Remember?" And then she was naked. Naked and giggling, her cheeks blushed scarlet, hands pressed against her cheeks as she waited for him to finish disrobing. With him still in his socks, she said, "Oh, Sam!" grabbed his hand, and counted, "One, two . . ."

"Three," he said, and they leaped from high atop a sunbaked rock into the cool, crisp water below. Both shouting as they fell away, down, down, down, into a triumphant splash that echoed off the far edge of the quarry and put two startled ducks to wing.

"THEY'RE CUTE, aren't they?"

The two ducks had returned. Sam and Laura, now dry and clothed in underwear, sat on the hot slate absorbing the strong August sun, she with her arms clasped about her knees, he, leaning back on his elbows, cushioned by his folded shirt. A warm wind drew lines on the pond and worked at drying her hair. She sighed happily.

"It feels good, doesn't it?" she said.

"Wow . . . that's all I can say; oh, wow . . . have I needed this!"

"I'm about ready to go in again."

"Me too."

They looked at each other and smiled. She said, "Did I surprise you?"

"Only for a second. Your blouse nearly hit me in the face."

"Speaking of which . . ." She let go of her knees and turned to look into the woods.

"It's back there somewhere," he assured her.

She too lay back on her elbows, immodest and lovely. He tossed her his pants and she used them as a pad.

"You're beautiful," he announced heartily. "And I don't mean just your body, though that, too. No, I mean *you*. You. You haven't changed a bit."

"Oh, yes, I have."

"Not to me." He closed his eyes. "If I shut my eyes and smell the smells and hear you speak, it feels as if we've never left here."

She shut her eyes and inhaled. "Umm."

"We're so lucky. Some people would say how unfortunate we both are, wouldn't they? But we're so damn lucky, you and I. We have our health, we have our lives, we have a warm August afternoon with the Corwin pond all to ourselves. Yes, we're very lucky." After a minute of silence he asked, "You okay?"

"I'm saying my last farewells to Tim, I think"—eyes closed, face pointing to the brilliant sun—"I knew this day would come. I've thought about it so often." She looked over at him, blinded by white orbs dancing in front of her. "We crossed a line back there, you and I—a very necessary line, mind you—it never happens the way you imagine it will."

"It's not the last time for Tim."

"Why do you say that?"

"You'll never lose him. That's the ghost we both have to learn to live with. That's the penalty for giving your heart, soul, and body so totally to another person. They never leave you."

A trout rose in the pond. The breeze died down and the sun baked even hotter. In the distance was the sound of a tractor starting up.

"You and I won't forget. The people we truly loved are still alive inside of us. We see them in us in our own actions, our expressions. We can't escape them. Nor should we try to. We learn to coexist. We learn not to let them interfere. There's no going back. We only have the future to deal with."

"I keep telling myself that. Easier said than done."

"It's easier when you're facing it with someone."

She rolled up on one elbow and looked over at him. His eyes remained closed, his strong body spread out to the sun. She studied the contours of his muscles, the hard line of his chin, his tight-set eyes and strong Roman nose. She thought him handsome.

"I'd like to meet your children," he told the sky.

"Really?"

"Absolutely. Right away. I have a plan. Here's what we do. I have inventory to do tomorrow. It'll take all day. So why don't we make a date for Saturday lunch. We'll meet at the mall. I'll knock off at noon. We'll take the kids for a bite at McDonald's or something and then go to the opening of the new pavilion. FunWorld. The kids'll love it. Tons of rides and things. How about it?" He looked over and caught her staring.

"It sounds wonderful," she told him, wishing she had the nerve to go throw herself on him, thankful that Georgine had coaxed her into seeking Sam out, thankful for Yankee Green and its few hundred stores, thankful Sam Shole had not left Hillsdale years before as she was sure he would have had the Green not existed. She stood up, her shadow covering his face, and, somewhat embarrassed this time, removed her small bits of underclothing, revealing herself fully to him. "Ready?" she asked, confusing him. He stood up and slipped out of his shorts. She reached and took his hand.

"One, two—"

"Three," he said.

And they jumped.

---12---

IN DISPATCH, sixteen nine-inch television monitors kept the various pavilions under constant camera surveillance. This one room reduced the security force by some one hundred employees.

Two guards, responsible for keeping watch on all the screens, sent messages to the dozens of uniformed and plainclothes guards on the floor, manipulating them like chess pieces to fill the security needs of the entire complex.

The room's ceiling lights, recessed in white Armstrong panels, were kept low to facilitate viewing. The room was small and well air-conditioned. Three of its four walls were occupied by counter space. The counter to the right of the video monitors held the Chubb computer, Security's nerve center; above it, mounted to the wall, was the large electronic map capable of showing any floor plan. Two attendants—usually the stocky Dicky Brock and the lanky Ralph Perkins—sat in chairs facing the bank of television monitors. Both wore small headsets with earpieces and wire microphones.

Some of the cameras operated from fixed locations, the corresponding monitors showing a specific framed image as shoppers passed below it. Other cameras pivoted automatically, tracking back and forth, sweeping the vast expanses of parking lots, service hallways, and large, open concourses. Any of these movable cameras could be interrupted by the dispatcher and controlled from the booth independently. Many of the fixed cameras had zoom lenses, enabling tighter shots.

Jacobs loved this room. From here, one had control of foot traffic for the entire complex. From here one could monitor arriving car traffic or action in the men's room. It didn't bother Jacobs that this whole thing smacked of Big Brother. Even though most of the mall's patrons had no idea their actions were being continuously watched, their privacy invaded, it was for their own protection. The system, if used properly, protected the innocent and helped to identify the guilty. And it was his job to see that it was used properly. That's why Dicky Brock and Ralph Perkins ran Dispatch. They were two of his best men.

Brock said, "I'm glad you hurried. I've got a woman who matches the description of the pickpocket you spotted yesterday. She's carrying a Harvey shopping bag. The bag alerted me. Not many people will carry a Harvey's bag when Harvey's isn't located here."

"Good eyes. Bring it on the big screen, would you please?" Jacobs dropped into a padded chair and studied the screen.

"I've got it now, thanks," said Jacobs confidently, taking the controls and manually directing the camera to   y with the woman.

"She seems to be following the bald guy with the camera," Brock added.

Jacobs switched cameras, zoomed in, and recognized her, "Okay. That's her. Let's get a hard copy and put someone on her."

Perkins barked instructions into the headset's microphone. Brock interrupted the video recorder, freeze-framed a shot of her, and sent it to the printer. A moment later a dot-matrix image of the pickpocket's face whirred out of the printer, catching even the subtle shading. Jacobs continued watching the various screens. He asked Ralph, "Which monitors have tape running?"

Jacobs saw her reach up and unbutton her blouse. "That's it. Here she goes. Damn!" The camera angle was blocked by a pillar.

He switched cameras, but too late. She was already walking away from her mark, the robbery completed.

"Damn!" he shouted. "Okay, let's pick her up before she dumps."

Perkins snapped orders across the radio.

Jacobs suddenly said, "Christ! Where the hell did *he* come from?" He watched as an older street hood ran toward the woman. "No!" Although the monitors showed only black-and-white, he knew the man's neckerchief was bright green. The pickpocket dumped the man's billfold in a planter. "We lost the drop," Brock announced. "I didn't have the tape running."

Jacobs cued the monitor back onto the large screen as the neckerchiefed man reached the pickpocket. He watched as she leaned her head back and evidently screamed. She broke into a run. The man chased after her. A uniformed guard collared the neckerchiefed man. "The woman," Jacobs yelled at the screen. "Get the *woman!*"

Jacobs tracked her on the monitor as she hurried down the stairs. Perkins kept the guards informed of the woman's position and direction.

Perkins said to Jacobs, "Robinson's made visual contact."

"Have him cover the exit to the parking lot," Jacobs ordered. "We don't want her getting outside."

"That'll have to be Robinson."

"Do it!"

Brock said, "She's headed for fifty and fifty-one, T.J. Those are the two that're out."

"Out?" inquired Jacobs.

"We lost a few cameras the other day. Something to do with the new construction."

"Why wasn't I notified?"

"I sent out a memo."

"A memo?" Jacobs recalled the pile of unread memos on his desk. "Oh, Christ. Call Robinson back." The pickpocket ran off one of the lower monitors, now unseen.

Listening to his headset, Perkins commented. "She's headed for the elevators."

"Or the stairs, or a car. Is Robinson with her?"

Perkins shook his head in disappointment. "No. We've lost her." Jacobs leaned back. Brock attempted to bring the dead cameras onto the lower screens with no success.

"I want to circulate copies of the printout to all guards immediately." He interrupted himself. "Speaking of which, any sign of our tunnel rat?" he asked Brock.

"No."

"Speaking of rats," Perkins added. "We heard that scratching in the walls again. Can't Maintenance do something?"

"I'll try them again. And listen, I want that kid in my office right away. How long have the Flock been in here?"

"First I've seen of them," replied Brock.

"Check this out," said Perkins, pointing out two more members of the Flock in one of the lower monitors.

"Goddammit, who asked for their help?" Jacobs said roughly. "Find Civichek. Our media people may know where to reach him. Set up a meeting immediately through my office."

"Right," Brock acknowledged. He'd only seen Jacobs like this a few times before. When he hit these moods, you stayed clear.

"YOU INTERFERED with my people."

"Shit. How was I supposed to know your people saw her? Hunh?" The man, in his early twenties, had stringy hair and bad skin. "I saw her make the hit. I chased her down. You got your job. I got mine. What's the difference?"

"Chasing her down is *my* job, that's the difference."

"I didn't see no one even following her. Shit, you have problems with me being here, you call Les. He'll straighten this out. Talk to Les." He hooked his thumbs in his pants pockets. "You can't keep me here against my will. I know my rights."

"You do, do you? Get lost."

The boy walked out of the office slowly, insolently.

What the hell was going on? One thing he didn't need was a squad of vigilantes trying to do his job for him. At least the man was a witness. If they could catch her now, they would have a shot at putting her behind bars.

Outside his window, a bright, clear summer afternoon shone down on the cars in the parking lot. Blinding spits of sunlight reflected off the chrome and glass. This was one of those rare days. It would be a beautiful afternoon for fishing.

Carmine DeAngelo knocked on his door, his cigar chewed raw and gripped tightly in his teeth. The moon-shaped sacks beneath his eyes held the color of a bad bruise. His hard, stubby fingers with their blackened, disfigured nails yanked the stogie from his lips. He wore a two-day beard and his eyes were disturbed.

"Carmine?"

"I been taking a look at that explosion. I think Rappaport is right. The cops are going over it again."

"Go on," Jacobs said.

The man looked tired. "We get tested on our pours every so many days. Never had any problems. I didn't think much of it when Rappaport got all excited about the stairway, but I went over his paperwork this morning and it sure looks like he's right to me. Our cement may be below code. The building isn't going to fall down, but we got problems. Even if the whole thing was poured this way, it's still structurally sound. You know how overblown the government regulations are. But if it gets into the courts before we have time to correct it—to inspect it, for that matter—we'll be in big trouble."

"What's next?"

"We wait for the results of that other test he sent out-of-state for. That'll tell us. I have a feeling he's right. That's one place to shave costs, you know. On a project this size the sub could pocket over a hundred grand by shorting us. I'll tell ya something: my name is on this job. It's my goddamned career, if this building is bad. I'm the one in charge. Truth is, I never pay much attention to the cement men or the lab tests. They come in, they do their job. Romanello's as good as any of them. Least I thought he was.

"You're in charge of safety," he continued. "I think we should run some additional tests before we get all out of joint. We can drill some core samples and run them to independent labs as well. It may be an isolated problem. Thank God most of the structure is precast."

"Meaning?"

"We used a combination of precast sections tied to support columns that we poured. In certain places we poured sections of walls too, depending on the size and shape the plans called for. The upper-level staircases were poured by us as well. There are a million reasons for cement going bad. But there's no excuse for a lab failing to detect the problem. At the very least we're going to have to shore up some walls."

"At the worst?"

DeAngelo shook his head. "I hesitate to think. I'll tell you one thing: No one, but no one, had better hear about this. If word gets out, we may not have time to think through a plan. You and I both know there are people downtown who would *love* to see this new wing fail. If there's bad cement throughout—well, I think you get my point."

Jacobs leaned forward. "This could close it down?"

"Of course it could. It could be condemned overnight. That's why I say we better get some samples, and we better keep a lid on it."

"The explosion. Was it in a precast piece or a section you poured?"

"It was in precast." He paused, then added, "As a matter of fact it's about dead center between two of our columns." His brow knitted. "You don't have to look so disappointed."

"For a minute there, it began to make sense. Arrange for a bad pour, set off an explosion to tip us off to the fact. It would all fit neatly into a plan to sabotage us."

"It was a precast section for sure."

"Get some samples for testing, Carmine. I'll brief Haverill."

"Right." DeAngelo turned to leave.

"Carmine," Jacobs said, stopping the big man. "Have any of your men been using the utility tunnels or shafts in Pavilion C?"

"C? Not that I know of."

"No electricians? Nobody?"

"Nope."

"How about the elevators in C. Any of your guys over there?"

"None of my guys. Maybe your Maintenance people," De-Angelo suggested.

"No. It's not us."

"You got someone in your tunnels?"

"Maybe."

"The bomber?"

"Could be. That's why I asked."

DeAngelo looked at the ceiling. "I can't think about it. I got too much to do. But I'll tell you something. I'll sleep a lot better when you have someone under arrest. It was my locker, you know."

Jacobs nodded. "Yeah," he said. "I know."

DeAngelo left in a hurry, his tension apparent in his stiff walk.

A FEW MINUTES LATER DeAngelo phoned Jacobs and called him down to the new pavilion. Jacobs spent nearly an hour walking the pavilion with a group of bomb squad police who had brought explosive-sniffing German shepherds along at Shlcit's request. No bombs were detected by any of the various means the police used to test for them.

At eleven o'clock that Thursday morning, the new pavilion was declared free of any explosives, and the bomb squad departed, confident the building was safe.

13

DESPITE THE LIGHT from his headlamp, the man had a hard time seeing in the tunnel. The air-conditioning ducts rumbled throughout the utility tunnels, making him imagine that he was inside the throat of a dragon with heartburn.

The pipes hung low, making the narrow tunnels difficult to move through and occasionally blocking much of the light. Only practice had afforded him his keen agility. He was not new to this.

He fixed a piece of tape to his wires. A fine job it was, too. They blended in with a variety of other wires that had been added over the years.

He thought he heard someone cough. He remained absolutely still. Alert, ad moving cautiously away from the sound, he headed down the tunnel, bent over and unable to see very far ahead of himself.

There! Again. That was no cough. That was someone speaking. Someone in the tunnels. A beam of light swept over him from behind without warning. He moved quickly, in an odd ducklike run.

Breathing heavily he continued his flight, pipes and conduits to his right, mounted to the wall. Yellow light from behind stretched his shadow before him, the hand-held flashlight jiggling with his pursuer's movements. Jesus, they were gaining on him!

He reached an intersection and turned right, leaving the path of the flashlight behind. This tunnel held more pipes than the others and was therefore more difficult to move through quickly.

His glasses began to fog from his exertion. It happened every time he hurried like this. His vision blurred. He pawed at the thick glass, still duck-walking at a full clip. The yellow light flooded him again.

They were right back there, moving along.

He crouched and began to move along himself, apelike, bent over severely to avoid hitting the pipes, shifting his weight between the balls of his palms and the soles of his feet, speed-crawling on all fours in a kind of primitive canter. He doubled his speed.

He continued down the narrow tunnel. But then the light from behind grew stronger and he realized his pursuer was again gaining on him. He stopped, turned, and began kicking on a pipe marked with a red arrow. The man behind him gained ground. The bomber continued to strike out against the pipe. It flexed with each kick but resisted breaking.

He isolated a connection in the pipe, reared back his foot, and kicked hard. The junction broke and steam spewed out, blocking the way for his pursuer.

The bomber went back to his ape run, feeding off pumping adrenaline, pulling away quickly.

Reaching an intersection with a vertical shaft, he began a hasty descent, taking chances by skipping several rungs with each step. A fall would mean injury, quite possibly death. He paused and looked up. No one there. He reached up and switched off his headlamp, angry at himself for not having thought of it sooner.

If he remembered right, there was a room off Sub-level 3 that connected with the storm sewers. He was real familiar with the maze of sewers. If he hurried, he could be lost before they figured out where he had gone. Down into the darkness he sank, hand over hand, the dragon still growling high overhead.

14

"MAY I COME IN?" Susan asked from the door to his office.

"Please." Jacobs stood and moved toward her. She shied away, offish.

"Thank you for the flowers. I called home," she explained. "I'm told they're beautiful."

"My apologies."

"Accepted." She sat lightly on the edge of the chair, as if she expected to leave quickly. It made Jacobs feel uneasy. "And I also accept your dinner invitation. Social amenities over, we have some business to discuss.

"First, I haven't been able to see Russo. I doubt if I will, but I'm still trying. I've had two meetings with a former Russo employee, a man named Proctor. A friend in the DA's office sent me to him. He was evidently set up as a scapegoat, and he isn't too pleased about it. At the same time, he's scared of Russo. I met with him last night, but it was fruitless. He was too afraid to talk. Thanks to some pressure from my DA friend, applied through Proctor's attorney, he was more willing to cooperate today.

"Proctor claims," she continued, "that Russo had several meetings with a man named Danny Romanello. Romanello took over the concrete work on your new pavilion when DeAngelo effectively broke the union. Now, one would think that would grate on Russo's nerves, and in fact he evidently pretended it did—"

"Pretended?"

"Ranting and raving around the office, that sort of thing. Come to find out, one afternoon when Proctor showed up at Russo's office door, he overheard Russo and Romanello getting along like buddies. And why not? As it turns out, the two are brothers-in-law. When Proctor knocked, they put on a show. They argued, and Romanello stormed out. Proctor claims that just before the arguing he overheard them talking about someone here at the Green who was in on something with them."

"Could be one of the workers Russo planted to keep an eye on things."

"Proctor thinks it's someone in management."

"What?"

"I'm just telling you what he said."

"How reliable is he?"

"Unfortunately, not very. I'm under the impression he'll do about anything to get out of his legal problems."

"It does tie into something else. . . ."

"You look worried."

"I am," he admitted. "I'm not sure which way to go with this. If it's what I think it is, we've got some big problems. Big. Capital B."

"Russo fits into it?"

"I think so, yes."

She flipped through her small pad and said, "Okay. Point two. I did some more library research. I've modified the list I gave you yesterday. Anderson, the first name, spread himself over a three-block area a few months ago. An investigation by the FBI revealed he was trying to make his own plastic explosives. He's out.

"Number five, Greenwood, was arrested in New Haven on a drug charge. He's in on a twenty-year sentence. No chance of parole for another four years. He's off."

"You *do* take your work seriously."

"You told me to read between the lines. I'm doing the best I can. This is all from the newspapers. The three names I added are arsonists who have been implicated in crimes having to do with explosives. No convictions. Thought they should be included in the club. There are a couple of things on the other list that are still eluding me: the rent-a-car bombing, the explosion on the yacht, and the killing of the judge. I have access to a computer later on today that should allow me to do some keyword searches. The indexing system for the periodicals isn't all that extensive. The computer should help out considerably."

"Do you have a spare copy of your new list?"

"You bet." She handed it to him.

"I really am impressed, Susan. And I'm deeply sorry for jumping to conclusions."

She pursed her lips, clearly uncomfortable.

He said, "If your Mr. Proctor can find out anything more about who at Yankee Green might be connected to Russo and Romanello—"

"He's looking into it. He's desperate. I think he may come up with something." She hesitated, blushing. "Is dinner tonight for real?"

"Absolutely."

"Time?"

"How would you be with an hour's notice?"

"Hungry, I'm sure."

"Good."

"I'll call."

"Do that."

She left. Jacobs called Haverill immediately. "I have to talk with you as soon as possible. . . . No, I'd rather it be just the two of us. Before the afternoon meeting, if possible. . . . No, it's about the cement. . . . Yes, that's right. . . ." After a long pause on Haverill's end, he added, "I think we can expect a visit from Russo soon, and if we're not prepared for it, it could turn against us. . . . Good, I'll be right up."

─────────── 15 ───────────

RAPPAPORT HAD YET to see the full picture, but he knew that both his discoveries were important. He couldn't be certain the bad cement was tied to the explosion. Where the hell was the connection? Without core samples, he couldn't even be sure the cement *was* a problem. If a single isolated pour had failed to cure properly it would hardly be anything new. On a job the size of FunWorld that could be expected. If only the emergency stairway failed to meet code it wouldn't make a bit of difference. One afternoon, a few yards of cement, and everything would be back to normal.

He pulled down the garage door. The Caddy was tucked in nice and tight. Light flickered at the corner of his eye. "Who's there?" he questioned.

The neighborhood was quiet. Hot afternoon sunlight beat down, warming the cement underfoot. Rappaport could feel it coming through his shoes. "Hello?" he said, feeling a presence nearby. "Anybody there?"

He pushed open the gate on the high fence that connected the garage to the small house. A strong hand grasped him from behind and shoved a rag into his mouth. Rappaport struggled, but to no avail. A heavy man stepped in front of him wearing a ski mask; another held his arms from behind, restraining him.

He knew what was coming.

"Stop poking your nose in other people's business, or you'll find your fat wife carved into little bits," said a gravelly voice. This man struck Rappaport hard in the stomach. "As far as your wife's concerned, you got mugged for your wallet," the man instructed, hitting him repeatedly above the groin, where the pain was intense but evidence of a mugging minimal. There would be no bruises. No cuts.

As the man behind released him, Rappaport slumped to the flagstone walkway clutching his abdomen, pain shooting through him. The two hurried off.

Rappaport dragged himself toward the back door, a gargantuan effort that required all his strength and presence of mind. The few feet felt like a hundred yards. He struggled up the steps, one by one, finally collapsing on the small back porch alongside a stack of old newspapers and a yellow plastic bowl of cat food.

Reaching up, he tried for the doorbell and fell short, skidding back down the molding. He pounded on the porch, but little sound resulted. Again he forced himself to his knees and directed his finger toward the lighted button mounted in the molding. *Come on, Jessi,* he mumbled.

He could picture her watching the tube.

His finger stabbed the button.

A moment later, Jessi opened the door, looked down, and screamed.

"Call an ambulance," he hissed.

"Marty! You've had a heart attack. Oh, my God, you've had a heart attack!" She slapped her pudgy hands across her breasts, feeling her own heart race out of control.

"I was mugged," he managed to gasp. "Call the ambulance. Quick."

He watched his panicked wife turn and scurry back inside. He heard her demanding an ambulance. "Atta girl," he said as their cat joined him on the porch, rubbing against him for attention.

Jessi yelled into the phone hysterically, repeating the address several times.

I'm on to something, he thought. *Hell, yes. I'm really on to something.*

16

"WHERE'S PETER?" Haverill asked his secretary.

"I've been trying to reach him, sir."

"Trying isn't good enough. I want to see him this minute."

Unlike Rappaport, Haverill had a fair idea of who was involved in the cement conspiracy. Following a private afternoon meeting that his Director of Security had requested, Haverill had taken a look at the accounting for the construction of the new wing. Although his own countersignature filled the lowest line on all the canceled checks, Haverill knew damn well *he* hadn't received any kickbacks. The only other signature on those checks was that of Peter Knorpp. Knorpp, who drove a twenty-five-thousand-dollar car. Knorpp, with his perfect teeth and designer suits.

Knorpp.

A moment later his phone beeped. "I just checked with Security, sir," said his secretary over the speakerphone's intercom. "He used his ID card to access the private elevators twenty minutes ago. Mr. Brock, in Dispatch, assumes he's in one of the model apartments because the computer shows the private elevator still at the top of the shaft, and Mr. Perkins remembers seeing him in the penthouse hallway on the monitors."

"Do I have a card to those apartments?"

"I can get you one."

"Do that, would you? Just as quickly as possible. I'll meet you by the doorway. Oh, and have Jacobs join me as well."

Haverill hoped he might have stumbled onto a meeting between Knorpp and whoever else was involved in the cement conspiracy. He wanted a witness to the meeting.

A few long minutes later, Jacobs joined Haverill at the doorway that led to a hallway and the two model penthouse apartments. The carpets smelled fresh. The air was chilled, the recessed lighting, subtle.

"After our talk I looked at some figures. I think Peter may be involved," he told Jacobs. "Your people think he may be up here in one of the models. The models would make a damn clever place for a meeting. He can always use the excuse of showing the apartments—he's responsible for sales, after all."

"What do you want me to do?"

"Back me up. Isn't that what it's called?"

Jacobs suppressed a smile.

Haverill led the way down the quiet corridor.

The first apartment was empty. Jacobs eased the door shut silently and they moved on to the next. Jacobs placed the card in the slot, but Haverill brushed him aside and did the actual opening of the door.

The two men stepped inside. Haverill leaned against the wall as if acting out a movie role.

As they crept down the narrow apartment corridor, their shoes brushing the long strands of the white shag rug, both of them indifferent to the bold modern art on either wall, they could hear the soft slap of wet, determined flesh. There was no mistaking that sound. The two men looked at each other. Haverill motioned for Jacobs to stand back as he continued toward the living room.

Jacobs was only too happy to oblige. Interrupting one of Knorpp's trysts had no appeal to him.

Haverill rounded the corner and saw two naked people entangled right on a chair in the middle of the spacious living room. The woman's long, slender back faced him, its muscles flexing as she rose and lowered herself. Time seemed to slow to a crawl. Involved with each other, they didn't notice Haverill. The woman continued to ride her partner, her pace and efforts increasing. The top of Knorpp's blond head could be seen over her shoulder as he suckled her. Haverill heard the spongy slap of excited flesh. The room smelled of her.

Say something! he told himself, nonplussed. He grew lightheaded, for something in him recognized this woman's back. It looked like Kate's back.

He reached out for support and, in the process, bumped into a lamp, knocking it to the floor. The woman's head rotated slowly. She glanced over her shoulder.

Haverill stumbled toward her: his baby girl, Julia.

She screamed.

"You bastard!" Haverill thundered at Knorpp. The lovers fell apart as Knorpp stood to deflect the first blow.

Julia's face held a horrible, paralyzed expression.

"My baby," Haverill gasped as he swung wildly at Knorpp. The younger man blocked the hit with a forearm and delivered a strong right to Haverill's jaw. Knorpp was not a fighter and gave away a full forty pounds to Haverill, but the right caught Haverill perfectly on the chin. A tiny pop and the big man went down.

The last thing Haverill saw was his daughter's flushed and naked body.

17

JACOBS GREETED CIVICHEK cordially, having already decided on a game plan.

Civichek took a seat. Jacobs elected to remain in his desk chair. The soft *whoosh* of air conditioning droned steadily. To both men, the office seemed smaller in silence.

Jacobs said, "I wanted to talk to you about your people."

"Surprise."

"We have our own security force here."

"That's part of the problem, from what I hear."

"Earlier we had an incident involving one of your people."

"So I heard."

"Then you can understand my concern. We have a job to do here. Yankee Green isn't exactly the subways of New York. We have adequate staff and more than adequate equipment to get the job done."

"The presence of groups like the Flock deters crime, both large and small. I have the results of several surveys confirming that. My people are here legally."

"Nevertheless, you've interfered with my operations."

"When the Flock is present, there is less vandalism and less serious crime. Anyone is allowed in this place. This place is a city —its own little city, that ain't so little. Since when can people be kept out of a city based on the color of their neckerchief?"

"We don't judge people by neckerchiefs." Jacobs was reminded of the lawsuit Haverill had told him about. Late yesterday, a young black attorney had filed suit against the Green for one million dollars in damages. Brick had been down to talk about it, since the arrests involved Security.

"We had the opportunity to nail a pickpocket who's been working the Green. One of your members interfered and the pickpocket got away. Your people," Jacobs continued, "are *interfering* with the performance of my staff. That is a situation I can't tolerate. And won't. You're a maverick, Civichek. You make up your own rules. The idea of society is for everyone to try and work within the same set of rules, not create their own. That's a dangerous attitude."

"You don't know what you're talking about," Civichek said offhandedly.

Jacobs said, "I spoke with the police up in Portland. I'd say your performance there was less than satisfactory."

"Portland?" Civichek's brow crushed down over his recessed eyes.

"If a single member of your organization is found to be carrying a concealed weapon, I won't hesitate to take action."

"I don't know what you're talking about."

"You don't remember Portland? They remembered you just fine."

"The police were on us from the moment we arrived. Don't pay any attention to that knee-jerk liberal."

"Until the courts decide differently, this shopping center is private property. You're in my back yard, Civichek. I can deal with this however I please. I'm going to pull a raid on your people, and if I find a single weapon, I'm going to throw all of you out and keep you out. If there's one thing you've been called by the press of the other cities you've visited, it's a publicity hound. You think about how it would be to have your so-called law enforcers caught violating the law."

"Listen, Jacobs, we train our people the way we see fit. Have any weapons charges been filed against us? No. And when we've had court problems in the past, we've been exonerated. So get off my case."

"Get off mine. Take your people somewhere else. Your man cost me that pickpocket. I have reports that your people have stirred up trouble with some of the youth groups. That's not supposed to be the way it works. You're making my job harder, not easier. The idea is to work together."

"We are working together."

"I wasn't even told your people were on the grounds. You call that working together?"

"Get off my case."

"Listen to me, Civichek. From everything I can determine, you are in the Green for two reasons: One is to recruit new patrolmen for the Flock by generating enthusiasm and hitting the media; the second is to generate publicity. I'll offer some free advice. If you really want some good PR, lead your people down across the tracks, past Washington Avenue, where the rate of violent crimes has tripled in three years—where you can *really* do some good."

The hard-faced young man stood. "We're here because we heard you had a problem with youth gangs. We'll leave when that problem has been resolved."

"I'm going to come down all over your people. One slipup and every paper and TV station in the Northeast will have it. Think about that."

"Likewise." Civichek pulled the door shut with a bang and signaled his two guards, both of whom were looking at pictures in magazines.

———————— 18 ————————

As THE OVERWEIGHT Larry Glascock stepped into the men's room of the Dela Vista Theater, on Sixth Street, one of Bob Russo's men jammed the door with his foot. Another of Russo's men, in the lobby, was ready to warn of anyone approaching.

Glascock's triple chin made him look like a fat turkey. The head man of the testing laboratory was nervous and sweated profusely, staining through the underarms of his suit.

Russo finished washing his hands and then dried them on a paper towel. He walked calmly to one of the stalls and retrieved his jacket where he had hung it. "What was our agreement?"

"I beg your pardon?"

"You had a simple job to do. Nothing fancy. And now you go and play like Al Capone."

"I don't know what you're talking about."

"Oh, yeah?" Russo's face turned crimson. He took the whimpering Glascock by the tie and led him to the front of one of the stalls. When Russo kicked it open, he pointed to an unconscious man sitting fully clothed on the toilet, white floor tiles splattered with blood. "He looked familiar? It took my people less than an hour to find him. He didn't feel like talking so we used some persuasion. I don't like having to persuade people. But I'll persuade you too, if you don't feel like talking."

"I—"

"You had that Jew beat up. Why? What could you have possibly hoped to gain? That was a costly mistake, Glascock. If I didn't have a few friends in the right places, I might not have known about it in time. As it is, I may not be able to salvage the situation. You're breathing like a fat pig. Talk."

"He figured out the cement was bad," choked out Glascock. "He knew we had either misreported our findings or switched cylinders. What the hell was I supposed to do? I knew you wouldn't do anything. You're so far removed from all of this no one will ever make the connection. I have my job to protect."

"We had an agreement."

"He sent a sample to another lab in Connecticut. He told me he did. By tomorrow, Monday at the latest, he would have had the results of those tests."

"What the hell did we pay you for?"

"I—ah . . . ahh . . ."

"What the hell did we pay you for?"

Noticing the anger in Russo's eyes, Glascock answered the question. "We okay the cylinder test. We sit on it for about a year, and then we discover that we switched cylinders by accident. The cement is bad."

"And who takes the fall?"

"The guy out at the mall, Knorpp."

"And what's so difficult about that?"

"Rappaport knew the cement was bad."

"You *idiot*, that was the entire point, wasn't it? So the timing's a little off. All you had to do was look alarmed and run a few more tests and discover the cement was bad. What's so fucking hard about that?"

"I—ah. . . . That's not the way it seemed."

"So, instead you play Al Capone and hire a couple of thugs to rough the old man up. How much sense did that make? Now look at what you've done. Jesus Christ! You've got fat for brains, Glascock. Look at you. I pay you ten grand, and you go off and do this. I don't believe it."

"He won't say a thing to anyone. Mark my words. I had him all cased out, him and his wife. . . . He won't let anything happen to his wife."

" 'Cased out'? What's wrong with you? You sound like some slob off the 'Rockford Files.' 'Cased out?' " Russo spun and hissed. "For your fucking information, Rappaport *and* his wife are under police protection. An investigation is under way. If I can find your hoods in less than an hour, how long will it take the cops? Two hours?

"Now let me make something clear to you, Glascock. You fucked up. All by yourself. I have two options here: I can have my boys hang you and your henchmen on butcher hooks in some deep freeze in Providence for a few months, or I can suggest you take a leave of absence and disappear for a while. I can offer you the same conditions you evidently offered Rappaport. You have a daughter in college in Kansas—"

"No, you can't—"

Russo grinned. "But I can, Glascock. And I will. No matter what you may be thinking you can get away with, you're wrong. The police can't help you. You enter a protection program, I'll find your daughter. You understand?

"What you do is head straight to Bradley Field. Don't use the local airports. You charge your trip on plastic, so there's a nice clear trail where you went. You fly to Cleveland. Are you getting this, fat man?"

"Cleveland."

"At the Hilton, there will be a package waiting for you. Use the money in that package to fly wherever you want, except Kansas. You stay away for at least two months, living off the cash in that package. Is that clear?"

"I—"

"Do you have that? No going home. No going back to the office. No phone calls. You disappear just like that. You understand?"

"I—ah. . . ." The harsh lighting gave Glascock's pale face a greenish pallor. He twisted his plump, stubby hands in his handkerchief. "Cleveland," he said.

"Right away," said Russo.

"I can do that."

"Get out of here."

The fat man hesitated, looked into the toilet stall at the bloodied man, and then hurried out the door.

Russo said, "You and Rusty follow him, Tommy. Once he's on that plane, call our friends and tell them Cleveland, tonight."

The man guarding the door nodded.

Russo straightened his tie in the mirror and then left the bathroom.

------------ 19 ------------

JACOBS HAD COME HERE only once, nearly a year earlier, and had left upon reading the prices. But, accepting his invitation to dinner, Susan had asked where he had in mind, and this had been the first name to pop into his head. He didn't know restaurants. He cooked what he called "poor man's food" at home or else caught some fish and chips at a local diner. The rest of his meals he ate at one of the family restaurants at the Green. But tonight had to be special.

A few cars lined the side of the street, far fewer than even a year earlier. Jacobs watched the signal lights ahead of him change in succession as he walked slowly around the aging Volvo and opened the door for her. Wind hurled a single sheet of newsprint down an opposing street and out into the intersection. An errant funnel of wind lifted brown dust in its path, like a miniature tornado.

He wore a tie and tan sports jacket. Susan Lyme wore a pale blue dress with spaghetti straps made of soft cotton that swished gently as she walked. She carried a cream-colored linen jacket. He took her hand and helped her from the car.

"Doesn't look very crowded."

"It used to be the talk of the town. I must confess, I haven't been here in quite some time. I hope the food's still good."

"I've never been. I hear it's delicious. It's probably that darn mall out of town." She winked. "It's ruining everyone's business."

"That's what I hear."

"So, anyway," she said, continuing their conversation from the car ride, "I ran those computer searches this afternoon. Much of it was done with a phone modem, using the databases of the newspapers in the various cities, and the modem had a high baud rate so I had to save the information to disk and then print it up. As a result, I haven't been through all of it. The two stories that intrigued me were the rent-a-car bombing and the killing of the judge. In both cases dynamite was used. I found out that much."

They paused by the door, Jacobs listening intently. He opened it for her and followed her into Fontaine's. The ceilings were low, the atmosphere enhanced by soft lighting and candles on all the tables. A wrought-iron gate separated the raised entrance from the sunken dining room. Well-dressed couples occupied several of the tables. A solo violinist worked his bow through Ravel in the far corner.

"Stolen?" he said.

"Nice," Susan whispered, clutching Jacobs's arm.

He seemed uncomfortable with the contact. He gave the maître d' his name, and the man excused himself and headed over to check with the headwaiter.

"I was able to download a number of articles on both incidents, but I haven't had enough time to go over them thoroughly," she said.

Moments later they were led through the small dining room, passing curtained private rooms to their right. The maître d' stopped at the third curtain and held it back.

"Ladies first," Jacobs gestured.

They stepped inside. Two oil paintings, individually lighted, faced each other on the end walls. The remaining wall was muraled with a scene of Rome. The table had a candelabrum, sparkling crystal, and a white linen tablecloth with matching napkins. The maître d' seated Susan. Jacobs picked up the wine list as he sat down.

"If Mr. Violin comes by and plays 'Some Enchanted Evening' I'll turn to putty. I think I'm nervous."

"You're lovely."

"Now I know I'm nervous."

"This is my way of apologizing for jumping to the wrong conclusions. That was very unfair of me."

"Agreed. Apology previously accepted."

"Wine?"

"Most definitely. That is, if you're going to."

"By all means. Red or white?"

"When in Rome . . . red, I think."

He opened the wine list. It was not something he knew a great deal about. He saw two Cabernets and picked the more expensive.

He heard his father say angrily, *"You don't know what it's like out there. You'll never make it out there. You belong here with your family. You're a fisherman."* His mind went blank.

He set down the wine list and opened his menu. Then, trying to sound indifferent and polite, he said, "What are you going to have?"

"Could we split an antipasto?"

"Sure."

Once the wine had been delivered and poured he asked, "Anything else?"

"It can wait."

"Agreed." They chimed glasses.

"I like you better without the hat," she said, studying his face like an artist inspecting a canvas.

"I only wear it at work." He blushed under her gaze.

"Not in bed and not in the shower." She repeated what he had told her.

"Right. Now tell me about you."

"What about me?"

"Your life. . . ."

"My private life? You want to know if I'm seeing somebody, something like that?"

"No, that's not what I meant."

"I'm not." She paused for another sip of wine and lowered her voice. "I've had two major relationships. Both with married men. When you're young and in New York—no, let me start over again.

"I'm an overachiever. Ever since college I've had this incredible need to excel. It's not altogether healthy. My parents—my mother, actually—arranged my first few jobs," she said, disappointment coloring her voice. "A couple of phone calls is all it took, I'm sure. I didn't argue. But I decided I wanted any promotions to come from my own efforts.

"I quickly found out there was no room for a permanent relationship in my life. No time for it. I was younger then, of course, and I saw my close friends get too caught up in it all. I decided married men were the safest." She was clearly uncomfortable. She repositioned herself in the chair, eyes on the tablecloth. "I established my priorities. Marriage wasn't in the picture."

"And?"

"And both times I found out I don't know much about priorities or devotion. In all, I had two relationships with married men. They both worked out great for a while. I never allowed myself to become too involved emotionally, which is what I wanted. The first affair ended amicably enough. He was devoted to his wife. I met another guy a few months later and liked him a lot. We started seeing each other. He had a family. I accidentally met his wife and kids. It was at a Harvard tea. It really wrecked me. I felt like a real—you get the picture. I called it off. Then he gets all upset, shows up at my place, and tells me he's moving in; he's going to leave his family. I tell him no. He falls apart on me. That was a year and a half ago. That was it for married men. In fact that was it, period. How about you?"

"Me? About the only quote *relationship* I had was in college. That seems like the Stone Age now." He forced a smile and shrugged. "I don't know. She broke some promises. It fell apart."

"What sort of promises?"

"I told her some stuff. She told everyone else."

"That hurts."

"Yes, it does."

"You're still angry."

"I'm still angry."

"So Toby Jacobs has secrets he keeps."

"We all have secrets."

"Yes." She looked down at the tablecloth. Her mood turned somber and she whispered, "My father's a drunk." She wondered why she had said it. This was not the stuff of first dates. This was how to wreck a nice dinner. Yet, she continued. "He's gone from top-notch doctor to drunk in about three months. He blames himself entirely for my mother's condition and won't listen to reason. I've done my best to cover for him, but it can't last much longer. He went back to the office this week. I'd kept him away as long as I could. He shouldn't be practicing medicine. I have no idea what to do."

Jacobs listened.

"I don't know what to do," she repeated. "Things aren't going particularly well lately."

"Have you talked to him?"

"I can't get through."

"I know what you're feeling. My grandfather died of alcoholism," he said. "He owned a tavern in Ireland. I'm afraid it runs in the family. After a big catch, my father and uncle go at it pretty hard."

"Catch?"

He felt his cheeks flush. He looked at her, unable to speak. What could he say to that? Why had he said that? It had just come tumbling out of his mouth. And now, if he didn't say something quickly, he'd never hide his obvious embarrassment.

"Did I say something wrong?"

He shook his head. "No, nothing."

"What is it?"

He shook his head again.

The waiter entered. He stood at attention in red jacket and gold vest, hands clasped behind his back. She ordered the calamari and scungilli salad with onions and garlic, for two.

"It's served with a cold vinaigrette," the waiter told her.

"Yes. Fine." She continued, "The Pasta Primavera à la Genovese for my main course, please."

The waiter nodded and looked to Jacobs.

"Veal?" Jacobs asked.

The waiter cocked his head. "Vitello Tonnato?"

"Please."

"Anything else at the moment?" The waiter gave them a few seconds. They were staring at each other. He slipped through the curtains and was gone.

Jacobs poured her another glass of wine. They toasted. She said, "To good company."

He felt as if he had to tell her now. He felt dishonest keeping it to himself. They sipped and he said, "My father is a Portuguese fisherman in New Bedford."

"You make it sound like a criminal offense."

"I left home at eighteen. Haven't been back since. I would appreciate it if you didn't repeat it."

"Of course not."

"I mean it."

"I understand." She hesitated. "You're embarrassed by it?"

"My mother's Irish."

"My great-grandmother had an illegitimate child by a slave. So what do I care?"

"I care. You see my father . . . well, he's very strong. His life is directed by what has come before. He believes we—our family—is supposed to fish. Forever. His adherence to tradition has always stifled me. He won't even modernize his equipment. It took him six years to finally break down and buy a sonar device that helps locate schools of fish. All the other boats were bringing in twice the catch, and my father remained steadfast in his determination to resist the new technology. That's him all over. He expected me to live his dreams, not have any of my own. I've always resented that—always resisted it. I *am* embarrassed by him. He's a stubborn, ignorant old man. It has always embarrassed me that I'm the son of a Portuguese fisherman." He paused. "It still does," he added.

"People don't measure you by where you come from," she said quietly.

"Don't they?"

"Do they?"

"Of course they do."

She thought about this and then nodded. "Yes, I suppose they do. And you think I'd care?"

"I wouldn't have told you, but I felt dishonest."

"I'm glad you did. So where's your New Bedford accent?"

"I'm working on it."

"You *must* be. So that's Toby Jacobs's big secret?"

He nodded. "I made up my mind when I was about fourteen. I hated the boats, the cold, the killing. All of it. I hated it all. I decided to leave, whatever the cost, and that's just what I did."

"You learn something new every day."

After a few minutes of silence he said, "I hope I didn't wreck our dinner."

"If it makes you feel any better, I never would have guessed your background."

"I got out of there as soon as I could. I applied to college without them knowing. And then one day I told them I was going to the store. I never went back. I had to get out or I'd have been on a boat the rest of my life. I can't explain it to you, but that would have been the end of me. I just couldn't have done it."

"No explanation needed. I believe you."

A large antipasto was delivered along with two chilled plates and forks. The waiter served them both from the platter and retreated silently.

"To good friends," she toasted. "I don't know how you figured it, Sherlock, but nothing pushes my button better than a charming man in a candlelit Italian restaurant with waiters who don't carry pads."

"Good friends," he echoed. "And I promise to ask next time before I jump to unjust conclusions. I should have given you a chance to explain this morning, but the thing is, I still carry that college memory with me. You see, I told her about my family. She promised not to tell. A day later, the whole campus knew. Suddenly it was like I was diseased. That's a year of my life I won't soon forget."

"Or forgive."

He nodded.

"It's funny what becomes important to us."

"I'll drink to that." He raised his glass again, wondering about the balance of his own priorities. "Now your story."

The food was delivered. They were well into their entrées before he asked her again.

"Born Susan Anne Lyme," she obliged.

He studied her. "That much I know."

She shrugged. "Spoiled rotten most of my life." She tried to make it humorous; neither of them smiled. "Grew up with a front-page view of the world and the proverbial silver spoon in my mouth." She paused for a moment and ran her fork through her salad. "I have this thing about being female—a complex, I suppose. I'm convinced all anybody ever wants is a chance to go to bed. Not because I'm so special, nothing like that, but just because I'm female. I've been hit on by teachers, professors, a dean, and several editors. I resent it horribly. I'm sure it has to do with my fascination with married men. Married men have already made an emotional commitment. That makes them different. Anyway, I'm changing, you know. Here I am in my late twenties and suddenly I feel like I'm growing up. Maybe it's my mother being so ill, or maybe it's seeing my father is human with all sorts of problems; whatever caused it, I'm starting to wake up, I think. The drive to be successful blew a fuse. Success is important, yes. But not as important as good health; not as important as love.

"I haven't ever allowed myself to really love anyone. I was always suspicious of their motives. I loved my parents, but almost unfairly." She wound a strand of her sandalwood hair around her index finger. "I'm coming around. It's just a little late in life."

"I'm in the same boat—if you'll pardon the expression—and I must be five years older than you."

"You said you left at any cost. What *did* it cost you?"

"My family," he tried to say casually. "My father is a third-generation fisherman. I was supposed to be number four. He'll never understand. I'm still in touch with my mother, though he doesn't know about it. Their lives change very little. There's something beautiful in that, and there's something tragic. He fishes. She takes care of his home. Around and around it goes."

"You miss him." It was a statement.

"In the last few years, very much. Before that . . . too much resentment before that. You want to know something?" he asked with a faint accent.

"What's that?"

"It feels good to talk." He toyed with his wineglass. "I've been so caught up in that damn Yankee Green." He hesitated. "Until the explosion I felt good about it. I have a weird feeling inside. One of these days I'll have to move on."

"When would that be?"

"Soon, I think. The really fun part was figuring out how to make the Green safe. Implementing the changes. I'd like to do it again somewhere else, on my own terms."

"Is that what you'll go after?"

"Something like that. My own security company, maybe. Testing established security systems. Who knows? Get people to pay me to break into their places. That would be something. I love the challenge of getting into someplace people think I can't."

She wasn't about to point out the sexual connotations to that, but inside she was thinking how she had spent the last several years keeping people out. It was just another sign to her of how they were complete opposites. He had a blue-collar background he had fought long and hard to hide; she had been born into opulence, with her biggest challenge which car to buy, something sporty or something practical. She started to reach out, to take his hand, but stopped at the salt shaker and spun it around.

He had obviously sensed her approach, for once she picked up the shaker, he shoved his hands into his lap. "Can I tell you something?" he asked, breaking the silence.

"Please," she said softly.

"You're very lovely."

She blushed. "I'm flattered. Thank you."

"I mean it. You look radiant."

"I feel radiant. I feel wonderful."

"Dessert?"

"No. I don't think so. Go ahead, though."

"Can't. Filled up to the brim."

She was silent. She toyed with the salt shaker.

After a moment he said, "I like to walk after a big meal. Do you?"

"Sounds delightful."

"You know Redman Park?"

"Not really."

"It's near my place. We could walk the park, maybe have a cup of coffee afterward. . . . I mean, if you want."

"Sounds perfect."

"Only if you want."

"I want," she said, reaching out and taking his hand in hers.

They didn't say much on the walk. They held hands and circled the pond twice, lamplight flickering off the ripples caused by an evening breeze.

He led her up the long stairs to the third floor, anticipation beginning to make his heart pound.

THE DOOR OPENED and she was overwhelmed by the sweet smell of salt water. The apartment was very different from what she had expected. It had hardwood floors as old and brown as pirates' teeth. Stark and bare. The furniture was mismatched. It was something of a loft: large multipaned windows with the ropes and pulleys in plain sight. No curtains. He looked out on the mall, way in the distance, a single insignificant speck on the horizon of tiered buildings and rooftops. Stark. Hot. Bare in the way that made her kick off her shoes immediately. She spun in a graceful arc, her hem rising, head back in what seemed almost a trained position, but with the expression of someone intentionally losing herself. She spun once, as if she heard music: jazz, perhaps, with a swaying, lilting rhythm, provocative and secure all at the same time.

She stopped and laughed, embarrassed, wondering if she had made a fool of herself.

She threw her dress back and landed on her knees next to the fish tank. Color blurred past her eyes, focused on the bed beyond. The Four-eyed Butterfly Fish turned lazily in the water. "What beautiful fish," she said, feeling a bit heady from the wine. Jacobs had smuggled it out of the restaurant and helped her consume it on the drive over.

"A *marine* aquarium," he emphasized. It obviously held significance to him.

"Salt water?" she wondered, suddenly placing it with the smell. "It's like being on a wharf," she told him before he answered.

"My pets," he said, as if in apology, and moved alongside her to examine them. "That one there has been sick. Could affect all of them." Seeing her expression, he said, "I'm treating the water for it."

"And the boat?"

"The boat?"

"The bottle."

"Oh, yeah. A project. Something to do at night."

"There are other things," she said, stretching an arm around his neck and pulling him close to her. The nape of his neck was warm beneath her hand. He took her head in his hands, rocked her gently to the left, and kissed her. He pulled away and swallowed nervously. She touched him carefully, pulling him quietly toward her lips again. They joined. He touched the edge of her neck and pulled away from her.

"You can see the Green from here."

"Yes, I noticed."

"Oh."

"What kind of fish?"

"That one?"

"Yes."

"Butterfly Fish. Four-eyed Butterfly Fish."

"Four-eyed?" She giggled. "He must wear thick glasses."

Toby laughed with her.

"Will he be all right?"

"She. Yes."

"And the ship?"

He glanced over at the table. "It takes a long time. I never seem to have enough time to make much headway."

"Any boat in particular?"

"The *Angel*," he said, moving toward the table. "I can only guess at her, really. My great-grandfather captained her."

"You're kidding." She pulled herself up and followed him over to the table. The project was laid out in little groups. The carved balsa-wood hull sat next to a small bottle of black paint which had been used to color the decks and draw a waterline on her. The thin-tipped brush rested improperly in a juice glass half filled with turpentine. A group of what looked like small chopsticks with tiny holes drilled in them and string tied all through lay adjacent in their own pile. "What are these?" she wondered.

"Spars and rigging." He pulled his head down close. She stopped several feet farther away than he did. "Masts, sails, the intricate parts."

"It's all so small."

"That's the idea,"—he smiled privately—"isn't it?"

She ran her hand up his back and let her fingers wander. "It's nice to see this side of you."

"Which?" he seemed suddenly embarrassed.

"We're so different."

"You and I?"

"Yes."

"Oh, I don't know."

"I like it. It's not bad."

He bent down and kissed her. She welcomed him and drew him against her. He pulled her tight, lowered his arms, and held her pressed to him.

"Do you suppose . . ." she managed between kisses.

"Ummm . . . ?"

". . . that we could . . ."

"Yes?" He ran his hands down and across her buttocks. She rocked against him, squeezing with her arms.

". . . find a place to lie down?" She leaned away and stared him in the eye.

Slowly a grin stole across his face. "No," he said, grasping her tightly, his hands wandering up her back. In the same motion he propelled her into a dance step. His left hand sought her right, and they began to move around the spacious room. He hummed a vague out-of-tune melody in her ear that had no rhythm yet paced her right with him. She closed her eyes and left with him. When she opened them the walls were spinning, light flicking past the windows and the dull green glare of the fish tank. His hands roamed over her, and she felt herself come undone. She wanted his touch.

She drew away, not interrupting their step, and let her fingers worm between his buttons, suddenly drawing the shirt, tie, and jacket off him in a single urge.

He picked her right off her feet and continued to twirl. She spun with him, giggling without intention. She floated in his arms, the sensation wonderfully out of control. "Oh, yes," she said, pressing her breasts tightly against him.

Then she jerked away, him refusing to let her go entirely, and pulled her dress off her shoulders and down, exposing herself to his skin, pulling him in again. A button ran noisily across the floor. "Oh, God," she said, trying to excuse herself.

He had slowed their arc, his lips walking down her neck in delightful pecks and picks, his arms lowering, arching her back until she moved as she had earlier, hair hanging toward the dark hardwood floor. He took her in his lips and she hummed his song. She lost all track. All she wanted was him inside her.

He lowered her slowly.

"Not the floor," she whispered.

"Yes," he said. And she relaxed.

"I want you."

"Yes."

"Now. I want you now," she declared, fighting his belt.

"It's okay," he said, laying her back and undressing her. "We have all the time in the world."

Her face was pained with intention. "Please?" She reached out for him as he undressed her. When he had shed his clothes, she pulled him to her. "Please," she repeated.

HE HAD SOME VODKA, so he poured them Kamikazes. He remained naked. She had pulled his button-down shirt around her shoulders. They had settled on the edge of the bed. He thrust a second round out to her and she accepted. "That was wonderful," she admitted.

"Extraordinary," he agreed. "Do you suppose we're just drunk?"

"No."

"Neither do I."

He playfully knocked the empty glass from her hand. It

bounced on the wooden floor. He threw his own against the far wall and it shattered.

"Why—"

"A tradition," he assured her.

"You see. I told you we're different."

"I found that out." He kissed her willing lips until she allowed her elbows to unlock and found herself pressed into the bedding. Again.

AN HOUR LATER, she lay awake while he slept soundly at her side. He was not snoring, though his breathing was heavy. She watched as the lights and shadows of passing cars raced across the ceiling. As she rocked her head, she saw the aquarium—the *marine* aquarium—and the dimly lit table with the ship-in-a-bottle project spread across it. Out there somewhere was Yankee Green, a tiny white ball surrounded by amber parking-lot lights.

Who was he? Who was he really? Was it his complexity that attracted her, or his simplicity? He seemed to be juggling both, like the two jugglers at the Atrium every morning. It was almost as if he wasn't sure, and yet he showed none of the insecurities that other men showed. He wasn't afraid to reveal himself to her. Not quite true, she checked herself. He *had* been afraid, and yet he had gone ahead and done it. He wasn't *scared* of her. He wasn't even *infatuated* with her. He was *intrigued* by her, excited by her. Stimulated. He had the raw uncertainty of a cornered animal. His lovemaking had been eager and yet cautious, a strange combination of passion and concern, as if every touch had to please, every nuance had to have value and meaning.

He was patient and caring. Understanding. He held himself back and waited. He had known somehow what she had been feeling, but with none of the fluidity of a seasoned lover. He spent his nights working on his ship-in-the-bottle, just like he said, or else he was a very good actor. And he simply wasn't the type to act.

That's it, she thought. *He isn't acting.* He wasn't after any role. The hat had fooled her. She had immediately wondered if he had some mid-forties image of himself: the Humphrey Bogart of the 1980s. But it was nothing like that. She guessed that the hat was really an effort to hide the tiny clearing up on top. Toby Jacobs was no longer twenty-two.

She supposed the rough edges had been rasped smooth a few years before, when the anxious Toby Jacobs had been fighting his way up. *You're still fighting,* she thought. *But like me, you're not certain where that leads.* She realized they were more similar than she had earlier thought.

He stirred and rolled away from her. She let him go, then pulled down under the sheet and snuggled in close against him.

The warmth of his body felt wonderful.

THE JET TOUCHED DOWN in Cleveland at twenty minutes past midnight. Glascock walked down the jetway nervously, wondering what his wife was thinking. Perhaps he should call her, even though Russo had told him to disappear.

He feared Bob Russo. He regretted having become involved. Ten thousand dollars suddenly seemed very insignificant.

The airport was nearly deserted. He followed the stream of passengers toward baggage claim. He had no baggage, but he hoped to catch a taxi from the lower level.

He didn't see the two men following him.

Most of the passengers headed toward the carousel, as Glascock continued toward the automatic doors.

The two men closed the distance and caught up to within a step of him.

Glascock waited for the doors to hiss open and stepped outside. He felt the bump from behind and thought nothing of it until the needle stung him. "What the . . . ?" He spun around.

The two men were walking away from him.

"Hey, you," he called out, choking on the second word. He felt dizzy. His heart raced out of control. The injected adrenaline went to work quickly.

He staggered toward a cab, a lumbering bear on its hind legs.

A young woman stepped out of his way, a distasteful look on her face.

"Help," he gasped.

And then his heart stopped beating.

Friday
August 21

----------------- 1 -----------------

HER NOTE READ, *Don't go anywhere, and don't eat. I'll be right back. P.S. I stole your car.*

"How could I go anywhere?" he asked the note.

He had the coffee going a few minutes later, and then showered. He stood in the swirling steam feeling dreamy. They had made love twice. All he could think about, all he could feel, was the two of them entwined together. *You're not sixteen, stupid,* he told himself, but the image wouldn't go away. For the first time in years he found himself not caring if he was late for work. He didn't care about Yankee Green. It felt wonderful.

Relaxed beneath the hot water, the usual tension and tightness in his lower neck nonexistent, he inhaled steam deep into his lungs and felt refreshed. Would she want to make love again this morning? God, he wanted her right now. Did she have regrets?

He fed his fish, checked the pH, and added some sodium carbonate. He didn't talk to them this morning; his mind was elsewhere. Each noise he heard out the open window he imagined as her arrival. He would hurry to the sill and try to see down to the sidewalk, looking for the Volvo.

He stood next to the spot they had made love and grinned. The first time had been so primitive, clawing at each other, an almost desperate joining. The second had been so delicate and careful, long and warm, with her wrapped around him like wisteria clinging to a sapling. They had been aware of each other's needs and mutually cautious, holding back, prolonging it, cautiously building something together until neither could resist finishing it. Flooded. Bonded. Clutching at one another in a way only lovers clutch.

He drummed his fingers on the edge of the cluttered table and allowed himself to slide into the chair. The pieces of the *Angel* lay scattered about.

He could picture his great-grandfather on her deck, shouting commands, wind at his face. He could feel the ship being rocked by swells, tossed by huge waves. He wondered what it had been like on the morning of May 14, 1891, the date the family Bible listed as the day of the man's disappearance and death. The stories of the *Angel*'s demise, legends to Jacobs, ranged from a school of whales capsizing the vessel to a mighty gale that snapped her masts and tangled her rigging. Or had his great-grandfather been blown into different seas? Looking at the rigging on the table, he could picture the wrecked *Angel* out at sea, her parts bobbing in the water, her crew struggling to hold on.

It seemed to him that the *Angel* was why his family, for generations, had remained fishermen. His great-grandfather had become a martyr; the family carried on his martyrdom. But here it stopped. Here, in this chair, the last and only male of this generation sat making a toy image of the craft that had determined his family's fate for the last hundred years. Jacobs no longer felt the guilt he once had. He felt removed from his past. And yet his past still pulled at him. The story of the *Angel*, romanticized over the decades, gave him a sense of pride, of family strength. It was hard to fully disconnect from the *Angel*. Perhaps that was why he felt drawn to this table every time he passed by. Perhaps, no matter how hard he tried, a part of him would always remain at sea with his father. Perhaps it *was* in his blood.

He used the tweezers to secure the thread through another miniature mast and tie off the rigging, the image of his great-grandfather struggling for life still present in his mind.

The smell of the coffee returned him to the kitchen. The coffee had cooled enough to drink. He poured himself a cup and changed into his suit, leaving the tie for later.

She had obviously left early—early enough to go home, change clothes, and shop on the way back. She had fresh croissants and half a dozen gladiolas, which she quickly put in water, using a mayonnaise jar as a vase. She wore a brightly colored flowered skirt, white blouse, and pink running shoes.

"You look beautiful," he told her warmly.

"Thank you." She beamed. "I feel beautiful this morning. I feel wonderful."

"I missed you when I woke up."

"I didn't sleep much." She sauntered up to him and hugged him, nestling her head against his chest. "I was worried . . ."— she paused—"that by now you might have second thoughts."

"Great minds think alike," he whispered.

"None. None for me. No regrets, no expectations."

He squeezed her into him. "We part company there. I have great expectations."

"I'm glad to hear that." She looked up at him, refusing to release him. "I lied. So do I."

They laughed through a continental breakfast of his cowboy coffee and her croissants. *So different*, they both were thinking. She made him laugh with a contagious youthfulness that was as refreshing as the cool morning breeze that streamed through the open window.

IT WAS JUST AFTER EIGHT by the time he drove them to the Green and began the short tour she had requested. "We are in C, which is easy to remember because it's in the center of the complex. Like all the other pavilions, C has four groundfloor—or Level One—doorways: north, south, east, and west. In this case, C also has a set of doors over there that will lead into FunWorld, and those beyond the Atrium that lead to the Sports Pavilion and on to the convention center and hotel. C was finished three years ago, at the same time that D, E, and F—that whole wing—was added." She walked by his side, a contented smile curling the edges of her lips.

It would be a while until he felt secure with her. He kept worrying that she might turn and walk away. "Each doorway actually has eight doors, but we number them in groups anyway. Exits lead outside; junctions lead to other pavilions, though the doorways are numbered consecutively. We numbered them clockwise: one through fourteen on Level One concourses, fifteen through twenty-eight on the upper levels. You get the picture.

"Like we talked about before, if I want an exit closed I can tell Dispatch; a single computer will mag-lock all the doors to Exit Three, say, or Junction Four. We have twenty-eight exits, for a total of two hundred twenty-eight doors." She whistled. "Dispatch also has control over all the service entrances to the mall and all the restricted areas—what we call our service hallways—within the various pavilions."

"That must be one heck of a computer."

"It is. Specially designed for security use. Best they had when it was installed. I don't know how I got off on this. This has to be the most boring tour in the world."

"I asked, remember. The free-lance article. Money. Survival. If I don't know the details, I can't paint an accurate picture. I find this fascinating. You come here and shop and you never consider the other aspects of keeping a small city running."

He led her into Pavilion B. "Okay, you asked for it. This was the second pavilion added. Work on the stadium started at the same time, though the stadium took much longer to finish, nearly a year longer. Originally B had no entertainment in it. The concept of entertainment didn't come until High Star had owned the Green for a couple of years. In fact, it was about the time I joined that someone came up with the idea, after a visit to West Edmonton, as I understand. Anyway, the wild thing about Pavilion B was that, when it opened, foot traffic in Pavilion A fell off tremendously. It was like a ghost town in there. No one had expected that kind of reaction. That's when the idea for rides came up. Following Edmonton's lead, High Star experimented by adding several rides in A.

"The idea worked. Foot traffic picked up again, and merchants' complaints receded. From then on, it was like dominoes. When we opened C, D, E, and F, we added rides to B. In fact, we lost a major anchor about then, and we converted the empty space into a mini-amusement park, with more than fifteen rides. It's still the major hangout for the teens. You want to see something crazy"—he pointed—"go there some Friday or Saturday night. It'll stun you. The place is totally crazy for about five hours."

"How about the space shuttle? How did that come about?"

"The shuttle came as an afterthought. After the loss of Challenger, we were offered an unusual opportunity by a company up on Route One Twenty-eight that did simulation for NASA. With the shuttle program on hold, they needed some quick capital. One of their geniuses happened to shop at the Green, and he came up with the wacky idea of selling us one of their simulation packages as a kind of ride. The package is super-expensive, all computer-driven, computer-animated, that sort of thing. It was way out of our price range. I mean *way* out. And then Haverill pulled off one of his typical miracles—and the rest of this has to be off the record, I'm afraid. He somehow talked the federal and state governments into giving us a tax concession on the purchase of the simulation, delaying income and property taxes on Pavilion B for three to five years—something like that—all because we were 'supporting the space program in a time of need, and enhancing the public's appreciation of the shuttle program.'

"Well, whatever he did, it worked. We not only could afford it, but at the same time we made the manufacturer sign a contract promising we would be the only civilian corporation to be offered the simulation, essentially giving us a monopoly on it."

"Haverill sounds sharp."

"He's sacrificed almost everything for his career. Keeping Yankee Green fiscally sound has taken more out of him than he expected, I think. He's a completely different man from when I first came on. He's something of a loner since his wife left him. Very driven. He's a nice man who works too hard. I suppose he'll sell the Green at some point and make a bundle. He deserves it."

"His wife?"

"Since his wife left him, he's tried to use his work to keep himself busy. But it's a losing battle. It's like trying to dig a hole in dry sand: it comes in on you as fast as you can throw it out."

She threw an arm around him briefly. "I'm glad to hear you say that. My first impression of you was workaholic. You seem to have twenty things going at one time. Sometimes those kind of people are hard to get to know."

"It's not much longer for me, Susan." He stopped and glanced around the spacious pavilion. "I depend on this place too much. It's become too routine, no longer a challenge. I'm out of here soon. Last few weeks, I've really begun to feel it. It's time for a change."

"Nothing wrong with change," she suggested.

"Nothing wrong," he said, "except it scares the hell out of ya."

"I could use a cup of coffee." She yawned. "A friend and I were out late last night."

Jacobs moved along with her, but his attention was elsewhere: thinking about starting out fresh.

THE METAL LATTICE GATE in front of Mykos Popolov's Greek Deli remained locked in place.

Pavilion A, empty except for a few Greyhounds, their numbers dwarfed by the structure's overwhelming size and openness, reminded Mrs. Popolov of what seemed like a lifetime ago: she and Mykos at the train station, fleeing for their lives. The determined footsteps of the Greyhounds reverberated through the cavernous enclosure.

Mrs. Popolov carried her square body in short little steps, moving cautiously and slowly. She held a shopping bag containing four white aprons and a half dozen dish towels she had washed in the machine at home. Her purse dangled from her shoulder. Puffy ankles bulged out of shiny black shoes, covered by flesh-colored hose to hide her blue-veined legs. She huffed shallowly and often, in unison with her gait. When she reached the cage in front of the café she sighed and placed the shopping bag by her side.

Mykos had not returned home last night, which meant he had, once again, worked through the night trying to prepare the new store for tomorrow's opening. She wondered how Earl Coleman's first overtime had gone. So typical, she thought, that after all these years, Mykos should still work so hard. Perhaps he was still trying to prove he wasn't handicapped. He had never cared for that word. Despite all the jokes, his good humor, the apparent relaxation, Mhykloteus would never fully accept the loss of his arm.

She reached out to rattle the cage but hesitated, changing her mind. Why wake him? She searched her purse for her ID card, knowing there was little chance it was there. She always forgot the card. Not finding it, she decided to call Dispatch. Foot traffic was light enough this morning. Despite the Green's requirements, they were already late in opening. What could a few more minutes hurt? She ambled down the concourse to the emergency phone and picked it up. This had become fairly routine for her.

HIGH ABOVE, on Level 3 of Pavilion C, the Dispatch emergency phone rang, its information strip lighting up with a number corresponding to the phone she had called from. Brock threw two switches and had a shot of Mrs. Popolov on the television monitors, the emergency phone in hand. He chuckled privately. He knew before he said "Hello?" that she needed to be let inside. Mrs. Popolov tended to forget her card.

She told him just that, apologizing so wonderfully as she always did, and he assured her someone would be over in a minute to help out. He radioed his nearest guard, Pollano, and sent her to the Greek Deli. Using a card, the guard could override gate security and open or close a store's gate. This was necessary in the event of a real or false alarm or other emergencies. Although Jacobs's card allowed such access without additional computer clearance, all other security cards required the Chubb's permission as well. Brock typed in the necessary command to approve Pollano's attempt to open the Deli.

On the small box outside the Greek Deli an LED turned from red to green. Mrs. Popolov pushed O for OPEN, and the cagelike gate rose electronically.

She tied on an apron, started a pot of coffee, and looked in the office. Mhykloteus, stretched out on the office floor, snored from a bed made of unfolded tablecloths, a pillow of piled napkins beneath his heavy white-haired head. Mrs. Popolov had no fear of waking him. Until his name was whispered in his ear he would sleep deeply. Then at a moment's notice he would be on his feet, alert and eager to tackle another day.

She felt heavy this morning. She promised herself she would find a way to lose a few pounds before her doctor's warning of a failed heart came true. My heart will never fail me, she thought. Perhaps the muscle will become fatty and small, a valve will clog, the blood will stop pulsing through this old plug of a body. But my heart will never fail. My true heart is right here with my dear and loving husband.

She was certain that Mhykloteus would outlive her. He would outlive half the world. He was a survivor. He had survived the resistance fighting of the big war. He had survived his struggle against the Germans. He had survived his poverty and had helped her to survive the six-week ride on the Spanish freighter that had eventually delivered the two of them to New York City. He had endured the months of learning a new language at an age when the mind cannot fully grasp new concepts. He had worked long hard hours for long hard years on a produce dock, one-armed. Yes, he was a survivor.

She turned on the espresso machine, checked the refrigerator bins for milk, cream, butter, whipped cream, relish, mustard, mayonnaise, lemons and limes. Low on shredded chocolate, she moved slowly back to the walk-in and liberated a heavy bar of Swiss chocolate from the third shelf. She placed it on the well-worn wooden cutting board that was bolted to the edge of the stainless refrigerator chest and shredded half a pound of chocolate, making sure to nibble a good amount throughout the process. Humming to herself, she put the pastries on display and, when it was ready, poured herself a cup of coffee.

If only she could return his sense of purpose. Oh, he was jovial enough, he had a wonderful lust for life, but something was missing. *It* was missing. Perhaps she had dominated too much. She hoped not. She had only tried to do what she thought necessary to keep from being a burden on him.

He had burden enough. The problem was, Mhykloteus needed to win at something. Making sandwiches, cleaning tables, pouring coffee was never going to do it for him. *I can't give you back the war,* she thought. Yet all else had seemed insignificant since that time, even to her. They had been young then, fighting for their lives.

She looked out the open mouth of the store in time to catch a glimpse of Toby Jacobs walking with that young reporter toward the Atrium. They were chatting and obviously enjoying each other's company. How strange it was to see Toby Jacobs arriving so late—eight twenty-five was two hours past his usual arrival time. Ah, the young, she thought. The young have so much flexibility and resilience.

She enjoyed seeing him walk so gaily with a young woman. Toby was, by nature, a loner. She knew her husband and the young man got along so well because of their mutual respect for one another. Both worked two days to every other man's one.

The two young people turned at the last moment and headed toward her as if they had overheard her thoughts. At first, the spring in their step didn't match the tired look around their eyes. Then she smiled knowingly and felt a warm little tickle at the nape of her neck, reminded of a springtime morning in Italy so many years before, when Mhykloteus had led her down a path in a blooming orchard and had opened a world to her.

Jacobs made the introductions.

She poured them black coffees to go. Toby bought two pastries. "Where's Mykos?" he asked curiously.

"Asleep," she explained. "He set up the new store last night."

"Doesn't surprise me. I hope he conned Bill Francis into letting him use one of Housecleaning's golf carts again. Your husband could con the president out of politics, Mrs. Popolov. How'd the first day with Coleman work out?" Jacobs had had to approve the young man's working at the mall and had discussed the matter with Popolov the day before.

"I have not yet spoken with Mhykloteus. It seemed to go fine."

"Give him my best. It's a courageous thing to do. If it goes well, it could mean a big difference for the Green."

He left with Susan a few minutes later, the two picking up their conversation where they had left off.

Twenty minutes later Mrs. Popolov completed a small sign in her crude block printing that read:

WE ARE OPENING A NEW STORE IN FUNWORLD.
SEE YOU SATURDAY FOR THE GRAND OPENING.

Within the last twenty minutes the concourse had begun to fill, not only with shoppers but with several workers from other shops frantically carting supplies toward the new pavilion. Mhykloteus and five other owners of existing stores had opted to lease additional space in the new wing. Pavilions A and B would have limited business for the next few months. The Popolovs had witnessed this phenomenon too many times to count—a new pavilion comes on-line and business at all other pavilions falls by 30 to 50 percent. It was one of the hidden penalties for growth that retailers didn't find out about until well into a ironclad five-year lease. There were other equally annoying aspects of the Green from the retail point of view: The required advertising fee, like a maintenance fee, seemed exorbitantly high; the variation in lease prices, running to thousands of dollars per month, seemed totally unfair; the organization of the stores, direct competition often as close as two spots away, seemed a ridiculous oversight by management.

For the Popolovs, these were all valid reasons to open a second store in the new pavilion.

To their credit, she thought, sipping her second cup of coffee, Haverill and Knorpp had finally organized a pavilion properly. The new pavilion had several interesting retail sections, all modeled after a central theme: Four Corners of the World. Gardens of the World, Toys of the World, Foods of the World, Fashions of the World—the new pavilion, home of FunWorld amusement rides, had been well-planned. Popolov's café was located on the west side of the new pavilion in Foods of the World. He had elected to work through the night in order to avoid today's crush by other retailers anxious to set up their stores. It would be a madhouse today.

The mail arrived precisely at eight-thirty. The order of delivery was rotated each day.

She dropped the pile, scooped the letters up, and flicked through them quickly, anxious to see if any word had come from the consulate. She scanned the return addresses.

She slapped the stack with her hand. What was wrong with those people? Didn't they have any sense at all?

2

"Toby Jacobs here to see you, sir."

"What's that?" Haverill noticed his secretary standing in the doorway.

"I'm sorry to interrupt. I buzzed you—"

"It's fine, send him on in."

"Sir."

Knorpp and Julia had left the penthouse apartment by the time Jacobs had brought Haverill around. The CEO had harangued Jacobs for several minutes about letting Knorpp leave, obviously embarrassed by being knocked out. Last night he had taken a room in the Convention Center Hotel in Pavilion F. Alone, he had spent the night stewing, confronting the failure that was Julia. Despite his many business successes, Haverill considered himself a failure. He had failed with Kate. He had failed with Julia. Was there any greater failure than failing those you love? He thought not. . . .

"Have a seat, Jacobs. About yesterday afternoon. Peter Knorpp is through here, that much is obvious. The rest is of a personal nature. End of discussion, okay? As for my berating you, I apologize. Have you seen Knorpp?"

"No, sir. Not yet."

Jacobs took a seat. Haverill looked terrible. His eyes were bloodshot, his limp, lifeless gray hair needed a comb. His shoulders drooped. A blue-gray bruise sat on his jaw. His suit looked like it had been slept in.

"I'll be as brief as possible," Jacobs said.

"I'm all right. Honestly. I'll be fine. What progress have you made on the investigation into the bombing?"

"I've just spoken with Shleit. He and I have a meeting set for later. I told you about the note I received yesterday—"

"Yes."

"And that a couple of maintenance men nearly caught up to an unauthorized entry in our tunnels—"

"We should have had him," Haverill snapped.

Jacobs ignored the comment. "The FBI lab analyzed the individual letters used to paste up the note. He's right-handed, although he wrote my department number on the front with his left to try to confuse us. Most of the letters come from newsprint available here in Hillsdale. Several of the letters were from the August issue of *Hustler*—"

"My God, they can tell all that?"

"And the remaining came from *Byte* magazine—a computer magazine."

Haverill shook his head in amazement.

"The Bureau is cross-checking the subscription lists for this area for both *Byte* and *Hustler,* looking for someone who takes both magazines. But it's more likely they were bought from a newsstand.

"More interesting at the moment," he continued, "is that they lifted and identified fibers from both notes I was sent. The fibers come from a kind of cloth manufactured for OK-Optics of Hong Kong. The cloth is used as lining for the inside of their eyeglass cases and as a polishing cloth that comes free with a new pair of glasses. That particular line is carried in only three stores in all of Hillsdale. Again, an effort is under way to compare customer/patient lists from those stores with the subscription lists of both magazines. It's not much, but it's the first real hard evidence we've come up with."

"The dynamite? What about it?"

"Shleit confirmed that the stick, or sticks, used here were part of a case that was stolen six weeks ago."

"And how much damage can a case of dynamite do?"

"Plenty. But to ease your mind a bit, the police walked a pair of explosives-sniffing dogs around the new pavilion this morning, and nothing turned up. We're clean."

"Were the explosives buried in the wall, or were they in the locker? You told me they found a wire." Haverill rubbed his temples.

"Yes, sir. Late last night they discovered an extra wire in one of the electrical conduits. It would appear McClatchy connected the wire inadvertently and, in doing so, set off the explosion."

"The poor bastard killed himself." Haverill sounded defeated.

"That's the way it looks. The subcontractor is positive about the extra wire. His people mark all their wires with something called EZ-Code. It's nothing more than numbered labels they stick onto a wire to tell them which circuit the wire is on. The bomber overlooked that. His wire had no labels. The police pulled the wire and have given it to the FBI for tests. No report yet, as far as I've heard."

"Damn frustrating."

Jacobs sat in silence.

"So we can't be sure there aren't more explosives in the walls."

"No. We can't be sure. The dogs wouldn't be effective for that."

"I'll tell you something. If I have to, I'll call off the opening. Obviously that would be a terrible setback both in the public eye and financially. I'd like to avoid it if possible."

"I have a suggestion, one that will cost money but might give us peace of mind."

"What's that?"

"I've been thinking about this for some time now, mainly because of the two hundred thousand in cash we're going to have on hand. Mary-Jo did some research, and it's a feasible option, though somewhat costly."

"Let's hear it." Haverill slumped into his chair.

"SureGuard, outside Boston, can supply us with enough metal detectors to cover all entrances to the new pavilion. They're the main supplier for airports. It would slow us down a little, but—"

"No, I don't like it. Not because of cost. It's the idea of the thing. It would put people off immediately. Think how the press would play it up. No, that's unacceptable."

"If someone walks in with a firearm, it's anybody's game."

"Yes, but this security company the police are working with will be armed, correct?"

"Yes."

"And we will have some undercover guards, will we not?"

"Yes. . . ."

"Then that's that. I don't think that will be a problem."

"Whatever you say. One thing I plan on doing is stationing

most of our uniforms outside the pavilions. We gain higher visibility there, and it may discourage and help reduce the chances of an incident."

"Whatever you think the best use of your people is. You know I'll support you there."

After a pause, Jacobs said, "There is one other item worth discussing, sir, though it is mostly speculation."

"Go on," Haverill said, annoyed.

"Mind you, I don't have all the pieces yet."

"You know your problem, Jacobs? You tend to be overly cautious. I'm not going to fire you if you have a bad idea. Get down to business, that's my motto. Now what the hell is it?"

"It's Russo, sir."

"What we discussed yesterday?"

"Yes. The way I see it, we complete the new wing, get all our retailers in place, and then it's discovered that we're poured from bad cement."

Haverill lost his color and his right hand shook noticeably. "How could something like that happen?"

"According to DeAngelo, if the right people were involved, it would be fairly easy to orchestrate."

"Good God." The two men sat in silence for what seemed like minutes. Haverill finally said, "I wouldn't put it past Russo."

"No, sir. He knows what this would do to us."

"We couldn't survive something like this. Who knows what the insurance people would say? Oh, Christ!" Haverill breathed as if on the edge of tears. He looked up, glassy-eyed. "It had completely slipped my mind: the reason I was looking for Peter yesterday. . . . After we talked, I found some discrepancies in the accounting, just as you thought I might."

"It was Peter?" Jacobs asked. "He was their inside man?"

"Could be."

"It would fit."

"How so?"

"Russo couldn't very well have it traced back to him, he'd need a scapegoat. If Romanello, the cement subcontractor, convinced Knorpp to take a kickback for overlooking the cheaper cement, then it all looks financially motivated. Knorpp ends up the guilty party. Russo, not having taken a cent, stays out in the clear."

"But Romanello would be indicted as well."

"Sure he would. But someone has to testify. Romanello plea-bargains with people who are already in Russo's back pocket and ends up with a slap on the wrist. The Green not only ends up in trouble but gets all the blame as well."

"That fits. I don't like it."

"Neither do I."

"We better find Peter, and fast. They may have screwed up somewhere. At least we better hope to hell they did."

"Remember, none of this is confirmed—"

"Thank God. If we wait that long, it will all be over." Haverill noticed Julia's picture on his desk and felt his blood pressure soar. He tried to relax his hands, which remained clenched in tight fists. Fear filled his deep voice, belying his usual confidence. "Where the hell *is* Knorpp?"

3

THROUGHOUT HIS MEETING with Haverill, Jacobs had found himself distracted by thoughts of Susan, who had left him earlier for continued research. Back in his office, he tried to clear his head and concentrate on the number of tasks ahead of him. He was thankful that he had delegated much of his daily work to Dicky Brock in Dispatch, who seemed to relish being overworked; for Jacobs had plenty on his mind just working on the explosion and the developing conspiracy he, Rappaport, and Susan had uncovered.

He flipped through the stack of memos and separated two from the pile that would need follow-up. Then he tackled his mail. The third envelope down caught his eye: a Green business-return envelope.

He opened it carefully, aware of what it was. The pasted letters read:

...AnD GIve you a CLUE...

I must play fair and give you a clue. . . . He immediately called Shleit and left word to call back. He was still staring at the note when Mary-Jo knocked against the open door and stepped into his office. He thought it odd that, in married Mary-Jo, he detected a hint of jealousy and standoffishness.

"You just got a message from the hospital," she informed him clinically.

"The hospital?"

"County Hospital. A Mr. Martin Rappaport was assaulted yesterday. The message is that he is recovering well and that he or the police will be in touch with you sometime later today."

"Assaulted?"

"That's the message," she said pointedly, turning to leave.

"Mary-Jo, what is it?"

"What's *what?*" she said, blushing.

"Why the crisp attitude?"

She squinted and for a moment he feared she might cry. "Some fantasies die hard," she managed with a forced smile.

He didn't know what to say.

4

ROY WALKER LOOKED straight into the camera. He had watched Jesse Jackson speak on television many times, but he had never fully realized how intimidating cameras were. Behind him loomed the mall's enormous facade. "We face a grave situation. Our city has deserted many of its people. The Yankee Green has deserted the city. Hillsdale exists in a divided time, when equality gets passed off for profit. What kind of society are we?

"What kind of city promises to shelter evicted tenants only to repeatedly break that promise? Is that *our* city? Is that what the citizens of Hillsdale want? Black or white, it doesn't matter. The common denominator of the people who now live near Washington Street is not color but economics. We are called 'poor' people. But we're not poor. We're just poor*er*. Where the Green now stands, our homes once stood. Where do we live now? Away from the jobs. Away from the stores. We've been sent away."

"Is that why you're calling for a protest tomorrow?" The reporter was a young man in a blue blazer. He was clearly impressed by Roy Walker and excited by the interview.

"This protest is about equality. It's about downtown politicians put in office by Yankee Green; it's about evictions and promises made that were never kept. This mall is not what you may think. Ritzy? Sure. Glitzy? Sure. Entertaining? Probably. But don't be deceived. It stands here for only one reason: to take your money from you. It's a big hungry monster that will keep eating until there's nothing left. There's no end to its appetite.

"Nearly two thousand people were evicted to make room for the various stages of Yankee Green. Our homes were bulldozed by direct order of our own city government. We were promised restitution, and we were promised low-income housing. We have received neither."

"What do you expect to gain from the protest?"

"To gain?" Walker grinned. "Sore feet," he said. "I'm here addressing the community because we need support. We intend to picket in front of the Green's five major street entrances. Gain? We'd like more than promises. Results wouldn't hurt anybody." Again he grinned, comfortable and self-assured. "I'll tell you what. Most of the minorities in this town were picked up and moved across the tracks ten years ago with promises of better living conditions, more jobs, and better schools. Don't get me wrong; it was all quite legal. The mall was coming to town. It was the perfect opportunity to clean up Hillsdale. But once this mall was in place and the politicians were in office, those promises went down the tubes. Maybe all we hope to gain is a little self-respect. Maybe all we're hoping to do is inform the concerned citizens of Hillsdale of what is going on while they're shopping their six hundred stores and riding their eighty-some rides.

"This mall is a monster. It ate up Hillsdale's poor, and pretty soon, if everybody doesn't wake up, it's going to eat up the rest of Hillsdale as well. Think about that this November. It's time we returned political power to people who understand Hillsdale's problems. I'm not endorsing any particular candidate. I just think it's time we wake up."

The camera panned away from Walker. The giant walls of Pavilion C rose from the sea of cars like a castle from a moat. On the roof a single satellite dish pointed toward the blue sky—a beastly ear cast to the heavens. The complex looked impregnable. A monster, perhaps, but one with a clean coat and brushed teeth.

The interviewer thanked Walker and saw him to his car. "We'll be here tomorrow. Good luck," he said enthusiastically.

Walker nodded and drove off.

Back at the van the young reporter told his cameraman, "We'll edit that down to twenty-five seconds of raw juice." He beamed. "When we get back, see if we can get in edit room A. I want to show this to Max just as soon as possible. This stuff is gonna knock him out."

"You're new here. I wouldn't get too excited," the cameraman said casually, wrapping up wires.

"Why not? That stuff was dynamite."

"Maybe so, but Yankee Green is our biggest local account by a long shot. Don't fool yourself. By the time Max gets through with this, it'll look like a mall endorsement. Mark my words. You don't go bad-mouthing your biggest sponsor. That's bad business."

"They'll edit the content?"

"Edit it? I doubt if they'll even run it."

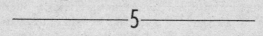

5

SUSAN CAUGHT JACOBS in his office just before his midmorning rounds. The room smelled lightly of perspiration despite the air conditioning. His hat and jacket were tossed casually over the typewriter, and the blinds were pulled against a sun that had battled with the clouds and won.

She pushed the door closed.

"Come in," he said, standing.

"Sit. Please." She took a chair.

"It can't be that bad," Jacobs said, returning heavily to his chair and concentrating on her.

"Does it show?"

He nodded.

"Are you familiar with anagrams?"

"An anagram is a word made by rearranging the letters of another word."

"That's what I feel I'm doing. Only I'm working with events. I'm trying to create the bombing you had the other day from other bombings that have come before. Anagrams can be a game as well. When you play it as a game there is that moment when you are looking at all the letters and suddenly a word jumps out at you. That happened to me today, only when I put it all together, it became a puzzle again. May I try it out on you?"

"You have my undivided attention."

"I read through all the computer printouts—all the articles—today. I was able to rule out a few more suspects. Our list is growing smaller, thank God. As is typical in this kind of thing, it was the one I was least interested in that ended up the most interesting. I do this every time I research something. You'd think I'd catch on after a while."

"Coffee?"

"Not now. Let me run this by you."

"Go on."

"It was the judge. Remember? One of the items we had on our list was a judge who had been murdered by a car bomb nearly six years ago. A man was arrested, sentenced, and convicted. I gave it less priority. But it's like we talked about, you have to read between the lines. I was hitting one dead end after another on the other leads. Like I said, I was able to narrow down the field. I took another look at the judge. I used his name and searched several databases. The problem was, it was really a Hillsdale case, and *The Herald* doesn't have a computerized database.

"I found it on a Boston database. Same judge. I was able to trace a number of cases he tried before his death. He served on an appellate court. One of the appeals was brought by a John Steuhl. S-t-e-u-h-l. It rang a bell. I went back to my other articles on the judge's death. John Steuhl was the man who killed the judge with a car seat full of dynamite. That renewed my interest in the judge."

Jacobs adjusted himself and concentrated. She was talking quickly.

"I called my friend with the District Attorney's office—the one who gave me Proctor. He didn't remember the name, but he asked a friend in Boston to pull the file and give me a call. I just hung up from that call."

"You're even prettier when you get intense. You know that?"

"Don't change the subject. This is where it gets good, Sherlock. John Steuhl was appealing a case he lost against the owners of Yankee Green. Ever heard of the place? His father died of a heart attack while being evicted when the Green first underwent expansion. You remember that?"

"How long ago?"

"A little over six years."

"Before my time here."

"I found an article on it. The old guy refused to leave his apartment and had a heart attack while the police were trying to roust him. Died before he reached the hospital. What never made the papers was that the son tried to sue High Star. And lost. Twice. The second time, he killed the judge who tried the case.

"My anagram started to come together. I had a man who had used dynamite to kill a judge, and his motive was anger at the Hillsdale mall. So I looked into John Steuhl.

"Anagrams are fun because once you see part of the word, the rest of the word comes pretty easily." She looked to the ceiling, collecting her thoughts. Jacobs could see her fitting the parts of her anagram together.

She said, "As a young man, John Steuhl joined the Navy as a SEAL. He went through all the usual training—it's very rugged from what I hear."

"Demolition work. That would explain his knowledge of explosives."

"Yes, exactly. Anyway, about the only thing of any importance is that he suffered a near-fatal injury on a training exercise. The

Navy crossed signals. Steuhl and his squad were assigned a night exercise to blow up a ship planted by the Navy. Problem was, some pilots were assigned to drop bombs on the same dummy ship. What it boils down to is that Steuhl's patrol was incredibly close to the ship when the bombs were dropped. Two of the frogmen died—I found an article about it in the LA *Times*—and Steuhl lost a full third of his skull. Nearly died. Spent months in a naval hospital. When he came out he had brain damage. Learning disabilities, slurred speech.

"He was finally released two years later and continued psychiatric counseling at a military hospital. About this time his father died. A year later, he blew up the judge. Police were baffled until a series of notes led them to Steuhl."

"Notes!"

"Evidently, he wanted to be caught. He didn't feel safe in the outside world—this according to his doctors. They sold it well. He was declared criminally insane. His attorney plea-bargained it to second-degree manslaughter. And here's the kicker. They put him in a home for the criminally insane. No parole from those places, as I understand it. That's where my puzzle fell apart. He was our best bet by far. And he's behind bars for life."

Jacobs was anxious in his chair. "Any photos? Did you see any photos of him?"

"No. Most of this was done by database and telephone. No pictures. There may have been some in the papers. I could try and find—"

"Would you, please?"

"Of course."

He stood, encouraging her out of her chair and over to the door. "I'm going to run this by Shleit. Like you said, Steuhl's our best bet by far."

"But as far as we know, he's locked up. Might be smart to have Shleit check that for us. I have a couple of other candidates—"

"Can you leave me the stuff?"

"Sure." She handed him a stack of pages which he tossed carelessly onto his desk. Her eyes stayed with her papers.

"I'll take a look at it," he said, nudging her toward the door.

He bent down and kissed her. "Meanwhile, try and find me a picture of Steuhl, okay?"

"You think he escaped?" When he said nothing, she returned the kiss. "I'm on my way."

6

ALEX MACDONALD TOOK a seat directly across from Haverill's desk and looked into the eyes of the young woman in the photograph. Macdonald was known for his casual air; today he seemed to have a lot on his mind.

He glanced around the office. It reminded him of something from a TV show—*Dallas,* maybe. He wondered if the couch folded into a double bed, and whether or not the bookshelf contained a wet bar.

His normally jovial expression absent, he said to an equally pensive Haverill, "Let's cut through it, shall we, Marv? You gained access to some very private information and then passed it along to certain powerful people. Although I don't want the debt load, I went looking for the five hundred K to make up the difference on the Treemont deal, and lo and behold, I couldn't find a single investor willing to play ball. Imagine that."

"You're overextended. What I did was look into your investment in that development in Florida. It was a fluke, actually. I read in the *Times* that the county wouldn't grant any more water to developers, and I remembered hearing you were into a big operation somewhere down there. It didn't take long to find out the rest."

"So you knew where I stood when we talked the other day. I'll say one thing for you, Marv; you certainly play a good game of beating around the bush."

"We need each other, Alex. That's all it comes down to. I've admired your work for the last several years. You get things done where other people simply talk. I'm cut from the same cloth. My commitment to a downtown office center is a matter of public record. It's going to happen at some point. Why not profit from it?"

"Here's how it works," Macdonald said matter-of-factly. "You put up eight hundred and fifty K, not four hundred. For that you get a hundred thousand shares of preferred, which will give you about a twenty-three percent interest in the downtown development corporation. The extra cash helps me shed some of my debt load and make things a little lighter. If and when we go to the development stage, you pull your weight by having a talk with your friends downtown and working a badly needed tax concession for the project, like you did for the Green.

"We arrange financing through Forest Long's venture group—maybe offer them thirty percent—and get the project moving. After five years—five years from date of completion, that is—I have an option to buy half your hundred thousand shares back with a preset ceiling at ten a share. That returns you to about a thirteen percent ownership, which is what you expressed interest in."

"The details will have to be worked out. The ten-dollar ceiling is unacceptable, but I see what you're driving at. On the whole, I favor the plan. However, as you know, if I'm to be involved, it would have to be silent, so the idea of me negotiating your tax concessions is out. That will have to be done by your people, but I'm more than willing to share my experiences with them.

"We need each other, Alex. You need a partner with ready capital. I need The Hauve and could use some diversification into downtown. What do you say?"

"Let's put it on paper and see where we stand. Since we're such good buddies, we'll split the legal fees whether or not we reach an agreement. How's that for partners?"

"Done." Haverill rose and approached Macdonald with an open hand. The two men shook hands, Macdonald the less enthusiastic.

"To be quite honest, Marv, I don't like the way you operate. No matter how legal it is."

Haverill shrugged. "We do what we have to do. Isn't that right, Alex? It's not always pleasant, but as long as it's effective . . ." He shrugged again. "Let's shake on it. We can work out the formalities in the next few weeks. I'm perfectly willing to make the stock transaction." He paused. "You will make your offer on the Treemont building this afternoon, won't you?"

"As soon as I get back."

"Timing is everything to me."

"Yes. I know."

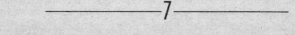

THE BOMBER had problems. Yesterday, the string he had attached to the EMERGENCY switch in the elevator had broken. Later, he had been chased through the tunnels. These two events had forced him to check his tape recordings at shorter intervals. And now he had just heard his *name* mentioned. It was obvious that this woman, Susan Lyme, considered him a likely suspect. She knew about the judge. To his relief she also believed he was still in jail.

He knew, from listening to the bug that monitored Jacobs's office, that Security would be watching all entrances to the utility tunnels carefully. He couldn't enter as he had this morning, too risky. By now they might have a photo of him. Dispatch controlled several hundred surveillance cameras, and late yesterday afternoon the cameras in the new pavilion had gone on-line. They were now being tested. Movement through the new pavilion would be impossible.

Once he made it inside the utility tunnels he felt confident he could avoid detection—and escape if necessary. But how to find a way inside? The only absolutely foolproof way he knew of was through the tops of the elevators. But the elevators would be closely watched.

The elevators were out. If you want to hide something—really hide something—put it in plain view. He decided to try the obvious.

He parted his hair along his scar and changed into blue work pants instead of jeans. He tried moving around his apartment without his glasses. He moved awkwardly and knew it. He left his apartment for the last time. He left the note in plain view. He left everything in his closet. Let them find it. Tonight would be spent in the catacombs of Yankee Green.

At a corner drugstore he bought a clipboard and some paper and carried them for effect.

Thirty minutes later he reached the southernmost end of the Green's parking lots. Even with the cloud cover, the sunlight hurt his eyes.

He waited ten minutes until he saw a delivery truck arrive. Glasses on, head low, he walked nearly a quarter mile across jammed parking lots to the delivery access on the south end of Pavilion C, a long wide alley between the new pavilion and the sports pavilion. He tried his best to look important. He didn't know how to look important.

As he approached, he pulled off his glasses. A fuzzy man-shaped object pulling a hand truck struggled with the service door. Steuhl held the door for him and followed inside.

Nothing to it.

The cinder-block service hall was painted a dull gray. Steuhl followed behind the taller man, on the lookout for the security camera. Blurrily, he spotted the box that was the camera overhead in the center of the hallway, tracking back and forth. Back and forth.

The delivery man wheeled his hand truck into the back door of a toy store and disappeared. Steuhl saw where the pipes entered the utility tunnel.

The camera was moving, but his eyesight was so poor he had to stare at it intently. It seemed to be moving away from him. Now! He slid a large, white, empty ten-gallon plastic container marked VEGETABLE OIL under pipes near the opening to the shaft. He set down the clipboard, stepped onto the container, and leaped up, taking hold of an overhead pipe and pulling himself up.

The camera tracked back toward him. It was hard for him to tell if he was out of view of its fish-eye lens or not. He climbed up into the relative darkness of the utility tunnel.

He was inside. Just like that. Nothing to it.

He hooked the wire stems of his glasses around his ears and blinked several times. Finally, placing his foot on the bottom rung, he began to climb.

8

JULIA HAVERILL STARED listlessly into the mirror. She drew a brush through her full hair, wondering what to do. How would her father react? She knew him well enough to know the answer. She felt tempted to run away. All things considered, it seemed the best alternative.

She had snorted up the remainder of her coke the night before. She hadn't slept a wink. She promised herself she wasn't going to buy any more. How many times had she made that promise? The coke was part of it all, somehow: the self-confidence, the desire to be older, the desire to show her maturity.

She cried hard. Her mother had left her for the same throbbing of flesh against flesh, the same quick shudders of electric bolts jumping up the spine, the tight little convulsions down there, the shortness of breath. Her mother had not had time to fall in love. It wasn't love that had drawn her away from them, it was sex.

Julia moved slowly through her morning routine. No rush. Her world no longer threatened to come apart—it had been torn wide open. The stuffing poured out, like the stuffing from the eyes of her teddy bear that sat on her bookshelf. Her father had not come home. The phone had rung several times but she had not dared answer it. What would she say?

For the first time she saw her affair with Peter through her father's eyes. She recalled her risk-taking with Knorpp: making love on the Green's rooftop tennis courts, in the private elevator, in Knorpp's office, in the penthouse suites. Had it all been in hopes of being caught? Had she *wanted* her father to find them together?

She pulled the brush through her hair, wondering where the next bend in the river would lead. Would he throw her out? Would she be left to fend for herself, spoiled by years of his doting, and his money, his influence? In the Green she had been treated like a little princess.

How strange it was that now, only now, after her insane few

weeks with Knorpp, did she find herself hopelessly in love with her father. Even yesterday, at this same hour, she had felt little love for him, only distaste at his selfish drive for more money and more power. He had seemed like an animal to her. Now, somehow, in his absolute anger, he had showed himself a human being.

She ran downstairs and dug out the family photo album, thumbing through the pages slowly. She reached a shot of her father, taken years before, and gently touched his face with the tip of her finger. So strong and handsome back then. He seemed so complete and invincible. Her finger traced the lines of his strong shoulders. She could feel his hard hands take her chin lovingly and pinch her ever so softly. His life had been so full of success at one time. The photo album attested to that. The pretty wife. The little daughter with the cute blond curls. The big house. A gigantic shopping complex—the third largest in the world—under construction, and all under his authority.

She slammed the album shut and cried again. God, what was she going to do? Run away? She'd been snorting and smoking drugs and drinking for several years now, such a grown-up woman.

The anxiety crept through her slowly. She rubbed her arm with a closed fist. She felt restless and afraid. The house was big and empty. Her father was gone. Her mother was gone. She felt sorry for herself. She wanted company. She called Peter again—it seemed like the hundredth time—but he didn't answer. Wouldn't answer. She wanted some attention, some company; she wanted to feel good about herself, to feel wanted. No one wanted her now. Her father hated her. Peter wouldn't be caught dead with her.

All she wanted was some company.

She ran back upstairs to change. She would get dressed and go find Peter.

Peter had to be at the mall. She would sneak in quickly and ride the private elevator to his office.

She would run away with him.

WHAT A STRANGE PLACE to die.

Steuhl could picture the thousands of people in the new pavilion tomorrow. What a sight. He sat in the tunnel, legs crossed, his foot tapping to the dull rhythmic thump of music emanating from the stereo shop directly below him, and continued twisting wires together. In all he had laid nearly a mile of wire. He had already set his timer for tomorrow at four o'clock. Now, even if they caught him, his plan would be carried through. The timer would detonate the main charges, and the pavilion would fall like a house of cards.

Only if he was successful in getting the money would the timer be stopped. They *owed* him.

His final step would be to connect the end of the detonation wires to the telephone system's matrix outlets, making the electromechanical switching matrix for the crossbar telephone exchange both his detonator and his timer-interrupt: one telephone number would explode the initial charges; another would bypass the timer and detonate the charges if necessary; the third would disconnect the timer, rendering the charges harmless. It all depended on the outcome of his attempts.

He twisted two wire nuts in place.

His escape route would be through the utility tunnel behind Dispatch, down the central utility shaft in C, to the storm sewers that led to the river. The route would require less than eight minutes. He planned one last dry run later today in order to time himself again. Once in the storm sewers, he was confident he would be clear of any effects of the blast, if it came to that.

He pitied the poor bastards inside the pavilion if they didn't pay. It didn't matter to him anymore. He would give them a chance. If they chose to ignore him, like the courts had ignored him, like the judge had ignored him, then that was fine. As far as he was concerned, he had a score to settle: his father's life for two hundred grand.

To hell with them all. They deserved to die.

Shleit appeared to have been up all night. He drank the cup of coffee hungrily, as a dog laps up water after a long run. He had the strong hands of a dockworker; it seemed he might crush the coffee cup if he squeezed too hard. "I checked out Steuhl for you. I'd have to agree; he sure seemed possible. Trouble is, you were right: Our records show he's locked up at the Funny Farm. One of my people is following through on it. I'm on a pager. If he comes up with anything, we'll know about it."

"Any report on the wire you pulled from our utility room?"

Shleit grinned. "I told you the lab boys would come through for us. They're a weird bunch. They work at their own pace, send stuff up to Boston when they need the bigger gear. But in the end, they deliver. They find the evidence.

"The wire was Number Twelve THHN. Nothing unusual about that, I'm told. Typical for a commercial project. We're now certain that the wire detonated the charges that killed the electrician. The end of the wire in the light panel had partial prints from McClatchy's right hand, confirming he was the one who connected it. That much we know. We pulled a nice set of prints from the flex conduit, but they could have been anyone's. We're running down the electricians who worked that area, but it'll take forever, and I guaran-fuckin'-tee ya it won't do us any good. We pulled a smudged set—a southpaw—from the plastic of the wire itself. We compared it with the partial print they pulled six weeks ago when the dynamite was stolen. No match. But we did get a possible match when we compared the prints on the wire to some of the prints we lifted from the top of your elevator. Nothing conclusive—too smudged—but enough for a good tickle. We couldn't find a set of Steuhl's prints on file anywhere. They got mixed up a couple months ago when they started putting everything on computer. Still trying to sort things out. We've requested a copy of his prints and a photo from the Navy." He looked at Jacobs and shrugged. "Why not?"

"So, we're closer."

"We'll get the bastard. The Number Twelve wire had some of the same fibers that we found on the notes you received: a cloth used to polish eyeglasses. So we assume our bomber wears glasses."

"The man we spotted at the elevator wore thick glasses."

"I know that." Shleit referred to a note. "We also found fibers from other material. Samples were sent to the FBI lab in Boston. Their report says the fibers are from a khaki-colored work shirt, sixty percent cotton, forty percent polyester. It's made in Taiwan and is sold by J. C. Penney."

"Incredible."

"So our bomber owns a khaki work shirt made by Penney, wears glasses he keeps in a case made in Hong Kong, and was careless when he installed that wire. He wore surgical gloves to steal the dynamite, but not to install the wire."

"Which indicates he believed no one would ever find that wire, and that means he intended to blow it up all along."

"I'm glad I don't have to explain everything. Whoever he is, when we catch him, we're going to have a nice circumstantial case built up around him. We can thank the lab boys for that."

"What about the magazine subscriptions? Any tie-in there?"

"Haven't heard. It would take some kind of stupid to use pieces of magazines you subscribe to for a threatening note."

"Not if it's someone like Steuhl. Remember, he wanted to be caught. Whoever this is may be trying to help us."

"That gives me the chills," said the big detective. "The crazy ones . . . I don't think I'll ever get used to the crazy ones."

An anxious knock on the door was followed by Susan's inquisitive face. Jacobs waved her in and introduced her to Shleit, who stayed seated.

"I thought you would want to see this," she said, handing Jacobs her folder.

He sat down and opened the folder. His brow crimped down over his eyes and he drew the computer enhancement of the man by the elevator to the folder for comparison. Then he spun the two around and let Shleit have a look.

"I'll be damned," said the detective softly. "Thought he was locked up."

"HERE'S HOW IT happened," Shleit said after six phone calls and as many cigarettes. Susan had gone. "They committed Steuhl to a hospital for the criminally insane. Because of budget cuts brought on by the new tax referendum, the hospital was eventually closed and inmates were divided between a variety of maximum, medium, and minimum detention centers.

"Steuhl was placed in a medium. They kept him there for two of the last five years. Then, eighteen months ago, the facility became overcrowded. Way overcrowded. A federal judge ordered the facility to release a full third of the inmates. The order bounced around some appellate courts for the last year. Roughly eight weeks ago, the release finally happened. Steuhl was among those paroled."

"We still don't have much. We know it's him, but we can't prove it."

Shleit said wearily, "One of my calls was to his former doctor. He's furious about all this. Steuhl is incapable of taking care of himself, says it was right there in his papers. He was never to be released. He belongs in an institution."

"Terrific."

"I got an address from his parole officer."

"Then we've got him," Jacobs said enthusiastically.

"I have two options. I could kick the place or put it under surveillance. If he does have this place wired, the last thing we want to do is panic him. I sent a plainclothesman in to talk with the super of his building. He confirmed Steuhl. He checked for us—Steuhl's not in. I put his place under surveillance. I'd rather catch him before we kick his place. If we don't pick him up by morning, we'll bust the place and see what we find. There's no use tipping him off until we have him locked up."

"It's a difficult call."

"It's my decision. I made it. That's how it stands. Right now we have nothing substantial to hold him on. We could bring him in and he could skate an hour later. If we ever get the damn prints from the Navy and can match them—something like that —then at least we can hold him, if and when we find him."

"It pisses me off that we can get this far and still be nowhere."

Shleit grunted and lit another cigarette. Jacobs went back to staring at Susan's photocopy of the newspaper photo and the computer enhancement of Steuhl. He wished she were still there.

Shleit thought aloud. "Somewhere he's got to have a detonation switch, maybe a whole bunch of them depending on the number of charges he's planted. I think we should bring the dogs back in. They didn't check the whatever-they're-called—"

"Utility tunnels."

"Right. And we have to assume the charge that killed the electrician wasn't the only one he planted."

"We also didn't check this pavilion at all, and it was in this pavilion we spotted him at the elevators. That was an oversight."

"I'll make the call."

"I'll have my people search all the utility tunnels while we're waiting. He could still be here, couldn't he." It was a statement.

"It's a big place."

"Yes, it is."

"Let me tell you something," Shleit said. "There's nothing more dangerous than an amateur, because he doesn't know when to stop. And this guy's an amateur."

11

MYKOS POPOLOV SIPPED his beer, his thick hand grasping the can, his sandaled feet in clean white socks planted firmly on the floor as he watched his wife clean up. "I have been thinking that if the new store is successful, maybe we should start a small chain of Greek Delis. What do you think about that?"

"First I think we should see how hard it is to run two stores."

"Always the practical one, you are, Mother. Without you . . ."

"Hush." She approached him with some difficulty—her legs hurt badly—and leaned down to kiss him. She straightened up and marched over to the cash register to her pile of morning mail, to look through it again.

"What is it?" he asked.

Her instincts had been right. Two envelopes were stuck together. She tugged them apart. The upper left-hand corner read

The Italian Consulate and had a New York address. She felt her heart begin to pound. "It's nothing," she said, her finger knifing open the envelope. She withdrew and unfolded the letter, reading it quickly. Then her head fell forward.

"What is it?" he asked.

Her shoulders shook.

"What's wrong, Mother."

"It's nothing, Mhykloteus." And nothing it was. For months she had awaited word from the consulate, hoping her husband's war service would finally be recognized by the government.

But the letter read:

> *I am sorry to report that the committee could not consider your husband's application for reasons of naturalization. It is our policy to only recognize citizens of Italy for such service.*

There would be no Military Order of Italy.

She turned, eyes glazed.

"Mother?" he asked.

If only there was some way to make him feel—

"Mother?"

Earl Coleman entered the deli pushing a hand cart. He said, "All done. What's next?"

She wiped away her tears and went back to cleaning up. "It's nothing, my love. Nothing at all."

"All done?" Popolov questioned. "That was fast."

"What's next?" repeated Coleman.

"Did you already stock the shelves as well?"

Coleman handed Popolov a poorly written note. "I kept track like you asked. That there's how many I put out on the shelves, and that there," he said, pointing, "is how many is still in the boxes in back."

"And the walk-in?"

"All clean. Mopped it up. No more smell of fish."

"Take a break, then. You deserve it."

12

"She shouldn't have come back," insisted Dicky Brock from his seat behind the wall of television monitors in the dimly lit Dispatch Room.

"If our people had scared her off, she probably wouldn't have. Maybe I should thank the Flock." Jacobs admired Brock's ability to keep the cameras on her. Ralph Perkins spoke into his headset, coordinating radio communication with the sixty guards, uniformed and plainclothed, on duty on this Friday.

"Ralph, let's get a couple of guards at the mouth of A, and also between B and C." Jacobs took control of the Chubb. He entered a command that caused the computer to request and wait for his password.

He now had complete control over the Chubb, enabling him to magnetically lock any of the several hundred doors in the complex. Yesterday, had he had enough time, had the member of the Flock not interfered, this was the procedure he would have followed to trap the pickpocket. Now he had his chance again. He asked Brock, "Did you take psych in college?"

"Sure."

"I remember the rats in the maze. You remember that?"

"Sure. You could train them to find their way out."

"Depending on the technique and bait."

"Right."

"Controlling the doors reminds me of that."

"Hadn't thought about it."

"We can stop her at any exit—force her to try someplace else. Manipulate her. She's our rat. The Green's our maze. Any plainclothes on ground level?" Jacobs asked Perkins.

"No. We have Stapleton on Level Three, but it'll take him too long to reach her."

"Agreed. Okay."

"Here she goes," announced Brock.

The pickpocket, seeing the uniformed guards behind her, turned down a public-access hallway that led to the rest rooms.

Past the rest rooms was a door leading to a service hallway that eventually led to several outside exits, ALL HOURS emergency exits.

"She spotted us," said Brock.

"Stay with her, Dicky. Ralph, send one of the women down there in case she tries to hide from us in the john." He checked the large electronic floor plan mounted on the facing wall, numbers at each exit. It revealed that the service hallway she had entered led to a T intersection that split: emergency exits to the right, delivery bays to the left. On the electronic diagram, emergency doors with ALL HOURS panic bars were marked in a vivid orange, corresponding numbers alongside each.

Ralph Perkins spoke clearly into his mouthpiece, one eye on the rows of monitors, directing the guards.

Dicky Brock mumbled to himself, announcing his moves as he used the manual controls on the cameras to follow her down the hall. He switched the picture on the smaller Emerson monitor to the larger RCA screen.

Jacobs typed several numbers into the Chubb terminal. Each number represented a particular exit. A separate command would now seal an exit by tripping the magnetic lock, or unlock the exit if it was previously locked. Anticipating her moves, he locked the exit to her right and instructed the computer to disable the use of its ALL HOURS panic bar. The screen showed:

EXIT: Pavilion C - # 19 . . . MAG LOCK . . . ENABLED
EXIT: Pavilion C - # 19 . . . PANIC BAR . . . DISABLED

He continued to type commands furiously, occasionally checking the monitors for her movements and referring to the electronic map in front of him for the proper exit numbers.

"She went left," announced Dicky Brock, "heading toward the delivery bays."

Jacobs typed the additional exit numbers into the Chubb, locking doors that normally allowed emergency exit.

They all watched as the pickpocket slammed against the panic bar, expecting the door to open. She tried it again and again and then quickly attempted to open the doors to the right of each loading bay, but the Chubb kept these doors locked as well.

These doors could only be opened from Dispatch when a delivery was requested.

She panicked.

"Got her!" triumphed Brock, slamming his hand on the console.

Jacobs barked to Perkins. "Move to intercept."

"Already done. Check out monitor nine."

Jacobs watched two uniformed guards run down the long service hallway. He felt the amazing power this room commanded. They ran drills like these from Dispatch twice a month. The real experience proved much more exciting. Even exhilarating.

On the larger RCA monitor he saw her slam into the ALL HOURS panic bar on another exit. It warned in large orange letters that an alarm would sound if used. She rammed the panic bar several times and appeared to read the ALL HOURS EXIT sticker again. Her lips were moving.

"I wish we had sound," Jacobs commented.

She hit the panic bar again with all her strength.

Jacobs smiled.

13

AT THE SAME TIME that Julia Haverill arrived at Yankee Green, hiding herself under the large brim of a Panama hat, Marv Haverill was knocking fruitlessly on the door to Knorpp's luxurious apartment across town.

His patience expired. He bumped his shoulder heavily against the door several times and it opened, dislodging the doorjamb. Knorpp sat in a chair on the other side of the living room, a drink in hand, a day's growth on his face, an empty bag of pretzels on the floor beside him.

The room belonged in a design magazine. Or so Knorpp thought. White shag rug. Oversize potted plants. A glass coffee table that appeared to have no legs. Copies of *Architectural Digest* and *Gentlemen's Quarterly*. The sectioned couch ran the length of the room and turned the corner. It butted up against a stainless steel end table holding a white porcelain lamp with a bold Chinese character that probably meant something like *love* or *many children*. Oil paintings cluttered the walls and a large bamboo sculpture rose from behind Knorpp, its limbs suspended above him like fingers.

"Come in," Knorpp said in a raspy whiskey voice.

Haverill's acute anger subsided at the pitiful sight. He had half expected, half hoped to fight Knorpp. But there would be no fight. He tried to push the door shut but it would not close.

He hadn't recognized the smell at first, but seeing the spent joint in the ashtray he knew Knorpp had been getting high on grass as well.

"We're going to have a talk," announced Haverill.

"So talk. You caught us. What is there to say?" He hoisted his near-empty glass. "Should I resign, or have you already fired me?"

"Take a shower. I'll put on some coffee. You'll do me no good in this condition."

"I can't move."

"I'll put you in the goddamned shower, if you don't get going."

Knorpp lifted himself from the deep chair with difficulty, leaned against the wall, staining it with a hand print, and staggered around the corner.

TEN MINUTES LATER Haverill had the pot of coffee brewed and awaited Knorpp in the kitchen. They sat at the white Formica table, each at one end. Knorpp's wet blond hair looked greasy. His eyes were bloodshot and glassy. He looked as bad as Haverill himself. They sipped their coffee in silence.

Haverill finally said, "I'm not here about Julia."

"I'm supposed to believe you busted my front door because you missed me at the office?"

"We know about the cement, Peter. You're in big trouble."

Knorpp paled and hung his head. "Oh, shit." He swallowed hard.

It was enough of a confirmation. Haverill was surprised it made him feel better to know. "If we don't move quickly we'll be behind the eight ball, and that'll be the end of it. They'll shut us down."

"Who?"

"Who did you deal with?"

"How'd you find out?"

"Too long to explain. Who approached you?"

"Romanello. He said he could arrange it so no one would ever know. I had to divert ten grand over to his account so he could pay somebody off. After that we would split the difference between the cost of the two grades. I was in over my head moneywise, Marv. I realize that's no excuse, but that's the reason."

Haverill tried to contain his anger. He knew if he showed his true emotions he would scare Knorpp away from explaining the deal. He realized that Knorpp's intoxication was playing in his favor. The man's tongue was loose. "How much?"

"Forty-some grand over the last two years."

"Not money. I mean concrete. How much of the building was poured below code?"

"How much? The whole damn thing as far as I know. Once DeGrassi was off and Romanello on, they changed the grade of concrete. It's done all the time." Knorpp finished his coffee, setting it down with both hands. He tried to pour himself some more, but Haverill had to finish the job for him.

The gray-haired man shook his head in disgust and sighed as he sat back down. "Do you know what they have in mind?"

"I don't follow you."

"They're going to *use* you, Peter. It's Russo's baby. Romanello is Russo's brother-in-law."

"You sure about that?"

"Hundred percent sure. The way we figure it, they pour the new wing out of cement that's below code. They don't tell a soul. They make it look like you arranged most of the deal in order to keep themselves as far out of the picture as possible. Who knows how long they intend to wait? Probably a few more months, maybe longer. Then they either blackmail us or simply let it be discovered that the lab made a mistake. We end up with a two-hundred-million-dollar white elephant. And the damn thing isn't even covered by our insurance. Has to be up to code to be covered. High Star takes a two-hundred-million-dollar loss, and that's all she wrote."

Knorpp shook his head. In the silence the air conditioning seemed to grow louder. The refrigerator kicked on and hummed for a few minutes. Haverill impatiently tapped his foot.

"I had no idea, Marv," Knorpp finally said. "I know that doesn't help, but I didn't see the bigger picture."

"We need time to run some more tests and consult with architects as to how we can get the structure up to code—if that's even possible. It's not going to fall down or anything. De-Angelo's convinced it's safe. But because of the rigid codes, it could be condemned. It could end up in court. In the meantime we have to beat them to the plea-bargaining. This is going to be one hell of a case to try and win. Our only hope will be to move it to a federal court where Russo may not have as much influence. Between him and the Vinettis, we're up against one tough battle."

"Plea-bargain? You mean I have to turn myself in?" Tears began to fill Knorpp's eyes. He hung his head.

"It's all over, Peter. Somewhere inside that pitiful mind of yours, you must have known that before it ever began."

14

BACK IN HIS OFFICE, Haverill studied the glum faces of Jacobs and Shleit. Both men looked exhausted. "So, what do you recommend?"

Shleit said, "The dogs uncovered a dead space behind the wall of one of the utility shafts—"

"Tunnels," corrected Jacobs.

"Whatever. We found all sorts of gear inside. Some of it is stolen goods. My guess is his prints are all over that stuff. The five switches mounted against the wall are not shown in any of the plans—"

"We assume they are his detonators, sir," added Jacobs.

"My feeling is that we stand a better chance of catching him if you go ahead with the opening." Shleit waited for a reaction from Haverill, but the eldest of the three just sat in his chair listening passively. Shleit continued. "We placed two men inside the hidden storage area. When and if he shows up, we've got him cold. If you call off the opening, he may shy away and we may miss our chance at him."

"We're not even sure, of course, that the opening tomorrow is his target," reminded Jacobs.

"But it very well could be," said Shleit. "The man is on record as having threatened to destroy the Green. My guess is he'll try and keep his word. Between his apartment and his storage area in your utility-tunnel, I'd say we've protected ourselves well. Jacobs's men will be watching the various entrances. In order to get inside, he'll have to enter one of the pavilions."

"Toby? Your thoughts?"

"It depends how the rest of the search goes. So far, we've turned up no other explosives. I think you know how I feel, sir. I'd rather call off the opening and have a chance to trace the wires leading into those switches. But as we discussed, tracing the wires could take days, even weeks. And as you said, I don't have a hundred thousand dollars of my money riding on the opening as you do."

"Indeed." Haverill isolated himself by folding his hands over his eyes. The combination of events over the last twenty-four hours weighed heavily on him. Eventually he spoke to Shleit. "You say we're better off not spooking him by changing plans at this late date?"

"The decision is yours, sir. That's just an opinion."

"But that *is* your opinion, is it not?"

"Yes, it is."

Haverill looked at both men. "And someone will be in this crawl space at all times? There's no chance he'll get to those switches?"

Shleit answered. "We have his apartment under surveillance and we have his storage area guarded from the inside. Your entrances will be watched closely, as will your surveillance cameras. Yankee Green has some of the most sophisticated security technology available. He's one man, unstable and carrying a lot of hate around with him. Granted, he got this far nearly without detection. I happen to believe that was a fluke. I don't see how his luck can hold out much longer. As long as he thinks everything is still as is, he's going to walk right into our hands. I 'suspect we'll have him before the day's out." He hesitated. "If you close the pavilion, if you call off the opening, there's no telling how long he'll react. We don't want to force his hand. Currently, we have the element of surprise in our favor."

"Yes, I see." Haverill brightened. "Well, then, that's it. The opening is on. I hope to hell you're right, gentlemen." He added, "Toby, I'd like you to stay for a minute. We have other matters to discuss."

Shleit rose to leave. Haverill offered his hand. "Good luck, Lieutenant."

———————— 15 ————————

BY SEVEN O'CLOCK that Friday night, the entire southwest corner of Pavilion B was teaming with teenagers. All the rides had thirty-minute waits, the food concessions had lines twelve deep. Among the several hundred teens, four uniformed and two plainclothes security guards patrolled. As the uniformed guards approached, small groups of kids would break up and disperse.

Susan had never seen anything quite like it. In her day it had been movies and rock concerts. In some ways this wasn't all that different, except it was so *social.* She could never remember her friends being so social. This section of the pavilion was deafening from the constant chatter going on and the rock music piped through the overhead speakers. For these few hours, the Green was clearly catering to one age level. The kids milled about and moved from one group to the next, all dressed in colorful fashions, sporting peculiar hairstyles, smoking cigarettes.

She had been told the meeting would be over any minute and had left word he could find her here.

She noticed a few girls in skintight Lycra. They looked almost naked in the stretch fabric, and the boys obviously thought so too. The girls found attention wherever they walked.

This was tremendous stuff, really. It showed a side of the mall few people probably knew existed, the complete opposite of the Greyhounds' morning walks. Multi-function structures beneath canopies of glass. Exercise centers, retail centers, social centers. It was nothing less than a social phenomenon. A terrific article.

"Here you are."

She looked up into the handsome face of Toby Jacobs, his dark eyes tucked under the brim of his hat.

"Unbelievable."

"I told you you'd like it."

"This place is frightening. Every corner you turn . . ."

"Yes, I know," he agreed.

"I missed you," she admitted, blushing.

"I've thought about you all day."

"Where do you stand? Will you open the new pavilion tomorrow?"

"Yes, Haverill agreed to open."

"Did the police find anything?"

"Yes, they did. We've set a trap for him."

"Then we were right?"

He nodded. "We wouldn't have found out about him without you."

"In some ways, I wish we hadn't."

"I'm going to be here all night."

"I understand."

"I thought you would." He reached out his hand, and she took it eagerly.

16

THE NIGHT WAS particularly dark, caused by an overhead cloud cover. A light wind blew the day's warm air around; it was getting cooler. The same wind carried a piece of litter in the air, tossing it carelessly over her head.

The lights at the rest area glowed an unusual tint of blue. The map mounted to the small building that housed the rest rooms showed the state of Massachusetts, indicating mileage and exits.

Julia Haverill studied the map, clutching the purse at her side. She wasn't hungry.

She had two of his credit cards, forty-six dollars in cash, and her mother's address in France.

It wouldn't be hard to hitch a ride to Logan. She planned to take the shuttle to New York. She was booked on a Pan Am flight to Paris at one o'clock tomorrow afternoon, which meant she would have to sleep in a chair at the airport or take a motel room nearby.

She was excited by the chance to see her mother. France in the fall would be lovely.

Things hadn't worked out here. Her mother would understand. Mother knew all about running away.

Saturday
August 22

---------------- 1 ----------------

THE HEAD of the bomb squad nodded his okay. "Kick it," said Shleit. Two uniformed cops worked quickly with crowbars and broke open the door to Steuhl's apartment.

The apartment was filthy. Fast-food litter covered the floors.

"It stinks in here," said one of the cops.

The bomb squad gave the apartment a thorough going-over and a subsequent clean bill of health.

Photographs were taken, and then Shleit had it to himself.

He walked directly to the far wall. Pinned there he found yellowed newspaper clippings that mentioned the death of Steuhl's father. The tattered clippings had been refolded dozens of times, obviously carried in soiled pockets for many years.

The closet door was open a crack. Shleit used his pen to pull it open farther. On the floor was a pile of newspapers and magazines and a few pieces of dirty clothing. He moved several pairs of stiff socks and a pair of blue jeans off the pile. The khaki shirt was on the bottom of the pile. Shleit didn't smell the foul odor of the dirty laundry, he smelled success. Using his pen he stirred the shirt until he found the collar. The label read Big Mac by J. C. Penney.

"I need a bag," he called out, and left another detective with the task of bagging the shirt for evidence.

The glasses case made by OK-Optics was under a Styrofoam container for chicken McNuggets. It was bagged as well. Shleit found the box of disposable surgical gloves under the bed. Kneeling there, in the stench of collected garbage, in the glare of the single bare bulb of the ceiling light, Shleit felt a tremendous wave of pity. John Steuhl was as much a victim as a felon. The system had failed him, the very system Shleit was part of.

"Lieutenant."

Shleit looked up. One of the lab crew, a man named Horton, said, "It has your name on it." He was pointing to an envelope taped to the back of the door to the room. *Detective Doug Shleit* was written in a crude handwriting across the front of the white envelope.

"Shit," said Shleit, reading his name. "Open it."

A moment later, Horton held the notepaper with forceps so that Shleit could read it.

WhERe uNdEr The SUN DOEs 4.12 maKe doom??

"Oh, Christ." Shleit looked frantically for a phone. Unable to locate one, he ran from the apartment as fast as his feet would carry him, his subordinates close on his heels.

When he reached the sidewalk he looked both ways and not seeing a pay phone, ran ungracefully to his unmarked car. He placed the call by radio. Unable to reach Jacobs, he was put through to Dispatch and left Steuhl's cryptic message with Brock. He finished by saying, "Tell him we're sure it's Steuhl. We missed him here. He may be there already. I'll be there as soon as I can." He pulled the door shut and drove off quickly.

2

JOHN STEUHL had not slept last night. As a result, he felt somewhat numb. He had spent the night reviewing his cassette tapes that had surreptitiously recorded the goings-on in both Jacobs's and Haverill's office. As a precaution he had checked these tapes every two hours on Friday, but to make sure he hadn't missed anything, he listened again, all through the night.

He pictured himself with two hundred grand cash in a brief-case, boarding a plane for Mexico. He retrieved the handgun from the hiding place and jammed it down into his pocket. It had been there for over six weeks. He trusted it would work if he needed it.

He checked his watch. Now hidden in hardened cement, his timer would be counting down toward four o'clock. Only he could prevent it from detonating the hidden charges in the walls and support columns of the new pavilion.

If anyone messed with him at this point, the pavilion would blow on schedule. He held all the cards.

His stomach growled. He wondered if this was how rock stars felt as they walked out on stage: heart pounding, butterflies in the stomach, weak legs.

He tried to sit still, crammed into a narrow space between pipes he used as a seat and the cement ceiling above him. Below the pipes hung the nondescript Armstrong panels of the sus-pended ceiling in the telephone utility room, Pavilion C.

Not too much longer, he told himself. *By now, they're totally confused, totally convinced.*

He thanked God for giving him the foresight to plant the listening devices in the air ducts of the offices. Without those listening devices. . . .

He tried to think of what might go wrong. One of the biggest threats to his plan succeeding was the Level 2 entrance to Span-ner's Drugs. The second level of the new pavilion could not be sealed as the ground level could be. People could evacuate through the drugstore.

For this reason Steuhl had planted charges at the top of each of the four escalators. These charges could be detonated by phoning one of the three telephone numbers he had placed in the memory of a small telephone autodialer he now carried in his pocket.

He had the entire operation mapped out in his head.

3

THE SUN CLIMBED HIGHER in the sky with seemingly little effort, unleashing its August heat on the protestors who had gathered at all six of the major traffic entrances to the malls. *"Niggers" have rights too!* read one of the hand-painted signs. The unusually heavy traffic backed up for over half a mile from every entrance. Six overheated cars and a stalled delivery truck killed any hope of a quick solution to the traffic jam. By five minutes past noon, a commuter helicopter en route from Boston to Hyannisport reported the mess to the State Police, who relayed the message to the Hillsdale police. Police cars sent to investigate also got caught in the traffic and found that cars were using the sidewalks and, in one instance, even opposing lanes.

The few police who had been assigned to keep an eye on the protest found themselves with a nightmare on their hands.

To his dismay, Jacobs had been forced to reassign a full third of his personnel to try and cope with the traffic jam. He now stood in Haverill's office overlooking the mass confusion below. Even through the thick double-pane glass he could hear the horns.

Haverill said, "We need those traffic lanes open. This has been going on nearly two hours."

"We waited too long to make our decision. They were too well organized. By the time you authorized filing complaints to have them arrested, we had lost the jump on them. We'll get it straightened out, but it'll take another hour, at least."

"Damn. I didn't want the blame on us, that's all."

"I think they realized that. That's why they're on our property, not city property. That's how they got around the need for permits."

Haverill not only looked exhausted, he sounded it. "Walker's a smart kid. He gets everyone all worked up over this housing issue, and yet I have a feeling all he's really doing is drumming up public support for his lawsuit against us."

"Speaking of which, what do our attorneys say about Peter?"

"He's turned state's evidence. They have him locked up downtown. We were able to keep it out of the press, but that won't hold more than through the weekend."

"Did I tell you about Larry Glascock?"

"Who?"

"He ran the lab that falsified the tests on the concrete," Jacobs explained.

"Ran?"

"Died of a heart attack in Cleveland on Thursday night. No one can figure out what he was doing in Cleveland. He was due home for supper. He was our one link to Romanello and Russo. With his death, all we have is Knorpp, and all the evidence is stacked against him. It's funny, I suppose," he said softly, "but it would appear it's going to work out the way Russo intended all along, despite the fact that we made the first move. Some things are like that, I suppose."

"It's up to the engineers now. If the building is tested and is found to be below code then we start looking for solutions. I'm told they may be able to pour some outside columns that wouldn't look too bad. We won't know for a few more weeks."

Jacobs said nothing.

"What about Steuhl?"

"I got a message from Shleit. He was on his way over here nearly an hour ago. Must have got caught in the traffic. He thinks Steuhl is here, or on his way. We got confirmation last night, about one o'clock, that the prints in the storage area we discovered are in fact Steuhl's. We have two men in the storage area waiting for him. If he is here, if he makes a move, we'll get him. Dispatch is paying particular attention to all the utility tunnel entrances. We just have to wait him out."

"It's nerve-racking, isn't it?"

"Yes, it is." Jacobs added, "If I'm not needed here . . ."

"Go on, go on. I'm sure you'd rather be down on the floor."

"If it's any consolation, sir, the people are still pouring in. We're getting a hell of a lot of foot traffic. We had a record attendance, for the hour, at nine this morning. I'm sure we'll have a good crowd even with the protestors." Jacobs was at the office door.

"I had no idea they would have this kind of support. Look at all those people carrying signs. When we were told they planned this, I thought maybe twenty, thirty people. There must be two, three hundred down there. You know what the sad thing is?"

"What's that?"

"There are a lot of people who hate us."

"I'll be on the main concourse, sir."

"Right."

Jacobs left.

Haverill felt the tears coming again. He walked over to the door and pushed it shut. She hadn't been home last night when he had finally gotten up the nerve to go speak with her. He had decided to forgive her, to accept all the blame himself.

He had tried phoning her good friends. No one had heard from her, or, if they had, they were protecting her. He had spent most of the night cruising the town, hoping to find her in a bar or at an all-night food joint.

He had discovered the hashish on the floor to her closet and had flushed it down the toilet. He was worried sick about her. Why hadn't she called? Why hadn't she left a note?

His decision-making had gone to hell. He couldn't think about the Green. It all seemed so unimportant. How could that be? He didn't care about the damn protestors. He didn't care about the new wing.

All he wanted was his little girl back.

4

"WHAT ARE *you* doing here? How did you get in?" Mykos Popolov, busy putting the final touches on his store, tried to ignore Civichek.

Mrs. Popolov, consternation plaguing her aging face, listened from behind the counter.

"I figure it was you who called in Jacobs on us. I just want you to know that the Flock will stay in Hillsdale as long as we're needed."

"I don't know what you're talking about. Now get out of here before I call Security."

"I'm entitled to be here, just like any other citizen."

"The building isn't open yet. You're not allowed in here. Besides, one of your people was caught with a gun. I was told no members of the Flock would be allowed back inside the mall."

Civichek untied his green neckerchief and shoved it into his pocket. "Who said anything about the Flock? I'm here as a private citizen."

"What's going on, Mr. Paplav?" asked Earl Coleman, arriving from the back of the store with an armful of cans of black olives. "He bothering you?"

"Back off, sonny boy, this is none of your business," Civichek said.

Coleman dropped the cans of olives. He stepped quickly over to Civichek and pushed the man away from Popolov. "I work here. It is my business."

"Earl—"

"And if you go giving any more grief to Mr. Paplav, then we'll work this out between you and me, hotshot."

Civichek stepped toward the smaller Coleman, but Coleman didn't budge. Confident of his street-wise abilities, he found himself wishing Civichek would take a pop at him.

"I said back off," repeated Coleman. "We aren't open yet." Still staring down Civichek, he said, "Mrs. P., call Security and tell them we got a problem."

Civichek looked over at Mrs. Popolov and saw that she was dialing a number.

"You make trouble, you get trouble," Civichek told Popolov.

"Same goes for you, hotshot," said an unwavering Earl Coleman.

Civichek grunted. "I'll see you later," he told Coleman, and left the store.

"You didn't have to do that," insisted Popolov. "You could have gotten yourself hurt."

"Just protecting my own interests, Mr. P. Can't get paid if I don't have a boss." He stooped down and retrieved the fallen cans.

The Popolovs' eyes caught just as Mrs. Popolov hung up the phone. She nodded her head, looking over at Coleman and back to her husband. She smiled.

5

"YOU RESPONSIBLE for this squeeze play?" were the first words out of Chester Mann's mouth as he sat down in a chair facing Haverill's large desk.

"Don't know what you're talking about, Chester."

"I wish I could believe that. I'll play along for the sake of expediency. Alex Macdonald has met the price the Treemonts set on our building. We have two options. We can see our lease through—it lasts another fourteen months—or we can pack it up and move now. If we stay, we have to tolerate construction on three sides for the rest of our lease. The plans have been sitting on Macdonald's desk for a year. A contractor's all lined up. They break ground in less than a week. It'll kill the business. There's really no choice at all."

"To answer your question, Chester, I wasn't involved. But if I said I was sorry, I'd be less than honest. Does this mean we might work out an arrangement after all?"

Mann rubbed his forehead. "This is something of a shock. The Treemonts have had our building overpriced ever since Macdonald started snatching up pieces of our block. It's priced so damn high, even we steered clear. Now, all of a sudden, Macdonald agrees to their asking price and I hear they'll close the deal Monday. How do you like that? We can stay, but with jackhammers and Cats working behind us, how many people are going to shop?"

"We have a nice space in our new wing. I'm about to go downstairs and wax philosophical for our adoring crowds. Come with me. Mentioning that The Hauve plans on moving in would certainly be welcome news, and the attention of the media can't hurt."

"Are we still talking about the same figures I have back on my desk? Peter's offer of August twelfth, minus the twenty percent you agreed to come down?"

"Let me see. . . ." Haverill searched his files and pulled out a copy of the letter. He put on his reading glasses and reviewed it carefully. "That looks about right to me." He placed the letter down where Mann could see it.

After Mann had reread the letter he said, "Will a handshake do for now?"

Haverill smiled warmly. "You bet it will." He rose and the two men shook hands. "Have you ever been on TV, Chester?"

Mann blushed, uncharacteristically. "No, I haven't."

"Look over at the cameras and keep smiling. That's all there is to it." Haverill came around his desk. "Welcome aboard."

THE LINES, eight to ten people wide, stretched for a hundred yards from every entrance. Dicky Brock, in Dispatch, reported by walkie-talkie that the estimated head count in the parking lot had swelled to two thousand. Jacobs knew another thousand to fifteen hundred had already jammed the Atrium in Pavilion C, awaiting the opening of the doors there as well. Total attendance of the entire mall at this moment pushed eighteen thousand—a record.

Jacobs knew that most people would be at the opening ceremonies of the new wing and the drawing for the lottery prize. The two hundred thousand dollars in cash had arrived fifteen minutes earlier, under security and police escort—and much fanfare, Jacobs thought—and was now on display in a well-guarded Plexiglas case.

Jacobs had spent the last ten minutes making rounds. Everything appeared to be in order—except his nerves. He checked one last time with Brock. Still no sign of Steuhl. Still no attempt on anyone's part to enter the discovered dead space in the sublevel tunnel below the new wing. He began to wonder if they had the wrong suspect again. He felt uncomfortable okaying the opening of the doors and stalled a few more minutes as he continued his rounds.

The three soap-opera stars and the baseball player arrived on the podium right on time, press agents waiting in the wings.

Everything set.

FunWorld would open as planned.

He spotted Haverill and Mann from a distance. They ascended the platform's steps and sat down side by side. Jacobs wondered what that was all about.

A technician blew into the lone microphone, causing a wind sound to swoosh through the cavernous structure.

"It's time," he called up to Haverill. "You all set?"

"All set."

Jacobs nodded, shifting the hat on his head up his brow. He unclipped and spoke into the walkie-talkie's handset. "Dicky, give me all units."

A moment later, Brock's thinned voice said through Jacobs's hidden earpiece, "Go ahead, T.J."

"All units, this is Jacobs. We're about to open. Any problems down-line please report now." He waited a full fifteen seconds for any reports. "Dispatch, are we go?"

"All set."

Jacobs paused, looking once around the empty building. "Okay, Dicky."

Brock typed the commands into the Chubb computer to release the magnetic locks on all doors at each entrance. He watched on a monitor as one of the female guards pushed against a single door between the new pavilion and the Atrium entrance, signaling the crowd that it was time.

Jacobs winced at the alarming flood of people that heaved through the doors. Squeals of awe and unsolicited applause rose above the high-pitched murmurings of excited spectators as eager eyes delighted in the sights before them; cheering crowds surged forward toward the huge roller coaster from all directions.

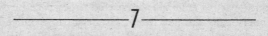

7

LAURA HAFF and Sam Shole each clutched a child, Keze in Laura's arms and the older Shelly reluctantly in Sam's. Neither had expected this many people. It bordered on the frightening. Sam shouted to Laura, "Once we move through the entrance and into the new wing it'll get better."

"I hope so," she yelled back. The crowd was beginning to separate them. Shelly called out for her mother. Laura turned in time to see Sam elicit a smile from her.

As Sam had expected, once they were propelled through the doors by the surging crowds, the vastness of the new pavilion absorbed the numbers easily and Laura's paranoia subsided.

Sam immediately bought each girl a helium balloon advertising FunWorld. The balloons cost a dollar apiece. Laura tied Keze's onto a belt loop. Shelly gripped hers tightly in her hand at Sam's instruction.

"How about a ride on the Saucer?" Sam asked Shelly.

"Sure!"

Laura Haff smiled, her eyes sparkling. Contentment at last. Sam was clearly enjoying the children, and she couldn't help but notice that Shelly had wrapped her arm more tightly around Sam's strong shoulders and neck. Her daughter turned to face her and whispered loudly, "This guy is neat, Mommy."

Laura caught the grin on Sam's face. Looking him in the eye, she said, "I know."

8

"LADIES AND GENTLEMEN, welcome to the grand opening of Stage Three of the Yankee Green Shopping Center." The strident voice was that of pudgy Lloyd Beggs, a public relations director for Haverill's High Star Redevelopment Partners. "This is the first time New England has seen a shopping environment of this magnitude. We hope everyone here will take note of the large variety of rides, the new stores which cater to your every need, and the fine food. . . ."

Jacobs focused on the crowd, his eyes searching for Les Civichek, his ears ignoring Beggs's dribble. Now that Mrs. Popolov had called in a complaint, Civichek could be thrown out, neckerchief or not. Jacobs had arranged for a number of his guards, both plainclothes and uniformed, to head off Civichek. Concerned over the fact that Civichek enjoyed publicity, Jacobs hoped he could get the young tough out of the mall without an incident.

He eased his way through the crowd and reached the northeast escalator that connected to the pavilion's upper concourse. As he was lifted up above the crowd, he checked again with Dispatch, making sure an accurate head count was being kept. Fire laws restricted attendance in this wing to five thousand five hundred and forty-one people. It was estimated that seven hundred and fifty-five worked as employees of the various stores. Another thirty ran the rides. Six of his guards—two at every entrance— were attempting to keep track of the influx of patrons, using small hand-held counters.

Looking down into the thick crowds, Jacobs wondered if they wouldn't be smart to mag-lock the doors temporarily until they could take a better head count.

The overweight woman in front of him smelled like a gymnasium and spoke with a voice that could shatter glass. Her husband had not wanted to come here, she explained to an equally unattractive woman at her side, that is, she continued, until he found out about the Hobby Shop, located in Toys of the World. A fan of model planes and rockets, he had gone off and she had lost him. Now, amid the swarming crowds, she was attempting to find her way to the Hobby Shop herself. Jacobs leaned forward and informed her that the shop was below, on the ground floor, behind the roller coaster. She told him it was none of his business, but as they reached the second level she stepped off, turned abruptly like a trained circus bear, and stepped onto the escalator headed back down.

"If I have my figures right," explained Dicky Brock's voice over the walkie-talkie earpiece, "we've peaked at a total attendance of four nine eight six, including all employees, so we're within the limit." The crowd had settled in to the festivities and rides on the ground floor, which made the building look dangerously overcrowded. Levels 2 and 3 had yet to see their share of the large crowds, which were just now finding their way up the escalators.

Jacobs caught up to Civichek and a few of his Flock, motioning his own guards back at the same time. "Mr. Civichek,"

Jacobs said formally, "I have been asked to expel you from the Yankee Green."

"I'm not here in any official capacity."

"Nonetheless, we received a complaint."

"That's bullshit."

"We have several options open, you and I. You can leave peacefully, which will better influence our decision to readmit you. You can put up a struggle, and my people will subdue you. Or you can put up a struggle and the police will subdue you."

"That won't make you look too good on TV, will it?"

"Fortunately, Mr. Civichek, my job doesn't involve 'looks,' only safety and security. Whichever way you decide it should go is just fine with me and my people. However, I should warn you that we will press charges. And if media people are involved, I will explain that we detained a member of the Flock yesterday who had in his possession a concealed and unregistered firearm." He added slowly, "These are the same charges, if I'm not mistaken, that were nearly brought against you in Maine. The choice is yours."

Color drained from Civichek's normally unwavering face. "Okay. Okay. I'm gone." He turned. "But this is bullshit, and I'll be back."

9

IN THE TELEPHONE utility room of Sub-level 2, Pavilion C, John Steuhl connected the three pairs of wires that ran from the phones in Dispatch to the three matrix switches on the crossbar exchange. At the same time he disconnected the one incoming pair at the top of the second line. Now, only the phone in Dispatch could call up the detonator and override the timer he had set. This eliminated the chance of a misdialed number causing the charges to explode.

He carefully taped the thin wires to the trunk line of pairs, so that even if on the off chance someone inspected this area today, nothing would appear out of the ordinary.

It seemed so strange to Steuhl to finally be doing this.

But the dry run had been yesterday. Today was today. He adjusted his thick glasses, squinting to read the face on his watch. Only minutes to go. He had to hurry now. Timing was everything.

He climbed up the pipes toward the darkened utility tunnel overhead, following the phone trunk and electrical conduits as he went.

He reached the mouth of the tunnel, tucked low, and went scuffling inside.

Twenty yards into this tunnel he arrived at an intersection with a utility shaft, running vertically, that serviced the east side of Pavilion C.

He knew from his cassette tapes that several guards awaited him at his hidden storage area below the pavilion. But he had set up the switches on the wall as a diversion. They ran nowhere. He had no intention of being anywhere near the storage area. His destination was directly overhead.

At the top of this shaft, he went down another utility tunnel to the backside of the wall to the Security Dispatch Control Center and the all-important Chubb computer. He could hear their voices on the other side of the wall. The trick was keeping the bolt absolutely still as he unscrewed the nut. The back of the large electronic map of the mall was woven with tiny wires, each leading to a different LCD.

He knew from his nearly fifteen months of study at the penitentiary that one of the RAM disks in the Chubb computer ran the map. The dispatcher could call up any one of the floor plans to any level of any pavilion with a single keystroke. The map measured four feet by four feet and was mounted on the wall, to the right of the monitors, out of the way of the Chubb.

Of the thirty-eight bolts that mounted the map to the frame, only two remained to be unfastened, the one on top, dead center, and its match on the bottom. This was where Steuhl had to be extremely careful. Too much pressure on the map at this point and it might move, alerting the two men inside to his intentions. As it was, he had just overheard one of them complain about the scratching of rats in the walls. Steuhl smiled at the assumption, squinting through his thick glasses and working on the next-to-last bolt and nut.

One hour and forty-eight minutes until the explosives would be detonated by the timer. Right on schedule.

He took hold of the back of the map as he removed the last nut on the top. His headlamp followed the motions of his head and lit the area in front of him. He rechecked his work, making certain that each of the thirty-eight hexagonal nuts had been removed. He couldn't afford to have the map stick. Timing was everything.

He removed the handgun and took a deep breath. After all the planning, his moment had arrived.

He pushed forward on the map, sending it careening to the floor. He pointed the gun at the two men and said, "Don't speak a word, and don't move a muscle." He'd been practicing for a week. He waved them a few feet away from the console. "No heroics. Hands visible. That's good."

Brock glanced at Perkins and back to Steuhl. At Steuhl's insistence, Perkins removed his headset and moved slowly across the room. He lay face down with his hands pulled behind him.

"You stay there," Steuhl told Brock, waving the weapon. "I want you to page Miss Susan Lyme. When she answers, tell her she is wanted here in Dispatch. Keep it very simple. Now go ahead."

Brock did as he was asked. To his disappointment Susan answered the page and after a second asked, "Is Toby up there?"

"Come up here as soon as possible," said Brock, replacing the receiver, feeling like a Judas.

Steuhl used the men's handcuffs to secure them to a leg strut of the counter on the far wall. He told them to stay still and kept the gun trained on them as he searched their pockets. He came up with three sets of keys, which he placed out of their reach. He took Perkins's ID card. A dispatcher's security card had high security clearance on the Chubb and could admit him to about any room in the complex. He moved over to the Chubb and sat down, placing the gun next to him and pulling the telephone over. "If you move at all," Steuhl told them, "I'm going to shoot you."

He withdrew the Radio Shack Memory Dialer from his pocket. The device was three inches square, ivory-colored, and held five push buttons. Within a matter of seconds he plugged the autodialer into the phone line between the receiver and the wall. With the touch of a button a number could be speed-dialed. He had arranged this because in the event of a raid on Dispatch he knew he wouldn't have time to dial seven digits of a phone number. The small box would do it for him with the single push of a button. The top three buttons had been colored with Magic Marker: red, green, and black.

He watched the monitors for several minutes until he spotted a woman he assumed to be Susan Lyme walking down the hall-way that led to Dispatch. He ducked down below the console and waited for her to push the doorbell, which she did within a matter of seconds. He admitted her by depressing a button and freeing the lock on the door. She stepped inside.

Steuhl poked his head up and she screamed. He held the gun on her. "Welcome, Miss Lyme. Over here, please." He forced the two men to lie down again and handcuffed Susan to the same post. "All the players in place," he said.

Susan's face was without color. She sat in total silence, trembling.

Steuhl took one of the two dispatch seats, depressed two keys on the Chubb's keyboard, and then entered Jacobs's master password.

He quickly cued the memory addresses for all the exits to the new pavilion and enabled all the mag locks, locking every exit. He then disabled the panic bars to the ALL HOURS doors.

Steuhl watched the numbers of the ALL HOURS exits scroll down the Chubb's screen. Everything was going perfectly. He studied the two topmost right-hand monitors, both of which rhythmically pulsed through various shots from various cameras in the new pavilion. As one reached a shot of a doorway, Steuhl threw a switch and held this picture on one of the small monitors below. When the other top monitor switched to a shot of the new pavilion's northeast escalator, he moved this to a lower monitor as well, his knowledge of the system operations total.

In the headset, Jacobs's voice asked, "Dicky?"

Steuhl pushed the black button on the small autodialer. In the telephone utility room a single spark connected the matrix switch, joining two tiny pieces of metal. Down the line, this switch tripped yet another, sending 120 volts racing down the

12-gauge wire Steuhl had so carefully laid. This current reached the blasting caps. Inside the cement, at the top of each escalator, the dynamite detonated violently.

The entire complex shook.

On the monitors they watched as the escalators in the new pavilion exploded silently and then fell away toward the crowded concourse below.

"God, no!" Susan looked away.

John Steuhl looked over at her and quoted, " 'Then Joshua rose early in the morning, and the priests took up the ark of the Lord.' "

Susan Lyme began to weep.

10

FOR JACOBS, it all happened too quickly. He heard Susan paged and curiosity gripped him. Who even knew her name? As he crossed the pavilion's main concourse, through the thick crowd, he spotted Shleit and caught up with him. The two of them, both wearing hats, stood in an eddy of foot traffic and talked quickly but softly.

"He's here," said Shleit, looking around.

"I got your message."

"We found enough to hang him: the magazines used for his notes, pieces of a chemistry kit. And another note. More Bible stuff. One of my boys says it's from Joshua, when they bring down the walls of Jericho."

"Not too reassuring," quipped Jacobs.

"I was thinking—"

"Why would he have left the note there?"

"Exactly."

"Unless he knew you intended to raid the apartment."

"Which means he either has a friend on the force—"

"Or he bugged my office. You mentioned you would raid his apartment when we talked in my office."

"Did I? I'd forgotten that."

"Yesterday. We also talked about searching the tunnels. What if he's been on top of it the whole time? That would explain how he's managed to stay one step ahead."

"You better have your office searched. If he knows what we're up to—"

"Then he'll never show up at his storage area. It was meant to lull us into thinking we had it solved. He played us against ourselves." Jacobs began to walk swiftly, and Shleit tagged along, though he found the pace too demanding.

"Where the hell are you going?"

Jacobs said over his shoulder. "I don't like the feel of it. A friend of mine was just paged. It doesn't add up. No one's answering my walkie-talkie calls. Something's wrong in Dispatch. I'm heading up there."

"I'm coming with you. You don't even carry a gun, do you?"

"No, but I'll be fine. You find Haverill, explain the situation. Tell him we need to evacuate immediately."

"But do we?"

"Do we?" Jacobs repeated.

"I don't know."

"Until we find him, everyone here is at risk."

"I agree. We evacuate. I'll tell Haverill."

"Yes. He'll listen to you. Give me a minute, and then call Dispatch."

"Right."

Jacobs dodged through the crowd, more frantic with each step. He remembered Brock's complaints of hearing rats in walls. How could he have been so stupid? Dispatch offered complete control over the mall; he had told Susan as much only the other day. He broke into a run as he saw people struggling to open the doors to Pavilion C. "Dicky, come in," he said into his walkie-talkie. The doors were mag-locked.

The doors were mag-locked!

11

THE EXPLOSION ERUPTED behind him. As the escalators fell the earth seemed to shake. Hundreds of people dove to the floor. A young girl released her balloon and it raced toward the skylight. A momentary beat of absolute silence followed the explosions, and then it seemed that everyone screamed at once. People surged toward the exits, finding no escape. Mass hysteria swept through the crowd.

"Dicky!"

Why had Susan been paged?

Jacobs pressed the button on the handset again and yelled above the roar of the crowd, "Dicky? Dicky?" He shielded his eyes and ran straight toward the origin of the blast: the escalators. All four had been blown clear of the second level. The injured were scattered about in droves. Children cried and screamed. He looked up: on Level 2 hundreds of people raced frantically toward Spanner's Drugs at the north end and found escape through the open entrance.

Seeing this, Jacobs immediately understood why the escalators had been blown. Steuhl had just taken the pavilion—and everyone on Level 1—hostage.

SECONDS BEFORE the explosion, Sam Shole stepped away from the bird cages to watch the Giant's Tail take a banked curve high overhead. The ride plunged down its steepest descent, and all the passengers screamed in unison. He didn't like the screaming.

As the explosions occurred he instinctively tucked into a crouch, spinning away from the blast.

In that same instant, he saw Shelly standing *beneath* the escalator talking to one of the birds. He moved in what felt like slow motion, reminding him of traffic accidents and bad dreams. Before him, Shelly stood frozen, looking straight up at the underside of the falling escalator; Sam heard Laura's scream behind him.

He took three long strides toward Shelly, scooped her up into his arms, and dove straight ahead. The escalator slammed down on top of his legs. Shelly cleared the falling machinery, as did Shole's arms, head, and waist.

Huge chunks of concrete fell away from Level 2. The falling debris enveloped Sam and Shelly in a thick, dark, gray cloud.

Laura Haff, surprisingly cool and collected despite her tears, rushed around the fallen escalator, Keze clutching at her neck. "Oh, thank God," she said, reaching Shelly and drawing her close. They embraced. Then she frantically dug through the debris. "Sam?" She dug even faster. "Oh, my God, no. Sam?" The dust was chalky and made her cough. The air smelled bitter, like the fourth of July. The screaming grew in volume. Everyone in the pavilion seemed to have gone mad. "Sam . . . oh, Sam." She spun around, dirty tears streaking her cheeks. "Shelly, dig! Yes, that's it. Help me. Dig. Dig. Dig! Come on." She touched his arm, jerked back and screamed, then leaned forward and worked even faster. "Here, Shelly. Over here." Shelly was crying too. Hearing her daughter's fragile voice, Laura paused briefly, looked at her daughter, and cried even harder. "Oh, God," she moaned, "no, please, no." She reached his head and threw herself forward, dropping her ear to his mouth and nose. Her shoulders buckled in what sounded like a laugh. She turned to Shelly and Keze, her face covered in gray dust and mixed with black mascara tear lines. "He's alive," she coughed.

Keze saw her mother's face and shrieked at the top of her lungs.

Laura continued her digging. Shelly reached down and took Sam's hand. "He saved me," she whimpered.

THE WALKIE-TALKIE BEEPED once in his ear. The calm high tenor of John Steuhl said, "Jacobs, listen good. It is now two fifteen. The rest of the charges are on a timer that is set for exactly four o'clock this afternoon. If those charges are detonated, the entire building will fold in on itself. That should be clear enough. I have control of the Chubb computer. I have mag-locked all the exits and prevented escape via the second story by blowing the escalators. I want the two hundred thousand dollars delivered to me by Marvin Haverill. He will place the money in a briefcase" —Steuhl giggled—"and when he shows up at the doors to Pavilion C, I'll let him through. If anyone tries to come through with him, I'll detonate the charges. He'll need a walkie-talkie so I can communicate with him." He giggled again. "Jacobs?" He paused. "Understand?"

"Yes," Jacobs said faintly, his head spinning.

"If I receive the money and escape from Yankee Green unharmed, then, when I am free and clear, I will interrupt the timer by remote control. No one will be hurt. If I am pursued, if I encounter any trouble at all, I will allow the timer to detonate the charges.

"I have called the police," he continued. "They have thirty minutes to evacuate the rest of the mall and clear the parking lots of people. I am monitoring everything. Any attempt to take me, any approach by the police, and I will override the timer and detonate the charges manually. Remember, only I can stop the timer. That is all-important.

"The Green *owes* me, Jacobs. And I intend to collect. Haverill will bring me the money through the north doors when I say so. And, by the way, I took out some insurance. Susan Lyme is up here with me. You like her, don't you?" Another giggle. "So do I. And I have the gun." He chuckled perversely. "The money, Jacobs. Haverill puts it into a briefcase. Remember, I'll be watching everything you people do. I can see everything from here."

The radio went silent.

--------------- 12 ---------------

THE LOSS OF THE escalators had trapped everyone on the main concourse. Jacobs ran through the hysterical crowd toward the elevators, reaching them quickly. He pushed the call button, but it was dead.

The injured cried out for help. Dust continued to settle. The rising heat indicated the air conditioning had failed at the time of the explosion.

So much to do. So few qualified people to help him do it. He had placed most of his guards outside as a show of force. Others had been reassigned to deal with the protestors.

He sorted through his priorities, his training beginning to focus him. Return order. Establish communication with the crowd. He tried to think how many of his people were inside with him. A half dozen perhaps, though he had yet to see one of them. Four uniformed security guards continued to guard the Plexiglas case containing the lottery cash.

The cash had done this. The cash that Jacobs had opposed.

He spotted Civichek across the way. The man had been headed out of the pavilion when the explosions had occurred. An idea struck him immediately. It would mean eating some crow. *Priorities*, he thought, pushing his personal feelings aside. *Return order. Establish communication.*

He'd seen that charisma at work before. He pushed his way through the crowd and reached Civichek. "I need your help."

"My help? *Now* you want my help? No way!"

Jacobs said, "You want to make people aware of the Flock, right? You want media attention, right? Here's your chance. I need someone to go up on that podium and bring this crowd under control. We've been taken hostage, Civichek. We have very little time. We must get organized. We must keep them away from the exits. I'm short-handed. What do you say?"

Civichek crossed his arms defiantly. "So that's how it is?"

"Yes."

"You've got balls asking me to help you."

Jacobs said nothing.

"Why should I?"

"Like I said: the press. The media." Jacobs was thankful that none of the governors had shown. Knorpp's attempt to use publicity to pressure them into attending had obviously backfired. "You'll be a hero, Civichek. Pardon the expression, you have a captive audience."

Civichek glared.

"I need you," he said. "It's that simple." He felt as if he wasn't getting anywhere. Civichek would be perfect for the microphone. He shifted his tack. "What's the matter? You not sure you can do it? Not quite the same thing as talking to a bunch of bored housewives, is it?"

"Screw you!"

Jacobs knew he had him. "Try to encourage some teamwork

among them, okay? You remember what teamwork is, don't you? Get them working together. That'll settle them down. First thing to do is call for any medically trained volunteers. Doctors and nurses. Keep the communication happening. Establish some order. You'll be the focal point of everyone's attention. For God's sake keep your head."

"Hostages?"

"He's sealed the doors with our computer. He has complete control." Jacobs tipped his hat back and found it in him to grin. "So do we have an agreement?"

"Right." Civichek pushed past him and shoved his way through the crowd.

LES CIVICHEK JUMPED UP on stage with an energetic bound—a gymnast ready for his routine, a comedian ready for the opening curtain. He blew into the microphone and shouted, "Okay, listen up." He scanned the disheveled crowd as he reached into his pocket and withdrew his bright green neckerchief, tying it back around his neck. "Ladies and gentlemen, may I have your attention, please? Ladies and gentlemen!"

The crowd ignored him.

"Hey! I'm talking to you!" he yelled, this time drawing the attention of a few. "Hey! Hold it down a minute!" he demanded, letting loose an ear-piercing whistle through the amplified system. Thousands of heads turned. "Settle down!" he demanded like an angry parent. Anxious people wedged at all three exits turned to listen. "I want you to sit down," he urged. "And I ain't asking. I'm telling you. *Sit down!*" The people closest to the stage cowered and sat down. A wave moved through the pavilion as others followed.

Jacobs pulled his hat back down and hurried to find Haverill and Shleit.

They were running out of time.

13

POPOLOV APPROACHED JACOBS at a stiff and unfamiliar run. He caught up and said, "What's wrong with the doors? The back exits don't work either."

Jacobs leaned into him. "We've been taken hostage, Mykos. He's after the lottery money."

Popolov's shoulders sagged as the full weight of the news sank in. Then he rebounded. "We can use my store as a headquarters. I've got hot coffee going. We can block it off with tables and put my CLOSED sign out." He added, "I've been in this kind of emergency before, Jacobs. I was buried alive in a cellar once with fifty people. We'd gone down there in an air raid. Believe me, you need an operational headquarters." This was the same old Mykos Popolov, a man ready to do whatever had to be done, ready for personal sacrifice.

"Okay, Mykos, your place it is. It'll be a few minutes." He patted the man on the shoulder and thanked the old Greek. They headed off in separate directions.

If there was one lesson Jacobs had learned from Haverill, it was that fifty people working together as a team can outperform any group of fifty people working as individuals.

He had no intention of making this a one-man show. He would draw on any and all resources he had and make the most of every one.

Reaching the edge of the stage he received a preliminary report from the emergency medical technicians: miraculously, no deaths; fifty-two injured, sixteen in serious condition, two critical, one of whom was still trapped beneath a fallen escalator. The EMT said, "Some old guy is over there getting everyone organized. He says we can get the man out."

Jacobs hurried toward the fallen escalator. He spotted Rappaport immediately. "I thought you were in the hospital," he said.

"Couldn't stand the food," Rappaport joked. "Sent my Jessi home when I saw the crowds, thank goodness. That's a blessing.

Got us a little problem here," he said, motioning toward the fallen escalator.

"So I see. Can you handle it?"

"I'll need some manpower. Tell that boy up on stage to send me some volunteers. This guy's in bad shape."

Jacobs could see the pool of blood. "Will do." He hurried off.

A FEW MINUTES LATER, Jacobs met with Haverill and Shleit inside the empty Greek Deli. Earl Coleman helped Mrs. Popolov prepare a tray of coffee for the men.

"Here's where we stand," Jacobs said, reviewing. "Steuhl claims to have the pavilion wired with charges. He has the charges on a timer. If Marv delivers the two hundred thousand and Steuhl gets away, he says he'll disarm the charges by remote control."

"And we're supposed to believe him?" Haverill questioned.

"What choice do we have?" Shleit removed his hat and wiped his brow, clearly upset.

"He has at least three hostages in Dispatch with him," Jacobs continued. "The timer is set for four o'clock." Checking his watch, he added, "That gives us one hour and twenty-eight minutes.

"All the exits have been locked by the computer system. He blew the escalators to keep us from getting out through the opening at Spanner's Drugs." He paused. "One thing's in our favor. He needs the computer running. If he sabotages the computer, the default settings will allow the doors to be opened. He must know that."

"Can *we* sabotage it?" Shleit wondered.

"Not without being inside Dispatch."

"Can't we cut the power or something?"

"Too many backup systems. Any attempt to mess with the backups sounds an alarm in Dispatch. He'd blow us up. There's no way around it. We installed all the backups to prevent anyone from sabotaging our computer from outside of Dispatch. The only way to get the doors open is to get inside Dispatch and take over the computer."

"Perfect," Shleit mocked.

"So much for technology," quipped Haverill.

"Can we bust down the exit doors?" Shleit thought aloud.

"It takes over six thousand pounds of force to open even one door. He's watching everything on our monitors. If we organized something strong enough to do the trick, which is doubtful—"

"I follow. He'd blow us up."

"So he claims." Jacobs addressed both of them. "Put simply, he has us trapped. He knows our system's strengths and weaknesses, and he's taking advantage of them."

"Damn technology," repeated Haverill.

"So we give him the money," said Shleit. "Big deal. That seems simple enough."

Haverill whispered coldly, "I should have never okayed the opening."

"That's behind us," reminded Shleit.

"Let's get him the money and get this over with. Agreed?" suggested Jacobs.

Both other men nodded, but Shleit said, "That's step one. Step two is that we set up contingency plans."

"Meaning?"

Haverill listened as the two men discussed the situation.

"If our information is right, Steuhl holds the Yankee Green responsible for his father's death. He may claim to want the money when in fact he wants much more. He may not intend to let us go at all. We have to consider that possibility and plan for it."

"Meaning?"

"As long as we have the money, we have at least part of what he wants. Once he has the money, what's to stop him from leaving and letting the timer run out? Nothing, as far as I can see." Shleit looked up to the ceiling in thought. "The minute he has the money, the minute he's out of Dispatch, we need another way out of here. You follow me?"

Popolov, delivering coffee and overhearing their conversation, said, "I may be able to help there. One time during the war when I was trapped in a bomb shelter—"

"Oh, Christ. A friggin' war story!" Shleit said. "Not now."

"Let him finish," insisted Jacobs.

"We were trapped in a cellar," said a determined Popolov. "The building took a direct hit, sealing us in. No one knew we were down there. There was no one to dig us out. The stairway to the outside was caved in. We only had so much air, so much time. What we did," he said, raising his stump arm to keep Shleit from interrupting, "was we made a bomb from what we could find in that cellar, and we blew our way out."

"You did what?" Shleit asked, noticeably more interested.

"We made a bomb and blew our way out."

Shleit said, "I don't see how that helps *us.*"

Popolov finished pouring the coffee and added softly, "I would guess I could find everything I need to make an explosive, right here in this pavilion. If we could hide my work, I could possibly rig a bomb in one of the walls that leads to the outside. It might give us the way out you were talking about, Detective."

Silence.

"Why not?" Jacobs finally said.

"You were the one who pointed out that if Steuhl sees us up to something, he'll blow us up," Shleit reminded.

"The point is, Lieutenant," Jacobs clarified formally, "you're right about needing an alternate way out of here. Mykos might have something."

Shleit huffed and picked his teeth nervously with a corner of a Greek Deli matchbook. To Popolov he said, "Okay. Look into it. Get back to us as soon as you know if it's possible."

Jacobs didn't think anyone else noticed, but Mhykloteus Popolov raised his half arm toward his head and saluted, a huge smile showing his crooked teeth and bright pink gums. "Take care of them, Mother," he said as he trundled off through the stacked tables that formed a barrier at the front of the store. "Earl, you're with me. We have things to do." Mrs. Popolov nodded to Coleman, who followed the old Greek at a quick pace. Her face tightened with worry.

"So what's next?" said an anxious Haverill.

In the background, Jacobs heard Civichek organizing the crowd.

Shleit said, "I see three possibilities. The first is that Haverill delivers the money and Steuhl gets away safely and stops the timer. The second is that he gets the money, gets away, and lets the timer blow the charges. The third is that once he's gone we either get control of the computer and get the doors opened, or the Greek blows a hole in the wall and we evacuate.

"Either way," Shleit continued, "we need to get the money to him. Either way, we need to have someone in place to get control of the computer. Those two things are the only absolutes I can see. And we're running out of time. What do you suppose is keeping him?"

"He's probably waiting for the other pavilions to clear. He said that was a prerequisite."

Haverill finally spoke up. "How can we get someone to Dispatch if we're locked in here? He's in Pavilion C. It's hopeless, isn't it?"

"Is that right?" said Shleit.

"There might be a way," said Jacobs.

"You designed the security system, Toby. Is there or isn't there a way to beat it?" Haverill's annoyance was obvious.

Both men looked to Jacobs for an answer.

14

"YOU, YOU, AND YOU," Laura Haff said, pointing into the crowd, her teacher instincts predominant, "will help me take care of the children." She glanced over her shoulder at the volunteers surrounding the escalator that had pinned Sam and tried her best to push it from her mind. What could she do? It was out of her hands. It was in His hands, now. *Thy will be done.* "I need some sitters over here. That's good. You too, please. . . . No, bring her with you. Good. Okay. We'll form a circle and sing some songs and play some games. We must soften this for the children however we can. They can certainly sense our fear. Let's get as many children as we can—children of all ages—to participate. You, please. . . . That's right. You too. Over here. Come on. Hi, sweetheart, you sit in with the other children. That's it. Okay, mothers, you can take turns helping with the children or tending to the injured. You heard the man on the stage; if you've had any kind of first aid training, they need you to volunteer."

As she spoke, she turned again to look at Sam. Her stomach twisted in unforgiving pain.

RAPPAPORT AND AN emergency medical technician named George Pepper ascertained that Sam's legs, though trapped and severely broken, had been saved by the fact that the cement bird pedestal had taken the brunt of the machine's weight as the escalator had fallen.

"He's losing blood badly," George Pepper told Rappaport in a whisper. "We've got to get him out of there. But quick. What if we try to roll it?"

"No, no," said Rappaport, himself in pain. "Look at the way its balanced there. If you try to roll it it's going to go that way, and it'll crush him. We'd kill him. How long do we have?"

"Not long."

"Okay. Wait here a minute." Spotting Carmine DeAngelo, Rappaport went over and brought him back to the accident. The two walked the perimeter of the fallen escalator, talking. "Can you think of anything?"

DeAngelo said, "Give me a boom crane, I'd have it off him in ten minutes."

"Right," Rappaport said.

They continued to the top end of the escalator, which was sitting on a chunk of concrete. As they watched, the escalator settled half an inch. Sam Shole came to with a cry of pain and then passed out again. "Oh, hell," Rappaport gasped, reaching out and picking up a handful of the concrete. It crumbled in his fist. DeAngelo did the same thing. The two men looked at each other.

"You thinking what I'm thinking?" DeAngelo wondered.

As they watched, the concrete settled yet another quarter of an inch. "The angle?" Rappaport asked.

"Yup. If this settles much further, the thing'll slip that way and crush him. It won't be just his legs either."

"Could we jack it up?" Rappaport asked.

"If we could find a jack that strong, and if it wasn't leaning so far toward him, we might be able to. But without something holding it back we might kill him trying."

"A crane, you said?"

"Right. Got a crane on you?"

Rappaport pointed overhead to the steel I beams of the roller coaster. "That's over a hundred feet high. Chain-driven, wouldn't you think? That means there's over two hundred feet of drive chain. If we could open that chain at the key link and use the extra hundred feet, positioning it over an I beam as a fulcrum, we might just have your crane. What about that?" he asked.

"I like the way you think, Rappaport."

OUTSIDE YANKEE GREEN, the evacuation continued at a frantic pace. Steuhl had called in his demands to Shleit's precinct. He made it clear that he would be monitoring the parking lot surveillance cameras, and if any attempts were made by the police to storm the building, the new pavilion would be blown up. Traffic became snarled, but the police untangled it quickly and professionally, using a combination of tow trucks and good management. Ten streets were made one-way heading away from the mall. All buildings were evacuated, and the crowds pushed back, over a three-block area surrounding the complex. Sharpshooters were established on rooftops. SWAT teams were deployed, but only on the outside perimeter of the property. Fire trucks and ambulances sat ready, their lights pulsing across the faces of anxious city politicians and police.

An antiterrorist squad was flown in by helicopter from Boston's Logan airport. Its members were specialists in both hostage situations and explosives. For thirty minutes, arguments pro and con were made concerning a surprise attack on the mall's Dispatch Room. The deputy mayor, in from a golf game, held a closed-door meeting with various heads of law enforcement and made an announcement on live television that the city was prepared to wait the situation out.

Forty-five minutes after Steuhl's takeover of Yankee Green— fifteen minutes beyond the deadline he had given them—all pavilions were declared empty, the parking lots were closed, remaining customers were forced from their cars and into city buses, and the three-block buffer zone around the area was fully patrolled and guarded by Hillsdale police.

In city hall there was a murmur of hope. Steuhl had allowed

the evacuation to run fifteen minutes overtime. The director of Boston's FBI described it to the deputy mayor. "It shows he's soft," he said. "We can take him. Give us the chance to take him."

The deputy mayor steadfastly refused.

15

"OUR PROBLEM IS THIS," Jacobs explained to Shleit, drawing on the tabletop. Haverill had withdrawn into himself. "Steuhl is in Dispatch. That's on Level Two of Pavilion C, the next pavilion over. He has us trapped over here on Level One."

"How did all the people on the second floor get out? What if we got someone up to the second floor?"

"Spanner's Drugs connects directly with the Level Two concourse in this pavilion. Its gate is keyed by use of an ID card. Steuhl must have known that, so he blew the escalators to trap the rest of us on the main concourse. The problem with what you're suggesting is that he'd be able to see any attempt to get to Level Two. He's got all the monitors up there. If he's smart, he has one aimed at the entrance to Spanner's. Besides, cameras in the lower level of C would pick up any intruder."

"What about an elevator shaft? Could someone climb up the elevator shaft and reach Level Two?"

Jacobs held up a finger as an idea sparked in his head. "Not the elevator," he said. "The utility shafts."

"What are you thinking?"

"The timing would have to be perfect, or he'd spot it," he said, continuing on his line of thought. "And at Level Two things could get tricky. Even though the buildings connect, I'm not sure there would be a way into the false ceiling of Spanner's. DeAngelo would know. If not Spanner's, it would have to be the rooftop. That's one hell of a climb."

"You lost me."

"Try to call him on the walkie-talkie," said Haverill, breaking his silence.

Jacobs and Shleit looked at him.

"Tell him I'm bringing the money."

"I don't think that's wise," Shleit said.

Jacobs agreed. "Neither do I."

"He asked for me. It sounds like you're going to need a distraction." He waited for Jacobs. "Well, aren't you?" He paused, and Jacobs shrugged. "Well, there you are. I'm your distraction."

"WHAT DO YOU THINK?" asked Rappaport.

"Yeah, I agree." DeAngelo was chewing on the soggy end of a partially smoked cigar, bobbing the stogie in his teeth as he spoke. "Let's see who we can find to help."

"We need somebody who isn't afraid of heights. And he has to be strong," explained Rappaport, moving deftly between the steel struts of the roller coaster and peering upward at the overhead maze of colorful I beams and machinery.

DeAngelo sent one of his crew searching for hydraulic jacks in the hardware store. "Danny," he called to another of his workers. The man hurried over. "Can you climb that thing?"

"Dunno. How high?"

"All the way up," Rappaport interjected.

"Haven't done any girder work in years. None of the boys have. We've subbed that out."

"Can you or can't you?"

"I'm willing to try."

"We appreciate it," said DeAngelo.

"*He* appreciates it," added Rappaport, pointing to the pale, unconscious Sam Shole.

—————— 16 ——————

REMOVING THE MONEY from the large Plexiglas display case caused a great deal of commotion. Shleit ended up in a heated argument with the head guard of the security company, finally assuming all responsibility for the two hundred thousand dollars.

Knowing he was being watched, he carefully placed the money in a brushed aluminum briefcase in full view of the cameras. The crowd's attention briefly left Civichek and focused on Shleit and the money.

When the money was inside, he closed the case and, using the security guards as an escort, returned to The Greek Deli, where Bob Russo and Haverill were in a bitter argument. He only heard Russo's last words. ". . . a blatant lie. Absolutely no proof. You'll be hearing from my attorneys." Russo pushed rudely past Shleit and stomped out of the café.

"What was that all about?" the detective asked Jacobs.

"You don't want to know." Looking at the case he asked, "That's all of it?"

"One small fortune with handle, ready to go."

"It looks so small and insignificant."

"Just what I was thinking. Can you imagine? We're trading this for a few thousand lives."

"We hope."

"We hope." The lieutenant added, "How 'bout you? Are you ready?"

"We've got to coordinate it all at once. The way it works is this. He has two rows of monitors to watch. On the top row of eight monitors each monitor is assigned to a specific pavilion. The various camera shots hold on the monitor for five seconds, then switch to the next shot. On the bottom row of eight monitors he can isolate any of these shots. Any combination at all. He can also use the RCA, our biggest monitor, for isolation.

"We have to figure he has chosen to isolate shots of this pavilion on the bottom monitors, maybe using one or two of them to keep an eye on the area immediately surrounding Dispatch to prevent anyone sneaking up on him. Meanwhile, the top row is flashing shots from all over the complex. No telling which camera is showing at what moment, so we have to assume he can spot us at any time.

"What we hope is that his eye will be on that money. He'll have to unlock a door for Haverill to get into Pavilion C. That will mean his attention will briefly be on the computer screen, not on the monitors. At that instant, we make our move."

"I follow you."

To the upset Haverill, Jacobs said, "You'll have to wear this." He produced a walkie-talkie setup he had taken from one of his guards. "When you get inside C, he'll tell you where he wants you to go."

"Can't I just go to Dispatch?"

"That's not the way he wants it. He sounds very sure of himself. He's going to have you make a drop, I think. Something to confuse us further, give him a chance to escape. If everything goes right, I'll be waiting inside the false ceiling above Dispatch. When he leaves Dispatch, I try and get control of the computer and get the doors open."

"That's all I do?" Haverill asked, sweating, heart pounding hard, eyes flicking about anxiously.

"You all right?" asked Jacobs.

"Sure," replied Haverill.

"You don't look so good," snorted Shleit.

"Nerves." He shook his head.

"What's important now," the detective continued, "is to give him everything he wants and hope like hell he makes good on his promise to stop that timer."

"If there is a timer," Haverill said.

"We have to assume there is," Shleit pointed out.

Haverill scrunched his lips. For years he had been the one in control. Now he was at the whim of a dimwitted madman. He simply couldn't grasp the concept. To him, he was still in charge.

"Two minutes," Jacobs said, checking his watch and speaking to Shleit. "You take my walkie-talkie. If you have to talk to him, adjust the squelch button. It'll fuzz your voice; he'll never know the difference."

"I don't like it. If he suspects we're up to something . . ."

"We *are* up to something. We're playing the odds. It's the best we can do. It'll take me fifteen, maybe thirty minutes, if I can make it at all. We have a little over an hour remaining. We're cutting it close—"

"Okay, I turn up the squelch. No problem," said Shleit.

"Let him do the talking."

"Right."

"Any problems?" Jacobs asked.

Haverill said, "Ready."

Shleit nodded.

"Off you go."

Shleit hooked the walkie-talkie to his belt and jammed the small plug into his ear. He led Haverill to the rear of the store and out into the gray cinder-block hallway. Above them, pipes and conduit ran the length of the hall, entering a utility shaft at the hallway's midpoint.

Shleit was reminded of walking death row with an inmate prior to execution, something he had done once in his life a long time ago and hoped to never do again.

Haverill carried the aluminum briefcase gripped tightly in his left hand.

JACOBS CRACKED the rear door open and peered into the gray hallway. The camera moved slowly from right to left. He pushed the door shut gently and kept his eyes on the face of his watch. The camera made a full sweep of the hall every thirty seconds. He waited ten.

He reopened the door after twenty seconds. The camera lens had swept past the Deli and was now aimed at the backs of Shleit and Haverill.

Jacobs ran across the hall, cutting in behind the constantly shifting view of the pivoting camera. He jumped up and grabbed hold of a strong pipe and pulled himself up. His eyes were on the moving camera, which paused at the far end of its course and then began its return. He struggled to force himself up in the narrow space between the pipes.

The camera continued toward him.

AT THE FAR END of the hallway, Shleit opened a door for Haverill that exited into the new pavilion's north end. As the door opened, the noise returned. Civichek continued to speak to the crowd.

Shleit pulled on the last door, as Jacobs had instructed. It was still locked. He waved up into the overhead camera.

STEUHL WAS HAVING TROUBLE fighting his impatience. He hadn't stopped sweating since he had broken in. The crowd bothered him. The guy up on stage bothered him. But he had played his only card by blowing the escalator. Now it was all or nothing. He had no way to show his annoyance, except to blow the whole pavilion. He saw the two men by the door in the monitor and typed in the command to free the mag lock.

TWENTY PEOPLE JUMPED UP and surged toward the door as Shleit waved. The cop pushed Haverill toward the door and held the encroachers off briefly. "Go!" he shouted.

Haverill tugged on the door and it opened. The loud crowd heaved forward, pushing Shleit into Haverill, who went through the doorway fast and pulled the door shut behind himself.

Shleit checked to make sure the door had locked again. An angry woman cursed and spit on him. "Bastard," she cried.

Shleit wiped her spittle from his cheek and dragged his wet fingers across his suit pants. He met her eyes. "I'd like out of here too, lady."

The small crowd pressed against the door. "What's going on?" asked one of the men.

"It's all up to him," answered Shleit softly.

They watched as Haverill, now in Pavilion C—a world away, it seemed—walked unsteadily forward.

17

THE WORKER COULD CLIMB no higher. Much of the crowd's attention had focused on this man's efforts to climb the roller coaster, though few knew his reason for the attempt.

Civichek saw a golden opportunity. It had been years since he had done any real climbing, but at one point he had been the best second-story man in Boston.

"We're going to give you a little show, people," he said strongly, trying to regain the crowd's attention, his voice carrying well and further amplified by the public address system. He had heard someplace that it wasn't enough to tell people, you had to show them. "You're a fine group of people. Why don't you give yourself a hand for getting it together so quickly. Go on, that's it . . . louder . . . louder." The crowd applauded enthusiastically. "Okay, how 'bout a hand for the volunteer medical people?" Again a roar broke. "And our volunteers with the children!" More applause. He had them with him again. "I'm going to give you some rest from my big mouth," he said smiling and drawing a laugh, "and lend a hand over at the Giant's Tail."

He bounded down off the stage energetically and weaved through the seated crowd, receiving appreciative pats from his admirers. Being emcee of this affair was the best idea anybody had ever had. How strange, he thought, that it should have come from the mealy-mouthed Jacobs. He knew damn well he couldn't buy his way into this kind of publicity. By day's end he'd be an all-out hero.

If he ever saw day's end.

As LAURA HAFF WATCHED the worker climb the multicolored superstructure, she was reminded of Tim. Tim had climbed up high every working day of his life, and on one occasion he had slipped. One mistake, one gust of wind, had cost him his life. Torn by the recollection of the phone call on that blustery day, she felt her throat constrict. She glanced over her shoulder at Sam, covered in blankets. A volunteer now lay next to him, connected by rubber tubing and needles, giving blood that was running from Sam's wound faster than they could fill him back up.

She willed him to stay alive, as much out of her newfound affection for him as out of selfishness. *You can't do this to me,* she thought, choking on her tears.

The children at her feet, happy-faced and enjoying a game of pass-the-beach-ball, seemed removed from reality. While some of us cry, she thought, others laugh.

Behind her, Les Civichek spoke for a few minutes with Rappaport and then began to climb the steel labyrinth of I beams, where the worker was frozen forty feet up, unable to move.

18

HAVERILL FOLLOWED Steuhl's instructions carefully, well aware that a good performance now might get this over with. Steuhl used the radio. Haverill listened to the voice of the disturbed man in the small earpiece. "You will go to the far end of Pavilion C. I'm watching you. Go on. Walk faster. Come on! Faster! No unnecessary motions. No signals. Hurry up!"

Haverill moved as fast as he could without actually running. His nerves were shattered, the pressure intense. Despite the cool of the building, he began to sweat profusely. His stomach knotted and burned.

"Stop there," the little voice said.

Haverill stopped, blood pumping, chest heaving. He dragged his handkerchief across his brow, mopping up the sweat. *Get it over with,* he thought.

"Turn to your right," came the voice. "Again. There. Right there. Now kneel down and open the briefcase. Yes, both knees. Open it. Good. Turn it around so I can see it. Not that way! Yes, that's right. Good. Show me the money. Take it out and stack it on the floor. Hurry!"

Haverill's nerves got the better of him as Steuhl's voice shouted into the earphone. He tore a paper band and a stack of hundred-dollar bills spilled into the briefcase and onto the floor. "For the love of God," Haverill said under his breath, attempting to restore order to the mess.

"Clean it up!" Steuhl demanded. "Neat piles, it must be in neat piles. The money . . ." His voice trailed off.

Haverill looked at the money as he put it in order. What an absurd notion that a box of paper was held equal in this man's eyes to the lives of several thousand people. Money, such a curse if you don't have it. Such a curse if you do. *Dear God, get this over with.* He had not spoken to God in over thirty years.

"Put it back. Put it back," demanded the childlike voice of John Steuhl. "I said put it back!"

Haverill tried to clear his head, tried to focus on the task before him. It was not easy. He felt vulnerable in the immense pavilion. Incredibly alone. He snapped the briefcase shut. "What now?" he asked aloud, though no one heard him.

"Back toward the fountain," said Steuhl. *"Hurry!"*

Haverill broke into a run, the heavy briefcase swinging at his side. It seemed like a full two minutes before he reached the Atrium. "Now, up the escalator on that side. That's right. Keep moving!"

His heart drummed on his chest painfully. His side ached. *Out of shape,* he thought. *I must get in shape. Must call Kate. Put it back together. I know what I want now. I know what's important.*

"I said hurry," reminded the impatient boyish voice. "Up the escalator and turn right. Wait by the popcorn stand."

The pavilion echoed hollowly to the percussive cadence of his hard heels striking the stone floor.

A vehicle on autopilot, he rounded the top of the escalator and headed right as Steuhl had instructed.

JOHN STEUHL GRABBED an ashtray from the counter and used it to prop open the door to Dispatch. If the door shut he would be forced to reenter the room via the utility tunnel, a difficult and time-consuming effort. In his frenzied state it did not occur to him that the ID tag he had taken from Perkins might open the door. In fact, the card would not have helped. Both Brock and Perkins gained entrance to Dispatch in a preestablished time programmed into the Chubb. That envelope of time had long since passed.

He tested the door, making certain the ashtray would hold. Satisfied, he hurried down the drab hallway.

THE MOMENT Steuhl left the room, all three hostages moved simultaneously. Brock stretched toward the Chubb but came up short. Perkins tried for the radio but couldn't even reach the chair. Susan strained to knock the ashtray out of the doorway. Her shoe came within a foot of the door. "Help me," she begged.

The two men saw her efforts and repositioned themselves to allow her to stretch. She clearly had the best shot at the door. Her lean calf muscles flexed with her efforts, toe pointed. "Push," she said.

Perkins adjusted himself and placed his foot on Susan's shoulders as she lay on the floor, and applied pressure. Her shoe came within inches of knocking the ashtray clear. . . .

STEUHL HAD AWAITED this moment for years. His father, though poor, had been a man of principle. He had believed in his right to shelter. Despite the eviction notice, Matthew Steuhl had been unable to relocate his family. Affordable housing simply could not be found. So when the law came to take him away, he resisted.

This was different from the judge. Much different. With the judge he had simply rigged a pressure detonator under the seat of the man's Mercedes-Benz and then had taken up a position a block away. The judge walked out of the building, opened the door, and sat down on the seat. The car had seemed to jump off the ground before disintegrating. That had been easy.

This was different, much more difficult. Steuhl aimed down the barrel of the small handgun and realized that killing a man face-to-face was a whole different story.

Haverill dodged to his left.

Steuhl fired. He saw the man's reaction: a slight stumble, an unavoidable movement backward as the concussion of the bullet threw him off balance. The wounded man fell, surprise on his face.

The money. So close!

Steuhl fired again.

The money!

The big man went down heavily, sliding toward the railing that overlooked the main concourse.

Steuhl saw him lifting the aluminum briefcase. "No!" he yelled.

But Haverill's last effort in life was to throw the briefcase over the railing, sending it sailing toward the concourse below.

Steuhl stepped forward reluctantly and finished him with a final bullet. The briefcase had fallen directly in front of a set of doors. The perfect location for a sniper's bullet to finish *him*.

He turned and ran back toward Dispatch.

SUSAN GROANED with her efforts. If only she could knock the ashtray out of the door. Toby had explained that the glass to the Dispatch Room was bullet-resistant. If only they could shut Steuhl out and buy some time.

"I need something more. I need an extension." Having heard the gunfire, her voice was ragged and tense.

Steuhl came running down the hall toward them.

Susan began to kick and scream in frustration, but to no avail.

The door remained open. John Steuhl reentered the room as easily as he had left.

Steuhl brushed his oily hair out of his face, removed and polished his glasses. He turned and said to his hostages, "It's all part of their plan, isn't it? It's a trap. They expect me to try and get the money. They expect me to walk into their trap. Well, I won't fall for that." He waved the gun high in the air. "I'm in charge here."

The three stared at him numbly. Ralph Perkins made no attempt to stop the tears that swelled in his eyes and began to run down his cheeks. "Don't kill us," he choked out.

Steuhl spun in his chair and slid the headset over his oily hair. Glancing over his shoulder, he told the hostages hysterically, "I can kill you. I can kill them all whenever I want." He stared down at the autodialer.

One button was all it would take.

19

AS THE CAMERA SWUNG back toward the north end of the service hallway, Jacobs reached down and cut the stiff black power wire that connected to the camera's pivot motor. Sparks flew and he tugged the cable out of the way and rested it against a PVC plastic pipe. The camera would not pivot now.

He jumped down and signaled Popolov and Coleman, joining them at the back door of the hardware store. "You're all set," he told the Greek. "If you work at this end of the hallway, you won't be seen by the camera. I'm on my way. If those doors aren't open by three-forty, that means I haven't made it over to Pavilion C. Shleit will make the decision."

"Did you see the parking lots?"

"No."

"I'm told the police and the national guard are surrounding the mall and that they have fire trucks and ambulances lined up."

Jacobs nodded. "Remember. Give me until twenty of."

Ridley Pearson

"If I'm ready by then it will be a miracle."

"We could use a miracle about now." Jacobs went back down the hall and jumped up, pulling himself into the web of suspended pipes. He crawled along the pipes awkwardly on his belly, threading his way between the metal supports that held the pipes from the ceiling. He followed the majority of the pipes as they turned right and entered the dark square hole in the wall. Inching his way, he reached the entrance to the tunnel and swung his large body into the dark hole. The tunnel's lights had failed as a result of the earlier explosion. It was dark.

Only moments later, he came upon the intersection with the vertical utility shaft. The shaft rose sixty feet toward the rooftop utility sheds that housed air-conditioning and ventilation systems.

As he ascended, rung over rung in complete darkness, he caught himself praying.

Popolov was right: they could use a miracle.

SHLEIT TURNED UP the squelch button to disguise his voice and answered the walkie-talkie. "No," he said. "Can't do it," he replied, keeping his response short. He clipped the handset back to his jacket. Steuhl had disconnected.

"What's wrong?" asked Popolov, just returning to the café. The Greek approached his wife, and they both walked over to Shleit.

"He says Haverill's dead," reported Shleit. Mrs. Popolov gasped. "He claims Haverill tried to set him up. He sounded bad. We're losing him."

"Losing him?" Mrs. Popolov asked.

"There's no predicting what he'll do next."

"What do we do?"

"There's nothing we *can* do. He expects Jacobs to deliver the money. Said it has to be Jacobs. The briefcase is on the bottom floor of C."

"But Toby is already on his way. I just spoke to him. Steuhl may know what he looks like. There's no way he can deliver that money."

"Exactly right," huffed Shleit. "No way at all."

CIVICHEK BENT DOWN and said to the worker who could climb no further, "I got it from here, pal. You think you can get down?"

The worker hesitated a second and said, "I'm a little rattled. I passed my limit."

"Can you get back down?"

"Yeah, I think so."

"Hand me the tools." The two men exchanged the wrenches. "Go on. I got it."

The worker pulled himself up to his knees and began a slow and arduous descent.

Civichek advised, "One step at a time." He then shinnied up another vertical strut and pulled himself onto the next I beam.

Within minutes, the nimble Civichek was only a few yards below the underside of the heavy chain drive to the roller coaster's main lift. The wrenches threatened to slip out of his back pocket. He reached behind and stuffed them farther in.

He understood why the worker had frozen. Even for an experienced second-story man like himself, this was rough going. The beams were only inches wide, slick because of the paint, which also tended to diminish the depth of field between levels. Civichek had climbed thirty and forty feet before. Eighty feet straight up I beams was for the American Indian gorillas who worked on New York bridges. Union work. He felt like he was thousands of feet above the ground. With all eyes trained on him, he wasn't about to quit, despite the sudden weakness in his legs. This was his big moment. And he knew it.

He paused briefly to rest, rubbing his right calf which had cramped painfully. Instinctively, he knew he should stop here. It was a Herculean job. Even if he made it up the next two beams, even if he managed to unfasten the key link, even if he could thread the heavy chain across the crisscrossed superstructure, how the hell was he going to find the strength to get back down?

His mind was wandering to his problems. It should have been on the job before him.

He pulled himself up to the final beam and made the mistake of briefly glancing down. At the same time, a good deal of the crowd broke into applause. His legs grew unsteady, danced beneath him, and he slipped, falling painfully to a beam. The crowd gasped. Civichek felt sweat on his palms. He steadied himself and dried his hands on his jeans. He slowly rose to his knees and then stood back to his feet. The crowd applauded again. He could feel their eyes on him. He reached up and touched the key link in the oversized chain drive.

LAURA COULDN'T LOOK. The last time she had glanced over to Sam he had seemed dead, his face pale and lifeless, the color drained out of him. It was torture to have the process going so slowly. She knew that that troublemaker was up there showing off, trying to be the big hero. She'd read about him, seen his picture in the paper. *Sam's the hero,* she thought, knowing Shelly would have died without his efforts.

Rappaport and DeAngelo moved the seated crowd away from the area. DeAngelo had pointed out that something might go wrong, and if people were too close, they might be injured. The chain could snap, the escalator could roll; any number of unpredictable things could happen. Rappaport moved slowly, still in pain from the injuries suffered the day before.

Everyone in the pavilion centered their attention on Civichek's efforts. A silence fell over the hall, broken only by a random cough or an infant's cry. Shafts of sunlight boldly filled the pavilion, catching the dust created by the earlier explosion and causing striking shafts of light to fill the upper air. The heat continued to rise—the result of the failed air-conditioning system. People in the crowd mopped their foreheads with their shirt sleeves. The distinctive smell of charcoaled beef filled the air—a fast food restaurant with broken ventilation.

Laura studied the faces of the children. Even they were watching Civichek. "Children, children," she said, gaining their attention. "Let's play a game of pat-a-cake."

SHLEIT ASKED, "Are you sure that you and the kid can handle this alone?"

Popolov, a headband tied around his broad brow, replied, "Right up until the last few minutes, yes. Positive. Once we have the charges in place, assuming we can find all the materials we need, we'll need to sandbag the area. We'll use whatever we can find."

"This other scheme can't possibly work."

"I'm telling you, you and Toby look something alike. Wearing this hat, with your coat buttoned up, you'll pass for him. Just don't let the cameras see your face. He may know what Toby looks like.

"Toby wears his hat," Popolov continued, adjusting it, "more like this." He turned Shleit around. "See, Mother?"

"Yes. Much better. I think you're right, Mhykloteus."

"I'm much heavier," complained Shleit.

"You must keep your jacket buttoned," reminded Popolov. "He'll never notice."

"Yes, that's good," added Mrs. Popolov.

"It'll never work," insisted Shleit.

"Let me tell you something," Popolov said sternly. "You can make anything work. I ought to know." He lifted his stump of an arm.

It was the first time his wife had ever seen him make a point of his own handicap. She stepped toward him but stopped herself. Perhaps this day was what Mhykloteus had needed all along. How strange that one man's peril can be another's reward.

Shleit nodded. "I still don't like it."

"It's our only choice," said Popolov. "What other choice is there? We're not going to give up, are we?"

"No," agreed Shleit with a twinge of a smile. "Okay, you old buzzard, I'll do it."

"Just remember to keep your head down."

"And you too."

"Yes," said Popolov looking into the eyes of his wife. "I learned that years ago." She reached out and touched him lightly.

Popolov stuck out his left hand, and Shleit shook it. "Here goes nothing," said the detective.

"Let's hope not," said Mykos Popolov. Shleit headed out the back door of the store. Popolov turned to his wife and said. "I must get busy. I am needed."

His wife couldn't hold back her tears. She could sense something final in his words. She threw herself around him and hugged him dearly. "God be with you," she whispered.

"And you," he whispered back.

STEUHL, LIKE HIS THREE hostages, was sweating heavily. With the air conditioning out, the mass of electronic equipment in the confines of the small cement room created intense heat. His attention was split between the monitor that showed the man he believed to be Jacobs walking down the service hallway, and an adjacent monitor that showed Civichek on the roller coaster.

The timing was all wrong. Only forty minutes remained until the charges would detonate automatically, but he still had to get the money.

His escape route would take him through the city storm sewers. Once he reached the sewers, it would be impossible to find him. He organized a route to direct Jacobs to the upper level. He had a trick in mind that would speed up his departure.

He sat with one finger poised above the autodialer, ready to detonate the charges if there were any sudden surprises. . . .

AS SUSAN GOT a good look on the monitor at the man entering Pavilion C, she suddenly realized it was not Toby.

The man in the hat moved wrong. He displayed none of Toby's natural athletic grace. The discovery gave her the first feeling of hope. They *were* up to something. There was still a chance.

————— 20 —————

CIVICHEK UNBOLTED the master key link that connected one end of the large drive chain to the other. The long section of chain disconnected, clanging against the steel I beam and chipping bits of red paint. The chips fell away, twirling like autumn leaves. The crowd applauded.

He signaled the clutch operator, who engaged the motor and advanced the chain a few feet. Civichek spent the next five minutes freeing a band of steel that held the chain against the drive gear and then backing the heavy chain over the gear to give him as much slack as possible. Since the gear drive only moved in one direction, he worked as much of the long chain free as he could, carefully placing the slack between I beams so he could work with it later. He then returned the steel collar that held the teeth of the gear in the slots of the drive chain.

With nearly two hundred feet of heavy chain draped over the I beam that he stood on, he located the end and began the tedious chore of lacing it across the beams, toward the outer edge of the roller coaster's support structure.

Civichek moved cautiously along the thin beams. The chain clattered across the steel as he pulled on it. Strut by strut, Civichek advanced the chain.

His legs betrayed him with the continual twitching of tired muscles. The chain was heavy and hard to move.

After nearly ten minutes Rappaport yelled, "That's it!"

The tired Civichek established a routine. Drag the chain over an I beam, hook the end over the next, inch his way over to this next beam, pull the chain up and over, start again. Loop by loop, he advanced the chain to the far side of the roller coaster's superstructure. Finally, he lowered the chain toward the fallen escalator below. He was seventy feet up and on the farthest extremity of the intricate interlacing of steel beams that supported the ride. This outermost beam would act as a fulcrum for the chain to slide across. As the motor of the ride was engaged, the chain would tighten. Held above the escalator by the I beam, it would serve to support the fallen piece of equipment as workers attempted to jack the lilting escalator off Sam Shole.

Civichek felt winded and even a little bit dizzy.

"That's perfect," shouted Rappaport, helping the others as they dragged the end of the chain toward the escalator.

Civichek stepped forward to rest a hand on a vertical beam and again looked down. The multicolored beams created an odd illusion of distance. He suffered a brief moment of vertigo. He blinked and reached for the security of the beam just ahead of him.

His hand missed the beam. He fell forward in a dive.

Several in the crowd screamed.

He free-fell ten feet before striking a cross strut. Bouncing off this beam, the wind knocked out of him, his ribs broken, he continued the fall. He smashed into the next I beam and the next, unable to grab onto anything to stop his fall.

He yelled, defending himself as best he could, protecting his head.

Off in the distance, he heard people screaming. Like a boneless doll he fell toward the ground floor, striking beams and bouncing clear.

He could vaguely make out the faint sound of voices. Blurred images swirled inside his eyelids. Red flashes of light. Blackness stole in from the edges and swallowed him, removing his pain.

Finally, he thudded onto the hard cement slab and was still.

———————— 21 ————————

COLEMAN CAUGHT UP to Popolov in the hardware store. "What can I do?"

"We'll need a larger container. A pipe bomb will not work. It has to be something much bigger." Popolov stood staring at the shelves in the hardware store. "There must be something."

Both men looked down the aisle. Coleman finally said, "How about a fire extinguisher?"

"Perfect."

"They must sell them here someplace."

A clerk who had been watching Civichek from the front of the store interrupted the two. "What's going on here?" he asked.

Popolov said intensely. "Nothing is going on. That is, as far as you're concerned. Go back and sit down."

"I don't like it."

Coleman said harshly, "You don't have to like it. Do as the man says."

"Okay, okay," said the young man, backing off.

Popolov located stacks of fertilizer in aisle two. At the same time, Coleman found the fire extinguishers in aisle seven.

Popolov read the contents carefully. The third stack of bags read: ACTIVE INGREDIENTS: Ammonium Nitrate. He dragged the heavy sack back toward the rear door.

Coleman stood in an aisle emptying the contents of four fire extinguishers onto the floor, piles of yellow powder at his feet.

Popolov located the paint supplies and took several cans of paint thinner toward the back door.

Coleman caught up to him with the empty fire extinguishers. Together they studied the nut on the top of the steel canister and just before Coleman went off in search of a wrench, Popolov said, "These will be heavy once they are filled. We'll move into the hallway now. We'll work there. We'll need some picks to try and cut holes in the walls. If that fails we'll need some sort of system to contain the force of the explosion—bags of cement, that kind of thing. We'll also need an electric drill."

"I'll get a cordless," Coleman said.

"Good."

Popolov and Coleman moved their gear into the service hallway.

Coleman loosened the top nuts on each of the four fire extinguishers, enabling him to remove the nozzle hardware and leaving him with an empty steel canister.

"A few more things," Popolov instructed. "We'll need a threaded cap from plumbing supplies for each of the tanks. See what you can find."

"What else?"

"Check the toy store across the way, the one that caters to specialty items. If they carry toy rockets, we're in luck."

"Estes rockets?"

"Black powder rockets."

"That's Estes rockets."

"We need the igniters the rockets use and some fusing."

"Okay."

"And don't go directly to the store. We don't want him noticing you. Head over to the roller coaster first. Pretend to lend a hand. We are in a hurry, yes. But we can't let him suspect anything."

"I got ya."

"Go ahead." Popolov studied the empty red tanks. Each was big enough to make a good-sized explosion. He stood one of the tanks between his legs and then tore open a bag of fertilizer. A smile swept over his face.

STEUHL'S CONCENTRATION was focused on the man he believed to be Jacobs. He said into the radio microphone, "Up the escalator to Level Two, and then again to Level Three. Go to the middle of the pavilion to the hallway with the phones and the bathrooms." He set down the microphone. On the screen, the man, head hung, rode the escalator.

It felt good to wield so much power. Steuhl leaned back and sighed.

JACOBS CLIMBED slowly up the narrow utility shaft, a vertical chimney containing a spaghetti of pipes and aluminum conduits. It was stiflingly hot inside. Toe holds in the cinder block, along with small steel bar hand grips, acted as a ladder. The going was slow and difficult, the darkness overwhelming. The shaft, like a narrow chimney, packed with water lines, air-conditioning ducts, sprinkler feeds, and power conduit, was claustrophobic.

He bumped into a darkened bulb and broke it. It seemed to fall forever before finally shattering several stories below. The long time it took to reach bottom gave him extra pause for thought.

Two minutes earlier he had passed the intersection with the utility tunnel to Level 2, which left him another forty or so feet to go. Somewhere above his head was the entrance to the rooftop utility shed, though he still saw no sign of it.

He had already made the decision to try for the roof. DeAngelo had confirmed that there was no opening above the doors to Spanner's Drugs. That meant if he didn't go via the roof, he would be forced to go through the doorway to Spanner's, which would expose him to the cameras and the chance of being seen.

The roof attempt would mean climbing the actual pipes themselves for the last fifteen to twenty feet.

He stopped and rested. If he lost his grip here, he would freefall fifty feet or more. Just like the light bulb.

The shaft was eerie in silence. His breathing was short and rapid. His heart pumped strongly.

He wondered what it would be like if Steuhl's timer went off now, what it would be like to be buried alone, perhaps alive, amid the plastic and metal of a hundred pipes. The thought drove him on. He climbed another twenty feet and paused to rest. In the darkness he could not read his watch. But he knew his situation. He was quickly running out of time.

The decision to climb to the roof was a final one. Whether or not it was the correct one remained to be seen.

CIVICHEK HAD BEEN quickly tended to. A group of medical volunteers helped move him to the EMT medical station, where he could be more properly cared for. He had broken a leg, a few ribs, perhaps a hip, and was suffering internal injuries. But he was still alive.

Marty Rappaport checked the connection himself. The roller coaster's chain had been looped around a strut on the escalator and then bolted to itself. There was no way to tell if the chain would be strong enough to support the escalator; there was only one way to find out.

He signaled the roller coaster's operator, who moved the clutch handle forward slowly. Slack pulled out of the chain. An unrequested hush filled the enormous pavilion.

"Clear away," DeAngelo told those people standing by.

The medic tending to Shole disconnected the second volunteer blood donor, and the two moved away from their gray-skinned patient. Workers moved in, set the hydraulic jacks in place, and prepared to try and lift the fallen escalator. The cement pedestal supporting much of the weight made a puffing sound, and the escalator slipped noticeably.

"Hurry up!" ordered DeAngelo.

"All clear," Rappaport announced.

Volunteers formed a human fence to keep the pushing crowd at bay.

"All clear?" Rappaport checked a second time.

Behind him the video cameras of three local television stations recorded the event as they had since the first explosions.

The initial fear that had swept through the crowd had waned. A group spirit, inspired by the singing and the efforts at the roller coaster, had overtaken the hostages.

Laura Haff's circle of children, which had grown to over two hundred, staffed by mothers and volunteers, reminded adults of the need for optimism. The children, nearly oblivious to the situation, played pat-a-cake, sang, and drew pictures on the cement floor with crayons supplied by the Art Shop.

COLEMAN, WHO HAD WAITED near the roller coaster on Popolov's orders, ducked into the Hobby Shop and quickly located the Estes rocket section, procuring two rocket igniters and a length of fuse. He stepped out onto the main concourse as Rappaport's hand dropped.

The children stopped singing and looked.

THE HUGE CHAIN TIGHTENED and pulled. Volunteers pumped the hydraulic jacks furiously. A group of three volunteers, led by the EMT, prepared to pull Sam from the wreckage.

The metal superstructure of the roller coaster cried out with pops and whines. Additional binding lugs began to work free of the cement. Looking overhead, DeAngelo noticed the falling dust and knew the problem. He hurried over to Rappaport. "We're losing the binding lugs. The whole damn thing could come down if they go."

Rappaport encouraged the workers—"We're not stopping now"—and motioned for the volunteers to push the crowd back farther.

"We're losing it!" shouted one of the workers.

The escalator tipped and began a slow roll toward Sam Shole. Rappaport immediately signaled for more clutch. The escalator's roll was checked.

"He'll have to hold it while we reset," announced the lead worker. The group busied themselves with relocating several of the hydraulic jacks.

"Come on, you bastard," Rappaport whispered below his breath. He raised his voice. "More clutch!" The chain popped across the I beam. *Ping!* DeAngelo knew that sound: a rivet had blown; the I beam was coming loose. "No time. Go for it."

The workers jacked the edge of the escalator up again, but as they did, it began to roll once more.

Rappaport shouted, "More clutch." To the workers he shouted, "Jack that son of a bitch!"

The escalator lifted. Another rivet snapped from an I beam. It whirred like a bullet into a nearby mirror and shattered it. Knives of broken glass fell to the cement pad of the roller coaster, missing the spectators. The air smelled bitter from the overtaxed electrical motor.

"Come on," Rappaport encouraged. "It's moving. Come on!" He closed his eyes and whispered, "Dear God, move that son of a bitch!"

The escalator jerked and lifted.

"Now!" one of the workers hollered.

The EMT and his three volunteers dragged Shole out from under the twisted pile of metal and cement.

"Stand clear," Rappaport shouted, anticipating the chain of events to follow.

Several remaining overtaxed binding lugs pulled free from the weak cement. An I beam broke loose, dangled, and then fell into the guts of the roller coaster. The sudden slack in the chain allowed the escalator to roll forward. It smashed to the ground where Sam Shole had been lying.

The crowd cheered, jumped to their feet, and applauded.

DeAngelo wrapped a hairy arm around Rappaport and gave him a squeeze.

Laura, hands folded in prayer, collapsed to her knees.

DETECTIVE DOUG SHLEIT was wondering just how one goes about behaving like another person. He moved along with his eyes to the ground, careful to keep his face from the cameras.

He moved as fast as he could. The briefcase was heavy.

As he reached the far end of the concourse, there lay Haverill, dead as dead, a bullet in the back. The image haunted him. Would Steuhl kill all his errand boys?

It explained the shots heard earlier. The hole in the man's back indicated a surprise attack. Somehow the briefcase had fallen over the railing—that much was obvious by the dent in the side.

He checked his watch. In a little less than thirty minutes the timer would level the new pavilion. Time was working against them all. The less time, the more chance that Steuhl would simply allow the timer to run out—if that had not been his intention all along.

Shleit reached the top of the escalator and tried to catch his breath. The thought that Steuhl could be around the next corner waiting to put a bullet through him was overwhelming. He tried his best to concentrate, but his paranoia won out. The image of Haverill's dead body—bullet in the back—hung with him. His career had been a hodgepodge of bouts of independence. He had always been a loner, yet he had always gotten the job done. How strange that all the years with a badge had led him to this point —an errand boy with a briefcase, pretending to be a rent-a-cop, four thousand lives in the balance. He had begun with the noble cause of public service; and this act, right now, represented what that stood for. Thousands of lives depended on his ability to perform his job. And a performance is what it was.

EARL COLEMAN CONTINUED his pickaxing of the wall. He had dug out one hole large enough to get a section of the fire extinguisher cylinder inside. His second attempt was proceeding much more slowly. "How much time, Mr. P? I ain't getting nowhere."

"A few more minutes on the tanks. Another ten to sandbag the charges. We're behind schedule. You better give that up and go round up some volunteers to help with the sandbagging."

Coleman set down the heavy pickax. "Good idea," he said.

"We'll place three charges at the bottom to create the biggest force. The hole you made up above should initiate fracture lines and cause this section of the wall to collapse downward," Popolov mumbled.

Coleman didn't understand, but he wasn't going to argue. He believed in Mr. P. "Be right back." He headed off at a run toward the back door to the hardware store.

For Popolov, assembling the four small bombs with only one hand was not easy. It was times like these that he could actually *feel* his right hand, would start to use it, and then would discover its absence. After all these years, his mind still played tricks on him.

"WALKER?" The preppie-looking reporter pushed his way through the teeming crowd and reached Roy Walker. Police barricades held the crowd three blocks away from the mall's parking lots. From where Walker stood, the new pavilion was in full view down an empty street. "Move aside, Eyewitness News, move aside," shouted a cameraman's gaffer, leading the way behind the reporter.

"We've got some down time," explained the television reporter. He was jacked up by all the excitement. His voice was loud and grating. "We have a live feed to most of New England. It's all being taped by the network for inclusion in the evening news. This mess kind of took the wind out of your sails. My producer edited the hell out of you last night. I thought I'd give you another chance. What do you say?"

Some youths behind Walker mugged for the camera, thinking it was running.

Walker nodded, his mood heavy.

"Clear back, would you please," requested the reporter of the kids, motioning with his hand. He hand-combed his hair once, faced the camera, looked back at Walker, and said, "Okay, here we go." He nodded to the camera and counted backward from five. He paused and introduced himself to the camera, motioning to Walker. "With me is Roy Walker, lawyer and activist for the rights of minorities in the Hillsdale area. Mr. Walker, what do you think of this tragedy?"

"I came to Yankee Green this morning with hundreds of concerned citizens in protest of this city's refusal to deal with its poor minority. At that time, it seemed appropriate to single out the plush, extravagant Yankee Green, which in some ways was itself responsible for the displacement of many minority families and the loss of skilled-labor jobs in the immediate Hillsdale area. Our efforts to correct the situation will continue, certainly. But I think I speak for everyone who joined me this morning when I say our hearts and our prayers are with each and every hostage inside the mall at this time. Our needs are secondary to the more immediate need to free those hostages.

"There will no doubt be blame placed for what has happened here today. We seem to be a society often too eager to blame, too afraid to accept that blame ourselves. As I understand it, the man inside that pavilion responsible for all this is a man who feels Yankee Green cheated him. If I've got the story correct—and God knows you people have been broadcasting it for the last several hours," he said to the reporter with disdain in his voice, "John Steuhl used the American legal system to seek restitution for his grievances and lost. That, I think, is the important lesson here. We—all of us—have agreed by virtue of our citizenship to live by a certain legal code. Right or wrong, good or bad, fair or unfair, it is the adopted code of our country. Taking hostages is no solution to anything. Learning to work within the agreed parameters of constitutionality is the way to find a solution for our grievances."

Walker bit his lower lip and then said, "My fellow protesters and I came to the Green this morning to try and draw attention to a problem. In that we meant no harm. But upon reflection, in an abstract extreme, we intended to take this mall hostage. I can see now that we took the wrong approach. We had no permit for public protest. Instead, we stayed on private property, intending to put the management of the mall in the difficult and unpopular position of having to demand our arrest. We *manipulated* the situation to meet our own needs. I see now that this was wrong of us, and I apologize.

"I invite the viewing audience to join me now in a prayer for the quick resolution of this horrible situation, a prayer of thanks to the public servants who did such a fine job of securing the area, and a special prayer of hope for all those innocent people inside." Walker hung his head and folded his hands together.

The reporter handled the prayer awkwardly.

JACOBS PULLED HIMSELF up the warm pipes with difficulty. Reaching the intersection with the floor of the rooftop utility shed, he held on tightly and began to remove insulation that had been stuffed around the pipes. With the insulation gone, there was just enough space to squeeze through.

The huge motors in the utility shed ran noisily. He located a light switch. The room was thirty by thirty. Pipes and conduit snaked along every inch of the walls and roof. Narrow aisles left small amounts of room for repairmen to service the equipment.

He edged his way past three warm steel-housed units that hummed loudly.

He knew the camera positions well. On opposing corners of each shed, cameras scanned the rooftop in overlapping patterns.

The windowless shed held only a single door facing west. He knew a camera was mounted immediately outside the door to the right, under the eave of the corrugated metal roof. It covered the west side of the rooftop in each pass.

Jacobs had to guess the timing of the swing of the camera so that he could open the door when the camera was facing fully north. He pulled himself atop a piece of machinery, up into the corner of the room, and pressed his ear against the thin, hot metal wall of the building. He could barely hear the pivot motor carrying the camera back and forth. He stuffed a finger in his other ear. The motor was too faint.

He approached the door, turned the doorknob slowly, and eased the door open just enough to peer through the crack. The camera pivoted back toward him. He pulled the door shut gently and waited a full twenty seconds. How could twenty seconds seem so long?

When he stepped out onto the roof and ducked beneath the camera, the soft tar roof oozed beneath his shoes. He looked up. The camera continued to move back and forth. He checked his watch and timed it. Since it rotated a full 270 degrees, it took forty-five seconds to make one full sweep.

He looked north toward the utility shed on the roof of Pavilion C. He could just barely make out the camera, could not see which way it was aiming. He kept himself pressed firmly against the wall of the shed, eyes jerking between the camera overhead and the camera across the way. The pavilions were separated by a twelve-foot gap that dropped fifty feet.

Suddenly light sparked off the lens of the opposing camera and he could ascertain that it was aimed due west and continuing to track. The camera directly over his head faced west at that moment, about to make its return swing. He timed the opposing camera until he again saw another glint of light from the lens. There was no dead spot between the fish-eye patterns of the two cameras. They were working as intended.

He had to have a dead spot in which to cross the roof. His only choice was to slow down the camera above him. He didn't dare stop the camera altogether: though not their primary function, these cameras showed a good view of the far streets, and Jacobs couldn't be sure Steuhl wouldn't be using them to keep track of the police actions. He blocked the body of the camera with his hard hand and slowed it. The servo-motor groaned under his efforts. He impaired its movement for twenty seconds, allowing it to track, but not at its normal speed. Now, when one camera faced west, the other did also. He had his gap, a twenty- to twenty-five-second lapse in synchronization that would allow him to cross.

"Hurry," Mykos Popolov said.

Coleman and several others continued to stack the sacks of fertilizer, silica sand, and charcoal. "A little wider," Popolov ordered.

The men continued their work.

Popolov had filled each of the empty extinguishers with a mixture of two thirds fertilizer, one third paint thinner, and a half bag of crushed Kingsford charcoal. He had placed the rocket igniter, which looked like an oversized firecracker, inside the entrance hole of each tank and had snaked the fuse through the small hole he had drilled in the threaded plug used to seal each extinguisher shut. Popolov had used some Super-Glu to seal the fuse in the hole. The threaded plugs had to maintain pressure for as long as possible; this would increase the force of the blast. He tightened each top nut as firmly as he could and examined his work. Combined, the tanks contained enough explosive material to do the trick. If the charges failed, it would be for one of two reasons: if any of the top nuts failed, then that tank would become a small rocket fueled by the combustion of the ignited chemicals inside, leaving the wall like a missile; or if the force of the blast could not be contained by the "sandbagging," then the explosion might not exert enough directed force into the wall, and the impact would be lost, the effort useless.

He checked his watch. Less than twenty minutes remained: he was behind schedule. "Any action out there?" he asked Coleman. The young black man ran to look and returned, shaking his head. "The doors are still locked."

"We're past time. Even if the doors open now, we won't have time to get everyone out through those exits. We'll have to blow the wall."

He looked at his creation. Four small holes had been left in the bunkerlike stack of fertilizer bags in order to reach through and light the fuses. It had taken Coleman and two of the hardware store staff the better part of fifteen minutes to stack the bags in the service hallway. This half of the long service corridor that provided a delivery area for the stores on the pavilion's west side was unseen by the immobilized cameras, and though an exit to the outside delivery bay existed at its far end, the door was maglocked and under the control of the Chubb. Popolov studied the stacked bags of fertilizer, potting soil, bagged sand, and cement. He hoped the man-made wall would contain some of the blast and redirect the shock back into the cement. He said, "We'll give him a few more minutes. If we don't receive a signal, we go ahead anyway."

THE TWO ROOFTOPS were separated by a twelve-foot-wide alley. The buildings connected in only two places: a short skyway at the south end of Spanner's Drugs and a passageway at Level 1. If Jacobs missed, it would mean a fall of fifty feet. He struck out at a full sprint, preparing for the jump.

He counted to himself as he ran, keeping track of his twenty-five-second dead spot in the camera tracking. It was a small envelope of time to work in. Five . . . six . . . seven . . . eight . . .

He reached the edge, leaped up onto the stub wall, and sprang forward like a diver, arms outstretched.

For a moment it felt almost like flying. Then he smashed into the opposing concrete. His strong hands slipped on the smooth sandy surface, his weight sucking him toward the asphalt below. Dangling in the crevasse between the two sheer walls, he dug his fingernails into the concrete, scratching and clawing.

. . . eleven . . . twelve . . . thirteen . . . fourteen . . .

He swung his knee over a protruding metal drainpipe and stopped his fall, his hands barely holding onto the small stub wall. A slight change in balance and he would go over backward.

. . . twenty . . . twenty-one . . . twenty-two . . .

Not enough time to reach the shed on the roof of Pavilion C without being seen by the cameras. He continued to count, waiting it out.

When he thought the cameras were back in position, giving him a second chance, he inched his hands in the direction of the drainpipe to better his leverage and managed to pull himself up and over the small stub wall.

He tumbled onto the soft hot-tar roof and scrambled toward the corner of C's utility shed.

With ten seconds remaining until his time envelope expired, he made his move. There was only one way inside: the vents on the top of Pavilion C's glass canopy. He took four large steps and threw himself onto the grid of large glass panes that covered Pavilion C's Atrium.

He moved quickly up the narrow steel supports like a monkey up a palm tree, ass in the air. Still counting, he reached twenty and flattened himself against one of the huge panes, remaining absolutely still. The camera would be aiming directly at him now.

SUSAN SAW JACOBS on the monitor at the same moment Brock did. Toby was climbing one of the glass canopies. Steuhl pivoted in his chair toward the monitors.

Panicking, she blurted out loudly, "How long do you think you can get away with this, Steuhl?"

He spun in his chair and faced her. Toby lay in plain view behind him.

She continued talking, eyes flicking to Brock, who had lost his color. "They know all about you," she improvised, trying to hold the man's attention. "They know about your accident in the SEAL. They know about your discharge, your father's accident, the judge."

"The judge? What do you know, lady? They killed my *father*. Dragged him . . . they dragged him from his home. All so they could build this piece of crap. This place is an open wound, lady.

This place is crap. Cheats and liars, every last one of them. Cheats and liars with their fine print and fancy lawyers. It ends today. Either they make things right by me or I put this place down."

Behind Steuhl, the camera in the monitor continued to track and Toby disappeared from view. Susan kept it up. "They are innocent people. How will killing them help?"

"Innocent?" He sneered. "There ain't one innocent person in this whole world, lady." He rolled his chair toward her. "You innocent, lady?"

"Keep away from her," Ralph Perkins said.

"You telling me what to do, crybaby?" Behind the thick glasses, Steuhl's eyes looked as fixed and hard as polished marbles, like the glass eyes of a wild game trophy. "You innocent, pal?" he asked Perkins. "You so fuckin' innocent?" Steuhl grabbed the gun. "I bet not." He shot Perkins in the shoulder.

Perkins passed out, blood running from the wound. The room smelled of the bitter powder.

Steuhl said calmly, "If there's one thing this great country of ours taught me, lady, it's how to shoot a weapon. You know what they told us, lady?" he asked, taking Susan's chin in his moist palm. "They told us there weren't no innocent people out there." He ran his hand down over her breast and she cringed.

Brock struggled helplessly. "Leave her alone."

On the same monitor, Susan saw Toby start to climb the frame of the glass canopy. If Steuhl turned around . . .

"You innocent?" Steuhl said, aiming the gun at Brock.

"It's all right, John," she said trying to cool him down. "You can touch if you want. I don't mind." It was the most difficult thing she had ever said.

"Up yours, lady. You and your fancy clothes." He started to swivel the chair.

"John!"

He looked back at her. "What the hell do you know, lady? You're ignorant. You live in your own little dollhouse world."

"The children, John? Do the children deserve it? Let the children go, John." Toby continued his climb.

"Listen to me, lady. The children grow up and they ain't no different than their parents. You ever been here on a weekend

night? You ever seen the *children?* There ain't no children anymore. The children have all gone. There ain't nobody innocent.
If they force me, I'll drop the place. You can bet on that." He
smiled again.

"But they know who you are, John," she reminded him.

Toby climbed out of the camera's view and disappeared for
good off the monitor.

"They'll never catch me. I got this all figured out. Got it
figured good." He tapped his chest. His teeth were urine yellow.
"I'm in control now. I know what I'm doing."

That's what I'm afraid of, she felt like saying.

THE TOPMOST COURSE of glass panes on each of the pavilion's
canopies opened like those in a greenhouse to allow for the vent-
ing of the hottest air, despite the air conditioning. When Jacobs
considered how to reach Dispatch, this ventilation system had
come to mind.

The vent panes in C worked off of thermostatically controlled
screw mechanisms that attached to the interior I beams. At a
preset temperature the vents would open automatically, allowing
the heat that collected in the apex of the canopy to escape. By
midafternoon in August, these vents were always wide open.

Except for today.

Because of the lack of crowds, the combined cooling effects of
the air conditioning and the Atrium's fountain had stabilized the
pavilion. The vents on C were nearly closed, now only a matter
of inches to go.

He couldn't believe his luck. Ten minutes earlier the vents
might have been open enough to crawl through. Now he could
barely fit his arm inside.

None of C's rooftop surveillance cameras showed the absolute
peaks of the glass canopy, so he would remain out of view as long
as he stayed up high. If he couldn't gain access here, his plan was
ruined. Several thousand lives hung in the balance.

He had little choice. He thrust his arm into the gap as the
automatic screws continued to twist. The metal frame clamped
down firmly on his forearm. He drove his arm deeper into the
ever-tightening space, tearing his skin open on the hooks that

locked the vents shut. His fingers groped for the cotter-pin that held the lifting mechanism together.

The screw continued to twist, severely pinning his arm. It felt as if a bone might break. His eyes began to sting. He attempted to lever the large pane of glass open with his arm, but the attempt failed. The screws shanks continued. With one last effort, he drove his arm deeper. His fingers touched the warm cotter pin. He took hold of the splayed ends and pinched them together. The metal resisted. Far too slowly, the ends moved together.

The gap continued to close against his forearm. Sweat streamed from his brow, into his eyes. He grew light-headed from the pain.

He pulled the cotter pin out of the hole, and it fell against the closed screen. He jerked his arm again, cutting it more deeply. With great effort, he tugged the bar attached to the screw mechanism out of the hole in the lifting device. The window freed.

He tied his handkerchief loosely around his bleeding arm and bound the wound. Lifting the heavy pane, he reached inside and tore the screen. Then he shoved his foot through and began to lower himself inside with only the flanged edges of the warm steel to grip.

Fifty feet below him, the unforgiving stone floor awaited a mistake.

SHLEIT HURRIED DOWN the concourse, the briefcase flapping at his side, his head to the ground. Time was running out.

With his head down, he felt vulnerable. Haverill had been shot in the back. He couldn't get the image out of his mind.

He turned down the short hall off of Level 3's east concourse, as he had been instructed. He stopped when the voice told him to.

A puppet in someone else's hands.

Something caught his eye. Steuhl? He snapped his head up in time to see a man—Jacobs!—dangling from the center of the glass canopy.

As he looked up, his face came into the camera's view.

"BASTARDS!" SAID STEUHL, on seeing Shleit's face. "They've tricked me!" His finger fell toward the autodialer.

"No," Brock yelled. "The money!"

Steuhl spun around, picked up his revolver, and waved it insanely at Brock. "You want it?"

"You think you'll ever get that money if you blow the pavilion? Use your head. The *threat* of blowing the pavilion is all you've got."

Steuhl dragged the handgun's barrel along his lips, as he considered this. He nodded and rose quickly from his chair, glancing over his shoulder to make sure Shleit was still waiting as he had been told. He opened the door to Dispatch and once again placed the ashtray down to hold the door open.

He disappeared down the back hall.

Susan stretched for the ashtray immediately, her joints nearly disconnecting. She could not reach it. "Where's Toby?"

"The canopy to C," said Brock, familiar with every inch of monitored area. "He's close."

"Damn!" she snapped. "I can't reach it."

"Here," said Brock, scooting in back of her. She slid farther, her toe now only inches from knocking the ashtray loose.

"Your shoe," Susan said. "Give me your shoe."

JACOBS WORKED HIS WAY down the canopy's superstructure, the Atrium below. Hand over hand, fingers gripping the edge of the girder with difficulty, he lowered himself down the steep incline.

His arms ached and his hands and fingers cramped under his weight. There was no way to rest, no way to support himself other than by his grip on the steel beam. He inched along, trying not to look down, trying not to think how painstakingly slow his progress was.

He had seen Shleit carrying the briefcase and wearing *his* hat. With a high perspective on the pavilion he looked around for Haverill and finally spotted what appeared to be the man, curled in a pool of blood at the far end of Level 2: dead by the look of it.

How pitiful the man looked. How helpless.

The sight of Haverill's corpse drove Jacobs on. He found a reserve of strength and increased his speed down the I beam.

As he finally reached the balconied edge of Level 3, he hooked his feet into the grooves of the I beam and punched a knee into an overhead ceiling panel. He couldn't drop to the concourse without risking being seen on camera.

SHLEIT AWAITED another order from Steuhl. What was keeping him? As the door behind him jerked open, he instinctively reached for his weapon.

Steuhl shot him in the back. Shleit spun and fell, momentarily paralyzed by the bullet.

Steuhl grabbed the fallen briefcase and shoved Perkins's card into the slot by the room marked MAINTENANCE. He entered, headed straight to the garbage chute, and pushed the briefcase into the hole. It fell away silently and then crunched into the bed of garbage far below. He debated following it down—the garbage chutes had hand grips—but he had mistakenly left the autodialer connected, which meant they could stop his timer, if they guessed which button to push. They had tried to trick him. They had broken the rules. They deserved the worst.

Shleit fired his gun, wounding Steuhl.

The man with thick glasses screamed wildly and grabbed his numbed shoulder, diving into the service hallway and away from Shleit's next bullet.

Blood on his hand. Bastards!

He ran toward Dispatch.

JACOBS TOOK HOLD of a sprinkler pipe and pulled himself into the darkness of the suspended ceiling.

Dispatch was fifteen yards straight ahead. His eyes adjusted to the darkness. He would be tipped off to its exact location by the thousands of wires that fed into the room.

In the tight space, he had to lie flat and pull himself along, spread-eagled for support between sprinkler pipes. Light seeped in from behind him.

The pipes bowed with his weight. He worried that a support might pop loose and give him away or that a joint would loosen and spray water out, announcing him.

Voices ahead. He hurried now, for one of the voices clearly belonged to his Susan—one of the voices just up ahead.

He lost himself in the narrow crawl space. Suddenly the voices were to his left. Following the pipes had led him away from Dispatch. He paused to try and get his bearings, his pulse rapid and loud in his ears. The voices stopped. *Where are you?* he wanted to shout.

He continued along, unable to see, dragging his hand occasionally overhead searching for wires. He struck a thick trunk of bound wires. They seemed to run left and back. Turning around on the sprinkler pipes was not easy. He groped to his right, resorting to using a leg while he held himself up above the ceiling panels. His shoe thumped as it struck the next sprinkler pipe over. It was too far away to cross it without risking going through the ceiling. Blind in the darkness, he returned his full weight to this pipe and continued down until he crossed an intersection with a heavy roof support. He guided himself along, hanging awkwardly from the support, which was sprayed with a foam insulation. He reached the neighboring sprinkler pipe, lowered himself carefully onto it, and continued back toward where he hoped he would find Dispatch.

The thick cable of wires ran along the ceiling to his left now.

He felt along the trunk line of wires. After several yards, it left the ceiling and headed down toward the Armstrong panels below him.

Dispatch.

Light filtered through gaps left where the bundle of wires entered the room, now looking like gilded spider webs.

Suddenly, he heard gunshots.

BROCK PULLED OFF his shoe as he heard the next two gunshots. "Hurry," he said to her, handing her his shoe.

She slid the shoe over her own: it added two inches to the length of her foot. She stretched out again, groaning from the pain the handcuff caused her wrist.

"Push," she demanded.

Brock repositioned himself and placed both feet on her shoulders. He leaned against her. She cried out and he eased off.

"Almost," she muttered, feeling her shoulder about to dislocate, her wrist on fire. "Push."

Brock pushed harder.

Every muscle, every bit of sinew in her body stretched to its limit. The toe of the shoe was less than an inch from the ashtray. She grunted with her efforts.

"Almost," Brock said.

The door to the back hall swung open. Steuhl saw the shoe just nudging the ashtray. He raised the gun and fired.

Susan kicked Brock's shoe off. It struck the ashtray and the springed door began to close. She watched, waiting for the click of the lock.

Without warning, a shoe filled the crack and stopped the door. Susan looked up through the wire-mesh safety glass and saw the evil grin of John Steuhl.

Jacobs hovered above the ceiling to Dispatch. He faced the decision of a lifetime. To attempt something could threaten the life of the woman he loved. If he didn't some four thousand people might be lost. *Priorities,* he thought. He hesitated, uncertain. What if he broke through the ceiling and gave Steuhl enough time to detonate the charges? Then his efforts would *cause* the death of four thousand people. What if Steuhl shot the hostages? Was this the right thing to do? His arm throbbed.

He heard Dicky Brock say, "Almost."

And then he heard her scream.

He dropped through the ceiling panel and landed directly atop the control system for the camera monitors. Steuhl fired wildly, exploding a monitor which caught fire. He lunged for the autodialer.

"No!" Brock yelled.

Jacobs wrapped his arms around the man and held him back.

Steuhl fired the gun into the man's thigh, broke Jacobs's grip, and ran from the room.

"Keys!" Brock hollered.

Jacobs caught Susan's eyes briefly as he knocked the sets of handcuff keys off the counter and toward Brock. "Radio," he said, rifling a storage locker filled with radios plugged into electrical chargers.

Jacobs hurried off, his leg bleeding badly.

BROCK'S HANDS were shaking so badly it took him three attempts with the keys. Finally he had the cuffs off. He unfastened Susan's and handed her the set.

She unlocked Perkins's cuffs and immediately tended to the man's wound.

The control board for the monitors was smoking: all the monitors were dark.

Brock hurried to the radio, slipped into the chair, and pulled the headset on. "I'm with you," he said to Jacobs.

"Roger," came back the panting voice. "My password is *Angel*. Open all the doors to the new pavilion. How much time?"

"A little under fifteen minutes." Brock didn't need the password. Steuhl had already entered it. He typed commands to release the mag locks in the FunWorld pavilion. How strangely simple it was to set them free. "The box is here," he told Jacobs. "Two buttons. I saw him push the bottom one before. Two others are marked. Red and green. I assume one triggers the charges, one stops the timer. That's what he implied. No way to tell which is which."

"I copy," said a breathless Jacobs. "Any ideas?"

"I'm not going to guess, if that's what you mean."

Susan was caught up in the ongoing conversation, hearing only Brock's comments.

"He'll have to tell us," said Jacobs.

"Yeah, fat chance of that," quipped Brock, still working with the computer.

"We're going to make him tell us," replied Jacobs, too winded to be heard clearly. "Lock every door there is, except those in C. Right away. And stay with me. Out."

Brock looked over at Susan, who was attending to Perkins. "How is he?" he asked.

"What's going on?" was her reply.

GLEE PASSED THROUGH the crowd as Brock's voice announced, "May I have your attention, please. Evacuation of the pavilion will begin immediately." Three thousand strangers embraced one another. Cheers resonated throughout the hall. Then, just as quickly, pandemonium broke out. The people rose to their feet nearly in unison, some pushing forward, a human tide surging towards the three exits.

Rappaport was among those swept away by the moving crowd. One minute he was standing by the Giant's Tail, the next he was being carried toward the south entrance. "Get control of yourselves," he shouted, his wounds causing him great pain. "Stop this!" he bellowed. But the crowd pushed on, taking him away. He, like others around him, was overcome by fear.

A woman screamed nearby. Rappaport saw her fallen child. The first people stepped around the child. Then a shoe came down. . . .

Rappaport clawed his way through the closely bunched group and reached the child before the mother. He bent down and was about to lift the child when he too was knocked over. "No!" he screamed, rolling under the thunder of trampling shoes. A man tripped over him. Then a woman came down on top of both of them. Rappaport forced his way up, clutching his bruised gut, and snatched the child from the floor just as the mother reached him.

"God bless you," she said, grabbing her child back.

LAURA HAFF WAS SEPARATED from Shelly and Keze by the mob. At first she thought everything was fine. She had a firm grip on the fallen escalator and was shielding the girls from the crush of people. The crowd slammed into the three of them. Shelly screamed. Laura lost her hold and was pulled into the surging crowd, away from her children.

She turned to fight her way back, but the crowd spun her around and carried her with them. "No!" she screamed. She clawed her way toward the edge of the crowd, pushing and heaving. Twice she fell to the floor, and both times she jumped back to her feet, determination pumping strength into her. She fought the strong current of human bodies, like a rescue worker in flood waters, carried along, yet progressing slowly toward the bank. She finally broke out of the swarm, into the tangled steel of the Giant's Tail. She hooked an arm around a support and stopped to catch her breath. Moving through the I beams, she worked her way back toward where Civichek had fallen. There was blood on the floor.

The girls had held on. They were kneeling on the other side of the escalator, arms wrapped around the bent frame.

Laura hoisted Keze onto her back. "Hold on tightly, honey," she said to her crying child. "You with me?" she asked the older Shelly, who faked a nod.

Before receiving an answer, she and the girls were again carried into the flow. Shelly screamed loudly and Laura grasped her hand tightly. "We're all right," she declared, wondering if it was true. "Aim away from the doors. Away from the doors, Shel. Cut across the crowd. That's right," she choked out as Keze gripped her more tightly around the neck.

She hunched over and plowed through the chaos. "There has to be another way out," she said. "There has to be."

COLEMAN CLIMBED on top of a fallen escalator and looked over the crowd. Although the west exit was open and people were pouring out through it, the south doors were, unexplainably, still mag-locked. A good part of the crowd had gathered there; people were crushed against the unbreakable-glass doors like moths trying to reach a light at night. Hundreds of people were stacked up, and the crowd was growing more impatient by the minute. The pushing and shoving was growing violent.

He ran back into the service hallway where Mykos Popolov waited with a childish glee on his face. Coleman said breathlessly, "The doors on this side are still shut. It's getting nasty. The others are open, but it's moving slowly."

"Stand clear," said Popolov.

The wall was stacked high with bags of potting soil and fertilizer, the homemade bombs held firmly against the wall.

Coleman insisted, "Let me do it. I can run faster."

Popolov shook his head. "Too risky. I made them. I light them."

"But Mr. P. You won't have time to get away."

Popolov lowered his voice and stepped close to Coleman. "Listen, my friend, the world is full of risks. You either take the bull by the horns or you lick it in the ass. You're a good kid. I'm old. I've had a good life. With any luck at all. . . . If anyone is to take the risk, it is me. Now give me your lighter and get out of here."

Coleman handed him the lighter. "Good luck."

Popolov smiled. "Luck is what you make it. Remember that."

Coleman ran down the hallway and into the hardware store. He headed straight to the marine section and grabbed an air horn off the shelf and then hurried outside the store, blowing the horn. It took five sharp blasts from the horn, but he finally got some of the attention of the chaotic crowd. He motioned for everyone to cover their heads and get down. It was too noisy to be heard, but he kept shouting, "Get down and cover yourselves." After several attempts to communicate, the crowd seemed to understand.

Popolov looked up toward the ceiling and said, "It's all up to You." He crossed himself and, one-handed, climbed the stepladder and lit the long fuse to the top charge.

He hurried down the ladder and thrust his hand into the first hole, flicking the lighter. He heard the fuse take. He moved down the line quickly. He had cut the fuses in different lengths, hoping for a simultaneous blast.

He ignited the second and third fuses. As he reached the fourth he looked up and saw that the fuse to the top charge had melted a section of plastic bag and had gone out.

He panicked. If the top charge failed to blow, the entire effort was useless. He reached the ladder and scrambled back up, one-handed, as fast as possible.

As he reached the top fuse, he knew he had taken too long. He bent down and bit back the fuse to a short stub barely a half inch long. He lit it.

When he was nearly to the bottom of the ladder, the first charge exploded. Then the second. Then the top.

The weak cement behaved more like sandstone than concrete.

Mykos Popolov was knocked off the ladder and thrown to the floor against the wall. A tremendous section of the wall fell away, burying him.

The last thing he ever saw was blinding, crystal-clear sunlight and a pale blue sky.

It was truly the most beautiful sight he had ever seen.

COLEMAN RAN into the blinding dust that choked the service hallway. "Paplav?" he called out, amazed at how much of the wall had fallen away. It was larger than any of the other exits.

No answer.

The hallway was littered three feet deep with boulders of jagged concrete.

Crowds of people broke through the doors behind him and climbed over the rubble, desperate to reach the outside.

Coleman began to dig frantically but abandoned his efforts as even more people found their way into the hall. There was no fighting the crowd. There was nothing to be done. Earl Coleman ran for his life.

THE SOUND OF THE EXPLOSION, and the sudden burst of sunlight, drew the crowd to the opening like insects to a porch light. Laura Haff followed the crowds. They had to be going somewhere, she thought, and it was much less frantic here than in the middle of the pavilion.

As she rounded the corner, the dust gagged her. A uniformed fireman reached out and offered his arms to Keze. "I've got her, ma'am," he said loudly. "Follow me."

"Thank God," said Laura.

JACOBS FELT THE BUILDING rumble and knew by the size of the blast that it had to be Popolov. With any luck at all the building would be evacuated in the next few minutes. But he couldn't count on it.

He could only think of one way to force Steuhl to tell them which button to push: he had to get him inside the new pavilion. *If there is one constant in this world,* he thought, *it is the value of life. One priority above all others has sustained the existence of every creature on earth since time began—the will to survive.*

But how could he trick Steuhl into walking into his own trap? The first thing to do was increase the pressure. Force the man to make hasty decisions. Split his concentration. Confuse him.

He grabbed the handset to the walkie-talkie and spoke to Brock. "Make sure all the elevators are running, and unlock the north door to the back hall on the east side of the pavilion. Repeat it." In his mind he was picturing the floor plan of the ground level of Pavilion C. Each step would have to be carefully choreographed, if his plan was to work.

Brock repeated the orders and Jacobs okayed them, finishing up with, "Start shutting down the main lighting when you get a chance. I want this as dark as possible."

"Emergency lights only. Got it."

Jacobs slipped the walkie-talkie's handset into his pants pocket and continued his slow, stiff-legged run.

Steuhl was directly below him, having already reached Level 1.

Jacobs didn't have time to run all the way around the Level 2 concourse and descend the escalators by the fountain. He had to pressure the man now. He had to force Steuhl either into the elevators or down the east service hallway.

He jumped up onto the rail and dove straight out, grabbing hold of a tree branch. He swung himself in to the trunk and slid roughly down its side, scraping the skin off the insides of both arms. He landed on his good leg, surprisingly close to Steuhl, who turned and fired the gun.

The overhead lights switched off, hardly noticeable because of the flood of daylight through the glass canopy. But Jacobs noticed.

He followed as Steuhl crossed the empty pavilion and tried to open the doorway to the west back hall. Their footfalls echoed in the cavernous building. The door was locked. Steuhl tried the door next to this one. It was also locked. Frantic, he ran down the line, tugging on doors. As Jacobs approached, he raised the gun.

Jacobs dove to the slick floor, sliding across the cool stone. The empty gun clicked in Steuhl's hand, who tossed it away, turned, and ran for the open elevator.

Right where I want you, Jacobs thought.

Steuhl ran into the first open car, pushed a button, and stepped to the side as the doors slid shut.

"Stay with me, Dicky," Jacobs said into the walkie-talkie just before stepping into the car. "I'm entering car number two. He's in one."

"With ya."

Jacobs hoped to trick Steuhl into his old habit of using the utility tunnels. The narrowness of the tunnels might allow a confrontation. Jacobs had to get the man's glasses off. A blind rat could be led through a maze by light.

The tunnels ran south from here toward the new pavilion. Still, the only connections between the two buildings were the passageway on Level 1 and the entrance to Spanner's Drugs on Level 2. He couldn't be bothered by this. One step at a time. First things first. He would force Steuhl to the far end of the pavilion. From there, with any luck, he could cause him to enter the service hallway on Level 2 and eventually chase him into Spanner's.

As the doors slid shut, Jacobs radioed, "I want to know where he stops the car, and I want you to cue me to stop mine alongside. Got that?"

"Got ya."

Jacobs pushed "3." The doors closed. He kept his fingers on the emergency stop switch as he listened for Brock.

IN DISPATCH, Brock typed the commands into the Chubb to show him a display of the elevator movement. Seeing Steuhl's car stop, and watching the graphic display of car two, he said, "Right . . . now!"

Jacobs threw the emergency switch.

"Looks good," Brock said. "You're a little above him."

"Stay with me."

JACOBS BUMPED the panel out of the ceiling and pulled the ladder down. He moved up it quickly despite his wounded leg. In the darkness, he stumbled and fell from the top of the car. His hands slapped around the thick cable of the next car over. He slid to the top of this car, palms burning, and landed loudly.

He looked down into the elevator car and met Steuhl's eyes. The little man abandoned his own efforts to climb out and dropped back to the floor of the car. Then he threw the EMER-GENCY switch.

The cable jerked, breaking Jacobs's grip. The elevator's motor engaged noisily, and the car began to move upward.

He landed first on the roof to Steuhl's car, taking most of the impact on his wounded leg. He tumbled forward, dangerously close to the high-voltage inductors, and then rolled off the car, catching one arm on the cross brace by the limit switches of elevator number two.

Steuhl's car climbed past him. Jacobs pulled himself up to the roof of car two and found his way back down the unsteady ladder. He reached for the EMERGENCY switch and flicked it up. The car popped into motion.

"Stop me where he does," he told Brock.

As THE DOORS to Jacobs's elevator car slid open on the second level, he saw the squat man running down the escalator steps toward the pavilion's main concourse.

His first attempt to box Steuhl had failed.

The sound of the fountain enveloped the slap of his irregular footsteps as he pursued. He looked at the huge clock on the wall: 3:49 P.M.

Eleven minutes.

Steuhl crossed the main concourse, its vastness dwarfing him. Jacobs followed, plotting another way to trick the man.

Steuhl hurried to the short hall, mid-concourse, that led to the public toilets on this level.

Jacobs grabbed the handset and said, "Open mid-doors, Level Two, east concourse." He ducked behind a huge mirrored pillar, in case Steuhl turned around, and watched him in the reflection of another overhead mirror. He whispered into the handset, stuffing the earpiece deeper into his ear at the same time, "If I give the word, lock that door immediately."

Steuhl pulled at several locked doors and then gained entrance to the service hallway. "Lock it," Jacobs said into the walkie-talkie, wanting to trap Steuhl in the back service hallway. He intended to direct Steuhl into areas that would grow progressively smaller and would thus offer fewer doorways—fewer choices for the bomber. Using the computer to lock and unlock doors, it might be possible to indirectly manipulate Steuhl into an area where he could confront the man.

"Mid-door locked," Brock acknowledged.

Jacobs hobbled back toward the elevator. So far so good.

BROCK INTERRUPTED and told Jacobs that he had sent Susan down to check on Shleit. She had returned to say that Shleit was conscious, though badly wounded. He finished by saying, "Shleit told her that Steuhl went into the maintenance room with the money and came out without it. Susan went back to check. The money's not in the room. He must have put it down the chute."

"Okay. We've got him." He stepped into the elevator and pushed the button for Sub-level 2. The elevator fell away.

The maintenance room off Level 2's service hall also had a trash chute. Jacobs depended on Steuhl's greed. The bomber would have only two choices: take the utility tunnel and try to escape, or take the trash chute and go for the money.

Jacobs bet on the money.

Disembarking from the elevator car, he headed down the dark hallway of Sub-level 2, which accessed a variety of utility rooms. The emergency lights issued a pale yellow glow down the length of the corridor. He limped down the hall toward the door, reached the trash room, and inserted his ID card. This room, like most of the utility rooms, opened only by ID access. This was necessary because of the dangerous machinery inside.

The door unlocked electronically, and Jacobs let himself in. The smell of garbage overwhelmed him. The room was huge, lit now only by emergency floods. Two gargantuan trash compactors faced him on the far wall, each the size of a tractor-trailer.

He spotted the briefcase. It lay atop the pile of trash in compactor number 2.

In his ear he heard, "Ten minutes, T.J."

He expected Steuhl to come down the chute into the compactor any second. Planning ahead, he whispered, "Turn the lights on in the east service hallway of Level Two." If he could succeed in removing Steuhl's glasses here, he could motivate the man with light. *The human condition prefers light, to darkness,* he thought. *I have to make him vulnerable.*

He moved across the room to the compactor and awkwardly climbed the loops of heavy steel that served as a ladder up the machine's tall side. He passed the dominant black and red buttons that controlled the machinery's operation. As he reached the top of the large bin he saw Steuhl's legs appear from the bottom of the chute. Steuhl jumped into the trash.

Jacobs had to get the man's glasses off at all costs. This one thought ran through his mind as he threw himself at the small man. He knew he had to lose the fight, but make it look convincing. At all costs he could not let Steuhl out of the trash compactor by any way but back up that ladder. Back up the chute.

The fight began.

-----------------23-----------------

THE CAB RACED OFF the highway ramp and bounced through a pothole on Green Boulevard. A cop motioned for the cab to make the detour to the left.

"Stop here," said Julia Haverill from the back seat, fumbling with her cash and finally throwing all forty dollars into the front.

She had been within minutes of boarding the Pan Am flight to Paris when she had overheard the news from a TV chair in the airport. Her heart had sunk and tears had come to her eyes. The announcement behind her called for boarding. Torn between the tiny world of a nine-inch black-and-white television set and an adventure in France, she grew weak-kneed and collapsed. No one paid any notice. The passengers were too anxious to get aboard the plane, and the TV chair had been abandoned. She pulled herself into the chair and wept.

She could not run. She could not sit on a plane for six hours wondering what had happened at Yankee Green. That place was as much in her blood as it was her father's. She could not leave him. Would the Paris papers even cover the event? Doubtful. It might take days to find out, a situation she found unacceptable.

Now, with the cab pulling a U-turn to the protests of the policeman, she looked at the gigantic complex. It seemed so still, cars stopped irregularly, abandoned. Parking lots nearly empty. No foot traffic. No movement whatsoever, except for the waving of branches in the breeze and the shimmering of the leaves.

Her father was in there somewhere. Strong Marv Haverill. She could feel it. He was one of the hostages. How had it happened? Where would it lead? How had she ever thought she could leave Yankee Green? She felt so at home here. She felt as if her home had been taken hostage.

The presence of the SWAT teams, the fire trucks and ambulances, intensified the dangerous urgency of the situation.

"My father's in there," she told the cop, not fully aware that tears were pouring from her reddened eyes. She felt so much pride for her father at that moment. "He owns it," she said.

"Julia! Thank God," a strong male voice called out. The cop stepped out of the way. Forest Long approached at a fast clip. There was sorrow on his face.

STEUHL PROVED surprisingly quick and nimble despite his stocky build. He had learned to fight on the streets. He kneed Jacobs in the groin and delivered a hard right to the security man's neck. Jacobs fell back into the spongy heap, clutching at his throat. Steuhl retrieved the briefcase.

With his right foot, Jacobs managed to hook Steuhl's leg and send him over backwards. He crawled forward through the paper and clawed at the bomber, going for the man's glasses.

Steuhl was up in a flash. He drew back a leg and kicked Jacobs in the face, bending the man's nose to meet his cheek. Jacobs scrambled and rolled into the short man's legs, which brought him down again.

Steuhl crawled away frantically, dragging the briefcase behind. Jacobs dragged his arm across his bloody face and cleared his eyes.

He lunged forward and caught Steuhl by the ankles. The little man fell forward and out of the compactor. There, nearly within Steuhl's reach, was the bright red button that engaged the compactor. He stretched to hit it, but his arm was too short. He began banging the briefcase against the side of the huge compactor. He heard a tremendous *clunk*. Contact.

The compactor's single ram began to move from right to left, carrying Jacobs with it, burying him beneath the trash.

Jacobs struggled his way through the garbage and fished his hand out blindly, grabbing hold of Steuhl's ankle.

The little man screamed.

The huge steel wall, covered with fetid matter, continued to crush the garbage toward the far wall.

Jacobs raked Steuhl's glasses off the man's face. They disappeared into the trash. Steuhl clutched the briefcase tightly, refusing to let go. Jacobs rose to his knees and spun the small man around so Steuhl was now on the inside of the machine, Jacobs on the outside. With one tremendous effort, he pushed Steuhl to the far side of the compactor, directly below the trash chute. The powerful ram reached the edge of the overhead chute.

Steuhl had a split second to make a decision. Briefcase in hand, he climbed up the trash chute, unable to see.

Jacobs dug through the trash searching for the glasses. The steel ram continued its path toward him. His hands groped through the trash. He searched furiously for them, the space closing in around him. His fingers touched the thin metal rims. He pulled the glasses from the trash. The moving wall closed against him. He pocketed the glasses and reached for the edge of the bin. The thundering wall of metal pushed him off balance. The trash began to rise from beneath him. As the compressing trash lifted him, his fingers finally found the lip of the bin and he struggled to pull himself free. He fell to the cement floor as bottles exploded inside the angry grasp of steel.

He ran for the door. "Mag-lock all the east side, mid-level maintenance rooms, except for Level Two. Do you copy?"

"All but Level Two. Copy."

"And cut all power to the sub-level trash rooms immediately."

"Cutting power," Brock said, typing furiously.

"You got those lights on in Level Two?"

"They're on."

"How much time?"

"Seven minutes," came the reply. As he rode the elevator toward Level 2, Jacobs tried to picture Steuhl's actions. Without his glasses, the man had to be really blind. Jacobs hoped he would continue climbing until he saw the light of Level 2. If, by any chance, he tried to exit the garbage chute on any of the other levels, the doors to the maintenance rooms would not allow it. He would be forced back into the chute. By cutting power to the trash room Jacobs had stopped the giant compactor in the middle of its cycle, thus sealing the bottom of the chute closed.

Steuhl had only one way out: the maintenance room at Level 2.

As Jacobs left the elevator he radioed Brock. "Set the computer to cut all the lights in the back hallway. Leave Susan with

the radio headset. Show her the ENTER button. I'll give her the
signal to cut the lights." He began to run, despite his pain. "You
go down to Spanner's and make sure all their lights are on and
the door to the service hall is cracked open. If I get Steuhl
through that door, I want you to scare the shit out of him and
head him toward the new wing. But don't stop him. Copy?"

"I'll do it," was all Brock said.

"TOBY?" came the eager voice of Susan Lyme.

"Hi, babe. You got that ENTER key?"

"All set."

"Nice to hear your voice."

"Likewise, Sherlock. Thanks for the rescue."

"All in a day's work, lady," he quipped. "Hang with me
now."

"Right here."

Jacobs used his ID card to admit him to the brightly lit service
hallway's north entrance. No sign of Steuhl yet. He knelt in the
corner and waited. Pain overwhelmed him. As long as his adrenaline had been pumping he had not dwelled on the pain. Now it
tried to pull him beneath a blanket of darkness. His head swam.
He fought against it. Unable to stand, he slipped to the floor.
The pain was winning. "No," he mumbled unintelligibly.
Through blurred vision he saw the door to Spanner's open a
crack. "Dicky," he called, but not even a whisper escaped his
lips.

He fumbled for the handset to the walkie-talkie. He drew it to
his lips but could not depress the button. He dropped the handset.

Again his mind swam.

When he opened his eyes, John Steuhl was staggering toward
him, eyes squinted, hands groping along the walls.

HOW MUCH TIME had passed?

Jacobs blinked. Had Steuhl seen him yet? The man was inching along, apparently sightless, the briefcase clutched in his
folded fist.

"Steuhl," he managed to gasp.

The little man spun around and hurried away, down the hall.

A frightened rat. Jacobs couldn't get up. He tried in vain. He looked down at the hole in his leg, lifted his fist, and pounded the wound. Pain shot through his body and charged him with adrenaline.

He yelled in agony and pounded again. He rose to his feet.

Steuhl, exhausted from the climb, frightened by the yell, stumbled and fell to the floor, dragging the briefcase.

Jacobs depressed the button on the handset and said, "Now."

The hallway went black, a blade of light seeping through the crack at Spanner's Drugs.

Jacobs thought about rats and mazes.

The blind man moved slowly toward the light.

Jacobs staggered slowly down the hall.

Steuhl reached the door and pulled it open. As he stepped inside, Jacobs heard Brock scream at the top of his lungs. The little man turned left at a full run.

Jacobs found a sudden flash of strength. He ran to catch up, entering the drugstore and passing by Brock, who gasped at the sight of Jacobs's bloodied face. "Get back up there," the Director of Security said over his shoulder. And he ran straight for Steuhl.

Steuhl stumbled forward through the open entrance of the drugstore, with no idea of where he was. Sensing more light, he began to hurry as he reached the empty concourse.

JACOBS TUGGED his ID card from his lapel and inserted it into the metal box in the corner of the store. The red LED changed to green. He pushed the square button marked "C" for close, and the wide metal lattice gate popped into motion, rolling toward the floor. It was no coincidence, he thought, that this gate looked like the door to a cage. He hesitated, standing there. Only a few minutes to go.

"Don't do it," said Brock from behind.

Jacobs spun around and glared. "Get moving."

The gate continued to roll closed from above.

"Don't do it. Don't lock yourself in there. We can still get away. Come on. It's over." He looked at his watch. "Two minutes. Come on."

Jacobs pursed his lips and shrugged. "Got to do it," was all he said. He dropped to the floor and rolled under the lip of the cage as it lowered and stopped.

He was sealed inside with Steuhl. "Get up there," he yelled to Brock through the gate. "Steuhl," he called out to the little man.

Steuhl had fallen next to a potted tree. He was mumbling incoherently to himself.

"I have your glasses," Jacobs said. He approached the fatigued man wearily and slid the glasses along the stone floor, landing them at Steuhl's feet. The little man bent down and slapped the floor hungrily; finally he fished the glasses around his ears. Then he looked around and said incredulously, "Fun World?"

"Right as rain," Jacobs said calmly. He checked his watch. "Two minutes till four."

"No," Steuhl barked, panicking. He surprised Jacobs, giving the security man no time to react; he ran down the concourse at a full clip and without warning threw himself over the railing, briefcase in hand. The large solar clock was mounted on the wide band of cement below the second level concourse and well above the floor to Level 1. This entire tier was covered with mirror. Steuhl lowered himself onto the upper edge of the giant solar clock and began kicking his legs against its face. He worked his way around the curved edge of its surface, still kicking. "Stop it!" he said hysterically. "Stop it!"

The round edge of the clock didn't provide enough purchase for him.

"No time, Steuhl," Jacobs yelled down at him. "Which button do we push?" Beads of sweat fell from his head and splashed on the stone floor twenty feet below.

Steuhl looked up at Jacobs. "Stop it!" he shouted.

"Which button?"

"The charges," he said. "Four o'clock."

Four plus twelve, Jacobs thought. *Four o'clock!* "Which button?" he yelled louder.

Steuhl kicked again. His foot cracked the thick Plexiglas face, broke through and the strained plastic bit into him. He screamed and released his grip, falling away from the clock but quickly stopped by his caught foot. He dangled upside down. The brief-case fell onto its corner and broke open. The cash spilled out onto the floor. The broken Plexiglas bent under his weight.

Jacobs limped as fast as he could toward the man. *Don't fall,* he was thinking, *you've got to help me.* "I've got you," he announced, climbing over the railing. As he stepped onto the top of the clock, the Plexiglas unbinded and Steuhl's foot came free.

Jacobs heard the man's head strike the floor. It sounded like a beer bottle being run over by a tire. Absolute silence filled the pavilion, broken only by the distant sound of sirens, and the rhythmic ticking of the large sweep hand on the solar clock.

He looked down. Steuhl's head lay in a pool of blood and money, his neck folded back ungainly. His mouth was open.

Steuhl wouldn't be telling anyone anything.

JACOBS LOOKED at his watch: one minute. He looked down at Steuhl, dead or dying, light shining off the plastic face of the oversized clock.

Why did he kick the clock? he wondered. *What had he been yelling?* Stop it! Stop it!

The clock.

The timer.

Jacobs remembered telling Susan that you had to look for the signs—the unintended signals that people gave you. You could gain as much from deductive reasoning and observation as you could from what people told you.

A solar-powered clock. One that wouldn't stop running even in a power failure.

He recalled the message Shleit had found: Where *under the sun* does 12 + 4 make doom?

Four o'clock, on the face of a solar-powered clock.

Stop it! The timer.

Jacobs lowered himself and kicked with his good leg. The Plexiglas was too thick. He directed his efforts to the photovoltaic cells in the solar panels alongside the clock. *Short the system,* he thought. *Blow the fuse. Stop the timer.*

He dislodged several of the cells. They plummeted to the stone floor below. He looked over—the clock continued to run. Breaking the cells wouldn't short out the clock. The cells simply supplied a battery.

He lifted up and dropped all his weight onto both legs, attempting to tear the panel from the wall. In order to short the system, he needed bare wires.

The edge of the solar panel separated from the concrete. The large screws pulled loose. The pain in his wounded leg made him delirious. He began to scream with each blow to the panel.

He couldn't look at the clock. He couldn't think of the time. He hooked his toes into the gap he had created and pushed hard, driving the panel farther from the wall. It groaned behind his efforts.

The panel tore loose and fell to the floor, burying Steuhl. A thick white cable protruded from the wall, three bare copper wires visible.

He couldn't reach it. He let himself hang from one hand, and still it was just out of reach.

He let go of the railing, pressing both hands against the warm cement.

The wire poked him in the chest and he clapped both hands together, grabbing hold of it. It slipped from the conduit. He fell several more feet before stopping in midair. He dangled from the end of the wire.

He let go of one hand and pinched the three wires together. Sparks flew.

Jacobs fell away, toward the floor below.

The clock stopped.

Epilogue
Two Weeks
Later

1

THE VINETTI YACHT, anchored off Hyannisport, barely rocked in the water. The only way Bob Russo could tell he was moving side to side was by the slight pitch of the surface of the wine in the crystal goblet. Russo took another sip and then cut the tenderloin with his fork and felt the beef melt across his tongue. "Wonderful meat," he said anxiously. Dino Vinetti had been unusually silent this evening.

"Bobby," Vinetti began, using a nickname Russo disliked, "you didn't clear the Glascock thing with me. I was very surprised at that. Upset, even. You used my boys and I never heard boo about it. Why is that?"

Russo halted the cutting of beef in mid-stroke and set down his fork. "Sir, the job had to be done quickly. Glascock had become a serious liability to the organization—"

"Not even our counsel was notified. What kind of dealing is this? What kind of man would call Cleveland and use my name without checking with my people?" The harshness in Vinetti's voice betrayed his calm eyes.

"He was a liability."

"To whom? To whom was this man a liability? To Dino Vinetti?" The don lifted a small brass bell and rang it. A waiter entered. The don requested wine and waited for his glass to be filled.

The waiter, a big stocky man, did not roll the bottle at the end of the pour. Russo failed to notice this. Yet he innately sensed the threat that this man represented.

"My problem is this," Vinetti explained over the lip of the wineglass. The waiter moved toward Russo with the bottle of wine. "I can't very well have my sons-in-law giving orders using my name, now, can I? Things could get quickly out of hand, could they not?"

"The way it was, sir—"

Vinetti held up his hand, silencing his guest. The waiter filled Russo's glass and then set the bottle down. He passed Russo heading for the door.

"I went along with your vendetta against DeAngelo and Marv Haverill. We talked, and we both agreed to a certain exploitation of circumstances. The Green has cost us a great deal of money. That is all being resolved, of course. But there are things I cannot go along with."

Russo felt perspiration bead up on his brow. He took a sip of wine and returned the half-empty glass to the linen tablecloth.

Anger sparked in Vinetti's black agate eyes, and his lips trembled. A drop of saliva rolled off his lip and onto his plate. "You take young women other than your wife out in public. What kind of man is that? What kind of husband are you? Ritigliano is my friend. We are blood. You are a playboy. You have always been a playboy. Never any respect for the family. Always pushing the rules to the limit. You never grew up, Bobby. You had such promise at eighteen, nineteen, but you never grew up. This vengeance you sought against Yankee Green. A fool's pipe dream. You lack the subtlety of a family member. You are undeserving of the family name. You have no imagination, no comprehension of delicacy. You ordered a man murdered in an airport! What kind of ass does that? What kind of fool ass does that?"

Russo rubbed his throat. It was exceptionally dry. He felt light-headed, and Vinetti's voice seemed more distant than only moments before.

"The wine, Bobby," Vinetti said with a devil's grin. "You see. No imagination. Look at my glass, Bobby." He held it aloft. "I haven't sipped it, have I? But you? You would drink water from a puddle if it contained alcohol. You see how predictable you are?

Predictability is a thief's greatest enemy." He smiled again. "And what are we but thieves?"

Russo found it hard to breathe. He tried to rise out of his chair but felt a thousand pounds of weight on his shoulders.

"It's a simple poison, Bobby. It shouldn't take too much longer. It affects the nervous system first. Go ahead, try to move. See? You can't even lift a finger. That's what makes it so safe. There's nothing you can do to harm me. Your days of harming me are over. All you can do now is die. You can't even speak, can you? No. All you can do is die.

"What will become of you? We'll hang you in the meat locker for a few days and then make sure you are buried nice and deep. Several hundred fathoms, I think."

A few minutes later, when Russo slumped forward into his food, Vinetti rang the bell.

THE OLD HARDWOOD-FLOOR auditorium in Brown University's Rand Hall echoed as the standing-room-only crowd watched the lights dim. Some of those in attendance coughed, clearing their throats. A young student at the back of the hall prepared his lips and fingers to release a deafening whistle.

Les Civichek appeared from the side of the stage and moved along slowly, unassisted, using his crutches well. The crowd rose to its feet. He didn't need the crutches anymore, but they added a wonderful effect. A young man in the back released an ear-piercing whistle. The ovation lasted a full four minutes. Civichek, glancing at his Rolex watch, finally began to speak, and the crowd quieted quickly.

Tonight he would give the same speech he had been giving for the last week. If the crowd's reaction was anything like it had been at his other stops, he would be very pleased.

Things were going just fine.

He thought it amazing that just a month ago his Flock had been on the verge of defeat. He had been ready to give up. Even now, the newspapers continued to warn the public of the dangers of "vigilante groups" like the Flock. Editorials spoke out openly against him. But they couldn't stop him. He could feel it. Momentum. The contributions were pouring in. The Flock was gaining immense popular support. All thanks to one afternoon at Yankee Green.

He started the speech with his standard opener. "I come here tonight as a common citizen. I come to free you of the fears you have lived with so long. . . ."

The crowd erupted into applause.

Les Civichek grinned.

IN A CHOWDER HOUSE in downtown Hillsdale, Laura Haff Shole sat across from her husband. Keze sat at her side.

"To freedom," she said, lifting her water glass. "You may be in a wheelchair, but at least you're out of the hospital."

"I'll be walking by Thanksgiving. I promise."

"I'll drink to that."

"Me too," echoed the animated Shelly. Keze played with the packets of sugar.

Laura spun the wedding ring on her finger. She thought of Tim and felt no regret. She was a new woman, full of love for Sam Shole and confident of the good fortune the future would bring.

"Are we ready for our first family trip?" Sam asked Laura.

"Should we?"

"Why not? I'll be fine."

"Where to?"

"I know. I know," insisted Shelly.

"Oh, you do, do you?" asked Sam.

Shelly nodded, then blushed, reconsidered, and shook her head.

Sam bent over and kissed the top of her head.

"I thought we'd take a drive up into New Hampshire."

"Oh, Sam, seriously?" Laura's eyes sparkled with hope.

"You bet." He faked an accent. "Had enough of this city life."

She reached out and touched her husband's hand. He took hers tenderly. "Can we go for one of those long, long walks, where we don't know where we're headed and we don't know when we'll turn back?"

"Just what I had in mind, sweetheart. Exactly what I had in mind."

THE EARLY SEPTEMBER SKY shimmered like polished turquoise, the sun still climbing toward its noon peak. Far below, tiny cars crisscrossed intersections; the occasional sound of a car horn shattered the still air. A blanket of Indian summer warmth lay over Hillsdale.

They sat in silence, he chewing on a piece of grass, she abstractedly using her fingers to comb the shaggy lawn. She wore madras Bermuda shorts and a white collared T-shirt. Her hair was pulled back. "You sure you wouldn't rather be there?"

"Positive," he said softly, toying with the stitches in his arm.

"Did you read my article this morning?"

"Of course. You're good, you know that? You're really very good."

"You don't need to sound so surprised."

They both laughed. Silence followed. She reached out and took his hand in hers, studying closely the fit of their entwined fingers.

"Here goes," he said, handing her the extra pair of binoculars.

Through the glasses they both watched as the crane swung the giant ball back and then unleashed it against the wall of the FunWorld pavilion. Dust fell around the ball and a large crack appeared beneath it. Again the ball swung back; again it struck the wall. On the far end, by the stadium, several hundred yards from the ball and crane, workers were in the process of erecting a brand-new pavilion.

She said, "Out with the old, in with the new. I can't believe they have to tear it down."

"No one would insure it. The cheapest policy they could find was astronomical. If they left it standing, it still had to be rebuilt. This was the only way out. The lawsuits will probably bring down High Star Redevelopment Corporation. But they won't own it soon anyway. Alex Macdonald will. It starts all over."

"You're sad." It was a statement.

"It's a funny kind of sad, like when the monster dies at the end of the movie. You know it has to die, but still, you kind of hate to see it go." He hesitated a long time and then said, "It's right that they do this. That wing was cursed from the beginning. Alex Macdonald will turn a profit. He always does."

"I don't know about that." She tugged him over to her. "It's been closed for nearly a month. People are shopping elsewhere. That'll be a big hurdle to overcome."

He tossed the binoculars aside "How much you want to bet that Shleit gets my old job? He asked me about it, you know. He said he wants a nice office and a good salary. I told him to buy foot pads."

"No bet," she replied. "You're probably right." She brushed his dark hair off his forehead. "So, what's next, Sherlock? You've been kind of quiet these last few days."

"Later on, I thought we'd go by and see how Mrs. Popolov's doing. Did I tell you that the Rappaports tried to talk her into traveling with them, but she refused?"

"I don't mean *today*. I mean *next*."

"First I have to live through that damn dinner you arranged. That could have been the end of us—you and me—you know."

"I took my chances. They're your family, Toby. He's your father. He wants this as much as you do. Besides, you have to show him the *Angel*."

"Oh, do I?"

"Yes, I think you should. It's beautiful."

He rolled over and looked at the pristine sky. "I'm scared of him. After all these years I'm still scared of him."

"It's good for you. He's scared of you too."

"It's going to be a terrific dinner," he quipped sarcastically.

"It's all what you make of it," she said stretching to kiss him on the cheek. "Just like us—like you said—the possibilities are endless."

He toyed with the buttons of her blouse. "You sure I said that?"

"Yes, I'm sure. I'm very, very sure."